Ace Books by Chris Marie Green

NIGHT RISING
MIDNIGHT REIGN

MIDNIGHT REIGN

VAMPIRE BABYLON
BOOK TWO

Chris Marie Green

ACE BOOKS, NEW YORK

THE BERKLEY PUBLISHING GROUP
Published by the Penguin Group
Penguin Group (USA) Inc.
375 Hudson Street, New York, New York 10014, USA

Penguin Group (Canada), 90 Eglinton Avenue East, Suite 700, Toronto, Ontario M4P 2Y3, Canada
(a division of Pearson Penguin Canada Inc.)
Penguin Books Ltd., 80 Strand, London WC2R 0RL, England
Penguin Group Ireland, 25 St. Stephen's Green, Dublin 2, Ireland (a division of Penguin Books Ltd.)
Penguin Group (Australia), 250 Camberwell Road, Camberwell, Victoria 3124, Australia
(a division of Pearson Australia Group Pty. Ltd.)
Penguin Books India Pvt. Ltd., 11 Community Centre, Panchsheel Park, New Delhi—110 017, India
Penguin Group (NZ), 67 Apollo Drive, Rosedale, North Shore 0632, New Zealand
(a division of Pearson New Zealand Ltd.)
Penguin Books (South Africa) (Pty.) Ltd., 24 Sturdee Avenue, Rosebank, Johannesburg 2196,
South Africa

Penguin Books Ltd., Registered Offices: 80 Strand, London WC2R 0RL, England

This is an original publication of The Berkley Publishing Group.

This is a work of fiction. Names, characters, places, and incidents either are the product of the author's imagination or are used fictitiously, and any resemblance to actual persons, living or dead, business establishments, events, or locales is entirely coincidental. The publisher does not have any control over and does not assume any responsibility for author or third-party websites or their content.

First edition: February 2008

Library of Congress Cataloging-in-Publication Data

Green, Crystal.
    Midnight reign / Chris Marie Green.—1st ed.
        p.   cm.—(Vampire Babylon ; bk. 2)
    ISBN 978-0-441-01560-3
    1. Women stunt performers—Fiction.   2. Vampires—Fiction.   3. Hollywood (Los Angeles, Calif.)—Fiction.   I. Title.

    PS3607.R4326M53   2008
    813'.6—dc22

                                                                        2007040247

PRINTED IN THE UNITED STATES OF AMERICA

10 9 8 7 6 5 4 3 2 1

A huge, heartfelt thank-you to everyone who read Book One: you've kept Babylon going!

Thank you to Ginjer Buchanan, Madame Ace; Judy Duarte and Sheree Whitefeather, critique partners 'til the very end; Wally Lind and the *crimescenewriter* web loop, mentors who show me where to start (and let it be said that any and all errors in this book are my own); and Pamela Harty and Deidre Knight, who take care of business so I can *just write*.

ONE

Starring

When Jessica Reese came home from her job at a Hollywood bar that night, someone was waiting in the bedroom closet.

Someone hiding amidst hanging party dresses and dry-cleaning wrappers that ghosted back and forth with every slight, controlled breath. Someone who sat patiently with a container of bleach and a long knife that would be used to slash the victim's throat and quiet her before that Someone could tear the woman's neck apart in leisurely delight.

Someone was going to become a star tonight.

The sheer plastic hangings leeched air out of the tiny closet, making the wait a humid, trembling vigil.

Patient, patient, wait, just wait.

From the kitchen, a set of keys jangled onto a countertop, a pair of high-heeled shoes hammered on the wooden floor.

Someone fought to breathe, running a tongue over the sharp points of fangs. Blood pumped like gun blasts, the resulting hunger pulsing like open wounds. *Just keep remembering why you're here. Remember how the Lee Tomlinson made himself a star through shock value, ripping out that other woman's throat? You can do it, too.*

Every night, entertainment channels and newscasts spotlighted stock footage of *the* Lee Tomlinson, the "Vampire Killer," the accused murderer wearing a ten-yard stare, handcuffs, and a harmless smile as he was led into the courtroom for arraignment. While breathlessly speculating about the upcoming trial, the press relished the charges: Lee had torn a woman's throat out with his bare teeth, then become a fugitive who hadn't even made it out of the county, thanks to a stop at a seedy motel. There, after getting his head together with the aid of some marijuana, he was found: a stoned and peaceful martyr who hadn't even questioned the "anonymous tip" regarding his whereabouts. He hadn't even fought the cops when they'd hauled him out of the room. They said he'd gone willingly, with that same smile on his lips, that same perpetual look of lost innocence in his gaze.

He already had a growing entourage of adoring women wearing the same clothing, makeup, and cotton-candy hairstyle that his victim—what's her name—had sported in the one headshot they always showed on the news. The fans camped outside of the bar where their idol used to work, holding signs proclaiming his hotness, his innocence.

A celebrity. That's what *the* Lee Tomlinson had turned out to be. A hopeful, Brandon Lee–look-alike actor who had never been anything more than a face in a mouthwash commercial . . .

. . . Until the cops had uncovered witnesses who'd placed Lee near the scene of the crime, then harvested the DNA evidence that led to the arrest of the "Vampire Killer."

But the press's nickname for Lee would become a joke tonight, right after they saw what a set of serious fangs could really do.

Footsteps exploded closer to the bedroom. Closer.

Someone shivered. If great care hadn't already been taken to shave every body part, the hair would be standing on end over each inch of skin, a body electric with skin-buzzing currents.

Tap, tap, tap went the victim's last footsteps.

The sound grew muted as she walked onto the bedroom carpet. Someone started to ache, aroused by the woman's proximity.

Stay calm. If the Lee Tomlinson can carry this off, anyone can. Now it's your time to shine.

The fact that murdering someone using *the* Lee's same patterns didn't register much. Killing this woman might cause reasonable doubt in a courtroom for him.

Instead, jealousy, even anger, twisted every heartbeat. Confusion and need pumped through each tangled vein like tainted blood.

You're smarter than the cops, so you won't get caught like he did. You're smarter than the Lee Tomlinson, too. You can beat him at his own game.

The thought of sinking fangs into flesh warped into a fantasy, one in which each violent bite was a thrust into Lee, a furious victory.

Through the slit of the sliding closet door, the victim came into view, ambling into the brandied darkness on three-inch heels. The steady drip of the adjoining bathroom's leaking faucet kept time with Someone's strangled breathing as the light from a dying streetlamp outside suffused the room.

The victim was on the midnight side of thirty, shrouded with August sweat and a dark red dress. She bent to work off the thin straps of her heels, her hair frizzed from humidity, her bodice gaping to reveal most of her small breasts.

Sex. I can smell the sex she wants so badly right on her skin. How will it taste?

Someone's belly went tight, body tensing with the yearning to join with a counterpart.

Lee.

Someone craved to become him, to fuse with him again in this substitute act of connecting. An act of beautiful violence. An act of hating and worshipping a fallen hero.

Unaware of what was in the closet, the victim sauntered to the bathroom, slipping the tiny straps of her dress down her shoulders on the way.

The bathroom light swicked on, slicing over the floor.

It's time. It's my turn to shine now.

Carefully, Someone grabbed the knife, then opened the closet door and crept to the bathroom, fangs gleaming in the mirror during the impulsive emergence of a smile.

And when Jessica Reese looked in that mirror to see Someone behind her, it was already too late for her to scream.

TWO

THE PLAYERS

EVEN with her eyes closed, Dawn Madison was aware of a vague, lurking danger.

Dressed in basic street wear—a sleeveless white T, black jeans, leather bracelets—she crouched, waiting for the next attack, senses alive. She caught the scent of old wood, paint, and must that lingered in the corners of the room. She heard a reporter's voice barking from the TV speakers her opponents had turned on in order to mask their movements. Her skin prickled as an air-conditioned breeze hushed over her.

But there was something else out there . . . stalking. . . .

A pop from her right split the air, and a projectile whizzed toward her. With the well-trained moves of an athlete, she banked to the left, using her shoulder to cushion herself while rolling to her knees. Another object came at her from the opposite direction. She dropped backward, grunting, her spine hitting the floor, her bent legs splaying to give her leeway. Immediately rolling to her stomach, then pushing up to her feet, she landed in another crouch, her hands at the ready.

"Not bad for the dead of night," yelled a tinny male voice that echoed off the windowless walls.

Heart pattering, Dawn exhaled, regulating her stress while keeping her eyes shut. She maintained her position, ready to withstand anything. "You guys take forever to reload. Can't you go any faster?"

She heard Kiko Daniels make an okay-you-asked-for-it sound as he inserted another beanbag into his gun.

Dawn tuned her ears in to what was happening with her second opponent. Breisi Montoya. Kiko wasn't very mobile with the back brace he was wearing, but his team member had been all over the room trying to whoop Dawn's ass during this agility session. The other woman's bare feet cushioned her stealthy attacks, aiding her in smacking Dawn with three damned bruises already.

The drone of the TV battled Dawn's concentration as she tried to detect Breisi's whereabouts. To the right? Left?

Temples throbbing, she stayed cool. She'd have no other choice if this simulation were real; although the three of them hadn't faced any vampires for over a month, the monsters were still out there. In fact, The Voice kept telling them it was just a matter of time before the vamps reemerged from their "Underground"—or whatever it was the team had gotten wind of.

Dawn blew out a breath, picturing herself outside at night, the moon shrouded behind the tips of pine trees. This training session was supposed to simulate the threat of one vamp variety they'd uncovered. The subspecies was bald, pale, clawed, with iron fangs and attacks that came as fast as those beanbags, especially when they used whip-quick tails with bladed ends.

Red-eyes, the team had called them.

But, Underground, she knew the group was named something else. Guards. Robby Pennybaker had revealed this and more before he'd turned into yet another form of vamp, a creature way more powerful than a Guard or one of the basic silver-eyed Goths the team had also encountered. Terrible to look upon and deadly to fight, Robby had thrown diminutive Kiko across a room and into a wall, breaking his back. The creature had also mentally violated Dawn's mind until she thought she would break, too.

And that's just one of the reasons Dawn had killed him.

Now, she was preparing to function without ever having to look any of those creatures in the eye—she'd never get mind screwed by a vamp again. Wouldn't ever allow them inside so they could see her weaknesses, especially her desperation to find her dad, who'd gone missing over a month ago. . . .

She heard a pop from across the room, straight ahead. Responding by pure instinct, she launched herself sideways, forcing her mind to act as a weapon.

Push . . . out!

But the trick didn't work this time, not like it had when she'd fought Robby. She'd accidentally belted the vampire with some kind of mental shove, and she didn't know how to re-create it, even if she'd surprised herself by doing it a couple of times during this last month of training.

That made it an undependable tactical option.

Whap! The beanbag punched Dawn's hip as she hit the floor. Shit. And ouch. Time for a new plan.

Before Kiko could get off a shot and Breisi could reload, Dawn opened her eyes and unwound a chain from around her waist. A nine-section whip chain, to be precise.

Holding the handle with her right thumb and forefinger, she coiled the steel-linked bars in her left hand. In a flash, she transferred the bundled chains to her right while securing her grip on the handle. Then, with a push, she sprung the whip outward.

Without pause, she was already cycling the weapon by her side, using a right elbow hook spin to create a blurred bubble around her body. The bars and links moved that fast.

Sure enough, Kiko's beanbag glanced off the steel arc.

"Dawn," Breisi yelled from the left. Her tone was laced with a heavier Spanish accent than usual, so she was clearly pissed. "I guess this means we're done."

"Aw, no, I wanna see this," Kiko said. "She's been practicing hard."

Just to be an ornery hot dog, Dawn spun the whip once over-head, winding up, then launched into a butterfly kick, circling the links beneath her body while jumping. She landed on her feet, grin-ning at Breisi and slowing the whip down. At the apex of its spin, she allowed it to fall gently back into her hand. There, the weapon rested like a happy snake that had struck out to get the best of Breisi and her damned beanbags.

"I thought I'd give my new toy a first run," Dawn said. She felt good about it, too, even though her right arm ached a little from the injuries she'd sustained during the throw down with Robby Penny-baker.

Breisi leaned against a mirrored wall, hand on one hip, beanbag gun at ease in the other. With her Louise Brooks–black hair, broad yet delicate features, and Mickey Mouse T-shirt—Dawn had just weaned the woman off those dorky teddy bear prints—you'd think she'd come off as some Latina cutie. But upon a closer look, she was more like an Aztec warrior ready to tear Dawn's chest open. A more minute inspection also revealed the tiny signs of age that had ended her ingénue acting career.

Not that a thirty-one-year-old should be worried about being ancient. At least, not in the real world. But this was Hollywood, where logic feared to tread.

As Dawn faced Breisi, she could see her own image in the wall mirror. Not exactly an L.A. poster girl herself, with her extremely average face, complete with a lovely scar riding an eyebrow, cour-tesy of a stunt gag. But that was nothing compared to the scar on her cheek from the fight with Robby. She also had a sleekly muscled antiwaif body and a low-maintenance, low-riding ponytail that banded her brown hair together.

A special delivery full of attitude. She'd been maintaining the package for twenty-four years, ever since she could first say, "Screw off." Ever since she realized that she would never live up to the gorgeous promises her mother, the famous Eva Claremont, had woven. *Mom.* The name tasted bitter.

Breisi spoke, voice flat. "Those are some clever moves, but I thought you'd left the stunt work by the wayside. Flashy show-off routines aren't going to keep you alive with vamps."

Dawn negligently inspected the dull practice dart on the end of her whip chain. It'd be the real thing if she used it outside. "Sharp, silver, and tipped with holy water. And I can use it to attack a Guard or maybe even one of those Goth Groupies. Blessed articles have an effect on both vamps, and we know silver slowly poisons at least some of them. If I could ward off spit with the chain's speed and slice the dart into a red-eye's tail or an exposed place—"

"It *is* just like one of those Guard's tails, ain't it?" Kiko said, making his way over.

A pretty blond guy in his late twenties with a soul patch under his lower lip, he was a struggling actor of a certain stature, a "little person" who was proportioned just right—only smaller. Right now, he couldn't audition because he was recovering from Robby's beat down. With a still-healing back, he also couldn't run, couldn't lift heavy objects, and sure as hell couldn't fight by Breisi and Dawn's side if it came right down to it. But his brain was still running on all cylinders. His psychometric, telepathic, and precognitive senses would always be valuable, not that Kiko was happy about missing out on any expected calls to action. During this past month, during all the days of dried-up leads to her dad's whereabouts and information about the Underground, Kiko had been in physical therapy, biting back the pain Dawn knew he wasn't showing.

He reached for the whip chain, wanting to inspect it, and she made a big deal of pausing, then running a challenging gaze over him. Afterward she grinned, handing it over, as if he'd passed muster. She hoped he felt like that, anyway.

"Those Guard tails kept nagging at me," she said. "I wanted to level the playing field with my own version of a barbed whip. Now, I know it's nowhere near as powerful as theirs, but what else am I going to do? Become a mutant monkey and grow my own freakin' tail?"

"Not a far trip for a primate like you."

Kiko scanned the dart. It was the first time Dawn had brought out the martial arts weapon around her team, even though they knew she'd been practicing off property.

"You can attack with this *and* protect yourself?" he asked.

"When the red-eyes spit at you, it will go right through that steel," Breisi said, referring to the Guards' lovely habit of expectorating burning-hot fluids.

"Your lab tests showed that the stuff isn't composed of acid, right?" Dawn asked. "Remember how their spit just charred the silver arm bracelet I used to wear, and that was it? Maybe steel will go unaffected, too."

She knew Breisi wouldn't refute her own scientific findings just to make Dawn put the whip chain away. Nope, not Miss Lab Rat, U.S.A., their appointed gadget wizard, the Bondian Q of their team. Which made Kiko their psychic Aragorn. Which made Dawn . . . what?

Memory washed over her: lifting a machete, hacking off Robby's head. Putting a silver bullet through his heart, just to be sure.

Dawn was what her father, Frank Madison, had once been to this team. Muscle. And maybe even something else . . .

Before she'd joined up with Limpet and Associates, a vision had come to Kiko. He'd seen her, Dawn Madison, covered in the blood of a vampire.

"It was the end of our struggles," he'd told her. "I *felt* that everything would be fine after that."

Supposedly, she was "key" to beating these vamps. That's what Kiko and The Voice kept telling her anyway. Their reclusive, as-yet-unseen boss had even used his employee, Frank, as bait to get Dawn the Prophecy Girl involved with all this craziness. She'd rushed to L.A. to help find her father, of course, but they hadn't met with success. Yet, according to the boss, whose agenda had more to do with the Underground than with Frank, the team was closer to both her dad and the vamps now more than ever.

She rubbed her arms, suddenly going cold . . . and way too warm. The Voice. The man who communicated with them only through speakers. The only entity the formerly oversexed Dawn had allowed inside of her lately in a strange lust affair.

When she held her hand out to Kiko for the whip chain, the psychic grudgingly gave it back.

"Don't even think about it, Kik," Breisi said.

He got a look on his face that Dawn had seen way too often lately. Hurt, resentment. "Why can't I just give it a go?"

"Because, honestly," Dawn said, "*I* shouldn't even be messing with the whip chain."

Kiko looked doubtful, like he knew she was just trying to make him feel better.

"I'm serious," she said. "I know full well I might hurt myself, even though I've had martial arts training for certain movies. But technically, I still don't have enough experience to master this. I'm just lucky I found an instructor, thanks to The Voice." He'd given her a lot of money to locate a teacher who would weigh her determination and knack for quick learning against common sense. And, lo and behold, it'd worked. Bribes could create wonders.

All in all, there'd been a lot of training this past month. A lot of healing, too. Kiko hadn't been the only one to sustain injuries from vamp fights but, aside from some stubborn aches, Dawn's wounds had been pretty well taken care of by a gel Breisi had concocted in the lab, as well as some rest and medical attention. But that didn't mean Dawn had sat on her butt, waiting to get better. Hell, no. She'd been working on perfecting her mind blocks—keeping others out of her head—as well as those mind pushes. She'd remained in shape, training physically according to her healing progress, and she'd caught up on studying her monster lore, poring over type-written case files housed in The Voice's library.

Obviously ticked, Kiko looked away from Breisi and Dawn, shutting them out. He fixed a gaze on the TV. To Dawn, the volume seemed to fill the room, emphasizing the awkwardness of having to leave Kiko in the dust when it came to fighting.

Not knowing what else to say, she glanced at the screen, too. It featured FOX News, where the entire day's coverage was devoted to Lee Tomlinson, a killer Dawn and the team knew all too well. They'd been keeping constant tabs on any updates: besides being a probable Servant to the Underground, Lee had murdered the woman who'd given them information about Robby, who was *part* of the Underground himself. . . .

On the TV, the reporter enthused about the career Lee could've had, how he might've been "the new Brandon Lee."

"Only on the surface," Dawn muttered, tucking the whip chain into her pocket and crossing her arms over her chest. She glanced at Kiko, hoping to draw him out with a conversation guaranteed to turn his attitude around. "There's a difference between people like Lee Tomlinson who just *look* like a famous celebrity and people like . . ." She swallowed, not wanting to mention the next name but, then again, sort of needing to if she was ever going to grow up and get over her neuroses. ". . . Jacqueline Ashley."

There.

Kiko perked right up at the magic words.

Dawn blew out a breath. Kiko's crush, their new friend Jac, had gotten a makeover that had changed the faceless starlet into an Eva Claremont throwback, a bloodcurdling almost-double who was persistent about becoming Dawn's buddy. She was continually calling with invitations to spar at the fencing studio where they'd met, but Dawn hadn't taken her up on it yet. Someday she would, just to get past the fears Jac's resemblance dredged up. Maybe.

"I guess," Dawn said, "there's something different about Jac when it comes to the hype. You can tell she's the real star and Lee's a poseur."

Catching on to Dawn's protective arm cross, Breisi rose to a stand and came over from the mirrored wall to pat her coworker's shoulder. The other woman had been in the room the day Jacqueline Ashley had revealed her Eva makeover. Just recalling the moment made Dawn dizzy, ill, longing for her mom to come back while, at the same time, hating her for leaving. Hating her for being so beautiful and perfect while Dawn was neither.

"Have you talked to Jac?" Kiko asked, all puppylike. "Is she still doing that 'buccaneer boot camp' for her movie?"

"Yeah."

"That's my girl." He performed his rendition of Happy Kiko, reveling in a geeky glow. "Her first big gig."

"She's trying to get me a job on the set, but . . ."

They all nodded. Even though Jac's movie wouldn't shoot for another month, Dawn had been forced to call all her industry contacts to tell them she'd be out of commission for a while. Did that finally make her an *ex*-stuntwoman?

Once again, she felt the machete in her hand as she winged it down to terminate Robby.

With one final squeeze to Dawn's upper arm, Breisi handed her gun over, dug into her cargo pants pockets for beanbags, and gave them to Dawn. "What do you say you muchachos take a run at me now?"

Kiko scrunched his nose. "I've gotten into a mental mood with this break, Breez. Unless you and Dawn want to go at it. I'd love to see a good catfight."

"Gross." Dawn made as if to punch him, and he flinched, even though he knew she wouldn't go there.

"I'm just being honest about my all-American, red-blooded maleness." He grinned.

"Kik," Breisi said, business in her tone as she moved to the opposite side of the gym. "You want to work or not?"

"Okay, okay."

As he left, Dawn busied herself by loading a beanbag into Breisi's gun. By chance, she glanced over, catching sight of Kiko by the far corner, turning away from her. He inspected his gun, slipping a hand to his back, holding it like it was paining him. But in the next second, he was loading a beanbag, acting as if everything was normal.

Frowning, she took off the rubber-soled work boots she'd been wearing for the gym floor, then her socks. Kiko was a big boy and she wasn't going to tell him to take a rest; she knew damned well that bringing up the subject would only encourage him to prove her wrong by playing that much harder. The best thing would be to keep an eye on him, and that was that.

Waiting until Breisi closed her eyes and settled into a defensive hunch, Dawn changed position, ready to give the other woman a few karma bruises.

But before the first shot could be fired, the TV blipped off, the room going quiet.

Her body readied itself, pounding, heating, because she knew what was coming next.

The Voice eased through the speakers, low and rough, still-of-the-night lethal.

"I need all of you in my office," he said. "We've finally got something."

THREE

THE LEAD

IF there was one way to describe the joint that housed Limpet and Associates, it was "Vincent Price on mescaline."

With its grand staircase edged with gargoyle-decorated balustrades, its creaky hardwood floors, its knight-in-creepy-armor sensibilities, the place floated in the twilight area between kitschy and truly haunted. Dawn wasn't sure which was more accurate because, based on what she'd seen so far, anything was possible.

As the team walked from the back of the house to the front, they passed under a massive iron chandelier that resembled a claw topped by melted candles. Then, while everyone climbed the stairs, she couldn't help eyeing a painting that hung over the granite fireplace mantel and dominated the room.

The Fire Woman, Dawn had started to call her. A seduction-postured temptress wrapped in a flame-red robe.

Dawn felt watched, just like she always did around The Voice's collection of portraits.

There was a good reason for that, too.

They made their way down the dark hall to The Voice's office, where the door stood open in dubious welcome. Inside, velvet curtains blocked the windows, books stood sentinel on the floor-to-ceiling shelves, and a magnificent TV surrounded by speakers reigned. There were portraits here, too, but oddly, one of the baroque wood frames enclosed a permanently empty field of fire. The rest of the pictures held the images of females, each of them looking like they'd been caught sliding their clothes off while webbed in an erotic fantasy.

Friends, Dawn thought. That's what Breisi and Kiko called the women in the paintings. She'd discovered they were spirits, that the portraits were something like beds where they rested. Where they watched. Always watched.

As Dawn took a seat in a velvet-lined chair, the faint scent of jasmine crept over her, the perfume of these ghosts who had fought Robby Pennybaker right along with Dawn and Breisi that horrible night.

Skin alive with sensation, just as it always was in The Voice's office, Dawn tried to relax. So many things confused her about being here: this new preternatural world, the raging impatience to find her missing dad, the strange ecstasy of what The Voice could do—and had done—to her body and mind.

Who was this man? she asked herself for probably the one thousandth time.

After the Robby incident, she'd done research, visiting an Internet café to bring up articles and images of Mr. Jonah Limpet—The Voice's real name. She'd found rare photographs of a young guy who held a hand over his face to avoid being caught by the cameras. He had short, dark hair that curled slightly at the ends. His body looked tall and wiry under long, untucked shirts and khaki pants.

Wanting more, Dawn had delved further, finding out that he was the reclusive heir to a medical supply fortune, that he never left any of his houses except to travel between them under a veil of secrecy. His aged parents had passed away years ago, but he'd held the funerals on Limpet property, being so wealthy that he'd never even needed to step foot into the actual world.

How had Jonah Limpet gotten this way? And why had he closed himself off from everything but the Underground?

Dawn crossed her arms over her chest, preparing to block out his well-established hypnotic powers before he could get the jump on her. He liked being inside her, liked solving her, too, bringing her to physical climaxes while lapping up her emotions.

Thing was, she liked it. Hated it. *Loved* it.

Realizing that she was getting all repressed again, Dawn sighed, resting her hands on her lap. All her life, she'd shoved her emotions into an inner box, but lately, she'd been trying hard to keep herself more open. She needed to face what The Voice was, and more important, what he'd become to her.

Nearby, Kiko arranged himself on a settee, sitting bolt upright because of his brace. The sight pinched at her. She was used to seeing him plop into chairs, then collapse into a sprawled mess of comfort.

He caught her sad gaze, his jaw going tight. Dawn glanced away, knowing the last thing he wanted was pity.

"You said you had something?" she said to The Voice.

Now that they'd settled, the TV screen bloomed with color. The Voice had started his meeting in the usual way: silently, arrogantly, efficiently, and with succinct visual aids.

The screen sharpened to reveal a press conference, and a familiar one at that. Dawn had seen Marla Pennybaker's announcement just days after Robby had encouraged his father to kill himself, then was finally exterminated himself. As the older woman stiltedly talked about her husband's suicide—a true enough statement, except that it'd been brought on by the man's refusal to join Robby in

a vampire Underground that his son had never fully explained—
Dawn evaluated Marla's body language.

Garbed in a white silk suit, she seemed more put together than
Dawn had ever seen her. Back when she'd engaged Limpet and Associates to find Robby, her face had been lined by grief and fear. Yet
now . . . there was acceptance, like she didn't remember the hell
they'd all gone through.

Kiko grunted. "We've seen this, Boss. And it *still* looks like she's
reading from a script."

"That would make sense if she was mind wiped by a vampire,"
The Voice said. "I've seen this type of reaction many times, though
it's not noticeable unless one is searching for it."

Breisi primly crossed her legs as she took notes. "We've already
speculated that when the Guards kidnapped Marla that night, they
made sure she wouldn't come back with memories of anything re-
lating to them."

Dawn could still picture the horror of Marla being whisked
away by the red-eyes. The team hadn't seen the older woman again
until a few days later, during the press conference. There, she'd insisted that her son's weird appearance in a film after he'd been dead
for twenty-three years—the catalyst for Limpet and Associates to
take her case—had been nothing more than a cruel joke perpetu-
ated by a few special effects artists having fun at the Pennybakers'
expense.

Without warning, the TV screen zoomed in on someone in the
conference's audience, a stately man with gray-tinged hair, wire-
rimmed glasses, and a natty suit. This was something they hadn't
noticed before; The Voice must've been scanning the images closely.

"Who's that?" Kiko asked.

Dawn knew. "Milton Crockett. He's a lawyer, a 'fixer' around
town. Basically, if you're a celebrity who murdered your mistress or
an actor who's been caught with your pants around your ankles in
front of an elementary school, he's your man. I recognize him be-

cause he took some meetings on the *Blades of Spain* set. He was helping Leland Richards when he got into trouble with some gigolo who was accusing our manly star of liking other manly men."

Kiko raised a brow. "Was it true?"

Dawn shrugged. "I guess we'll never know. Crockett did his job and the accuser never said another word in public."

Breisi's pen stopped moving over her clipboard. "I wonder if Milton Crockett could be the reason Marla would not talk to us after she reappeared."

Interesting. Upon attempting to contact her, Limpet and Associates had been threatened with a restraining order from Marla's new "personal assistant," so they'd never been able to interview her. Once, when Breisi had attempted to wheedle her way around the red tape by intercepting Marla during a shopping trip at The Grove, the assistant/bodyguard had intervened. He definitely could've been hired by Milton Crockett's firm.

Now, the TV whisked over to another newscast: Lee Tomlinson in handcuffs. The screen focused in on a man following in the shadow of the accused murderer.

Hello. "There he is again. Milton Crockett. I assume this is leading up to a big reveal, Voi . . . ?" Dawn stopped herself from saying the old nickname she'd given him. But she couldn't call him Jonah, even if he'd told her to during one of their more . . . *intimate* moments.

The TV blinked off, and Dawn's belly clutched into itself, anticipating The Voice. She despised her weakness in wanting to hear him so badly.

"There's been another murder," he said, tone melding with the high-quality speakers until it sounded as if he actually might be in the same room. "A cocktail waitress named Jessica Reese."

His words, etched with a foreign undertow, scraped over her skin, digging, biting into her with nips of suggestion. Dawn stirred, restless.

"When you say 'another murder,' " Kiko asked, "are you referring to a second victim, after Klara Monaghan? Is that why you showed us Lee Tomlinson, the guy who did her?"

Dawn thought about the reason The Voice had shown them the Marla Pennybaker clip, too.

Frank. Would the murders somehow lead to her dad and . . .

"You think this new killing might have something to do with the Underground?" she asked.

"And Klara's murder, too," Breisi added. "Crockett is a link between Klara and Marla and, by extension, Lee Tomlinson, the Servant, and Robby Pennybaker, the vampire. Boss, are you insinuating that Crockett is a vampire Servant like Lee?"

"That would certainly be something to go on," The Voice said.

Kiko came to sit on the edge of the settee. "So—"

"What're the details?" Dawn blurted, unable to wait.

Breisi glanced over at her, and Dawn knew exactly what she was thinking. Patience.

Knowing the woman was right, Dawn settled her ass down. But who could blame her for urging answers out of a man who rarely gave them? Could anyone fault her for doubting The Voice when he was so damned cryptic?

And when he'd betrayed her before?

A man named Matt Lonigan had told her something similar once: answers. Demand some answers about The Voice.

Sinking lower into her seat, she put thoughts of Matt, a possible vampire hunter and rival PI, on the back burner, where they still simmered no matter how hard she tried to turn them down.

The TV now showcased a grisly picture of Klara Monaghan, a glorified extra whom the team suspected had been murdered because she'd given Limpet too much information about Robby. On the screen, the blood leaked from her torn throat.

Dawn swallowed, going ill at the sight of red plastered over her mind's eye. Her mother's own crime-scene photos. Images she couldn't shake.

"Dawn," The Voice said gently.

"I'm okay." Liar.

As Klara's image hovered over the room, The Voice paused, as if he wasn't sure she was telling the truth. But he knew Dawn too well to pursue it, so he continued.

"The new victim's wounds are similar to Klara's, but with a few differences. Where Lee Tomlinson left DNA residue from saliva, this time the killer used bleach to wash it away. It isn't an ill-planned crime based on impulse. This one is methodical. So far, there are no helpful fingerprints at the victim's apartment, although there are some cloth fibers that might be useful. Teeth imprints could be salvaged, as well."

"The scene has been processed already?" Dawn asked.

"It's still occurring."

The Voice didn't need to confirm that he'd been talking to a paid source who was at the crime's location. He had connections everywhere.

Kiko shook his head. "So it's too late for us to do a bust-in on the scene, huh?"

Dawn didn't even tell him that he couldn't do bust-ins period. Reminding him of his injuries was overkill, especially since he was worried about other things, like losing his acting agent due to the injury, too. Not auditioning was killing Kiko; she knew that because, during long chats while sitting next to his hospital bed, she'd realized he was a closet overachiever. A GATE student and an honor-roll stud, he'd planned on a law career as a backup to acting, believe it or not.

The TV went dark again. "The authorities have set a tight perimeter around the scene, but let's see if Breisi can get one of those secret, late-night coroner appointments so we can view the body. Breisi?"

"I'm on it just as soon as you tell us more, Boss."

The Voice laughed, a sound that scraped through the center of

Dawn, stripping her from the inside out. Her tummy seized up, moved by the sparked friction between her legs. She crossed them to dull the hunger he always inflicted.

Dawn . . .

She knew that she was the only one who could hear him, *feel* him, saying her name.

Pushing the craving away, she ignored his silent supplication and asked, "Are we assuming this is the work of a copycat murderer?"

"It could be." Kiko stood, blue eyes glinting with the thrill of the chase. "Lee Tomlinson's DNA tells us that he's Klara's murderer, but he's locked up awaiting trial. He's been contained ever since the law caught up with him."

After Klara's murder, Lee had disappeared. The team had researched him, then tried to track him down for further questioning about the Underground, but to no avail. By then, he'd been found holed up in the very same county, stoned out of his gourd.

"Unless," Dawn said, "Lee wasn't the killer in the first place. Maybe someone planted evidence to frame him?"

"Or maybe a rogue vampire took up on Jessica where Lee left off on Klara," Kiko added.

"We need to lay this out." Breisi paged through the notes on her clipboard.

When The Voice spoke, it was easy to picture him with a finger in the air, now that she sort of knew what he looked like. "Before we start, we need perspective. Remember, our objective is to use this murder to discover an Underground."

"How could I forget," Dawn said. "The good of the many outweighs the good of the few. And if we just happen to solve a crime while we're at it, champagne for us."

"Dawn—" The Voice began, his tone reflecting a weariness she'd encouraged with her eternal arguments.

"I know, I know. We're here to save the world, and that's all the explanation the team requires."

She'd been told the vague, noble justifications for The Voice's secrecy ad nauseam. Limpet and Associates didn't exist to find Frank or supply Dawn with the answers she'd been thirsting for. No wonder The Voice generally hired people like Kiko and Breisi: salts of the earth with overdeveloped senses of justice, people who fought for good merely on faith alone.

"Spock. You just quoted Mr. Spock," Kiko said, facing Dawn in his enthusiasm. "Cool."

Then he continued, turning toward the TV as if it contained The Voice, which . . . it couldn't. Right?

God, who knew anymore?

"So, technically, we don't have a client this time? No Marla Pennybakers to deal with?"

"Correct." The Voice's pause seemed to stretch into a smile in the dark. "Just the Underground."

He said the last word with a mixture of reverence and vengefulness. She wished she knew why.

Damn it, if she didn't need to find Frank, she'd be out of here. But The Voice had her by the fine hairs and he knew it.

"All right." Breisi stood and walked beneath the TV. "Are we ready to piece some puzzles together? Maybe something we already know will connect our vampires with this murder."

"Ready," Dawn said.

"Ready." Kiko gave a little hop.

"All right. Let's start at the beginning and work forward. There's our objective: this Underground that Robby and his father, Nathan, mentioned. Robby told us that, as a child actor, Nathan had sent him to this place to 'reinvent' his image or make a comeback."

As the speakers hummed with The Voice's presence, Dawn's body fritzed. "The Underground. We know it contains a 'Dr. Eternity' Nathan talked about. And, in general, lore tells us that vamps are all about extended life. So maybe Robby would've stayed down there until his comeback, even if it was years away? A long life would've given him enough time to reemerge and wow a future generation. Then, the public wouldn't believe he could possibly still be alive or twelve years old anymore, and common sense would lead them to think he's someone else . . . ?"

"Or maybe something happens Underground that would've made Robby into a bigger star than ever, without the public catching on that he's still actually Robby?" Kiko turned to Breisi, making sure she was writing everything down. "So we need to fill that hole with an explanation, like plastic surgery." He chortled. "Vamps getting plastic surgery, that's . . ."

His laughter faded as they all just gazed at each other.

Dawn's head began to pound, her breath coming short. Jacqueline Ashley . . . her resemblance to Eva. But Jac hadn't been like vampire Robby, with the mind screw and crazy-colored eyes. Yeah, Dawn had been exhausted and wigged out when Jac had shown her the makeover, but . . .

No. God, it hadn't even been the same as when Robby had looked into her eyes. With Jac, Dawn had been too emotional, too messed up because Kiko was hurt and she'd just chopped a vampire's head off. Jac was only another starlet doing whatever she could to be successful. The Eva/Jac connection was all in Dawn's head, Breisi had even said so. . . .

Across the room, Breisi's eyes had gone wider, like she'd been thinking the same thing. But then she blinked, scanning her clipboard again, making Dawn believe she could be wrong.

Kiko cleared his throat, and The Voice's speakers continued their electric wait.

Finally, Dawn could speak again. "These vamps we met, they were all different, like various races or something, so maybe one of those breeds committed this murder instead of a human Servant like Lee? We know for sure that there're two Underground varieties—the Guards and Robby's death angel. They're tied together since the red-eyes were trying to get Robby back to the Underground. So should we assume that the silver-eyes and Servants are related, too? I mean, Lee Tomlinson knew some information about Robby, remember? And that's when the silver-eyes showed up, like they needed to shut his mouth. Could the murderer be a silver-eye who already knew Lee?"

Kiko oohed. "That's something I'd like to know. Why are there such different subspecies—ones that seem to coexist—running around in such a relatively small area?"

"Maybe they've found a biome that suits their needs," Breisi said, her speech quickening, as it always did when she got on a tangent. "Maybe they all evolved together and rely on the same environment *and* each other for survival. The variations can be accounted for through evolution. If humans can differ from continent to continent, race to race, and if we indeed can call a gorilla like *Proconsul africanus* our ancestor, then I see no reason to discount the possibility that vampires have adjusted to the passing of years, too, maybe even at an accelerated pace. They would have to adapt to anything that threatened to destroy them or that made surviving easier."

Dawn was still half catching up to the end of Breisi's impromptu professor lecture. It wasn't always easy being on the same wavelength as a girl who'd gone to college on an engineering scholarship. "But the vamps' powers really vary, Breisi. A *lot*. You'd think one Underground would hold a specific kind of vamp. The lore we've studied shows that, yeah, different types of vampires have been documented in different types of cultures, like that female vamp in Mexico that was reported last year—"

"The *tlahuelpuchi*," Breisi said.

"Right, or the one that was caught in Greece and destroyed three years ago—"

Kiko almost jumped out of his skin to beat Breisi. *"Lamiai!"*

Dawn sighed, seeing the beginning of yet another competitive event between her coworkers. "T-lah-lah-blah or lam-whatever, thank you, Breisi and Kiko. The point I'm trying to make is could all these vamps really exist together in one Underground without stealing each other's food?"

"Maybe they've found a way around that," Breisi said.

"Are you talking about vamps that don't feed on blood?" Kiko asked.

The Voice cleared his throat, sending a jolt through Dawn. He couldn't just stay quiet so she could focus? Yeesh.

"Okay, the taskmaster wants us to get back to the objective," she said, still keeping him at bay. "Maybe talking about the vamps' characteristics will connect this murder and the Underground."

"Excellent," Breisi said. "Let's start with our first set of vampires. The Guards. Red-eyes. We've seen that they can die from decapitation or a silver bullet to the heart. We don't know yet if other vamp lore staples like fire or stakes work. But garlic does repel them, and crucifixes. Silver anywhere else in their body might weaken them—"

Trying to top Breisi, Kiko fired off his own list. "You and Dawn know from experience that Robby's kind of vampire—if there's more than one of him—gets slowly poisoned by silver anywhere in his body. You said that he was begging for blood to cleanse the stuff out."

"So, silver?" Dawn said. "Bad for these vamps. And that means . . . What? How does this relate to Jessica Reese?"

She could almost feel The Voice's approval. It made her bristle.

"It doesn't relate so much," Kiko said. "But at least I can imagine a Guard tearing out a throat more than I can Robby's type of vamp. Animal wasn't his style—he had to ask Dawn's permission to drink blood, even though he didn't get it."

"Little prick," she said, recalling how Robby had trespassed into her mind instead. She still had nightmares about it. "But why would Jessica give permission, and then why would a vamp just leave her body out in the open when secrecy seems to be so vital to their existence?"

Breisi was giving Dawn a measuring gaze, as if she was checking her over for buried Robby wounds. "Good question."

Kiko went on. "Back to Robby—he had two forms, right? In human guise, he could pass for any Joe Blow walking the street, except for those eyes. He could mind screw you with them, even worse than those red-eyes do. But when Robby went all death-angel vampy . . . shee-it." Kiko started counting his fingers with every checked-off attribute. "Robby looked like a creature of the Rapture and was stronger than Godzilla. Oh, and the change brought on the fangs."

"As far as similarities to the Guards go," Breisi said, "Dawn killed Robby using decapitation, too, but we don't know if her follow-up silver-bullet shot to the heart was effective. Differences: garlic *didn't* work on the Robby type and neither did the crucifix—they only gave Robby pause and didn't repel him. And he hinted to us that he could tread on holy ground."

"Also, he can be seen on film," Kiko added. "But does this obviously higher-class vamp murder like a rabid wolf?"

"Hmmm." Dawn leaned forward, forearms on thighs. "Nathan Pennybaker ordered those Guards around like he'd captivated them, and he wasn't able to do that with Robby. That gets me to thinking. . . ." Nah, it was a weird idea.

"What, Dawn?" Breisi asked.

Okay, her life was all about weird nowadays. Might as well go for it. "Mind suggestion. Could the weaker vampires be open to some *other* commanding creature that wanted Jessica dead? Could the other party be, like, a puppeteer?"

"Excellent point," The Voice finally said. "This would leave us with Guards or silver-eyes as the most likely vampire suspects, excluding Servants."

"Silver-eyes," Kiko said. "Robby called them Groupies. We know they can try to mind screw, too, and that crucifixes, at least, fazed them. We haven't killed one, so we can only guess what would work best, if it came down to violence. I could see their type turning almost as feral as the Guards."

Dawn nodded. "But I'd never forget about the possibility of another Servant, like Lee Tomlinson. A human who gets off on being bitten, one with no obvious powers, could resort to using their own teeth to become a vamp. Remember how Lee dressed like he wanted to be one? Maybe this murderer wants to make himself into the real thing by just copying vamp habits?"

Kiko looked up at the TV. "You getting any ideas about how we catch the killer, then have them lead us Underground?"

"Not as of yet," The Voice said.

As his tone shuddered through Dawn, they all sat motionless, allowing everything to coalesce. Breisi got out her phone and dialed.

Okay, Dawn thought. *Underground.* Was it a literal reference to where the vamps lived? Or could they be housed in some old decrepit hotel, or even in plain sight?

She didn't think so, because at one point during Robby's death night, he had tricked his father into revealing too much to Dawn and Breisi. The vamp had been hoping to trap Nathan into coming Underground with him because there was some penalty for saying too much. That spoke of the importance of secrecy, and Dawn imagined vamps needed that to survive. Living in plain sight might be a clever upset of expectation, but she doubted vamps would be that brave. But, again, who knew?

And who knew why The Voice demanded the same secrecy?

As an almost physical invisibility nudged against her, she felt how he was attracted to her questions, how his essence was seething around as if to request entrance.

I need you to do the work I can't do, to uncover them so I can do the dirty work, he whispered, breathing into her. A pulse thudded in her belly, flowing lower, hotter. *You know I can't go outside, Dawn, because if I were to expose myself too early, I would never gain the initiative again.*

As he swirled inside of her, churning, escalating her hunger, she thought about all the seeds of mistrust that had been planted by The Voice's betrayals: his using Frank to lure her to L.A., his refusal to share information. What he *wasn't* telling her could even be worse. . . .

Get out, she thought. *I'm not giving you permission to come in.*

And he left, forming a freezing void that weighed her down, left her feeling abandoned.

But that was nothing new. Her mother had done the same thing, preparing her for times just like this.

Once again, Jac's makeover—from redhead to blonde—smashed into Dawn. *Eva,* she thought. *Dead. Gone. Accept it.*

Breisi's voice snatched Dawn back. As she blinked at the other woman, her vision solidified to reveal Breisi talking on the phone, brows drawn together in concern. She was just as invested in this case as Dawn was because she'd fallen in love with Frank before he'd disappeared.

We're going to find him, Dawn thought, repeating a mantra they both clung to.

Breisi got off the phone, tucking it into a pocket of her cargo pants. "My friend at the coroner's is going to let us into the office in a couple of hours. And tomorrow morning, I'll see if Lee Tomlinson is open to talking with us. I suspect his lawyer, Mr. Crockett, has advised him not to, but even a long shot will occasionally pay off."

"We should use fake IDs and disguises for that 'cos Crockett probably knows we'll be around." Kiko rubbed his hands together. "But tonight, we can go to the Cat's Paw since we have time to do a sweep there before getting to the coroner's. Let's go."

They'd been checking at Frank's favorite bar regularly, taking the chance that someone new would be hanging around with information regarding his last days among the nonmissing.

"Kiko," said The Voice. "I need you here."

It was as if the psychic had been smacked across the face—not hard enough to hurt, but gentle enough to sting.

"But I . . ."

"Your talents are too valuable to send you out at night before you're physically able to defend yourself. Additionally, Jessica Reese is dead, and you've never gotten a reading from a corpse before. It is not worth the chance."

"What about the clothes she was wearing—?"

"Part of the chain of evidence, Kiko. After they are examined by the bloodstain-pattern analyst and a forensic scientist, then we'll see if you can get a hold of them, just like you eventually did with Klara's clothing. We cannot risk contaminating the evidence before it's processed, especially if we've got additional options to explore first."

As Kiko's posture slumped, Dawn wanted to look away, but she couldn't. He seemed so lost, just like she'd felt so many damned times.

The Voice continued. "However, we can arrange for you to visit the crime scene later, when morning breaks."

"Whatever," Kiko said, turning to leave the room. "I've got a million things to do here anyway."

As he exited, Dawn and Breisi looked after him, their gazes connecting. Kiko felt useless, rejected, and neither one of them knew what to do.

"And you," The Voice said, addressing them now, his tone hardened, "report any vampire activity immediately. That's essential."

Callous bastard. "What about Kiko? Can't he just—"

"He's not ready, Dawn."

"At first, you said I wasn't, either. . . ."

But he was gone, leaving the room in stretched silence.

"Here we go then," Breisi said, already on her way out.

Sure, here they went, off to the Cat's Paw and then to gape at another casualty of a surreal war Dawn couldn't even begin to fathom.

They loaded up on weapons. Vials of holy water, crucifixes,

stakes, and Dawn's *shuriken* throwing blades, among other things. She also had her .45-caliber revolver with silver bullets, which she carried illegally since she was still waiting for her CCW permit. Not even Jonah had been able to secure it through his connections yet.

After rubbing themselves down with garlic, the two of them climbed into the 4Runner and hit the road, unaware of another party tailing them.

It was someone who knew about the murder, too, waiting, hoping that Dawn would eventually come out.

FOUR

The Extra

Low, cheap-whiskey lighting bled over the scruffy interior of the Cat's Paw, licking Maury the bartender's shiny head. Around the slender man, drunks who had no place else to go this late at night slouched in their chairs until last call, when they'd have to find another place to pass out. Fumes from doubled shots thickened the summer-night atmosphere, and the air-conditioning unit was on the blink, making the pockmarked tables slick with sweat from the melted ice of cocktail glasses.

But the stink didn't seem to bother Maury. And neither did the garlic Dawn and Breisi wore on their skin like nose-flaring cologne. He'd no doubt smelled much worse.

He stood behind the bar, flashing a gold-capped smile as Dawn and Breisi checked in with him.

"You girls don't give up, do ya?" Maury asked. Then his smile fell as he shook his head. "I wish I had good news. That'd make me and the boys a lot happier. We miss old Frank."

Dawn turned to scan the anemic bar crowd, her gaze snagged by a lush named Stanton, who was leaning his cheek against the rough wooden wall, just below a chalkboard announcing a woefully misspelled "French Frys" special. Every time she and Breisi walked into the Cat's Paw, they knew they were wasting their time. Thing was, they couldn't stop coming. There was always that one teeny, niggling hope that maybe, just maybe, tonight would be the night that yielded the biggest break of all.

Giving up on Frank's hangout was like giving up on him.

"I think we've chatted with every regular customer about five times over," she said.

Stanton the drunk's mouth opened and a thread of saliva rolled out.

"Believe me, Dawnie," Maury said. "These guys don't mind you and Breisi giving them the time of day. Not at all."

On the next stool, Breisi flinched at the nickname "Dawnie." It's what Frank had called his daughter. Hearing it must've brought him back to Breisi, even just a little. Unfortunately, the two of them had blown up at each other just before Frank had disappeared, leaving Breisi with hard regrets. Lately, she'd opened up more, hinting about the depths of her feelings for the ex–bar bouncer. Dawn understood Breisi's remorse. Definitely. All too well.

Since Frank and Dawn weren't the closest, she hadn't even known he'd been dating anyone, much less working with a freakin' paranormal investigative team. Talk about remorse.

Dawn smiled at her coworker, trying to soften the blow of missing Frank. Out of the corner of her eye, she saw Stanton slump a tad more against that wall.

"No," Maury continued, "the boys don't mind the two of you at all. I remember how Hugh Wayne pranced around here for hours after Dawn and that midget friend showed him some attention."

They'd interviewed the big, burly Hugh when Dawn had first started her hunt for Frank. It hadn't helped much.

"Haven't seen Hugh since then," Dawn said.

"Me, either." Maury tapped his hands on the bar. "He's probably doing another stint in the slammer."

"Yup, Frank's buddies. Gotta love them."

In the meantime, Dawn caught Stanton's face sliding down the wall an inch, then two. She sucked in a breath, anticipating the splinters the guy would be wearing.

Jeez. She hopped off of her stool, went over, and carefully faced him forward so as not to awaken him. Not that she could ever hope to. He was out. After looking him over for facial splinters—he didn't have any, thank God—she nodded to Breisi, indicating that there was nothing left here to do.

Before getting off her stool, Breisi ran a slow gaze around the bar. It was one final sip of Frank that would have to tide her over. Then, shoulders slumped, she stood, holding her hand out to Maury for a shake. "Thanks again."

"Yeah, Maury, thanks. And good luck with your daughter's wedding this weekend."

"Ah." The bartender flapped a towel in flippant dismissal. "They're eloping to Vegas to a tiny chapel that has scrub brush for decoration, I'll bet. Only the best for my kid."

Dawn grinned, walking with Breisi out the door, but not before she spent a glance on Stanton. He now had drool coating his chin and, since it wasn't going to hurt him, Dawn let it go.

Outside, the moon paled the sidewalk, turning it ghostly as they headed in the direction of Breisi's tricked-up 4Runner. She'd modified it herself, jacked up its speed and put in extra storage compartments that held an arsenal of monster-fighting equipment—everything from spirit-hunting temperature gauges to pump-action shotguns for more solid attackers, like ghouls. Not that they'd ever run into any. Yet.

"You okay?" Dawn asked.

"Why?" A gust of warm night wind stirred the sharp edges of Breisi's bob.

"I don't know." Dawn didn't want to get all mushy, but . . .
"You looked a little sad in there. More than usual."

A pause languished between them. Breisi shrugged. "Some
nights it's worse than others. Sometimes I can feel Frank walking
next to me, not in a preternatural way, but because . . ." Her voice
got tight. "Because I want to feel him there."

Dawn didn't know what to say. She'd never loved a man like
that. Sure, she'd slept with more than a few, but she wasn't stupid
enough to confuse sex with something more.

She stole a peek at Breisi, just to see if she'd maybe started crying, hoping she hadn't.

But her coworker's jaw was tensed, like she was warding off the
vulnerability. Dawn could relate to that, too.

The wind tossed Breisi's hair again and, absently, Dawn thought
about how different this woman was from Frank's first love, Eva.
Where Breisi was petite and dark, Eva had been elegant and light.
Where Breisi was feminine yet tough, Eva seemed absolutely unguarded.

As Dawn kept staring, Jacqueline Ashley, Eva's starlet look-
alike, superimposed herself over Breisi. Dawn's chest sucked into itself in utter fear and darkness.

Jac's resemblance brought all Dawn's competitive neuroses, her inferiority complexes, to the surface. Growing up, she'd done her best
to avoid comparisons with Eva, rebelling against being her daughter
in any way possible, even becoming a rough stuntwoman as a big
"screw you" to the Claremont glamour. Now, with Jac, Dawn didn't
know how to feel, how to react to a woman who seemed to have
Eva's magnetism within her.

A woman who might not be human at all. . . .

Stop it, Dawn chided herself. Jac wasn't a vamp. The Voice
would've said something if it was even a possibility.

Wouldn't he?

The night had gone quiet as they approached the curb-parked

SUV. As another car passed on the street, its moaning roar lingered, mingling with the wail of a soft wind.

The skin on the back of Dawn's neck tingled.

But when she saw someone step away from the front of the vehicle, where he'd clearly been waiting, she knew her heightened senses had nothing to do with the atmosphere.

Her blood pistoned through her veins. "Matt?"

Breisi positioned herself in front of Dawn, stiffening.

"Whoa, whoa." Matt Lonigan held up his hands and took a couple of steps to the side, into a pool of light from a streetlamp. He was holding something—flowers? "I know you don't believe it yet, but I'm one of the good guys."

His low voice abraded Dawn, and she enjoyed the gentle torture, the memory of how good his mouth felt against hers.

Hands still raised, he waited for Breisi to relax, his pale blue eyes running over Dawn with the usual hunger. He had short brown hair and a face of bruised beauty that intrigued her as much as it disturbed her.

Once again, Dawn couldn't help thinking that if life were a movie, he'd be cast as a street thug who carried a baseball bat and wore his shirts rolled over his forearms. But Matt being Matt, he wore no such thing. He liked his just-about-new jeans, boots, leisure shirts over a T, and in spite of the weather, the oversized coat he wore now—a coat that hid what Dawn suspected to be a machete in a back holster.

A PI or fellow vamp hunter? Dawn had no idea, but whatever his job, he was real good at planting doubts about The Voice in her head.

Demand answers, he'd said, encouraging her to investigate The Voice and his motives. And she'd tried during this past month. Yet she'd also researched Matt Lonigan at the same time. He'd changed his name after his parents' murders, from Destry to Lonigan, and she'd used that information to discover that he really hadn't been lying when he'd told her about his parents. She'd accused him of using the Batman mythos to concoct a fake history and, now, seeing him face-to-face after finding evidence to the contrary, she felt like an idiot who'd jumped to conclusions—something she was trying to avoid with Jac, too.

After all, the man was holding flowers instead of a gun.

Daisies. The kind of petals Eva Claremont had worn in her hair during the most famous film scene of her career. One day at lunch, Matt's eyes had gone woozy when she'd mentioned Eva's name. On the surface, they'd been talking about Frank, since Matt had been hired to find him. By who? Dawn still didn't know since client privilege barred him from revealing that information. But, truthfully, she and the team had been testing him to see if Matt was the enemy or a friend.

After his reaction to Eva's name, she'd gotten jealous, as she always did when men responded to the suggestion of her stunning mother. Sometimes Dawn even wondered if that was one reason she was attracted to this shy guy who wasn't her normal type. To win him over fully from Eva.

She nodded to the flowers, finally catching her breath, her balance. "Those for your sweet old grandma or what?"

He grinned, held them out to her, and took a step forward. Breisi stiffened even more.

Dawn put a hand on her coworker's shoulder. "Everything's copasetic."

"I can't believe you're so sure about that."

Matt laughed, a white flag of truce. "Keep friends like her around, Dawn."

She'd never introduced Breisi to Matt and didn't see the need to do it now. "Breez, can I . . . ?"

The other woman kept her eyes on the rival PI. "I don't like leaving you on a dark street by yourself."

"I'm not by myself. I'm with him."

She went dead serious. "I know."

"Breez . . ."

"All right." She backed away, shot Matt another glare. "I'm going to be in the car and I'll be on the phone to the office at the same time. Just in case."

"Yes, Mom."

It'd been meant as a jest, but as Breisi widened her eyes, Dawn realized just how uncomfortable the comment was. If it wasn't for Frank's disappearance, Breisi might've been her stepmom one day.

Her coworker went to the other side of the SUV, the slam of the vehicle's door reverberating. Matt shifted position, automatically drawing Dawn's gaze to him.

Unable to resist, she walked closer, feeling the heavy vibration that always filled the space between their bodies. He grinned a little, offering the daisies again.

"Long time no see," he said softly.

Dawn just about sighed. His voice. Graveled. Hot.

Taking the flowers, she awkwardly held them. Sad fact: she'd never gotten a gift like this from a guy before, so she didn't know exactly what to do with them.

"I guess," she said, "our jobs aren't the best for scheduling leisure time, huh?"

He'd asked her out before, and they'd decided to do an actual date once Frank had been discovered. That way, there'd be no conflicts. Hopefully. But it'd happened before she'd found Matt skulking around Klara Monaghan's murder scene. Before she'd felt the machete at his back. Before she thought she'd seen that machete fly through the air from an unknown assailant and whack off Robby Pennybaker's arm.

Had he been hunting vamps that night, too?

She couldn't even ask him. He wouldn't tell her anyway, just like she couldn't reveal the specifics about what she did with Limpet and Associates.

"How'd you know I'd be here?" she asked.

"Pure chance." He risked a glance at the car, where Breisi was staring daggers while talking on the phone. "I was driving home when I saw your one-of-a-kind vehicle parked here. I ran into that grocery for the flowers"—he pointed across the street to an all-night shop whose windows lit the darkness—"and . . . voilà."

"These are nice. Thank you." She smelled them. Fresh and simple. The stems were wet, making them as slick as the excuse he'd just given her. She didn't know if she believed it, but she didn't want to think he'd been following her, either.

Yet what had he said the last time she'd seen him, before he'd disappeared into the night again?

I know you better than you can ever imagine. I've had access to files, Dawn. I've done surveillance on you, watched your films, talked to people you've known. And bit by bit, I . . . I liked what I found.

A shiver traveled from her toes up to her neck. Along the way, the cold, white heat seared through her belly, making her wonder if she was turned on or afraid.

Either way, she liked it. Freak.

During one of the phone calls they'd engaged in lately—who had time to meet face-to-face?—he'd briefly apologized for springing the confession on her and causing the situation to sound creepy. But he'd likened his interest to a guy who had a crush on a girl whose locker was just two feet away from his own in high school. Maybe they never talked to each other, he'd explained, but he'd seen how she smiled, knew about her accomplishments from hall gossip. He'd told her that, once he'd seen her reaction to his confession, he'd been so mortified that he'd left her when a phone call had diverted Dawn's attention.

She could buy that. Matt had a bashful streak, and she found that sweet. And, even if he wouldn't admit it, she suspected he'd decided to court her on the phone, taking off the pressure to see him, giving himself a chance to test her out with the screen of a cell phone instead of getting rejected in person. The "I'm busy" excuses were a smoke screen, she guessed, and she liked that he thought enough of her to actually care.

Now, he reached out to touch her, skimming her ear, where she used to wear a blood-moon pendant before laying it to rest in a suitcase underneath a pile of clothing.

He paused, as if asking where it was. He'd liked to run his fingers along it, to see the fake silver-and-ruby strands stir.

"It's lost," she lied, not wanting to explain how she didn't feel right wearing it anymore. It belonged to the old Dawn who'd never hacked at a vamp in cold, vengeful fury.

The sound of the 4Runner's horn blaring made both of them startle. In the car, Breisi made an "oops" face and pointed to the wheel as if it'd been the horn's fault. Matt backed away from Dawn, hands up, respecting Breisi's rules.

"You know," Dawn said, grateful for the reprieve, "I really do need to go."

"Okay." Slowly, he tilted his head, like he was reading whether or not he'd scared her off again by showing up randomly in the dead of night. "I suppose I'll see you in some alley or during some kind of emergency again."

It was a tease, but it fell flat, underlining all the reasons she really *couldn't* feel comfortable around him. Until he was honest with her, there was no way she would ever come clean with him, either.

A hesitation tore the air in half. She realized the cadence of her breathing was pacing his own. Heartbeats from the last time she'd seen him echoed over from the past, reminding her of uncontrolled kisses, caresses that'd grown rougher and more needful by the second.

"Alleys and emergencies," she said. "You need to step out of the house more. Get some variety in your life. It'll give you some better ideas about where we *could* be meeting."

"You're right—I don't get out much." He glanced at her from beneath lowered brows. "But you just might like where I at least *imagine* meeting you . . . and how."

The innuendo made her melt just a touch. Boy, what she'd give to make him back up that comment right now—

The start-up of the SUV's engine headed off any emerging fantasies. Breisi revved the gas, somehow making the car into a strange version of the chastity belt Dawn so sorely needed.

"That's my cue," she said, holding up the daisies. She started to move away but stopped, wondering what he'd do if she pressed up to him, ran her mouth over his, just for a hint of what she'd been missing.

But she didn't do it. Especially not with Breisi here. Damn girl would throw a fit if Dawn didn't get her butt into that car right now.

With a slight wave, she sent him a smile that said she was anticipating a normal meeting, someday, then tucked herself into the vehicle. She slammed the door and rolled down the window, stretching out every last opportunity to be with him.

"Before you go . . ." He sauntered over, footsteps so stealthy she couldn't even hear them. "There's one more thing."

The engine purred. Dawn raised a finger to Breisi before she could take off.

Matt came even closer. "When you're ready to admit that we have more in common than you realize, I'll be around."

Apparently disgusted, Breisi sighed, taking off.

"Jessica Reese!" he said, holding up his hands in a you-should've-stayed-to-listen gesture as they pulled away.

Then he motioned to his throat.

Crap. Jessica Reese, tonight's victim. Was he saying she was connected to Klara Monaghan, who'd been the victim at the crime scene where Dawn had seen Matt sneaking around?

Did he know something about both murders?

"Go back!" Dawn told Breisi, but her driver had already gunned down the street with nowhere to maneuver at the moment.

"Why?" Breisi asked.

"Do it!"

Yet, two minutes later, when they returned to their parking space, Matt had already left.

Disappearing like he always did.

FIVE

The Emptiness

THE next morning, after getting a secretive up-close and way-too-personal look at Jessica Reese's body at the coroner's, Dawn took a break for sleep, only to be woken up by a call.

The blast of a Def-Leppard-guitar-lick ringtone set her heart to thudding. She fumbled for her cell, almost tumbling off the sheet-covered couch where she slept. "Mmmm?"

"Get up," Breisi said without preamble. "The Voice assigned our Friends to trail a few people, and one of them is Milton Crockett."

Even though Dawn didn't need more than a few hours of shut-eye per night, she was a little lagged right now. Maybe it was because of the mental hangover Jessica Reese's body had caused. "Our Friends are out of their portraits bright and early, huh?"

"They're also watching Lee Tomlinson while he's in custody. Looks like he's not talking to anyone but his family and legal team, so that means no interviews for us. There's speculation that he's hiding himself away because he wants to give an exclusive to Katie Couric. Accepting a lot of visitors takes away his mystique, I suppose. I wonder if Lawyer Crockett had anything to do with that." On the other end of the line, she huffed. "I'm betting he warned Lee about us. Bleeping jerk."

Bleeping. God, Breisi slayed Dawn.

She sat up, stretched. "If Crockett was the one who sheltered Marla Pennybaker after she got back from her vamp-napping, he'd do the same with Lee. Secrecy for the Underground, remember?"

"Technically, Crockett is not associated with the Tomlinson defense team. Not on paper, but he *has* to have his hand in this mess."

"Chances are."

"You know what I love the most?" Breisi didn't even stop for an answer. "That he has no idea our Friends are watching his client in jail. The surveillance could help if Lee decides to share tales with anyone else while he's locked up."

Her coworker laughed confidently, telling Dawn just how much she got off on this detective crap. It was further proof of The Voice's expertise in hiring just the right kind of person who wouldn't ask too many questions about his agenda. In fact, Kiko had once revealed that, upon recruiting them, the boss had told his underlings that they probably would never get answers. But they were fighting for capital-G "Good," and that was motivation enough.

For them.

"And here's more good news," Breisi added. "Thanks to the Friends, I think we might be able to corner Crockett today to ask a few questions and maybe get a reading through Kiko."

"In person?" Dawn frowned. "Can't we just sneak into the man's house to maul his clothes or something?"

"The boss thought of that, but he believes if Kik can touch Crockett's skin, he'll get more immediate information out of him. That's preferable to a secondhand reading, the kind that clothing would provide for Kiko."

"So Kiko's going with us." Dawn still couldn't believe The Voice had changed his mind about keeping their psychic safely indoors. Kik had probably talked the boss into it, just like he'd done when she'd first shown up and Limpet had resisted sending her out, too.

"Yes, and the boss already gave Kiko the news. As for you: be ready in an hour. And wear a dress."

A . . . what? Uh-uh. Dawn didn't do dresses. "Don't have any."

"Dawn."

Okay, she did have one, but just for emergencies. It was still in a suitcase, crumpled into a ball.

"The Friends have reported that Crockett is headed toward Beverly Hills," Breisi added, "so we want to blend. *Comprendes?*"

Dawn knew by now that she never won an argument with these people—not yet, anyway. Besides, Breisi was right. If Dawn walked into posh BH in her street clothes, she'd stick out like a good-morning boner.

"All right. I'll wear the damned dress if it means we'll get some information from this guy."

"Thank you."

"So, *Kiko's* going?" she asked, fishing for more of an explanation about The Voice's turnabout.

"We'll be in public, daylight, and in the past we've had no creature troubles then. Besides, early this morning, the boss arranged for Kik to visit Jessica Reese's crime scene with a few Friends. The body had been removed and the scene had been processed, but he managed to get a few readings."

Dawn got to her feet. "Really? Like what—?"

A click sounded from Breisi's connection. Call-waiting.

"The boss," she said. "Ask Kiko about it?"

Before Dawn could respond, Breisi signed off. Typical.

Last night's details slowly flickered back on in Dawn's mind, just like an old light clinking to life after being turned off for years. She snatched that damned dress from the corner of her suitcase and passed Kiko's closed bedroom door. Might as well grab the single bathroom shower before he might need it.

After taking care of business, she came back out to the common room to find him spry and ready, sitting back-brace upright on the couch and dressed in a navy mini–business suit. He was watching a soap opera while munching on a thick, turkey-laden sandwich.

Surrounded by Foxy Brown posters and the minimalist décor of a single guy who just likes his movies, music, and girls, Kiko spotted Dawn in her tan jersey dress with the matching low-heeled sandals. Once upon a time, she'd worn it to a fellow stunt double's wedding but she hadn't needed it since, thank God. In the shower, she'd steamed out most of the wrinkles, but that didn't mean she didn't feel like a moron in it.

"Woo-woo," Kiko said, giving her a canary-eating grin. "Mama's on the prowl."

"Meh." Dawn plopped onto the plaid couch next to him.

He snapped off the TV, putting down his lunch, blue eyes aglow as he faced her. The stiff movement forced a slight grunt out of him. "So our busy boss said you'd tell me about Jessica's body. What'd you guys find?"

Far be it from her to get ecstatic about a murder, but Kiko was almost manic. Maybe it was because he was now back in the loop and his manhood had been restored.

For her part, Dawn fought the image of Jessica: bled-out pale, throat a mass of pulp. The colors wavered in front of her, refusing to settle into a palatable picture.

Come on, she thought. *Stop hiding from it. You've hidden for too many years already.*

Resolutely, she allowed the mental portrait to sink in, but that didn't mean she let it affect her. No emotion: it was the only way to deal.

"Breisi took pictures of Jessica for a better look later," Dawn said, "but the visit didn't tell us much more than we already knew.

It looked like an animal tore into the woman, just like with Klara."
The first vampire murder. Lee Tomlinson's murder. "But there was
something interesting: they found one cut on the left side of Jessica's neck that the bites didn't cover. A knife cut, they think, and
they say her throat could've been sliced before the murderer laid
chompers to her. That's something we didn't see with Klara, unless
Lee Tomlinson covered the cuts with his own mutilations. And they
found hints of longer . . ." What did they call those teeth? ". . . *lateral
incisors*. So maybe we've got a weaker vamp—a real one?—who
had to subdue the victim before feasting. . . ."

"Valid theory, but . . ." Kiko raised his eyebrows, obviously
knowing something that trumped the morgue stories. "I didn't get
back from Jessica's crime scene until about an hour ago, and I
found something that definitely makes me think we're not dealing
with what we think we are."

"Spill, please."

"Well, mostly I got residual readings, memories, from Jessica.
Dates she'd brought to her bedroom, upsetting phone calls she'd
made to her mom, who was getting her second divorce, things like
that. But then . . ."

Kiko took a dramatic pause. *Acting!* He was like that Jon Lovitz
character from *Saturday Night Live*, but for real.

"What?" Dawn said. "Tell me before the Four Horsemen of the
Apocalypse arrive."

"You have zero patience, you know that?" He angled forward,
becoming Serious Kiko. "I kept getting vibes from the closet. I was
touching everything inside, and when I came to the carpet, it was
obvious. The killer had been waiting there for Jessica to come home
from work."

Oh, damn. Just . . . *damn*. Suddenly, Dawn never wanted to be
alone in a room again. Shit, shit, shit.

Containing a shiver, she managed to ask, "So you were with the
killer? Do you know who it is?"

"No, no, don't I wish. There weren't a lot of clues about this . . . thing. Human, nonhuman, I'm still not sure."

"You've admitted yourself that you're not very good at reading vamps, like, you're not sure when they're going to show up and all that."

"But it's always just been a suspicion, not something I entirely believe. Definitely only a theory." Kiko shifted, then touched his back. Sending a testing glance at Dawn, he quickly looked away. "Vamps aren't supposed to have souls, or so we think. But what about the human Servants? I'd be able to read one of them. I did it with Lee Tomlinson in Bava."

Dawn watched him squirm around, not liking the tension on his face at all. Had he worked too hard during the beanbag simulation yesterday? "What did you get from the killer, Kik?"

"Nightmares." He removed his hand from his back, his eyes going dark. "The images, the feelings were like stabs. I couldn't hang on for long. But what I saw was . . . God, you know those old Nine Inch Nails music videos? Flashes of hell?"

Concerned, Dawn put her hand on his knee. She couldn't imagine having to live with a mind that was a portal to another dimension. Seeing Eva's grisly murder photos over and over was enough. Maybe too much.

"Any details?" she asked.

He nodded, his gaze straying from hers, as if seeking cover. He came to stare at the coffee table, where a pill bottle was resting on its side. Next to the filled water glass where she'd put Matt's already-wilting daisies, it made for an inexplicably disturbing picture.

"The killer might've been having sex with Lee Tomlinson," Kiko said. "Rough sex, too. Brutal. That's what I saw."

"They knew each other?"

"Either that or the killer fantasizes about him."

"And that would make sense if this were a copycat. Wouldn't there be some kind of worship and desire to *be* him?"

"Right, right." He moved around again. "You should've seen the morning news. They're all over this story. Jessica's murder is casting suspicion on Lee's guilt now—"

Dawn couldn't stand to watch him anymore. "Man, are you okay?"

His only answer was to look annoyed, which wasn't a surprise.

Her cell rang and, dragging her gaze away from Injured Kiko, she checked the call screen. "Breisi. She's probably in front of the apartment complex."

Kiko stood stiffly.

"Maybe you shouldn't go," Dawn said.

"Maybe you shouldn't worry like a squawking hen. I'll meet you out there."

She glanced at the pill bottle, then at him.

He scowled. "I said I'll meet you there."

Something leaden weighed in her chest as she went outside.

Happy Kiko, Serious Kiko, Hurting Kiko . . .

She wasn't so sure which one would be coming with her and Breisi to their surprise meeting with Milton Crockett.

It didn't take Kiko long to stuff his sunglasses into a front pocket for later use, do whatever else he was doing, and come outside. Ready and raring, they headed toward Beverly Hills, where the Friends had tracked Milton Crockett, Esquire, to a power lunch at the Grill on the Alley, or "The Grill" to those who spoke L.A.

Even though they were in the dog days of summer, the team all wore coats of different sorts, the better to cover and hold weapons with. The SUV's air-conditioning and Dawn's light jacket over her sleeveless dress helped a little, but they didn't completely erase the heat.

Sipping from an iced water bottle, she stretched out in the front seat, which she'd grabbed since Kiko hadn't been there to do it first.

And because there was no Dodgers game right this minute, Breisi wasn't wearing her usual earpiece to block out any and all conversation. Instead, she was decked out in a white pantsuit, a filmy long robe coat, and sunglasses. A faux Greek heiress, if Dawn said so herself.

"The plan is to get Kiko near enough to Milton Crockett for a touch reading, and that's all," Breisi was saying as she turned onto Santa Monica Boulevard.

"Easy as pie," Kiko mumbled from the backseat.

Dawn turned around to glance at him. He was as relaxed as someone with a back brace could be, staring out the window. Even from here she could tell his eyes were bleary.

"How many pills did you take?" Dawn asked.

"Just . . . one."

"One." Breisi was confirming, not actually asking. "Because if you're off in dreamland, Kik, you'll do us no good. Maybe we should take you into the doctor today—"

"No, Breez, just drive. I'm on full power, baby."

He closed his eyes, conversation over.

Dawn turned to Breisi, but neither of them commented.

It wasn't until a full minute later that Breisi said, "I wonder if we should make contact with Crockett another day, when Kiko's at his best."

"And when will that happen?"

Did Dawn ever sound pushy. But why shouldn't she be? Frank needed her, needed all of them. A while ago, Kiko had discovered he could divine occasional vibes from her dad's clothing—like the T-shirts Dawn wore to keep him close to her. Since the readings proved that Frank was still alive somewhere, they checked on him several times per night. Yet, lately, Kiko hadn't been picking up anything. Yeah, sometimes there'd be flashes of Frank in what had to be either physical or mental pain, just like the ones they'd gotten before, but nothing that led them onward. But, hey, why expect

more? Not even Breisi's tracking inventions—locators—had produced any results.

"Hey." Breisi's smooth voice reflected a woman who had everything under control in her own world. "You keep saying it yourself,
Dawn—we're going to find him. Never doubt it."

She wanted to believe that, because Breisi made it seem so possible with her rationality. But Dawn wanted to find him *now*. Wanted
this all to be over, damn it, so she could know her dad was okay, so
she could go back to normal. Whatever that was.

Still, she followed Breisi's advice, taking in a lungful of oxygen
and allowing it to pacify her, to temper last night's visit to Jessica
Reese.

"There you go." The other woman smiled as they stopped at a
red light.

"It amazes me," Dawn said.

Breisi raised a brow in question.

"Your faith." Dawn shook her head. "For a woman with such a
scientific bent, you've got a lot of it. Way more than I do, even if I'm
always telling you that we really are going to find Frank."

"Faith is what has always kept me going." The light turned green,
and Breisi urged the vehicle forward. "Faith in my ability to defend
my mother when my father would go on a bender and threaten us.
Faith in my studies, because that was what would get me out of that
house and into a better life at college. Faith in the church."

Dawn wondered if Breisi's crucifixes might work better than her
own in a vamp fight. Did believing in what they stood for matter? If
so, she was in trouble. Having a mother taken away from you so
violently and needlessly kind of helped with the whole lack-of-faith
thing.

"So . . ." She couldn't say what she wanted to without choking
a little, so she took another sip of water, coating her dry mouth. "I
know you think I haven't cared that much over the years, but
there's a lot between me and Frank that—"

"That's between the two of you, Dawn."

She shut up at that. Really, truly shut up. Breisi was right. Dawn couldn't make anything up to Frank by apologizing to his girlfriend.

In a smaller voice, one that sounded like the little girl who only wanted her daddy to be sober or to stop locking himself in his room at night and crying over Eva, Dawn asked, "You *really* believe we'll find him?"

With no hesitation, Breisi nodded. "Even if I don't seem sure, I always believe it, deep down. I keep thinking that God would not have made me feel the way I do about Frank if I wasn't meant to play a more important part in his life."

A more important part. Oddly enough, Dawn didn't chafe at that. She imagined Breisi might've made aimless Frank pretty happy, balanced him out so he could function better. And, evidently, that's exactly what had happened in the time before he'd gone missing. He hadn't been Frank the screwup anymore; he'd held down a job, paid his bills. Unbelievable.

From the back, Kiko breathed deeply, so relaxed that he was snoozing. It gave Dawn some courage to finally go where she never thought she wanted to before.

"Were you the one helping him get his act together, Breez?"

The other woman hesitated, then shrugged. "I suppose. But it was his choice to begin the process."

"Maybe you were the reason he did it." She couldn't believe she'd admitted that, but it felt decent, as if she'd finally caught on to something *else* she'd packed away inside of herself. Something she hadn't dared open for fear of how much it'd destroy her.

Breisi seemed to savvy how hard this was for Dawn. She flashed an easy smile. "You'd be happy to know that he was even starting to drink less. I made him smoothies, hoping that would fulfill some sort of craving, and he gulped them down without complaint. Blueberry." She laughed softly. "That is his favorite."

A lump tightened Dawn's throat. "Is. Is his favorite."

"Yes, is."

As another stoplight halted them, loud rap music from the Buick next door thudded through the floorboards. They took off at the green signal, leaving the clamor behind.

"Did you guys . . . ?" Dawn stopped. Then started. "Did you ever talk about marriage?"

"We talked, yes."

Something snapped inside, a final link Dawn had been maintaining, one that joined Eva and Frank in all their romantic, whirlwind-marriage snapshots.

"But," Breisi added, "we had that big fight about Eva. I thought he still wasn't letting go enough and he disagreed." She bit her lip, then pressed both of them together before speaking again. "Now that I look back, he was right. I'm the one who wasn't letting go of her."

"I know what you mean."

Because she, herself, was holding on to Eva through Jac now, and it was time to claw herself out of this hole of bitterness and one-sided competition between a goddess mother and her mortal daughter. Time to just leave the hard feelings behind.

But . . . panic fluttered at the thought of deserting such a vital part of her existence. What would she be without Eva?

Rather than face down that question, Dawn relaxed, dealing with more immediate menaces instead. The menaces she was getting to know real well.

"It must've been crazy, dating a fellow investigator." She played with the label of the water bottle, tearing at it. "I mean, it's bad enough tapping a regular coworker, but at least in normal life you don't have to worry about your boyfriend fighting monsters for his paycheck."

"Not the best of circumstances, I agree."

"But it's natural, I think, to gravitate toward someone you spend so much time with. It happens on every nine-to-five job, and especially movie sets. Damn, if we could keep a tally of how many costars fall into bed, the numbers'd populate a small country."

"It might be even more natural with someone in *our* business."

Our business. Could that possibly include Matt Lonigan? And what about The Voice? Did that mean it was perfectly natural to be hitting *that*?

Dawn turned her entire body toward Breisi now. "More natural?"

"Yes." Breisi smiled, but it wasn't a happy gesture. "Who else could I ever date, assuming that I'd want to? What would I say to a regular man I just met in, for instance, the hardware store? 'Hi, I'm Breisi. I like building my own computers, taking long walks on the beach, and killing vampires.' "

Laughing at the other woman's candor, Dawn took up where Breisi had left off. "Because I did terminate a vamp last night, you know. One with red eyes and iron fangs—"

"And burning spit—"

Laughing even louder at how ridiculous it sounded, Dawn embellished. "And a belly button that can suck you inside and put you right in the middle of a tea party with Bigfoot."

Breisi laughed, too. It was nice to see. She didn't go there much at all.

"Yeah." Dawn sighed, leaning back in her seat again. "That would impress any candidate for romance, wouldn't it? He'd probably jet away from me on a stream of piss and fear."

When Breisi laughed again, then reached over to do a fist bump with Dawn, it was a jolt. Whoa—the two of them actually *fully* understood each other for what had to be the first time. To make matters more shocking, Dawn realized that she hadn't thought about the reality of life for a record ten seconds. She'd never, ever guessed that Breisi could be the one who would give her that relief.

Still, Dawn cleared her throat, the awkwardness returning in a small, yet obvious, dose.

"So basically," she said, "the key is finding a fellow monster enthusiast who understands my work."

A man like Matt Lonigan or even The Voice, right? Could they anchor her in the same way Breisi and Frank had anchored each other?

Dawn now understood how Frank had moved on from Eva and his old life, truly understood how someone who wanted to change might be able to do the same thing.

If they really wanted to change.

"Maybe you're right," Breisi said. "Perhaps life might be simpler than we imagine."

They'd entered the impeccable streets of Beverly Hills, passing clipped, lush median greenery, pristine sidewalks, chichi boutiques and restaurants.

Breisi inserted her earpiece and instructed her phone to dial The Voice. He answered, and Breisi checked in with their location.

"Good," The Voice said. "Mr. Crockett seems to be wrapping up lunch with a partner from his firm." Somehow, his tone was less emphatic than it had been last night.

But it always had the power to tear through Dawn.

"Can we make it to Beverly Hills before he leaves?" she asked, ignoring her yearning for him. Too much work to do. At least, right now.

"If we don't intercept him before he leaves Beverly Hills," Breisi said, "we can just tail Crockett to wherever he's going next. Actually, maybe that's even a fortunate turn of events. Mr. Crockett is a part of the community here while we're not, and if our attempted reading becomes a confrontation, *Dawn*, the local cops could interfere. Beverly Hills police are known for responding to their calls within a couple of minutes, and we don't want that sort of trouble."

Breisi had taken extra care to emphasize Dawn's involvement because Dawn occasionally got a little persuasive with her hands when it came to interviewing difficult people. Lee Tomlinson could testify to that.

"Boss," Breisi added, "where is he parked?"

"His silver Ferrari is in an underground valet area on Two Rodeo. Before lunch, our Friends report that he was shopping for a bracelet at Harry Winston. He told the sales clerk it was for his wife. Then he took a leisurely stroll to The Grill from there. Our Friends will track him until you've made actual contact, just in case you should lose him."

"Got it, Boss."

"Harry Winston," Dawn said. "Crockett bought a guilt present, I'll bet. The wives score every time. Man, I wish we were detectives on a cheating husband case instead of . . . well, you know."

"Yes, I know." The Voice's volume had diminished even more, as if he really might have feelings—like regret—after all. "I—one moment." He paused, then came back online. "Milton Crockett is exiting the restaurant and heading toward Rodeo. Godspeed."

And he clicked off.

From the backseat, Kiko sat forward, rubbing his eyes. "Did he say a silver Ferrari? Imagine that in Beverly Hills. It should be really easy to spot."

They all chuffed, knowing a facetious comment when they heard one.

They drove past The Grill, discovering Milton Crockett strolling toward the valet garage with the sun glinting off his graying hair and lawyerly glasses. Then they turned around, taking care not to look like they were casing any of the snooty stores. By the time he exited the garage in his Ferrari, they were in position to follow.

Backtracking onto Santa Monica Boulevard while staying a respectable distance behind the possible Servant, Breisi attempted to avoid being obvious. Soon, they trailed him onto Fuller Avenue, which led to him turning into a condominium complex that wasn't too fancy, but not downscale, either. The buildings were all two-story white adobe creations, resembling a nondescript pueblo village where the neighbors probably didn't take pains to know each other, even if they shared common walls.

"From Beverly Hills to this," Dawn said. "What's Crockett up to?"

Kiko was leaning forward against the back of her seat, so his voice was almost in her ear. "The Winston bracelet, that's what." He didn't sound as alert as usual, but it wasn't bad enough for her to remark on it. "I'm thinking it's not the wife who's going to get it, if you know what I mean."

There wasn't a security stop, so the team easily caught up to Crockett just as he was getting out of his car and heading toward a condo. Beyond the modest wooden gate, on the door, a golden kitty spread its paws, spelling out "Welcome" with childlike letter blocks.

As Breisi cruised past, Dawn slid on a pair of oversized sunglasses that her coworker had brought for her.

Veering around the corner and coming to a stop, Breisi kept the engine running.

"Go," she said.

Dawn and Kiko wasted no time, leaving the SUV calmly enough not to scare off Crockett yet quickly enough to make sure he didn't get away. Kiko circled around so he would be approaching the lawyer from the back. He stumbled once, and Dawn's adrenaline ratcheted up a notch.

But she didn't have an opportunity to worry about him.

"Excuse me, sir?" she said.

Hand raised to open the wooden gate, the lawyer turned around, just as Kiko came into view behind him, advancing on quiet feet.

Milton Crockett ran a gaze over Dawn, seeming to appreciate her bared legs most of all. He was shorter than he looked on TV, but he was still imposing, with his smooth suit and intellectual glasses. Even garbed in layers of silk, he seemed as cool as autumn.

His expression was politely inquisitive, well suited to greet a female stranger who was dressed for a lovely lunch.

Good. At least this asinine dress hid her real identity, one he'd probably be familiar with if he actually was a Servant.

Dawn rushed to speak, gesturing behind her just to divert Crockett from the advancing Kiko for one more second. "I'm sorry to bother you, but is that building nineteen over there?" She smiled winningly—or the closest she could come to it.

Acting!

Crockett followed her pointing finger, and that was all the distraction they needed. From behind, Kiko grabbed the man's hand, immediately closing his eyes in concentration.

Startled, the lawyer jumped back, just as Breisi joined them. In spite of Crockett's movement, Kiko still had a firm hold, his whole body clenched as he got a reading.

"Robby Pennybaker," Breisi said.

She was using a phrase that would hopefully force Crockett's mind where Kiko—and The Voice—needed it. On the Underground, not necessarily the murder. They weren't giving anything away by saying Robby's name, either, since it'd been public knowledge that they were investigating him.

Gasping in obvious shock, the lawyer raised his other hand to cuff Kiko away, but Dawn whipped off her glasses and sprang to her friend's defense, bolting Crockett against the gate. Sucking in a breath—of pain, terror?—Kiko backed away, out of Dawn's line of sight.

"Don't you touch him!" she grated.

Crockett's nostrils flared at her garlic scent, but he wasn't repelled, and she could look into his eyes without consequence, proving he wasn't a vamp. But, this close up, she could see some kind of recognition burst open in his pupils, expanding the darkness over the light brown of his irises.

He knows who I am, she thought.

Yet he covered that really well, his expression hardening into a mask of outraged cluelessness in the next instant.

"Who are you? I'll have you arrested—"

"Let's go!" Breisi yelled.

Taking stock of her position, Dawn noticed Kiko wasn't around; he must've gone to Breisi already. So she pushed away.

Then, on second thought, she straightened Crockett's fine collar, his tie, and looked into his eyes the entire time.

God help him if he was a part of the vamp nation, because if they had Frank . . .

"Sorry for the inconvenience," she said.

Letting go of Crockett, she held up her hands in mocking defiance, then walked backward as the growl of the SUV hit the air. Behind the outraged lawyer, the condo door began to open, and Dawn took off toward the sound of the engine.

It was a bitch to run in heels, but she'd done it as part of one stunt gag before. As she got to the car, she saw that Breisi had already flipped the license plates to false numbers so they could avoid getting IDed. Once they were clear, the press of a button would change the plates back to normal.

The moment she hopped inside, Breisi charged off, and Dawn fought to close the door.

"He's got to be one of them," she said, turning toward the backseat so Kiko could hear her. "Right?"

Back stiff, the psychic seemed to draw into himself, looking more fearful than Dawn had ever seen him.

"I don't know," he said, voice shaking. "I didn't get anything." He closed his eyes. "Nothing at all."

SIX

BELOW, ACT ONE

LATER, just after the sun buried itself below the horizon, Milton Crockett bowed before a powerful Underground vampire in fearful respect and remorse.

"You," Sorin said through clenched teeth, "have been compromised."

Merely moments ago, after awakening, the vampire had been reclining near the clear-water lagoon of the emporium, enjoying the attentions of a Groupie. The sounds of the waterfall had sluiced over him as lovingly as his partner's tongue, her fangs, her long body. This Persian female was his favorite pet, talented with her mouth. Though Sorin adored her, he had been slightly dismayed that she, along with three other male and female Groupies, had recently chosen to shave their heads in a fashion statement of modern chic. Certainly, as a whole, the fun-loving vampires were prone to the trends Above, but this time Vashti, who had so named herself upon taking her Underground vows, had displeased him. Her "punishment"—if their exotic activities could be termed so—was even now occurring, her lips worshipping him to arousal.

Now, as the Servant Milton Crockett submitted himself before Sorin, the vampire eased Vashti's smooth head away from his lap, his unfulfillment doubled by what the human had just revealed.

A single bead of sweat dripped from the lawyer's face to the lagoon sand. "Master, Dawn Madison and her friends can't be certain of what I am. I'm confident they're only following up on Robby Pennybaker's case, nothing more than that."

Master. No one but the elite citizens knew that Sorin was merely a double, a bodyguard who took the place of the true leader for security reasons. That was how it had been these past fifty years, since this particular Underground had been established. However, these days, the real Master disguised himself and mingled among the populace more and more frequently.

As he was doing now.

While mist from the waterfall gathered on the air, one cloud remained more solid than the others. The wispy tendrils wove through each other, beautiful and deadly.

The Master. Dr. Eternity, as the Elites had named him. The creator of this Underground paradise.

Do you hear this Servant? Sorin thought to the Master, accessing the Awareness a vampire and its child could use to silently communicate. *The threats Above are growing even stronger.*

Yes, I can hear.

Sorin gestured for Vashti to press her ear to his mouth so he could whisper an instruction to her. She complied, covering him with a swath of silk. Then, pressing her fingertips to her forehead in a sign of respect, she left to fetch another Servant, another lawyer who would do well to listen to this conversation with Mr. Crockett. All the while, her silver eyes flashed disappointment at the interruption of her punishment.

A thought tugged at the edges of Sorin's mind. Yes . . . he

remembered now. Vashti had been among the flock of Groupies who had first recruited Lee Tomlinson to the Underground. They had come upon him at one of the many so-called vampire bars humans loved to frequent.

Fitting that she should be the one to fetch the lawyer who would now see to Lee Tomlinson's fate.

Alone with the Servant, Sorin turned his full gaze upon him. "Rise."

Mr. Crockett wiped away the sweat that had gathered on his upper lip.

"You think Limpet and Associates is harmless," Sorin said, "even if their tiny detective—the one who is said to have the sixth sense—was touching you, as if to know your thoughts."

"I think they only suspect that I'm a basic familiar and that I know more about Robby than it appears to the public."

"You do not think this psychic looked into you?"

"I blocked my thoughts as soon as I felt him touching me."

That might be true, but Sorin was not a vampire who traded on maybe's. "I hope you are correct, Mr. Crockett. Surely you recall how Robby and Nathan Pennybaker leaked information about our home to these detectives."

The Servant nodded, gaze fixed to the ground.

It was not enough to assuage Sorin.

Having been present at the scene of Robby's final betrayal, the Guards had informed Sorin, their keeper, of every last detail. What Dawn Madison and her friends had learned concerned him a great deal, yet the Master remained insistent that they wait for a "better" time to attack. A time when they knew with absolute certainty that Limpet and Associates was hunting the Underground and not merely investigating Robby Pennybaker. A time when they could ascertain if this "Limpet" was perhaps even a master from a rival Underground, an "other" to be avoided at all costs.

Others forced takeovers, and Sorin knew this all too well.

Though it was true that, since parting ways over a century ago, not every master had become a dangerous one—some only had the ambition to peacefully join with existing Undergrounds out of pure loneliness—Dr. Eternity had been attacked and beaten before. And, long ago, Sorin and his Master had determined that this would never happen again. *Never.*

As Sorin's silence forced Milton Crockett to keep staring at the ground in his shame, Sorin thought of how the loss of the first Underground had negatively affected the Master. Fear of a second attack had plunged their leader into a recurring numbness. This depression had sapped his will, urging him to ignore the hint of another master in the area before the situation had grown more serious with Robby. Perhaps he had only been attempting to avoid repeating one of the most devastating moments of his vampire life by refusing to acknowledge the threat of another losing battle.

But now, after Robby's security breach, the Master was no longer ambivalent, thank the day.

The Underground was preparing to defend, not provoke, because if they should launch an effective attack against the PIs only to be mistaken, this would force an end to the Underground. Utilizing their full powers Above—going beyond simple shielding to avoid detection—would announce their whispered presence to those who knew how to read such signals. It would mean surrendering their safe haven, exposing them to perhaps a real master who could, in turn, attack.

Fear was no way to live.

Sorin felt his maker shift closer to the Servant, and he knew his father was restless.

"Mr. Crockett," Sorin said, calling the human's attention.

The lawyer, a man who loved the Underground as much as any full-vampire citizen, lifted his chin and spread out his hands.

"Please, Master, I can take care of this situation without any attention focusing on our society. That's what I do Above. That's what I have been doing for the Pennybaker case, as well as Lee's."

Sorin nodded. Since Lee Tomlinson had used vampire methods to murder Klara Monaghan for what he thought was the good of the Underground, he had marked their society for human attention. The lawyers Above knew there was no way around this, so they had improvised, taking great advantage of a subculture some humans embraced—a vampiric Goth lifestyle. They had convinced the public that Lee Tomlinson was one of those shadow numbers, diverting suspicion from the reality. Their philosophy was simple: cast a blinding, never-ending light on the lies rather than the truth, and the humans would never be able to look away from the one show to pay mind to the other.

Sleight of hand, that was the key.

The Master floated closer. *Tomlinson . . .* whispered his Awareness. His cloud darkened, seething at the name, echoing the hiss of the waterfall. *Traitor.*

It was a fitting description for Lee the Servant. He, too, had forfeited information to Limpet and Associates, just as Robby and Milton Crockett had.

Security at any cost, Sorin thought to his father.

The Master's cloud swirled, as if regretful of what must be done. *Your instincts are right, even though it took me longer to admit it. We weren't vigilant enough the first time. But we will be now.*

Vashti returned with the other Servant and left with a petulant glance at Sorin, who ignored her in favor of the new arrival.

This human, wearing a burgundy silk robe, was short in stature and fairly well padded around the middle, with bushy eyebrows, slick brown hair, and what humans on the television called a "five o'clock shadow." His presence increased Mr. Crockett's anxiety; he no doubt recognized the lawyer from a competing firm Above.

Enrico Harris bowed, fingertips to forehead. Sorin motioned for him to sit quietly.

"I'm begging you, Master," Mr. Crockett said, "I can take care of this. Secrecy for the Underground is everything."

"Yes, it is. Tell me, did you anticipate that the genetic material of Lee Tomlinson would lead to his arrest?"

The Master's mist rolled, as if he were positioning himself to hear clearly. The television program *CSI: Las Vegas* was one of his favorites, and Sorin was certain his love of it was piqued, along with the more important issues. He had utilized newscasts, shows, and movies in order to learn how to function in this modern world, and he had required it of Sorin, as well. He longed to be a part of the Hollywood he fed from, educating himself to be their equal. Sadly, the Master's adoration of these humans was a double-edged blade, infusing him with the knowledge that the narcissistic Elite could never return Dr. Eternity's overwhelming affections with the same passion.

"There was nothing I could do about the DNA." Mr. Crockett glanced at Mr. Harris as if searching for affirmation. "But I can keep that evidence out of the trial."

The second lawyer nodded at Sorin, assuring him that he would be able to accomplish this as well as Mr. Crockett could.

"Besides," the first lawyer continued, clearly making a case to prove his value, "you know Lee's mind was wiped, erasing all his vampire memories but leaving all the others, before you gave him over to me. It was just as effective as Marla Pennybaker's treatment, and it's not possible for him to slip up and reveal anything about the Underground. All the public will see during his trial is a wannabe actor who worked at a Goth bar. They'll know without a doubt that he was one of those humans who only wishes vampires existed. The world is used to people like him, and no credence is paid to their beliefs. They'll think Lee's need to feast on a woman's throat was the act of a psychotic. *He* doesn't even know what he was doing."

All this trouble because of breaking the rules, the Master mused to Sorin, hovering ever nearer to the unaware Mr. Crockett. *Always ask for permission to feed off our partners, we've said. Willingness to join us means they won't resist and they'll be open to never revealing us. Lee didn't understand that.*

This was true of the blood vampires imbibed to survive, but the Master, ah, the true Master was a Soul Taker. Souls were his manna, his sustenance, the only way he could feel real emotion. Sorin had never understood the Master's compulsion, never once in over three hundred years since his father had created him.

Not until recently, when there were times he . . .

Sorin discarded the very thought, setting his mind back on track.

Perhaps feeding on a human's life force was not so odd—for the Master. It had aided him in emerging from a lengthened depression, after all. Souls had helped to awaken the old vampire. Did they also have the power to—

Yes, the Master said. *It's sublime, my son. They have the power to make you into whatever you wish to be. I keep telling you to try it.*

Once again turning aside from the horrifying idea, Sorin stood from his relaxed position against the smooth waterfall rocks and sheathed himself in his long, black robes. "Are you telling me, Mr. Crockett, that Lee Tomlinson's case is well in hand?"

"Yes, Master. Even before I took care of calling in the anonymous tip that gave the authorities his location, I've had *everything* well in hand."

Excellent, Sorin thought. In the Servant's haste to seem indispensable, he had given assurance that Mr. Harris would be able to take over all "fixer" duties. The Underground had layers upon layers of Servants who handled surreptitious matters Above, and every familiar was rewarded with the joys down Below. It was a prize for vowing to never speak of the paradise's existence.

One less familiar would not harm the Underground.

The Master positioned himself over Mr. Crockett's head.

"You understand," Sorin continued, "that Lee Tomlinson is not our only worry, of course. This new murder Above echoes the troubling situation Lee Tomlinson brought upon us with Klara Monaghan. Hence, we are being forced to emerge from our retreat and risk using spies again to stop this killer from inadvertently revealing us. After what occurred with Robby Pennybaker and Limpet and Associates, your revealed identity is a risk we should not otherwise be undergoing."

Lee Tomlinson's actions, as well as the Elite Robby Pennybaker's, had caused an Underground lockdown. There had also been heightened concern when a Guard had discovered tiny mechanical devices on its clothing before it had returned Underground with Marla Pennybaker in tow. In response, many lesser Servants had not been granted access except for investigative purposes as well as blood-food for the rest of them. Additionally, Groupies were not allowed Above until Sorin and the Master were confident in the community's ability to withstand a takeover.

They were not at that point yet, but they were close. Sorin had been refining the manufactured Guards, polishing away their shortcomings, and they all had been training in war arts. In essence, casual vampire activity Above had been discouraged, so they could, as the Master would say, "lie low."

But with this new preternatural-type murder, they had no choice but to act. The appearance of the corpse, Jessica Reese, would only stir up groups such as Limpet and Associates, especially since no Underground vampire knew who *this* murderer was. Could it be a creature who was not related to the Underground? Or perhaps it was another Servant who wished to show the Master that they were worthy of being a full vampire, as Lee Tomlinson had reasoned. Sorin had already checked into the minds of the Guards, the Servants, the Groupies, and even many of the Elites to determine if the murderer had been one of their own. Thus far, it had not.

Milton Crockett was sweating in earnest now. "I understand

Robby's and Lee's actions might have caused harm. But you know *I* would never let that happen, Master. You know that I would sacrifice anything to be here."

"Even your family?"

Or your mistress? asked the silent Master.

Sorin dismissed the other lawyer, Mr. Harris, whose skin had gone very pale. Perhaps he realized his possible future, as well, if he was not careful.

"You would exchange blood with one of the Groupies to become a permanent part of us?" Sorin asked, knowing that, in spite of his marital infidelities, Mr. Crockett fancied himself a "family man" and this was the reason he had never become more than a human Servant. "You would give your soul?"

In the Master's cloud, Sorin detected the hint of fangs, of a terrible virtue not even *he* could look upon directly.

Mr. Crockett hesitated, still too attached to his humanity, and that was all the answer Sorin and the Master required.

Like the gaping jaw of a god, the cloud descended around the Servant's head. His eyes bulged as he suffered a glimpse of pure terror. Knowing that paradise was about to be washed from his memory, Mr. Crockett's lips opened in a scream that never came to be.

One fraction of a second later, it was over.

The lawyer crumbled to the ground. Efficaciously, Sorin enlisted Groupies to prepare the mind-wiped man for return Above. There, Mr. Harris would be his keeper, making certain Milton Crockett adjusted to life as it used to be.

Although the mind wipe had taken his memories of the Underground, it had at least left him his soul. And Sorin knew Mr. Crockett had come out the loser.

Task completed, the vampire rested near the waterfall once again, in no mood to summon Vashti, even if she was casting seductive glances at him from a satin bed where three other Groupies painted blood pictures over each other with fine-haired brushes.

Nearby, two Elites, whose money ensured the success of the Underground, languished. They wore no clothing, save for the jewels pasted on the female's skin. They were smoking from a hookah pipe, the concoction laced with blood to add flavor.

Jesse Shane, Sorin thought, running his gaze over the blond film legend's sleek muscles. The actor would be released in fifteen years. The other cocoa-skinned vampire, Tamsin Greene, was their newest Elite, born almost a month ago, transformed from a superstar singer/actress to a myth. Robby Pennybaker, the child actor who had caused such a disturbance, had been an Elite, as well.

Excepting Robby, the Elites found the Underground to be the answer to eternal fame. They had literally sold their souls for the Master's edification, sacrificing them so they could receive Dr. Eternity's treatment.

First, at the height of their careers, they staged their own sensational murders—ones that would guarantee infamy. Yet they were not truly succumbing to death. Far from it. Dr. Eternity exchanged blood with them, then continued to infuse them with his fluids each month since the Elite were not true children like Sorin, who had been gifted with merely one bite. Continual maintenance kept the emotionally unstable Elite under the Master's control, making them inferior in Sorin's mind.

After the initial stage of treatment, the Elite stayed Underground for years and years, knowing that Above, fans mourned their memory, wishing for them to return while worshipping their pop-culture images, keeping their legends alive. Just when public hunger reached a climax, the Elite underwent Dr. Eternity's final magic, a surgery that shaped him into "another" celebrity, a new creation with a different stage name, a budding star who would claim an eerie resemblance to his true self. The Elite was then released back Above to use his enhanced, naturally magnetic life force in a fresh career. In the end, he would build on his old talents while enjoying the new.

Hollywood was full of Elites, "the new so-and-so," "the next him-or-her." In fact, one of their earliest clients had recently been released Above a second time in anticipation of another chance at fortune and glory. She had returned Underground when the public began to notice her chronic youthfulness, and that was the cue for Sorin to arrange another death. Her second passing had been of a milder form since the first had already set the proverbial stage for her legend to be established, and she was now continuing a prosperous career.

The Underground was where a star's drug addictions became blood addictions. It was where they gave up their human entourages for the haremlike conditions of massages and Turkish baths, pampering, bodies frozen in perfection. The Underground even used Servant psychiatrists to fulfill the Elite's never-ending emotional crises.

It was heaven for so many of them.

Sorin breathed the incensed air, the languid pace of lovemaking behind the veiled curtains of silken beds, the laughter of Elites and Groupies drinking blood from golden cups, feasting on kisses and bites.

His Underground. A pleasure to die for.

In the meantime, the Master was reveling under the water's spray again, as if cleansing himself, allowing the liquid to separate the wisps of his disguise in masochistic ecstasy.

Mr. Crockett only proved that, to save ourselves, we must neutralize Limpet and Associates, Sorin tacitly said to his father. *Even if we are not certain they are connected with another master.*

No!

Sorin narrowed his eyes at the Master's ferocity. *For what reason? Limpet could be the beginning of the end.*

You know why. The Master traveled nearer, bringing a chill with him. *We cannot afford to show our hand to the world before we're sure. And attacking before they do would make us vulnerable. We can't give up the protection of secrecy, Sorin. We need proof—and*

*we need to draw them to us. Otherwise, the same thing will happen
as it did the first time, when, clueless, I was flushed out.*

The younger vampire tried to restrain himself, but he could not.
Images of the Master's most recent behavior—which included
spending hours in front of the television watching Eva Claremont
movies—disturbed him.

The Master grew colder.

I worry, Father, Sorin said, thinking again about how the elder
had always sought human affection, had always searched to replen-
ish the soul he had lost so long ago. In the 1980s, he had developed
a fascination for Eva Claremont, favoring her films and collecting
her photos. The pattern had gone beyond his usual adoration of the
Elite crowd, and it had even led to the troubles they were experiencing now.

I worry about this obsession you have, Sorin thought. *I worry
about your activities—*

Silence!

At that point, Sorin blocked off the Awareness between them.
He knew it would show his father how strongly he felt more than
any words. In the past, the Master had allowed his predilection for
Eva, the blond screen goddess, to cloud his judgment. Sorin did not
wish this to happen again.

The older vampire grew angry, his cloud hissing actual, soft
words. "Have you thought about the ways Eva's daughter might be
able to lead us to our enemy, if one indeed exists?"

Yes. Sorin had thought about it night after night.

He turned his Awareness back on. *I have thought of everything
possible.*

*Then allow our players to do the work Above, Sorin. Let us
trust the spy work again.*

Sorin did not respond. Instead, he glanced up at the ever-shifting
cloud, attempting to find his beloved father in the mist.

SEVEN

Somewhere in Transylvania, Late 1600s

If the night was slightly chilled, or even mild, Benedikte did not notice. These past months (or perhaps they were years?) had blended into a thick, ever-sifting fog, a murk that held no sense of time, place . . . identity.

He entered the forest, overtaken with such drunkenness that he did not heed anything save the aftermath of the kills he had impulsively enjoyed last hour. Blood still painted his tongue with the taste of a heavy, piquant honey, a hint of an elemental ingredient that yet escaped him, bite after bite.

The family he had taken unawares—mere sustenance—would not be discovered until morning at the earliest, when they would fail to creak open the door of their thatched cottage, fail to greet the sunlight and harvest the gains from their farmland. Perhaps it would take more than a few days for the neighbors from the nearby village to sniff out the carnage and raise the alarm so as to gather in their fortified church and barricade themselves from danger.

By then it would be futile. Yes, they would cry that a vampire epidemic had descended upon them, yet Benedikte would be long away, hunting for his next meal in another unsuspecting community, whether it be across the mountains or southward to more exotic lands already visited—*anywhere* that would satisfy his appetites.

Yet tonight, before leaving altogether, he was compelled to follow a trail. He had caught scent of this particular human, prey that fascinated him, weeks ago. He had been tracking the man from village to village, assessing, worshipping him from afar, fantasizing that his blood would be the answer to the unnamed recent hunger Benedikte felt for more than food. . . .

Yawning night enveloped the vampire as he threaded deeper into the mist-hushed cove of trees, up the gentle slope of a mountain. His sturdy jackboots, once stolen from an unfortunate western adventurer—English, perhaps?—crushed the fallen beech leaves. Quite near, he could sense the trickle of a stream, the crackling stench of a fire. Most of all, he could all but feel the warm skin and pulse of the human.

Drawing closer to the mortal aroma, Benedikte's own skin absorbed the prey's heartbeat, just as it did every time the vampire lurked near this man. Once again stunned by the awakened sensation—none of his food allowed him such a pleasure as this—he halted, clutching his belly. This echo of what Benedikte remembered to be life wrenched his stomach into painful knots of estrangement.

It had been so long. . . . How many years *had* passed since he had taken the blood oath? More than two centuries now? And how long since he had abandoned Tereza for these exquisite compulsions that had changed him from the rough, yet moral and Godly husband he had once been, to this: a lost creature who wandered the earth, glutting on blood and sin while searching for a way to alter the pattern of his nights, to feel alive once more?

And how long since Tereza had passed out of this world to leave him behind, never to allow him the opportunity to finally conquer his shame at his new appetites, to leave the shadows outside their home and approach her, to invite her to exchange with him and ease his sorrows?

Benedikte leaned against the bole of a tree, adapting to the wonderful shock of connecting with this human. Over the gloom, a wolf keened while moonlight drifted down through the branches, blading the ground with faint light.

Slowly, the pulse of the mortal insinuated itself into Benedikte's very veins. He followed the call of it, the thud enrapturing him, guiding him to a clearing in which a man sitting on a log held his hands out to a fire.

The light hushed over the brown hair flowing just past his shoulders. His bearing was that of perhaps a Magyar, one of many Hungarian conquerors who had stolen this land and called it their own. Yet the human wore clothing that contradicted this assumption of superiority: a longer coat hewn of coarse fabric, perhaps a Moldavian weave; breeches; low-heeled, practical shoes.

Though the fire's flames repulsed the vampire, this male still drew him.

Benedikte had first discovered him entertaining a small crowd on the outskirts of Cluj, where he had been made to flee when an old woman cried out in fear at the sight of the fire he had conjured from air.

"Sorcerer!" she had branded him while men chased him and his baskets of tricks into a copse of trees.

A magician. A being who proved that what the eye saw was not always what existed in reality.

Benedikte, who had served as an audience for a collection of performers during his wanderings, was enthralled by this man's kind. How this variety of person lived another identity onstage or how they fooled the eye with costumed playacting enchanted him.

In truth, the vampire craved the same magical escape from himself, some nights.

All nights.

After this sorcerer had been driven from Cluj and before certain attack from the community could follow, Benedikte had stalked the male: through the woods where he had sheltered himself to avoid detection, on the fringes of towns where he earned his meals. All the while, the vampire had remained spellbound by what the human had done with the fire—controlling it. The audiences had been utterly transfixed, and Benedikte so wished to hold that same power in his own hands. Perhaps he could absorb this sorcerer's secrets, just as he had taken in centuries' worth of education during his wanderings.

In the dark of shadow, Benedikte carefully breathed, softly and undetectably, as he watched the human. More than anything, he wished to find another being who would not turn away from him once they discovered what magic *he* held, as well. Long ago, his brothers had all scattered to the winds, pursuing their own lusts, though their blood vow assured they would come together if their maker ever summoned them.

Now, while the fire sparked, the sorcerer stiffened, as if sensing Benedikte. Quickly, he turned about to discover the vampire waiting under the black of the branches. On the human's lap, a cat arched to a feral stand, hissing, baring its teeth.

With one hand, the man reached into his far coat pocket. With the other, he lay a vigilant palm upon the feline, restraining the animal while awaiting Benedikte's reason for approaching.

"Good evening," the vampire said in his mother tongue. He had learned many languages during his travels, but these were the words that would always come first to him. "I am sorry to intrude, but I was seeking light in this darkness. I mean you no harm."

Stepping into the glow, Benedikte compelled the human to accept him.

The sorcerer narrowed his eyes, his clear gaze taking in this stranger's refusal to don a periwig as fashion dictated. Scanning the rest of Benedikte, the man assessed the vampire's simple *justaucorps*, which covered a linen waistcoat, and the cravat he favored, all of which spoke of modest means and a genuine apathy for the style of the day.

"Do you hail from a nearby village?" the sorcerer asked, his tone uneasy, though it did not cover an accent tinged with educated refinement.

"I am not from any village."

Finally, the sorcerer succumbed to Benedikte's mind grasp. His heartbeat calmed, yet only slightly. He stood rigidly, gesturing for Benedikte to sit on a stone that rested on the opposite side of the fire. The cat watched the vampire, green eyes wide. Its tail whipped around, as if readying itself to strike if necessary.

"I am Benedikte of Wallachia." Bowing, he awaited the male's name, his body livened by the delightful rhythm of the human's heartbeat.

"Sorin, the son of Ion. I regret there is no food for me to share in companionship."

Smiling, Benedikte rested on the stone, then arranged his coat comfortably. He knew his skin was flush with his last meal, creating a mortal complexion. As well, he was expert at controlling his natural urges regarding a human. He could subsist on a meal for weeks, though, as of late, he longed for a treat other than blood, something he could not name. . . .

As Benedikte's need quickened, the cat reacted, standing on its two rear feet, claws swiping the air.

Sorin kept hold of the creature. "She is addled this night."

Benedikte had witnessed the cat during one show. It had been docile enough, yet he recalled the animal balancing on two legs even then. The sight of a dancing feline had struck him as enchantingly human.

"This is a most astounding creature," he said.

"Yes." Sorin arose, tucking the cat into a lidded basket, latching it, then moving to yet another.

When he opened it, he searched among the contents, extracting a piece of cloth, a long pipelike musical instrument, then—

The flash of a crucifix blinded Benedikte. He reared back, hand uplifted to block the sight.

Forgive me, Father, please, forgive me for what I've become, he thought, unable to take his eyes away, struck with a horrific despair so profound that he could not move. *I am nothing, nothing at all. . . .*

Sorin tucked the silver object back into the basket, saving Benedikte from further anguish. He breathed easier, though the air pierced his lungs in the aftermath.

Upon returning to the fire, the human offered what he had retrieved from the basket. A bottle of wine.

Calmed, Benedikte refused.

The youngster nodded and drank deeply. Though he kept his gaze fixed on Benedikte, Sorin seemed more relaxed now that witchery or burning at the stake had not been mentioned. Superstitious mortals who had seen his sorcery would not take the time to sit before Sorin and converse with him as Benedikte was doing.

"I believe," the vampire said, attempting to keep his gaze from Sorin's throat as it worked to swallow the wine, "I read a pamphlet detailing the exploits of a sorcerer with an amazing cat who was run out of several villages in this area. I must say that it amused me."

"Mmmm." Relieved even further by another of Benedikte's smiles, this one testifying to a certain camaraderie and understanding, Sorin saluted with his bottle. "My fame spreads, does it not?"

"May I assume the rancor has not convinced you to refrain from entertaining more villages?"

"You may. I am afraid that it is the only way for me to eat my daily bread for now. Yet . . ." He lifted his hands and the wine sloshed against the bottle's sides, singing high and sharp in Benedikte's ears.

"I do suppose it is time for me to cross borders again and take up in another place."

"May I ask . . . how is it that you came to be a . . . sorcerer?" Benedikte leaned forward.

While Sorin licked a drop of wine from his full lower lip, the vampire's mouth flooded with juices. He silently asked the young man to expose all.

As always, he succeeded.

"On the estate," Sorin said, blinking slowly, "that is, my childhood home, we employed an old man who kept silent about knowing certain . . . tricks. Simple yet bewildering. I found him amusing his grandson one day and I wished to know his secrets. Much to my shame, I threatened to reveal him if he refused me, not that I would have actually. . . ." Sorin shook his head, a strand of hair falling over his young cheek. "All the same, he taught me the illusion of conjuring fire, then encouraged me in other, shall we say, pursuits."

Benedikte tilted his head in query.

Sorin took yet another draw from the bottle. As Benedikte calmed his instincts, he detected details: the temptation of a vein throbbing in the sorcerer's neck, the broadness of his shoulders, the obvious outline of a pistol under his coat.

Possibly his only defense, Benedikte thought. And it would not be enough, though it seemed to give the boy confidence.

"Other pursuits?" Benedikte prodded.

Leaning his forearms on his thighs, Sorin canted forward, encouraged by wine and the mind grasp. "Do you believe in the possibility of miracles?"

The vampire smiled yet again, knowing he would not show fangs at this stage. Not until he was fully primed to feed. "I do."

Sorin hesitated, as if deciding whether or not to demonstrate to this stranger how dangerous he could be. Then he, too, smiled.

"The cat," he said. "She has been improved."

Without meaning to, Benedikte laughed in surprise. In pure rapture at the memory of the standing, dancing cat.

"I am not jesting." Sorin motioned to the latched basket. "I cannot explain this fully, but I . . . I have a gift, the old man told me. I can 'manipulate,' he said."

And so can I, Benedikte thought, seeing before him a revealed brother, a soul worth clinging to. Joy speared through him, stronger than hunger, thicker than the blood with which he replenished his body.

"How is that?" the vampire whispered. "How do you . . . manipulate?"

Sorin spilled the information as easily as wine from the bottle. "I do not know. I . . . I lay a hand on the creature—small creatures, only small—and I think of what I would like them to be." The human flushed. "It does not always succeed."

"Have you performed your talents on a human?"

The young man's gaze went dark, as if the mere notion frightened him. Benedikte knew that Sorin had mused about this possibility, yet had never attempted it.

"This is the reason you hide in the woods," the vampire said softly. "Because of your great magic."

Sorin drank again, a trail of wine trickling from the corner of his mouth as he pulled the bottle away. "My family disavowed me. There were whispers among the servants, then fear in my mother's eyes. I had no choice but to deny the accusations, yet they cast me out. They . . . abhorred me."

The fire snapped as Benedikte calculated the distance between him and the ruthless flames.

"Family," he said, breaking eye contact and staring into the heat. He required the mind grasp no more. "I have not seen my family in . . ."

Yes, it had to be at least two centuries now. He had no concept of the year nor his whereabouts, but at least he knew this much. He had given life to no progeny and this agonized him most of all. His line was dead. Once, in an attempt to redeem himself and to quell the growing isolation, Benedikte had forced an exchange between himself and a Venetian noblewoman whose countenance recalled his bride, Tereza. She had screamed for hours afterward, and he had been compelled to silence her forever. He had never returned to his own pious wife; he had already become a creature she would have seen as an abomination, and he had ached too much for all the appetites his blood oath awakened to leave them behind for her sake.

Not that he could end it all. Once, and only once, he had tried and failed, even at the risk of the soul he no longer possessed.

After the death of Tereza, in search of a comforting balm, he had turned to blood, imbibing it, reveling in it until the liquid lost heat in his mouth. It was the only method that soothed the agony of knowing she had aged without him and passed into peace, just as their only son, dead out of the womb, had done.

Benedikte was truly alone. Or, at least, he *had* been.

Once more, he locked gazes with Sorin, a man who understood the anguish of being cast out just as well as he.

"I, too, have not seen my family in years," the vampire said quietly. "I have traveled extensively, and I have been . . . remiss in visiting, I am afraid."

The mention of travel lit Sorin's eyes and, as the fire burned on, the two began to talk of travel: the splendor, the dangers. They chuckled together, comfortable, slipping down from their seats to the ground.

Soon, Sorin's bottle was near empty. At a tale Benedikte told of a madman he had dined with in the town of Targoviste, the young man sprawled over the dirt in a fit of laughter, his coat now gaping to clearly show the long pistol.

Shaking his head while the gaiety trailed off, the sorcerer closed his eyes, sighed, and leaned back to rest his head on the wood. At the sight of his exposed neck, Benedikte's veins thundered, a violent hunger cutting through him. He so desired a companion. He so wished to know this human's secrets and to, perhaps, be animated by his touch and fulfilled by whatever magic he wielded.

All I want once more is to feel, the vampire thought. Did this man have the talent to alter his matter, just as he did with small animals? Could he imagine Benedikte with a soul again and make it possible?

Nimbly, Benedikte inched closer to the resting sorcerer. He settled by Sorin's side, breathing him in, his body exploding with thrusts of a shared heartbeat. He sniffed upward, traveling the path of a vein. The scent of young skin whipped his mind, his yearnings, into a frenzy.

"I am thirsty now," he whispered.

Eyes still closed, Sorin reached for the bottle, then flopped it toward his companion. "Then drink."

So invited, Benedikte roared to a change, body scrambling into a powerful mist, fangs springing from his gums as he pounded forward in a blur. When he pierced a vein, the sorcerer jerked awake, mouth opening, body convulsing as the vampire sucked in deep gratitude.

Do not fear the years I will give you, Benedikte thought, feeling his words infusing themselves into Sorin's head as his mouth and throat flooded with blood. So much blood, never enough, never, never . . .

Then it happened.

A different clotted, hot, numbing flow rushed into him. It filled Benedikte, blooming with the memory of true laughter, sadness, all the emotions he had forfeited upon drinking the blood of his own maker.

It was a soul, Benedikte knew, Sorin's soul, and it darted around inside of him with the confused ferocity of a trapped animal, seeking a path out while leaving sparks of that sublime emotion he so wanted. Yet he did not wish for it to leave, did not wish for it to—

With an agonizing tear, it screamed out of him. Benedikte

flailed, reaching for it, combing through the thick invisibility of air while his greatest dream fled.

"No!"

When his hand gripped nothing yet again, he smashed a fist to the ground. The wine bottle shook in the aftermath.

"There." The vampire aimed a stare at the container. "You go *there*. A haven. Safety. *Shelter*."

The soul wailed, lured and tricked, as it swished into the open wine bottle. Wildly, Benedikte grabbed the vessel, pressing his thumb over the opening. Capturing his new hope.

Life, he thought. What he had felt just now was finally life, not the mere existence he had been enduring.

Using a handkerchief to plug the bottle, Benedikte rushed to cut his misted wrist with a long nail, to force his blood into Sorin's mouth in hasty exchange so he, too, would not attempt to escape.

Just as his son once had . . . his child, blue-skinned, lacking in breath . . .

The sorcerer gulped as if he were an infant at a breast, taking in the blood that would nurture him. Taking in his new life.

Twitching his mouth away from the wrist, Sorin moaned in agony, screeching and reaching out, fingers clawed as he attempted to grasp the silvered murkiness of Benedikte's body.

Meanwhile, the old vampire hovered away, wisping back to his other, more human form. He watched, eyes tearing at the birth of his own line.

An eternity later, young Sorin shuddered to completion. Benedikte went to him, easing him into the cradle of his arms, stroking his child's hair.

"Son," he said, looking down upon the new, confused vampire as he leaned back his head, blood marking his gaping lips. "Finally . . . my own son."

For the rest of the night as he rocked his child to rest, Benedikte smiled to himself, listening to the wolf howling and the fire dying.

EIGHT
THE BROOD

AFTER the interview, there's a nice, plump cactus by the lobby where we can do pictures," said Coral Tomlinson, Lee's faintly inbred mother. "We been posing out in front of it all week."

The afternoon following the Milton Crockett ambush found Dawn aiming a digital camera recorder at the fiftyish widow Tomlinson. She was sitting apart from the rest of her family, in a zebra-striped chair here at the Adventure Motel off Sunset, a relic from the days of plastic-beaded entryways and turquoise shag carpeting. Stale smoke seemed like it'd worked its way into the safari wallpaper, and the atmosphere wasn't so much a throwback as an admission that the owner didn't have enough money to redecorate.

As Dawn watched the camera's flip-out monitor, she noted that Coral's hair was that bright red you could only get from a dime-store bottle, her skin tanned to the point of accelerated age spotting. She wore one of those paisley-patterned blouses that probably came from the same store as the hair supplies, plus polyester slacks.

Not that Dawn was some catwalk pro herself, but she could tell this was high fashion for Coral because of the way the woman tugged at the material, as if it didn't fit—or didn't belong on her. Generic pink terry-cloth sweats seemed more in Coral's ballpark, to tell the truth.

But Dawn wasn't complaining about the company; the team was damned lucky to be here, even if talking with the Tomlinsons was no substitute for seeing the accused murderer himself.

After the Crockett confrontation, Breisi had managed to secure an interview with the family, who was visiting from Florida in support of Lee. The Limpet team had needed to fudge their reasons for being here *just* a tad, telling the Tomlinsons they were journalists and carrying fake press badges The Voice had somehow procured. But if questioning these people would yield another lead, who cared about telling a few white lies?

Since Lee's attorneys were monitoring his interviews, the team assumed the lawyers were doing the same with the Tomlinson family—thus the false identities. And because Kiko was too distinctive, he was waiting outside, guarded by a contingent of invisible Friends, just in case. His part of the interview would come after Breisi and Dawn asked basic questions.

If he could handle it.

Dawn tried not to think too hard about his difficulties, but yeah, color her worried. Kiko had been sullen ever since yesterday, after his failure to read Milton Crockett. Were his pills clouding his mind? Or, even worse, was he taking more medication than the rest of them were aware of?

Breisi, who had been fetching a notepad from her equipment bag, came to stand next to Dawn. "Are you all set up?"

"Roger-roger," Dawn said, sending her partner a subtle let's-get-on-with-this-already look.

Clipping out an agreeable nod, Breisi turned to the Tomlinson family. She was wearing a slim beige suit and a long, curly brown wig gathered in a ponytail, plus much more makeup than usual. She could be a bitchin' local newscaster if this whole vampire-hunting thing fell through one day.

With well-prepared charm, she said, "The cactus sounds like a lovely spot for pictures, Mrs. Tomlinson. Anything you need. We're just happy to be able to talk with you."

"That's right," Dawn chimed in, watching through her viewer. She was also wearing a disguise: a long boho skirt with fringed boots, an untucked white blouse, enough thick makeup to cover her facial scars, and a wig: long, black, and straight. Since she'd decided to play a journalist from, say, Austin, Texas—hell, if actors could do their own stunts, she could sure as shit turn the tables and act—she was using an accent. "At first, we were afraid we'd have to go through a team of lawyers to talk to you."

"Oh." Coral waved her hand dismissively. "They might be tellin' Lee to keep his trap shut, but the rest of us Tomlinsons don't take orders from anyone but ourselves."

Damn. Maybe Milton Crockett, Esquire, didn't think the Tomlinsons could offer much information about the Underground if he wasn't keeping a tight rein on them. Did that mean the team was wasting its time?

One of the Tomlinson siblings spoke up, the older sister, Marg. "The lawyers came to *Lee*," she drawled. "We didn't search *them* out, so we don't take orders from 'em, especially since they ain't doing much good in making it clear that Lee couldn't have killed that lady anyway. It's more like they're . . . well, encouraging an image. Understand? It's like all they want to do is make him the most famous murderer ever."

Dawn had focused the camera on Marg, a woman who looked to be as old as swamp water but was really in her midthirties. She was wearing a long-sleeved Universal Studios shirt. Since an unseasonable film of clouds was covering the sky today, everyone in the room had buttoned up more than usual for August.

Marg, with her short, dark near-mullet, had a chain smoker's complexion. Her skin and clothing reeked almost as much as Dawn's own garlic essence, but that didn't seem to faze Marg's hubby, Herb, who sat next to his wife on the jungle-leaf bedspread. He was a man who existed in his own sphere, almost literally; his wiry body seemed ready to ball up, his hunched shoulders getting a head start as he stared at the floor. Light from the nearby vanity played over his bald head, and he kept fidgeting with the seam of his faded jeans instead of adding to the conversation.

Breisi was scribbling everything down in shorthand. "Marg, why do you think Lee wouldn't have been capable of this murder?"

Another sister cleared her throat, as if to take attention off Marg, who seemed like the loudmouth of the bunch.

Cassie. She was younger, a little more hip than most of the other Tomlinsons, with her dark cornrowed hair worn under a kerchief, hippielike. She and the other remaining sibling, older brother Lane, were the only two who didn't appear totally at home in this tacky L.A. motel hell room. How they both managed to avoid turning out like Marg, Dawn would love to know.

She steadied the camera on Lane because he was, to put it mildly, worth staring at. He had his brother Lee's firm jaw, chisled cheekbones, slightly tilted blue eyes, and longish black hair. But he wasn't as pretty as Lee. Nope, he had more of an edge, a kind of car mechanic–poet vibe that could also go over really well on film, if he chose to stay in Hollywood.

Yup, he'd be a great target on any day except for the ones she'd been having lately.

At the randy thought, Dawn ignored a niggle of conscience. Matt wouldn't be so open to her Lane lusting. And who the hell knew what The Voice would think, if he cared at all.

"I guess you would've had to know Lee while he was growing up," Lane said, mouth tilting in a sad smile as he avoided looking at the camera. Dawn didn't know if that was because of modesty or because he didn't need to be assured that the lens was eating him up. "After our dad died, Lee got . . ."

"Into his own badass world," Cassie supplied from her seat next to her brother. Hippie girl looked a little sickened at what Lee had done.

"Badass world." Lane shook his head, obviously agreeing with his sister. "We all shared rooms, and he'd lock us out and listen to music that got angrier and angrier with each album. It seemed to encourage him to isolate himself. And he drew a lot. I can still see him sitting with his back to the wall in a corner, penciling away."

"He was *creative*," Marg said, putting an emphatic spin on the last word, a master of PR for her beloved brother. At least she wasn't blaming Lee's behavior on pop culture. "One of them geniuses, I'll bet."

Lane continued. "He drew pictures of . . . I guess they were dragonslayers. Then he started hanging out with the drama crowd, the artsy types. He got cocky around them because, suddenly, he stood out. He was a star in these fringe plays the group would put on in town. The powers that be would always shut down the productions because of 'indecency.' Lee just said the subjects were too cutting-edge for the boondocks, and he'd laugh about it and think all of us were such hicks."

A muscle ticked in Lane's jaw. He glanced at the carpet, just like Herb.

Mama Coral had been sucking at her teeth while listening, but she stopped at the mention of the plays. "Those other kids put such ideas in Lee's head. They're what got him out here to Hollywood. They come out here in a pack, like a bunch of wild dogs, and Lee kept callin' and askin' for money because none of 'em were makin' enough to pay the rent on that hole they were sharin'. They were a bad influence, and Lee was like anyone else, open to what they told him." She glanced at Breisi. "You getting all this?"

"Yes, ma'am, I am."

Dawn tightened the focus on Coral. So that was Mama's explanation for Lee's fall from grace? Peer pressure?

"Ma'am," she said, "are you saying Lee got talked into going down the wrong path—one that eventually led to . . . this?"

Mrs. Tomlinson wiped at one eye. Mascara had smudged beneath it. "If Lee did do that murder—which he didn't—sure, that's what I'd be sayin'. He's a good kid, deep down."

Sister Marg got off the bed to wander over to a table that was littered with vending machine snack packages. Brandless cheese puffs, peanut butter chocolate bars, cigarettes. She slipped a death stick out of a carton and tamped it against her palm. "Lee got a commercial, so he was on his way to doin' some good. You seen it? It's the 'Ahhhhhhhhh, so fah-resh!' guy swillin' mouthwash? That's when he stopped callin' so much. He damned near broke Mom's heart."

"He didn't mean to," Coral said off camera.

"Of course he didn't," Cassie said. When Dawn caught her on film, she was glaring at Marg. "Lee just got too busy. He had a lot of auditions, I'm sure." She turned to the camera. "He would always promise to spend his first big paycheck on a Cadillac for Mom."

"Just like Elvis," Lane added wryly, standing up and grabbing some chips from the table, then sitting again.

From the bed, Herb finally said something, and Dawn whipped the camera over, catching the phenomenon.

"We're a close family." His soft words were almost chalked away by a cough.

Dawn panned around the room, catching Marg staring at her husband. She got out another cigarette, this one clearly for him. Good medicine, those death sticks.

After sauntering back to the bed, Marg dropped the ciggie into his lap. He didn't touch it, just remained quietly engrossed in the carpet, like he wasn't enough a part of the family to add anything.

"A Cadillac," Mama Coral echoed.

Dawn turned the lens to her. A reminiscent smile widened the woman's painted lips. Red lipstick flecked her teeth.

"See how happy she is?" Marg said.

Out of the corner of her eye, Dawn saw the sister stuff a cigarette in her mouth, sit down, and gesture toward Coral. "Lee's promises made all of us want to bring Mom a smile, just like that."

"By coming out to Hollywood? Did you want to act, too?" Dawn zoomed over to the Universal Studios logo on Marg's shirt. Then she traveled upward to the older sister's choppy mullet, thinking The Voice, who was watching, might appreciate this ironic moment just as much as she did.

"Can't anyone act?" Marg said, laughing.

Touché.

"Anyway," Cassie said, rolling her eyes at Marg's remark as Dawn turned to her now. "After a while, Lane and I got in touch with Lee's roommates. They'd all gone back home, but Lee was the only one who stayed behind."

Goosebumps rose on Dawn's arms. Had he lingered in L.A. because of his servitude to the Underground?

Breisi jumped in. "So he pursued his career further?"

All of them just stared at Dawn and her partner.

In her chair, Mama Coral leaned forward. "*I* think his acting wasn't the only reason. He had a *lover*." She said it with such flair that Dawn almost wondered if she was playing to the camera, creating a sympathetic romance for the interview.

"We just found out about her," Coral added. "Our Lee was in love."

"Mom," the siblings all said, obviously warning her to stay quiet. Cassie and Lane even seemed angry, as if this information wasn't meant to be aired. Herb glanced up at Coral, eyebrows furrowed.

"What?" the mother said. "Lee has a good heart. Everybody should know that. He ain't capable of nothin' but love."

"Mrs. Tomlinson," Breisi said, "how do you know Lee was having a relationship?"

From the way her coworker asked, Dawn knew it was the Fourth of July and Christmas all rolled into one for Breisi.

A lead, Frank, Dawn thought, feeling the same adrenaline rush, too. *Maybe this is it. . . .*

"I know he was involved with a significant other," Coral said, "because the final roommate to leave California called last night and told Lane, here. That's why." Coral shot her family a satisfied look. "She said Lee was spendin' a lot of recent time with someone while workin' at a bar between auditions. He might've even met the light of his life on that job."

Breisi quickly wrote something, then flashed it at an angle so Dawn could read it. WASN'T JESSICA A WAITRESS?!?

A chill zinged up Dawn's spine. Holy crap, yes. But they hadn't found any indication during their research that she'd worked at Bava with Lee. Then again, Dawn had come to discover that monster-affiliated bars weren't exactly known for laying all their information out on the table, so what if Jessica had quit within the last month and no one was talking about it?

What if the Underground had erased all traces of her employment there?

"Now, you all tell me," Coral continued, repeating her point. "How can a boy who carries on in a relationship all of a sudden do murder? Everyone should ask that."

In a way, Dawn pitied the woman for having no imagination. People who killed could also be really great at covering it up. People weren't always who they seemed to be—especially in L.A.

Speaking of which . . . Who else had Lee met in this town? Did he have any friends who were also in the Underground?

"Mrs. Tomlinson," she asked, "did he hang out with anyone else after his roomies left, any people this last roommate might have mentioned in particular?"

Coral opened her mouth to answer, but Marg cut her off.

"Not really." The cigarette bobbed with her tight words.

"Mom's right," Lane added, obviously trying to get this interview back to the whitewash job it was supposed to be. "The fact that my brother could carry on a dedicated relationship makes it obvious that he functioned normally. Even if Lee dressed weird, he wasn't that different. He never even hurt a bird when he was a kid. He didn't have that in him."

Cassie was clutching the sides of her chair, staring at her mother.

And that made Dawn all the more curious.

"Are the cops aware of this lover?" Breisi asked, a polite bulldog after the real story.

"I guess they will be." Marg plucked the still unlit ciggie out of her mouth, holding it like a security blanket to cling to.

Herb's was still waiting like a forbidden goodie in his lap.

All the siblings were shooting mommy dearest the death eye, and she frowned at them, as if asking what she'd done wrong.

Had she revealed something she wasn't supposed to?

There was meat here, all right. Breisi kept scribbling, so Dawn knew it.

And they obviously weren't the only ones. Herb finally stood to his full height, thin as a matchstick. The cigarette fell to the carpet, and he absently stepped on it while moving toward the door, crushing tobacco into the shag threads. Lane followed, then Cassie.

The interview was over.

"How about those pictures?" Marg said, as if the room hadn't just suffered a tiny mental explosion.

Breisi nodded cordially, but Dawn could still sense her disappointment.

When Herb opened the door, cloud-hued gray light slithered into the room. Head down, Cassie was the first to rush outside.

On the way to the cactus outside the lobby, Dawn saw that

Breisi had written something else on her pad: LET'S FIND LOVER. MAYBE LEE SHARED SOMETHING WITH HER?

"Exactly," Dawn said so only Breisi could hear.

Mrs. Tomlinson was the only person who agreed to pose, but the rest of the family had obviously followed her to make sure she kept her mouth shut. As the matron put on a suitably sad expression—one tailor-made for the grieving mother of a man wrongly accused—Marg sauntered over to Dawn.

"You have enough for a good story?" she asked, not seeming to mind the stench of garlic on Dawn's skin.

"Well, we'd like more. But we can do a decent human-interest piece." She hoped she sounded like a real reporter.

"You might wanna take Mom's comments with a pinch of salt. She ain't altogether here. Know what I mean?"

"I understand. These are hard times."

This acting crap was totally easy. If Dawn wasn't morally opposed to actually being an "actress," she might even be dumb enough to fall into the sparkling lure of it.

If she hadn't grown up in L.A. knowing better.

Marg put the dead cigarette between her lips again. "It'd be real nice if you respected Lee's private love life and stuck to a story about how much his family supports him. That's why we invited you here. That's all we came here for—to buck up little Lee."

At the mention of the lover, Cassie had wandered over. Her face was mottled. Boy, was Mama going to get an earful from *this* daughter later.

Dawn thought how she'd react in the same situation, chiding a mother who'd done wrong. But she couldn't dredge up a connecting emotion. It sent a split of pain through her chest, reminding her of why she'd never wanted to need a mom anyway.

Swallowing away the ache, Dawn joined the daughters in watching Coral adjust her blouse, then run a finger around her mouth to absently clear away stray lipstick.

"So, now that we're done here . . ." Marg said, changing the subject. "You know any hot spots?"

Hot spots? Was she kidding? She was asking about places to party? Wow, Marg was definitely in mourning.

"What kind of action are you looking for?" Dawn asked.

"Like places the celebrities hang out."

Star screwing. God. Dawn wanted to tell Marg the reality of Tinseltown: it was all fake. From the limos driving bankrupt stars around, to the glossy magazines that crowed about family-oriented producers who held orgies in their second, off-limits mansions, Hollywood was a lie. Not even Marg would be able to find the fantasy of it if she knew everything.

"Marg," Cassie said.

The woman held up her ciggie as she spread her hands. "You don't wanna know, too?"

Her sister presented her back and left. Marg didn't seem to care much as she turned to Dawn again.

"The thing is," Dawn began, "once the public knows where the celebrities hang out, they kind of never go there again. Most of the really big stars enjoy their privacy, unless they're in the mood for PR."

"That's what I'm talkin' about. Where do they show up?"

Before Dawn could answer, she was saved by what looked to be a boy in a back brace dressed in a striped shirt and jeans. He'd pulled a baseball cap down so low his face was barely visible. Just above the bill, the sign of the cross blazed in full glory. He was carrying a bucket and handing out candy bars attached to small Bibles.

"Peace and love," Kiko was saying in a modulated, higher kid voice as he gave each Tomlinson a gift, holding their hands in the process. He was so anxious to get readings this time out that he'd sacrificed the patch of hair beneath his lower lip, shaving it off so he would look years younger.

Lingering over every touch, especially Coral's, Kiko made his rounds, then disappeared behind the motel. He'd meet the team at the SUV.

"They let their kids Bible-thump out here without parents around?" Marg asked, staring at the tiny book in her hand.

Dawn shrugged. "L.A. kids get geriatric when they're, like, five."

The other woman shook her head. "Poor little cripple boy. He doesn't even have a good mom."

Minutes later, the photo session was completed, but Breisi attempted to wheedle a few more rounds of question-and-answer from the Tomlinsons. Lane just gave her a knowing grin, then personally escorted his mother back to the room. The rest of the family trailed behind.

Ultimately, Lane was the last one in and, as he closed the door behind them all, Dawn caught a sincere glint of sadness in his gaze. It struck her that his emotion seemed much less dramatic than his own mother's.

Wasting no time, Breisi and Dawn rushed down the street to the SUV, where Kiko had already crawled into the backseat. Wasn't he even going to call shotgun?

The women climbed in, too, locking the doors. Breisi flicked on a dashboard switch that allowed The Voice to listen in from wherever he might be.

Even though he wasn't here, his presence felt real and solid, a perpetual thrum in Dawn's body.

"What did you get?" Breisi asked Kiko.

The psychic didn't answer, not verbally anyway. Instead, he reached out to Dawn. She was wearing one of Frank's sleeveless T's under her blouse, and she knew exactly what he wanted to do.

Slipping the white blouse off of her shoulder, she allowed him to touch the undershirt, allowed him to close his eyes and summon whatever nightmares Frank might be having today.

But when Kiko's mouth twitched, she knew it was out of frustration. He wasn't getting anything, and that meant . . .

"No readings from the Tomlinsons," she said.

Almost out of desperation, he darted his hand out to touch the shirt again, but Dawn grabbed his wrist.

"I just need to concentrate more," he said, voice strangled. "Please."

"Kiko," Breisi said, taking his arm from Dawn. "Don't worry. It'll all come back."

"When? My talents are as useless as—"

He stopped, grabbed his arm from Breisi, and fell back to the seat, where he stared out the window.

Dawn could've finished his sentence for him. His talents were as useless as his body.

Pressure gathered behind her eyes. Shit.

Without another word about Kiko's difficulties—because what could they say?—Breisi started the engine and the briefing. They talked about how at least they knew that the Tomlinsons weren't low-level vampires since they hadn't reacted to Kiko's cross on the hat or the blessed Bibles. The team touched on their impressions of the family, too. Breisi's instincts matched each one of Dawn's, and Dawn wondered what the hell was going on that she all of a sudden wasn't arguing with the lab rat every second of the day.

"Back at the house, I'll contact these old roommates of Lee's," Breisi said. "I would especially like to get in touch with the one who knew about the lover."

Dawn was watching out the window as they drove back up to the Hills. Palm trees swished by, mocking the clouds. In the side mirror, she saw a hint of movement, and her gaze fixed there.

Kiko. His hand had arched up to his mouth to pop something into it.

Dawn's gaze went red. "You really need one of those?"

He hesitated, like he was mortified to have been caught.

She waited, not letting him off the hook.

Finally, he chuffed. "My painkillers are safer than yours any day. So back off, okay?"

She should've been pissed about his reference to her habit of using sex for a cure-all. It was a weapon in her personal war against Eva, a way to make Dawn feel like she was just as attractive, even if it was only temporary.

With all her effort, she did back off, knowing he wasn't in a receptive mood. She kept her eye on him though, and he damned well knew it.

After they parked, then walked up the path leading to the Black Dahlia dollhouse, UV lights flooded the Gothic entrance, emphasizing the iron cross hanging over the doorway. Once inside, none of them talked, just went their separate ways. Kiko headed for a bed, where he could get the rest he was required to take each day, whether he wanted it or not. Tomorrow, he had a therapy appointment, but before then, Dawn was going to talk to his counselor about those pills.

In the meantime, Breisi veered toward the huge wooden door off the parlor. She unlocked it, making Dawn wonder, once again, just what was behind the barrier. Previously, she'd seen blue lights, heard a metallic buzzing. Breisi guarded the sanctuary like her life depended on it, and every time she got all secretive, Dawn got even more curious.

With a squirrelly look, Breisi disappeared into the dungeon, leaving Dawn alone.

Hell. What to do?

She decided to head up to the computer room to see if she could research any info about Lee's roomies and then dial up Kiko's keepers to ask about his meds.

With a sigh, she climbed the stairs, gradually consumed by the dimness of the upper story. The eerie silence was like perpetual twilight, an unexplained place between all the worlds crashing in on her daily.

As always, she came to the first portrait hanging on the wall. A desert spanned the canvas: sandy, desolate, warm in its emptiness.

Barely glancing at it, she began to pass by on her way to the computers.

But when the picture suddenly filled with the image of a beautiful woman, Dawn froze.

NINE

THE FRIENDS

GAZE locked on the portrait, Dawn held her breath while the woman formed into a vision. It was like an invisible paintbrush was swiping over the canvas, breathing jasmine-scented life into the vivid texture: a golden turban against sand, darkly slanted eyes against brown skin, bare shoulders against the falling collar of a silken robe.

One of the Friends had just returned home.

Pressing her fingertips against the rough oils of the woman's neck, Dawn found a pulse, as if she could actually absorb energy from the paint itself. Then . . . something else.

The sibilant vibration of a laugh, a sigh.

She yanked her fingers back. What the hell?

All the while, the woman in the painting stared at her, watching in silent assessment, unmoving in her dreamy-eyed rest.

From the end of the hall, the door to The Voice's office gasped open. It wasn't really the sound of it that attracted Dawn—it was the gape of its movement, the shift in balance and temperature. She glanced sidelong at the door, thinking in the back of her mind that it resembled the vertical slit of a reptile's gaze, one that fixed on her with night-prowling intention.

A soft giggle floated from that room, or maybe from over Dawn's head, or . . .

She glanced at the portrait again.

From there?

She ran her palms down the intricate wooden frame, not knowing what she was searching for. Sound devices planted just to screw with her? Doubtful. But she couldn't stand here, listening as another laugh danced around her.

Dawn, giggled a female's melodious, foreign-accented voice.

Wracked by a chill, Dawn eased away from the painting. The light voice was more inside her head than anywhere else. Still, that didn't mean it hadn't come from the picture.

Dawn Mad-ee-son . . .

Ignoring the mind games, she tried to slip her fingers to the back of the portrait, expecting it to move away from the wall. But it didn't. The frame was bolted permanently, like a flat fortress that could never be breached.

Then it happened, right in front of her.

In slow—or was it fast?—motion, the woman's eyes closed, as if in sleep.

Dawn's breath chopped past her lips.

Why was she still what-the-helling all this? She knew the pictures contained spirits. She'd at least been told that much. Or maybe she'd just inferred it. . . . Anyway, seeing one of them in the flesh, or whatever, made this all too real—much harder to deny, because even with all she'd been through, all she'd learned, that's what she still wanted to do.

Keep denying everything.

"Dawn," said a much lower, much more immediate voice.

She gazed toward the office again, toward the slightly open door. Had it been the boss this time? His tone seemed different, maybe because it was unfiltered by the constraints of those high-quality speakers. She'd heard him sound that way only once before but there was a less ominous quality this time. . . .

"Jonah?" she asked. It seemed okay to call him that right now, with him sounding so human . . . so *here*.

The door scraped open a few more inches, an invitation.

Her body went Pavlovian, a throb working between her legs like the stiff ticks of circular seconds. Heat primed her in anticipation, in the hope that she would get a sexual fix to tide her over again.

Just until she could get back to normal.

Her heartbeat banged in her ears, through her belly, as she made her way there. She pushed open the door, greeted by cool air and a faint, unidentifiable scent that did more to stir her up than calm her. She felt like she was listening to a crack of thunder split the sky, like she was waiting for a bad storm to hit.

But fear didn't stop her. She was lured beyond endurance, and it wasn't for the first—or probably last—time, either.

Stepping inside his dim office, she saw the lone flicker of a candle ensconced in its iron-and-glass casing behind the massive desk. A tongue of reflection teased the surface, where a scar marked the wood, hinting at a ripple of violence in The Voice's past. It looked like an ax blade had made itself at home there, not that he'd ever told her the story.

Or ever would.

The candle flame imitated the waver of her heartbeat. "Jonah?"

No one answered as she scanned the rest of the room: the lifeless books and heavy, closed curtains, the ever-watchful TV that seemed to have been lulled to a nap.

The portraits of the other women.

She stopped near the picture of an empty field of fire, but as her eyes focused on the familiar scene, she did a double take.

Like the portrait in the hallway, this one wasn't empty anymore.

The fiery landscape now showed a person she'd never seen. The subject faced away from the room, a red cape covering any hint of a body, a long sheen of tousled dark hair masking everything else. It reminded Dawn of the woman downstairs above the fireplace mantel—the colors, the tone. . . .

Entranced, she began to move toward it.

A gust of jasmine perfume spiked through the room, mixing with a sound that made Dawn think of a torch being brandished in attack. With the accompaniment of a deep, sirenlike laugh, the candle behind the desk guttered.

Adrenaline burning, Dawn crouched in response to the sudden darkness. The door slammed, and she spun around, darting toward the now-barred exit.

What was The Voice trying to do? Control her through fear this time?

"Shhhh," he whispered from somewhere on the right as she tested the locked doorknob. "Quiet, Dawn."

It seemed as if he were actually here in the flesh, standing in the corner near a bookcase. The situation made her think of that other time Jonah had come to her like this, when she'd confronted him about luring her to L.A. with Frank as bait and he'd tried to tell her he hadn't planned it that way, even though that's how everything had worked out. Of course, he'd gone invisible when it came down to interacting with her; at least, that's what she thought he'd done. Even though his touch had felt more real than usual, she hadn't been able to see him in a mirror across the room, a mirror reflecting *her* every movement—not his—even as his hands and mouth had remained on her body.

As she listened to him stir in his corner, she halted, remaining low to the ground near the door, tuning her ears in to his movements.

This was a guy who usually preferred to enter her during mind play, never physically. So what was he doing now? What did he have planned today?

"I've been waiting for you," he said. "Waiting a long time."

He sounded so . . . strange . . . without the speakers. Not as low-pitched, and the foreign accent . . . gone? Why? Maybe the speakers just warped his tone whenever he spoke. But wouldn't she have noticed this the last time he'd come to her without the cover of the audio system?

"What's going on?" she said. "Spill it or I'm out of here."

"Trust me."

She heard clothing rustle as he moved closer.

A thought clicked into gear: had he gotten braver and finally decided to forgo all the masquerade crap he loved to hide behind?

Her blood went hot, rushing and stomping until she got light-headed, light-bodied, a rhythm beating deep and low.

"I want you to turn from my voice," he said, only feet away now. Games. *Their* games.

Her skin awakened, but it was more out of an odd inner alarm than desire. Yet, weren't fear and lust entwined? Hadn't she gotten off on other short-lived, rough-and-tumble boning sessions too many times to count?

So why was she hesitating? She'd already decided that it was okay for The Voice to "anchor" her crazy new existence, right? Wild sex had always stabilized her. Why not now?

Before she could answer him, frigid heat enveloped her, like someone had wrapped her in a column of numbing flame. She startled, unable to move her arms, her hands, her legs.

Another of The Voice's provocative moves?

Why didn't it feel as good as it usually did?

Dawn thought she heard him breathing just inches away now, but when she caught a whiff of jasmine, she realized that Jonah wasn't touching her at all: it was one of the Friends binding her.

"Relax," he whispered. "All I want you to do is relax."

Listen to him, let it happen, she told herself. *You always feel better afterward, so don't fight it.*

Her pulse escalated, liquid gusts flooding her veins.

He came to stand behind her. At the feel of silk against her forehead, then over her eyes, she sucked in a quick breath.

A blindfold.

As he tied it, the sensual material whispered, harsh and sleek, into a knot. The pressure vised around her head, cutting into the long black wig she was still wearing from the Tomlinson interview. Her temples thudded in time with the rest of her body, kicking out a coded message that she couldn't translate.

The world was all black, a mass of heartbeats and razored hesitation—

Something crashed against the closed door, and Dawn startled away from it. A rain of thumps followed, like fists pelting the thick wood.

She thought she heard cries, thin and rushed, like voices threading through a wind tunnel.

Kalin, stop, Kalin . . .

In back of her, Jonah made a sound of disgust. "Damn it, you'd better go to your sisters, Kalin. *Go.*"

The cloak of cold fire unwrapped itself from around Dawn's body, spinning her mind as the door's lock snapped, allowing the wood to whoosh open, then slam shut. In the hall, there was a screech, then what sounded like a thousand wails of responding anger.

"Go!" Jonah yelled.

With a clipped cry, all the voices merged into one long scream that traveled down the hall, through the house, into oblivion or wherever the Friends resided.

Something, no, *a lot* of things, weren't right. She had to get out of here, now, before—

At the same time Dawn reached for the blindfold, she angled away from Jonah. But before she could maneuver away, he gripped her wrist.

Solid, real—

"No . . ." he began.

But his words sliced off as he jerked back from her. Still blindfolded, she heard him fall to the ground.

As she fumbled to take the material off, she didn't even have time to ask another what-the-hell. She got rid of the silk, but when she squinted her eyes to see, she couldn't. With the candlelight gone, it was too dark.

Meanwhile, Jonah writhed and grunted on the floor, and she frantically slid her hands along the wall, coming to the light switch.

"Stop, Dawn!"

It was The Voice she knew.

She was bolted back to the wall by the command's power . . . and also by the thrust of a carnal presence, exponentially more debilitating than before. She realized that, earlier, she'd only been anticipating The Voice, that her body had just been reacting to the promise of what would definitely come.

For a few seconds, she couldn't move at all, could only gasp at the erotic waves consuming her.

The darkness covered the sounds of Jonah moving—was he sliding along the carpet?—toward the bookcase, then the mild roar of wood slipping back into place.

A secret door, she managed to think. It was probably where Jonah had first entered the room.

And . . . silence, except for her erratic intake of oxygen. She clawed for it, hampered by the pounding of her body, the sharp ache between her legs.

Melting, she thought, wanting him to come back, to finish what he'd started.

What had just happened?

Again, she grappled for the light switch, finally turning it on.

Illumination flooded the room, but not her mind. She looked at the bookcase, finding it opened to a slit, just as the office door had been.

But she didn't think it was so much of an invitation this time.

The next moment, she felt his essence, expanding around her, taking up the air she so sorely needed.

"Are you all right?" he asked softly. His dark, low accent was back, and it didn't sound like he was coming through the speakers. Still, it didn't sound like he was quite in the room, either.

Even so, his obvious concern threw her off balance. "Nice, *Jonah*. Was that your take on the female version of blue balls? Because I don't like that game so much."

"I am sorry, Dawn. I . . . I didn't mean to get so out of hand."

Her lust was evening out to a slow rhythm, no less stimulating but definitely less frenzied.

She slid down the wall, resting on the floor before her legs gave out. "What happened?"

"I lost control. This time."

Her brain finally grasped all his foreign allure again; his tone brushed over her with the same rough strokes that always escalated her desire.

Back in familiar territory, she relaxed, allowing her head to rest against the wall, her neck exposed. She ran a hand over her throat, her beating jugular. Tempting him, she played dirty so he would consider telling her more.

Again, she thought back to that one sexual battle they'd had after she'd found out that The Voice had used Frank as bait. She'd been enraged, tearing around the house to find him. Then he'd come to her, offering scant answers but somehow managing to get her back on his side—as much as possible anyway.

Inevitably, they'd fallen into their usual pattern, raw and starved pseudo-sex, leading up to the moment she'd given him permission to enter her. And she never failed to give it: he supplied her with such a high that she didn't mind when he used her lust to avoid answering her questions.

Maybe that's why he kept doing it.

"I went too long without sustenance." Why did he sound so different . . . sad? "That must be what got to me."

Sustenance, she thought. *What* kept him going? Sex?

When he hushed around her, his presence fluttering the strands of her wig, Dawn realized that *sustenance* was just a double entendre for what he really wanted right now.

Her.

She started to quiver, shaken by her need for him. "You looking for permission?"

In answer, a caress of air skimmed her earlobe, as if marking where her earring—a sign of the old Dawn—used to be. The pressure of his essence was a disarming sigh telling her how much he needed her, too.

"Why is it always me?" she asked. "Why not Breisi? Or—"

"I need you more than anything."

His admission made her heart clench just as ferociously as the rest of her body. She didn't like how that made her feel: vulnerable, open to attack.

"Why?" she asked, being difficult, defensive.

His essence stroked and memorized her face, making her feel beautiful. She closed her eyes, taking it in, holding on to it before she had to get back to reality.

"When I'm in you, I'm fortified," he said. "You surround me in comfort and strength." He brushed down her body then back up in one, long, endlessly lulling drag. It was almost as if there was something else going on with him though—something so uncharacteristically emotional she couldn't possibly get a bead on it. "You are the only true safety I've known in . . . years."

An anchor, she thought. Just like Breisi and Frank.

"In other words," she said, unwilling to roam into this new territory without at least some armor, "you're using me."

"Don't say that."

"I use you, too."

It was true, she realized. She'd gone from one-night stands to an even more dangerous form of supposed intimacy with The Voice, an entity she couldn't even see. But maybe that's how she wanted the bedroom lies to go: invisible, easy, and addictive. He was so intoxicating because he always made her believe she was one of a kind, more spellbinding than Eva. The fact that he had to ask permission to enter gave her a power unlike any other. She controlled her intake.

He was combing over her wig now, pace melancholy. "This gives you the appearance of a Russian Cold War spy. And these clothes . . ." He tugged at the long white blouse and Gypsy skirt. "A brilliant disguise."

"Not as brilliant as yours."

"Yes." He seemed to sigh. "You're right."

She'd slid farther down to the ground, unbuttoning her blouse, bending and parting her legs and allowing her skirt to rustle down to her hips. He skimmed her inner thighs and she reached down to touch herself, to assuage the buzz of his presence.

"Why don't you come on and make yourself feel better," she said. "I don't know what's wrong with you today, but—"

"There it is again. The 'using' reference."

What was he talking about? Ever since they'd found out that she could block him out of her mind, he hadn't attempted to read her again, so that left their relationship purely physical. As much as it could be anyway. Why did it sound like that wasn't enough for him? What was going on?

He paused, then laughed a little, a huff of air blowing back the strands of her wig. "I don't bring flowers, but I hope I offer something . . . more."

She flushed with twisted contentment. "You talking about Matt Lonigan again? Why, I didn't know you cared."

"Don't be flippant. Breisi and Kiko are uneasy about him, you realize."

"And you?"

Instead of answering, he bathed her with swirls of movement, light yet insistent, urging her to stroke herself harder. She bucked, getting wet, slick with vibrating excitement.

Okay . . . ignoring the whole Matt thing.

Not to be trumped, Dawn reached up with her other hand to part her blouse, showing her undershirt and bra. The last was a pretty standard satin creation, but it didn't matter. With The Voice's attentions, she was the hottest lingerie angel on earth.

While still working her, he stretched upward, over her belly, which jumped with his pressure. Fingertip-light sensations traced over her ribs.

Her skin prickled as his touch seemed to go below the skin, saturating it with gnawing heat, flowing to the core of her.

It turned Dawn on so much that she lifted a leg, hooking it under the arm of the chair next to her for balance. Slowly, she opened her legs farther for him, swollen, stiff, aching. Ready. So damned ready.

"How much experience in this"—she blew out a breath—"have you . . . had?"

"Why would you ask me that?"

"Why not?" It'd keep her sane, pinned to her old habit of keeping this interaction casual and simple enough to leave behind after she'd gotten what she wanted out of it. "You've been in my head. You know I've banged a lot of guys."

"Never say it that way." His essence went cold. "That's not what you are to me."

Power overcame her, building up until it pushed against her skin. It felt good, and bad, to upset him. He'd used her for bait and she could bait him just the same.

"I'll bet," she said, shifting her hips and reminding him that she was the one who would or wouldn't be letting him in, "you've had quite a few partners yourself. Your technique tells me you aren't exactly a virgin."

Something like a hand came to clasp itself around her throat, harshly, delicately. Body swamped with adrenaline, Dawn swallowed but didn't back down.

"Many women," he said, his tone so low it seemed to scratch the surface of hell. "I have had *many* women. Is that what you'd like to hear?"

He squeezed slightly, and she arched her hips against his invisible form, taking in the escalated danger, the chance of losing everything with her need to push him.

And to push herself.

"Yes, I like to hear that, *Jonah*." His name was a reminder of everything he refused to tell her, and she reveled in using it against him. "I'm not surprised you've had many women. You seem to like them."

She was talking about all his female portraits. A collection.

He squeezed again, and she gasped. Immediately, he released her, as if horrified by what she'd brought out in him.

Fascinated, she pushed it even further. "Who's Kalin, the Friend you talked to when I came in the room?"

"Stop—"

"Do all the other women in your portraits have names, too? Who are they? Why—"

The air rumbled, whipping up a combination of lust and fear around her—*in* her. Did he compel her so much because she didn't trust him? Was that another part of his appeal?

She was drawn to his danger, needed it inside of her because that's what had kept her going for most of her life: fury, confusion, and now terror.

"Come in," she whispered urgently, fully opening herself to his destruction, his intangible power.

He obeyed, crashing into her with such searing rage that she cried out, devastated and completed.

As if reflecting his fury, the lights blinked out, plunging the room into pitch black. He hammered into every cell of her body, stretching them to the point of explosion. He shredded her membranes, pieced them back together, then ripped them apart again. She allowed him the fevered pleasure, her emotions so scrambled she didn't know what to cling to or who she was anymore.

As she came, shuddering while she strained against the pressure of him, she reached out and grabbed the leg of the chair, holding on, afraid to let go. When she cried out, she yanked at it, toppling it over, the wood crashing to the ground. Brought down. Beaten.

Panting, she opened her eyes, still electrified, even though something inside of her was dying back to its original form. Inner sparks buzzed on, then off, jittering to the occasional flash of something lost as she lay in the dark.

She felt The Voice hovering above her, his essence clenched in what she thought might still be anger.

"Why can't it be any other way with you?" he said, his tone edged with devastation.

She couldn't answer, because she really didn't know herself.

TEN

THE LOV-AH

POSTORGASM, Dawn left the office, then methodically shed the wig, cleaned up, and got dressed into regular garb: comfortable jeans, another of Frank's T-shirts, and her worked-in motorcycle boots.

Of course, while slipping out of the guest room she'd been using as a changing area, she came face-to-face with another portrait. There was no way to avoid them.

This one featured a woman with Chinese features, her head bowed, her body barely covered in a blue silk robe. She looked like she'd just done some questionable canoodling, too.

Who were these ghosts? And how had they gotten into the paintings? More important, why did they stay if they had the freedom to move in and out of them?

Dawn waited a second, just in case anyone—including a freakin' portrait person—wanted to answer. But there was nothing. Only the sounds of an old house settling into a night of creaks and moans.

"So much for female bonding," she muttered, leaving the picture to itself.

It was time to get back to work. Sure, The Voice had let her punch out a little steam, probably knowing full well that the interaction made her more limber in both body and mind. And she did feel exercised plus . . . well, kind of exorcised, too. Even if today's session had been a little weirder—but hardly more mentally exhausting—than usual.

Beating back all the lingering questions from her time with the boss, she went into the computer room, a bland space lined with dark wood and a stand of work stations. No portraits in here. No distractions while she checked some items off her mental to-do list and forgot about everything else.

Even though she knew she should remember.

Flipping her shower-wet ponytail over her shoulder, Dawn sat and turned on a machine. As it warmed up, she took out her cell phone and accessed the number for Kiko's therapist.

Before she'd left Jonah, she'd done one of those awkward by-the-way asides that hadn't erased any of the tension between them. Avoiding any more mention of their sex, she'd told him about her worries regarding Kiko's pills, but the boss had already been aware of all that. In fact, he'd already called Kiko's doctor with his concerns, and he agreed that having Dawn get in touch with the therapist, too, could only help.

Then he'd disappeared into the TV, the walls, or whatever. She'd shut the door behind her, moving into the lighted hall, relieved and miffed at the same time.

The call to Kiko's therapist didn't rock the earth: Dawn let the woman know about how his medication was affecting his mind and, after asking general questions about his behavior, the other woman promised to conference with Kik's doctor and look further into it. Afterward, hardly comforted, Dawn clicked onto the Internet, promising herself she'd follow up.

Knowing that's all she could do for now, she got down to other business, doing a search on Lee Tomlinson, concentrating on the lover angle.

Unfortunately, there wasn't anything available that the team hadn't uncovered before. Premurder, Lee's PR exposure was low. The highest profile he'd enjoyed was on MySpace.com, where he'd trumpeted his one big commercial. Dawn would bet his legal team—or maybe those Underground connections—had tampered with anything and everything that was currently in the public eye.

Frustrated, she navigated away from all the murder-related hits his name brought up, typing in the name of Lee's brother, Lane, just to see what that would conjure.

Links were just flashing on the screen when Breisi stuck her head in the room.

"Busy?" she asked.

"Spinning in circles with Lee Tomlinson and . . ."

A memory of The Voice skimming over her, through her, shot a tingle under her skin.

Yeah, *not* going there with Breisi.

Dawn veered around in her chair to face her coworker. "Can I ask you something?"

Breisi stepped inside, having dressed back into street clothes, too: a black Buzz Lightyear shirt and cargo pants. Her expression remained neutral, telling Dawn that she could ask, but she shouldn't expect any answers. Huge shock there.

She went for it anyway. "It's about the Friends."

"Yes?"

Argh, the calm acceptance of this woman. "Who's Kalin?"

At the name, Breisi straightened her spine. "Where did you hear that?"

Ah-ha-ha. She was *on* to something. Breisi wouldn't be quietly having a cow if the name didn't matter. "I heard The Voice say it. I thought he was addressing one of the Friends, and I just wondered if you knew who she was."

"I don't know any of the spirits personally."

She looked stunned that Dawn had even heard the name, as if the rest of the team were adults who took great pains to spell out things like "h-e-l-l" and "i-c-e c-r-e-a-m" in front of a two-year-old who would end up decoding their efforts anyway.

Was saying the name of a spirit bad? But then why had The Voice done it in front of Dawn?

Breisi looked like she was turning something over in her mind. "Truthfully, I don't know much about the Friends, only that they protect us."

You should've told that to Kalin when the ghosty messed with me earlier, Dawn thought.

"I saw one coming back into her frame today," she said, referring to the Friend in the hall, "like she was being colored onto the canvas."

"That's when they return home. You didn't think they just floated around after chasing down lawyers or monitoring Lee in his cell, did you? They need rest, too."

Good time for another question. "And how's *that* going? Lee, I mean."

"He's keeping to himself in jail-land. That means no word about any of his vamp connections. He and his lawyers don't even talk about anything to do with an Underground."

Not the best of news, but . . . yee-haw, Dawn could be on her way to an answer about this Kalin. She got even braver.

"There was someone in that fire field picture that's usually empty, you know the one in The Voice's office? Has that Friend been away for a while?"

Breisi's throat worked around a swallow as she merely stared at Dawn.

"Is the subject in that picture Kalin?" Dawn added.

"I can't answer anything else."

"Why?"

"Because they help us, and that's not for us to question. Remember how they defended us at Robby's house?"

Dawn nodded, then spoke up just in case the Friends were listening in. "And I'm totally thankful, too."

"Then no more foolishness. We have a lot of other matters to focus on."

"I can't even wonder why the spirits don't know who this murderer is? Don't they have, like, their own contacts in the ghost world?"

Breisi started looking exasperated. "Many spirits travel in their own realms. It's not as if they have networking parties."

"I'm just saying. It'd be useful."

Under her breath, Breisi muttered something that Dawn suspected was the Spanish equivalent of "bleeping idiot." "I didn't come here to have the great debate with you."

Still, Dawn had to admit she'd gotten a couple of tidbits out of the stone maiden. "What's up then?"

Breisi narrowed her eyes. "I'm free now to give you the rundown on the case?"

Knowing she wouldn't get anywhere else for the time being, Dawn nodded.

Her coworker's eyes gleamed because she loved this part. She was like a spelling bee champion who got to stand up during a dinner with drunk adult relatives and show off the lists of words she'd learned that day at school. "First, I tracked down one or two of Lee's old roomies."

"How did you manage that when the Tomlinson family wouldn't give us names?"

She shrugged modestly. "I did the usual. A buddy with DMV connections got Lee's old address for me. I used that to find his roomies' names and current whereabouts."

Man, Breisi was link central. "Nice."

"Well, I didn't find enough to fill a jelly jar. And I haven't discovered anything that links Jessica Reese to Lee. But then I talked to the roomie Mrs. Tomlinson mentioned, the one who told her about 'the lov-ah.'" Breisi waved her hand while saying the affected word, just as Coral Tomlinson had done. "Her name is Torrey Sajen-Morgan, a mouthful, and she had kept in contact with Lee until about a month ago, just before he committed the murder and took off. I told her I was a friend of Lee's and I was planning to stage a rally to support his innocence."

"And she was all for that."

"You bet. She gave me names of people here in L.A. who would attend."

Dawn stood, suspecting what Breisi had found. "Including the name of Lov-ah?" In her excitement she ignored the links her Internet search had brought up for Lane Tomlinson. She'd get to them later.

Breisi made a subtle tah-dah motion. "Sasha Slutskaya. What a name, huh? I've got a work address."

"Damn, you're good."

"I try."

As Dawn made for the door and passed Breisi in her haste to get on with this, the other woman held up a fist.

Oh, Dawn thought. Another bump. Right. Okay.

They lightly smacked knuckles, both of them holding back sort-of smiles as they exited. After weaponing and garlicking up, they jogged down the stairs, just reaching the door when Kiko came up behind them.

"Wait!" He was tugging on his light jacket over a dark top. "Boss said I should go."

"But the sun's setting," Dawn said while scanning him. He seemed lucid enough and even kind of perky. Good signs, but she didn't trust her prognosis, seeing as she wasn't a professional.

Kiko shrugged off her amateur opinion. "I'm going straight into

Sasha's place with you two, and I promised I wouldn't pull anything heroic. Besides, I'll have the usual cover."

Friends, Dawn thought. Which ones would be with them, hanging back, watching, waiting, just in case?

Then he turned to Breisi, who didn't look any more convinced than Dawn was.

"Get off it, Breez. The boss just took some convincing is all. He knows I can handle myself. I'm fit as a fiddle."

Proving it, he kicked out with a tiny leg. The only sign of back agitation was his tight, smug smile.

"You slept off the last pill?" Breisi asked.

"Of course." Kiko widened his eyes so his coworkers could peer into them. "See?"

Breisi looked into his gaze, and when Dawn had her turn, she supposed he was focusing well enough.

"We don't want you to be in any discomfort, Kik," she said. "That's all."

"Yeah, yeah."

At his casualness, Breisi gave him one last, long glance, then powered out the door. The outside UV lights blared on, swallowing her up.

Dawn started to follow, but Kiko grabbed her jacket, stopping her.

"About earlier," he said, sheepish.

Her mind rewound. *Blur-de-blur-de-whir.* Past what she'd done with The Voice, past Kiko telling her off on the way home, past their meeting with the Tomlinsons. Then she fast-forwarded a bit, landing on Kiko saying, *"I guess my painkillers are safer than yours any day. So back off, okay?"*

"What about it?" she asked, not wanting to go there with him, either.

"I . . . I wasn't in the best of moods. Sorry about getting on your case."

"We just . . ." She cleared her throat. "I guess we just worry about each other. That's all. Now let's—"

"Because you've gotten a lot better about sleeping around lately." Kiko had clearly been rehearsing this speech and he was hell-bent on delivering it. "When I first met you, I couldn't help reading you because you were putting off such strong, needy vibes."

Awk. Ward. "But you stopped reading me after that because I'm not the massive ho you fear anymore, so no worries. 'Kay?" Rolling her eyes, she started toward the door.

"No, wait. You're right." He got red in the face. "I can tell that you're doing real good. . . . I mean, you're trying real hard to . . ."

A flash of The Voice inside of her, filling her, made Dawn flush with guilt.

Kiko sighed. "What I'm saying is that I admire how you've controlled yourself. And I can do the exact same thing." He gave her an admiring glance, then looked down as he shuffled his oversized shoes.

Oh. But, ah, hell, she could've told him that the only reason she wasn't going around slammin' half the town was because she was limited on time. A lot had changed about her, but she doubted she'd ever be able to give up sex. She'd just changed her own prescriptions, that's all.

Wanting this conversation to be over, she fidgeted. "Thanks" was all she could say without incriminating herself.

"So we're cool?" he asked.

"We're cool."

She offered him a white-flag grin, and he broke into a full-fledged smile, clearly Happy Kiko resurrected.

He headed out the door, leaving a blare of UV lighting in his wake. The chill of it swept into the foyer, bathing the portrait of Fire Woman over the mantel.

She peered straight through Dawn, as if to say, "If only he knew the truth, because *I* do."

Impulsively, Dawn flew the bird at her, then left the house, protected by the lights until she reached the SUV.

As they drove into the twilight, Dawn kicked it in the backseat. A shade-wearing Kiko had grabbed the front, which meant he was back to normal. Thank God.

While driving, Breisi said they were heading toward Santa Monica Boulevard, like yesterday, but tonight they'd be stopping in West Hollywood to intercept Sasha Slutskaya at work.

"Did you say we're going to the eight-thousand block of the boulevard?" Dawn asked.

"Yes."

Kiko glanced at Dawn in the backseat, and both of them seemed to come to an understanding at the same time.

"Boystown," they both said.

"Hot dog," Kiko added. "*Mr.* Sasha?"

When they finally reached the address, their suspicions were confirmed.

After parking in the street, which wasn't too challenging during an early weeknight, they stood in front of a bar called Red Five. It was innocent enough on the outside, wedged between a sampling of other gay Boystown bars, but on the inside . . .

Na-ht so innocent.

Dawn had never seen Kiko shut up so completely as he did when they strolled into the blue-lit building. Happy Hour was advertised on every neon-markered black sign, which explained the unexpected crowd. Oversized golden cages held boy babes in go-go gear. Gargantuan screens played scenes from a cool-attitude movie; Dawn thought it might be *The Usual Suspects*. Large metal buckets attached to the ceiling near the walls sluiced water over cavorting patrons every few minutes, much to their yelps of delight. It seemed like every man was holding a martini, creating a rainbow of alcohol-drenched streamers. Tight shirts, no shirts—it didn't matter as they all danced with their arms around each other.

Onstage, a performer belted out a lip-synching extravaganza. A Celine Dion twin. Holy crap.

She was standing in the spotlight with a microphone, dressed in a colorful mess of scarves, singing one of many silly tunes Dawn hadn't ever learned the name of. The audience yelled along during the "river deep, mountain high!" chorus, reminding Dawn of why she'd never bothered.

Unruffled, Breisi made her way to a bartender as Kiko laughed and took off his shades, then started snapping his fingers to the music.

Breisi was back in a flash. "Sasha's in the dressing room!" she said, raising her voice over the music. "Rolf said to go right back!"

Rolf. As they weaved through the water- and sweat-misted crowd, Dawn glanced at the beefy, shirtless bartender dancing his way toward a new customer. They were lax on security here, which probably meant this bar had nothing to do with vamps.

On their way, Dawn rubbed against some decent chests, so she could've called it a good night right there. But her better instincts were still on alert for Underground clues because *that's* what was going to lead to Frank.

In the dressing room, half-garbed drag queens primped in mirrors surrounded by big, white bulbs. The air was heavy with Aqua Net and the oily scent of makeup.

Kiko asked a Diana Ross look-alike where Sasha was, and the performer batted her lengthy false eyelashes and gave the psychic a sassy smile.

"There, sugar." She pointed a few mirrors down. "Wow, aren't you a darling thing? A sample-sized man, just like shampoo at a hotel."

Kiko laughed good-naturedly. Then they all made their way over to Sasha's station, where a robed performer was sitting in a chair, slipping off a long, dark wig.

It seemed such a personal act that Dawn actually averted her gaze. In that instant, the delayed images of what Sasha kept taped to the mirror infiltrated her: photos of recent ice skaters like Michelle Kwan,

Sarah Hughes, and then his two obvious namesakes—Sasha Cohen and Irina Slutskaya. The combination of the last two monikers made for a perfect drag queen.

She heard Breisi greeting the performer. Then, the next thing Dawn knew, she was peeking up again, finding that Sasha had already stuck a baseball cap over his head and was making quick work out of removing his heavy makeup with fingers full of cold cream.

"Too bad," he said in a deep voice. "You missed my Cher act."

Now, Dawn had awesome gaydar; a girl needed it badly in Hollywood. The thing was, Sasha wasn't setting it off.

Breisi took position next to the vanity, posture relaxed. "As much as we would have loved to see it, Sasha, we're here to discover if you can help us."

A finely tuned machine, the Limpet questioning method kicked into gear. Kiko stood on the other side of Sasha, getting ready to execute his touch-reading. Dawn hung back while Breisi consumed the subject's attention this time around.

"Help with what?" Sasha raised his darkly penciled brows and paused while taking off his lipstick.

"Lee Tomlinson." Kiko said it with command, seeing as he played "bad cop" to Breisi's "good cop."

Dawn, naturally, was the "ugly cop," so she saved her energy in case it was needed.

The performer ran a gaze down Kiko's body, then back up. It was a curious assessment, the recognition one social outsider might have for another.

He turned back to the mirror and finished cosmetic-removal duties. Impressive muscles lurked under his robe, and now that Dawn could see him better, she realized that his features were masculine and feminine at the same time. An ambiguously pretty boy who could end up starring in spy movies if he wanted to.

"Lee is as good as dead to me," Sasha said.

"What do you mean, he is as 'good as dead'?" Breisi asked.

"I mean he murdered a woman, they've got enough evidence to prove that. We were close for a while, but I don't cozy up to killers so, basically, I haven't talked to him since we broke up. That was before Klara Monaghan's last days."

Hearing him say Klara's name when everyone else in town seemed to have forgotten it, Dawn caught his gaze in the mirror. He grinned slightly, as if giving himself credit.

He knew the name, but the death didn't move him. Either this guy had no feelings or he knew how to hide them well.

Welcome to my club, Dawn thought.

"We heard you and Lee were an item," Kiko said bluntly.

Sasha turned an amused gaze on the psychic. "Yes, we were. Does it matter?"

"We're attempting to get to know him through his close relationships." Breisi fished out her PI license and flashed it. "And in just five minutes, you've been more forthcoming with us than his family and anyone else within a one-hundred-mile radius put together."

"Why're you investigating him?"

"Because there's been a similar murder," Breisi said. "We're looking into any links between the two. Unfortunately, that's all we can tell you due to client privacy restraints."

"So you're doing some good." Sasha seemed fine with that explanation as he tossed away a foundation-smeared tissue.

"We're trying," Kiko said. "But the leads are slow."

"Really. Then we'll see if I can't help. What do you want to know? I'm an open book. A regular exhibitionist, like anyone else around here."

As if to prove his point, he rose, sliding off his robe in the same fluid movement. Dawn caught a glimpse of smooth skin and hard body before she inexplicably looked away again. She came to lock gazes with Kiko, who'd angled his glance away, too, wide-eyed. She wasn't terribly surprised, him basically being a puritan and all. But her? Had this afternoon's bout with The Voice made her think twice about . . . well, being too hard-bitten about sex?

When Breisi said something else, it sounded as if she was still facing their interviewee. What do you know?

"How long were you with Lee, Sasha?"

Dawn heard him moving around, probably putting on clothes. "A few months. Then we broke up, he tried to flee, and the authorities hauled him back for murder."

"You had no contact with him during all this?"

"None. Before I knew about what he'd done with Klara Monaghan, I just assumed he'd taken up with another fling. Lee wasn't a relationship kind of man, not with males or females."

"He was bi?"

Sasha stopped moving, and Dawn looked up to find him fully clothed in jeans and an Eddie Bauer–like shirt.

"Lee didn't label himself," he said. "I don't do much of that, either. This queen stuff? I have a lot of fun doing it, but it doesn't make me something I'm not. Lee and I felt the same way—we are what we are. That's what attracted us."

"What did his mom think?" Dawn asked.

When Sasha turned his gaze on her, she felt a rogue shiver travel over her arms. Maybe what unsettled her was in his eyes, the intensity of the light green or gray or . . . some combination of color.

"I don't know about his mom," Sasha said, "but the sister I talked to didn't like the idea of Lee being with another man."

Dawn would put money on the notion that the sister—Marg or Cassie?—had told Mama Tomlinson about a lov-ah but hadn't mentioned he was male. Could it be that revealing this tidbit would've put the Lee-adoring Coral over the edge and the siblings were avoiding that?

"I'm starting to think there was a lot Lee's family didn't know about him," Dawn said, searching Sasha's face for any sign of her double meaning.

Kiko jumped on the Underground reference, having turned back around to the conversation. He reached out to Sasha, touching his bare arm as if to get his attention. "Before you and Lee broke up, did you notice anything different about him? Was he secretive? Did he go places and refuse to talk about where he'd been or did you catch him in any lies?"

Underground bait.

"Yes, I did notice some things." Sasha sent a deliberate glance to Kiko's lingering hand, then grinned at the smaller man. "He'd get moody when I'd ask him what he did the night before. And we had arguments about marks on his body. Bites that I hadn't given him."

At Sasha's cheeky expression, Kiko removed his hand, then loosely backed away, hands up, as if silently saying, *Hey, that wasn't me making a pass. Not gay. Sooooo not gay. But I respect you for your choices, dude.*

Dawn could've been wildly entertained by the Sasha/Kiko show, but she was trying to see if her coworker had gotten a reading. Also, she was wondering about that bite part.

"You were into biting, too?" she asked.

"Still am. Care to trade some?"

The feminine side of her preened. *Yeah, screw you, Eva. See how men can like me as much as they like you?* But her common sense was overriding everything else.

"Bites aren't my thing," Dawn said. "Where do you think Lee got his?"

As Sasha paused, Dawn noticed her partners trading a glance. From the way Breisi glowered, it was easy to guess that Kiko hadn't gotten much off of his Sasha reading. Damn.

"Biting was just playtime for me." Their interviewee rested his hands on his hips, coming off like the most masculine thing on the block. "But for Lee . . . ? He got more and more into the fetish. Obviously, he went to other sources besides little ol' me. I'm sure there're a thousand places in town you can check into, businesses or pleasure palaces that would've accommodated him."

Almost in desperation, Kiko watched Sasha's hand, no doubt planning how to touch him again.

"But," the ex-lover added, yanking his cap lower, "what do I care? Lee wasn't the love of my life. Hell, when he hit the big time, like he always bragged about, I was going to leech off of his grand career anyway until it was time to move on. He took what he wanted from me, and I've done the same with him."

Sasha tossed another charming grin to Dawn, making her wonder if he was full of shit or just the world's most honest individual. Something told her he wasn't kidding and wasn't remotely ashamed of it.

Once again, his eyes burned into her. Automatically, she reverted to training, jamming him out with a mind block. But after a second, she realized she'd gone overboard.

God, she was on edge. All this waiting for something to attack them since Robby died was eating at her.

"Sasha—" she began.

"My real name's Dave. Dave Nisro."

He seemed to catch something over her shoulder, and his smile grew wider, revealing a set of beautiful white teeth as he spread out his arms and ambled away from his dressing station.

Dawn followed him, discovering a young man walking toward Sasha/Dave to be enveloped in his embrace. The other male was somewhat familiar to her: slender, pale, his long auburn hair teased out to . . .

Oh, crap. Sasha's friend resembled Klara Monaghan.

Jaw tight, Breisi guided the team toward the back exit of the dressing room while Sasha nuzzled the new arrival. As the three of them passed, they thanked him, knowing they were anything but done.

"Give me a call if you need anything else," he said, eyes still only on the Klara doppelganger.

Kiko was the last one headed for the door. "Count on it."

The exit led to a back alley, where a Dumpster provided stale-trash cologne and a lone streetlight shone piss yellow.

Weirded out, Dawn stuck her hand in a pocket, fingers digging past some velvet to touch the reassuring, sharp tips of her silver, holy-water-tipped throwing stars: *shuriken.*

"That was disturbing," Breisi said.

"Which part?" Kiko wrinkled his nose at the Dumpster. "Where the male Klara clone sauntered in or where Sasha kept crossing gender lines to hit on Dawn? It was all . . ."

"Something to go on." Dawn couldn't hold back a smile because it was a lead, a reason to think Sasha was more invested in Klara or Lee than was obvious. "And I keep wondering—is Sasha vampire material or just a leech?"

"Guys, we gotta come back," Kiko said, hopped up. "I had a reading from him—mainly images of Lee, and I don't want to linger on those, thank you—but nothing about the Underground. I can get more, I know I can!"

Breisi motioned toward the alley's mouth and they all moved toward it. "Maybe he isn't vampire-related at all, Kik."

"Maybe he is and I need to dig deeper." His voice cracked on the last word as they passed the Dumpster.

Dawn felt terrible for him. "Hey, Kiko, don't . . ."

A shudder ripped through her, a warning that flinted against all the time she'd spent thinking that a vamp attack was just waiting around the corner for them—

She turned to find red eyes staring back at her, a dark shape huddled beside the Dumpster. Without pause, she extracted a throwing star, fired it at the looming threat.

"Dawn!" Breisi yelled.

But it was too late—she was already buzzing, glad to get back into action, to finally do something that would bring her that much closer to Frank.

The dark shape yelped, jumped away, red eyes dropping to the ground. Dawn's pulse imploded as she used this distraction to reach for her revolver.

But before she could fire, Breisi was yelling at her to stop again.

Vision blurred by memory, by the running red blood of Eva's crime-scene photos and Robby's mind rape, Dawn barely held back. Then . . .

No. God, no.

Her eyes focused to reveal a bare-armed homeless woman with blood on her arm from where the blade had glanced off. She was quaking in her ragged clothes—not shrinking in Nosferatu, blood-poisoned injury. She was pinned in terror like a moth that only wanted escape—not clawing at Dawn with gnarled fingers.

As Dawn's stomach turned, the woman's rickety-toothed mouth gaped in a scream, her brown eyes holding nothing but horror.

Horror at seeing Dawn, who had suddenly, easily turned back into the hunter who'd savagely beheaded a little-boy vampire.

On the ground, a stuffed animal tilted on its side, toy eyes glowing red. Bile crept up the back of Dawn's throat.

"It's one of them!" Kiko yelled.

When Dawn turned around, she found Breisi restraining the small man from joining in with his usual monster-hunting verve.

"No, it's . . ." She choked on disgust. "It's *not*."

She faced the homeless woman again, recoiling at her terrified gape while putting her revolver back in its holster. "She's human."

"How can you be sure?!"

"Kiko." Breisi's tone was forceful. "The holy water and silver are having no effect—"

"She could be one of those higher-level vamps! Let go of me, goddamnit!" Kiko grunted, trying to free himself.

Dawn couldn't feel anything—she was too afraid to. "I thought I saw . . . *felt* . . ." What? What the hell had she felt besides hatred and vengeance?

For one second, while the adrenaline coursed through her, she'd felt like she had a purpose. She'd felt defined.

Tentatively approaching the woman, Dawn reached out to her. "I'm sorry. So sorry, here . . . let me—"

With an ear-stabbing screech, the woman sprang up, swiped at Dawn with her jagged fingernails and sprang away. She sprinted down the alley, erased by the darkness.

Dawn's gaze settled on the woman's meager belongings: an army bag with torn pants sticking out, a plastic tarp, a ratty, stuffed pink bunny rabbit with dead pink—not even red—eyes. The last item had a bloodstain on it, fresh, livid.

"We need to find her," Dawn said, the words barely forming. "We should get her some medical aid—"

She took off running to the end of the alley. *Have to find her,* Dawn thought. *Have to make sure she's okay . . .*

But when she arrived at the exit, she zipped her gaze back, forth, everywhere.

The woman was gone. Hiding? Where?

Footsteps slammed the pavement behind her, and without really feeling anything, Dawn recognized that a hand had landed on her shoulder, jerking her back into the alley.

It was Breisi, frantic, pissed as hell. "Don't ever run off by yourself. What if she was bait for an ambush, or—"

"We've got to find her," Dawn repeated.

"No."

When Dawn looked at Breisi, she found her coworker angrier than she'd ever imagined. In back of her, Kiko finally arrived, slow to travel.

"Dawn, you know what's at stake," Breisi half whispered, but her soft tone was lethal. "We cannot tell a medical worker that you stabbed a woman with a martial arts weapon."

"But you can give her some help," Dawn insisted. "You've done it for me and Kik, with your gel. . . ."

Looking torn, Breisi glanced around. She was only being careful, Dawn knew, only analyzing the risk of a trap. Gradually, Dawn forced herself to admit the necessity of pausing; she'd already done enough damage by reacting too quickly. Was she going to make it worse by leaving her team?

Kiko kept right on going past both Dawn and Breisi, clearly intent on finding the woman himself.

"Kik—" Dawn grabbed at his jacket, holding him back from the unknown.

He resisted, and Breisi stepped back in, holding his jacket, too, keeping him with them, just as Dawn was.

"You're not to engage in anything, Kiko Daniels," Breisi said. "We've been clear about that."

He held up a finger, first to Breisi, then to Dawn, accusing them both with a heartbreakingly enraged grimace.

"You need my help," he said, voice trembling. "You can't stop me from giving it."

Feeling dead again, Dawn shook her head. "You're right. We do need you. But you're not . . ."

How could she say it without mortifying him?

He finished for her. "I'm not up to it right now. You've told me. I'm a gimp, physically and mentally. But that's just because you're coddling me. If you'd let me loose, I could get us back on track. . . ." He trailed off, probably because he, also, knew that he was lying to himself.

Without another word, he turned his back on them.

Slowly, Breisi put an arm around his shoulders, then guided him away, casting one last baleful glance at Dawn, who slowly followed, taking up their backs.

But before she turned the corner, she looked behind her, seeing the faint glow of the stuffed bunny's eyes by the Dumpster.

The pink lights sputtered out.

ELEVEN

The Haven

In the clenched silence of the SUV, Dawn sat on the edge of her front seat, vainly inspecting the passing storefronts and sidewalks. "Can't you slow down?"

Breisi complied as Kiko spoke up.

"If we haven't found her by now, we're not going to do it anytime tonight. The boss even said that none of the Friends can locate her. She's gone where all the other faceless people in this town go: through the cracks."

He'd grabbed the backseat, surrendering shotgun to Dawn, acknowledging that she needed the clearer view in this fruitless search. Lying flat on his back, he wore his sunglasses, as if blocking everything out.

"Kiko's right," Breisi said. "Chances are slim to none we'll find her."

"A slim chance is higher than zero." Dawn swiveled her gaze

back and forth, covering every streetlamp-lit patch of sidewalk and every shadow. This wasn't over. Not until she made up for her mistake.

"We can anonymously look around to see if a woman of her description checked into any ERs," Breisi said. "How is that?"

"Not enough."

Even as she said it, she knew her teammates were right, that they couldn't do this all night. L.A. wasn't a sandbox; the wounded lady could be anywhere by now. But, still . . . it was her own tangled thirst for payback that had injured the innocent bystander, and the more she recalled the thrill of whisking that throwing star at what she thought was a monster, getting it before it got her, the more her self-disgust grew.

The dashboard clock flashed 11:08, each pulse seeping into Dawn with stressful urgency. But when Breisi turned the SUV back toward the office, Dawn knew it was done.

I'd take it back if I could, she kept thinking over and over in useless apology to a woman who'd never hear it.

Wouldn't I?

The question stabbed at her, a knife point digging toward what she suspected was the truth.

Her weapons were real now: no more stunt fighting, no more movie magic that made the imaginary into a facsimile of life. She'd crossed that line a while ago, but it was only tonight, faced with the wounds she could inflict on a human, that she understood the full impact of drawing blood.

And, someone help her, deep inside she knew she'd do it again if the situation were repeated. She'd do it to get Frank back, and that scared her more than any monster.

Terror lodged in her throat, and when her cell phone vibrated in her pocket, she rushed to grab it.

The call screen read "Matt Lonigan," and even though Breisi, his biggest fan, was sitting right there, Dawn went ahead and took it. They'd been playing too much phone tag. "Hi."

"Hey." He hesitated. "What's wrong?"

She straightened in her seat, like that would change the flatness of her voice or something. Out of the corner of her eye, she saw Breisi glance over, then turn back to the front.

"I'm just tired." There. The most deflective excuse in the book. It was almost the *How are you? / Fine, thank you, how are you?* of meaningless exchanges.

A beat passed while he probably thought the same thing. Then, "You sound busy. I was actually expecting your voice mail since it's pretty late. . . ."

So polite. He often called late, knowing she'd be up. They knew each other's schedules by now, if nothing else.

"I'm just . . ." What? Worried about her id? ". . . puttering around right now."

From the backseat, Kiko grunted but didn't say anything.

"Just puttering?" There was a smile in Matt's voice. "Well, how about that. Me, too."

"No pressing PI duties tonight?" Her tone was still comatose, but it was improving. He had that effect on her. "No dead bodies to lurk around or shadows to jump out of? You must be at a loss."

He laughed. "See. I knew I could get you to say something scrappy. For a minute I thought you were in a bad mood. Well, worse than normal."

What she wouldn't give to allow him to help her forget. She managed her own smile, then rubbed a hand over her eyes.

"If you're not doing much," he said, voice going low, "I have a couple of ideas about how to cheer you up."

"Cheer? That sounds so . . ." Impossible. But if that were true, why did it send a blip of interest through her?

They'd reached the Hills by now, pulling in front of their Spanish Revival office. A small sign proclaiming LIMPET AND ASSOCIATES hung over the porch, near the iron cross that guarded the doorway. Like shaded eyes, the circular windows were blocked by iron grating and thick curtains. The red-tiled roof and tan stucco provided caked makeup for the building's aging face—a Gloria Swanson used-to-be who was creaking into modern times.

As Breisi pulled into the garage and cut the engine, she didn't make a move to exit. Even Kiko, slowly sitting up in the backseat, wasn't leaving.

Dawn cleared her throat at them, indicating that, perhaps, some privacy wouldn't come amiss.

Both coworkers remained rooted. Nosy.

Matt started to say something again, but Dawn stopped him.

"Can I call you back?"

"All right." He sounded a little baffled.

She hung up. "May I help you two?"

"Besides recovering from tonight, you need to catch up on sleep," Breisi said. "Things are picking up, so any rest you can get now might help later."

Kiko joined in. "I think that's Breez's way of saying some shut-eye will increase your powers of judgment, Dawn. And you know what? Not a bad idea."

Dawn got the impression that he'd wanted to add something like "for us both" to the end of his comment. She didn't remark on this near-apology for getting angry at her and Breisi. No sense in rubbing salt in his sores.

"Are you saying you don't need me for the rest of the night?" she asked Breisi.

"I'm saying you need to use your time wisely." The other woman gave a pointed glance toward the phone.

Dawn's rebellious attitude reared up. "Did it occur to you that I might be able to get a bead on what Matt knows about Jessica Reese's murder and how it's connected to Klara's?"

Breisi opened her mouth, but Kiko beat her.

"If that's why you wanna go, then go, Dawn. It's too late to make any other possible interview appointments tonight anyway."

With one sex-patrol glance back at her, he carefully got out of the SUV, sliding down the seat until he hit pavement.

He shut the door, leaving Breisi and Dawn alone. Genuine worry lingered in her coworker's gaze, and Dawn couldn't find it in herself to battle against that. It was kinda nice to be cared about sometimes.

"Don't get all fretful," Dawn said. "I'm defense-ready, just in case he turns out to be the mean man you think he is."

"You've got free will, but . . . If you insist on seeing him, would you refuse to have a Friend accompany you?"

"Breisi."

"Dawn."

Stalemate. Realistically, Dawn saw the sense in bringing extra protection; part of the reason she found Matt so attractive was his dark mystique. The other part of it was because, out of everyone else in her life right now, he really did make her feel that normalcy was not just an abstract word someone had stuck in the dictionary. In spite of all his possible closet activities, he was a genuine guy. Hollyweird didn't have many of those. She sure as hell didn't know any.

And, anyway, he *did* know something about Jessica Reese; he'd let on as much the last time she'd seen him. Why not subtly grill him about it in person?

Breisi traced her car key over the steering wheel. "I don't feel right about leaving you alone with anyone right now. We should all be sticking together."

It occurred to Dawn that maybe Breisi thought she owed it to Frank to watch over his daughter. Unable to help it, she smiled at the other woman, touching her arm briefly before taking her hand away again. Breisi merely nodded once, as if most everything was out in the open now. Right.

"I'll tell you what." Dawn felt like a kid bargaining for the car on a Friday night. "What if one of our Friends hangs around outside while I go to Matt's. I won't even stay long, just enough to get some information if he's willing to give it. No guts, no find-out-about-the-Underground, right?"

And maybe she could also get some of what Breisi used to get from Frank: smoothies, quiet nights, understanding from another person in their business. Daisies. God knows she needed that anchor tonight of all nights—and not the kind The Voice provided. No, she needed another human. A hu-*man*.

Breisi seemed to come to a conclusion. She glared at the door leading to the house, as if communing with it—or their boss. "I really don't like this. Not at all."

"But you'll arrange some Friend protection?"

She clipped out a nod, then got out of the car. "Just be careful. Stay aware of *everything*."

Finally, Dawn was able to breathe. "I will. And, Breez?"

She paused in closing the door.

Dawn offered a thankful grin, not finding it necessary to say anything else.

Because there was too damned much to say.

An hour later, she was relaxing on Matt's futon, a glass of water in one hand, TV remote in the other. She was surfing channels while Matt microwaved popcorn in his kitchen, which was connected to the family room by a wall with a window cut out of it.

Weird, weird, weird, she kept thinking. The two of them had never hung out like this, person to person. She couldn't get over it.

He lived in a real "regular guy" place that had been in his family for years and years—a cottage on Beachwood Drive. Palm trees and bird-of-paradise plants shaded his windows. White paint shimmered off the planks of the building's facade, creating a serene,

happy-in-a-pretty-expensive-neighborhood look. Inside, he'd deco-
rated in alpha-male style: a studio lamp aimed toward the ceiling. A
basketball backboard, complete with a net, propped against a
bolted door, as if waiting to be relocated to a permanent outside
home. An entertainment system much like Kiko's, except where her
temporary roommate was neat, Matt was not. He had the compo-
nents sitting on boxy steel structures, the wires nevertheless
wrapped in bundles. No pictures, no frills. Very Matt.

"Find anything good on the tube?" he asked as he carried out
the popcorn in a large plastic bowl.

At his approach, she'd stopped on a random channel, too compelled by him to notice what was on TV anymore. He'd showered
recently; his brown hair was still damp. She imagined he would
smell so good: soapy and male, tinged with a little bit of the spice
she'd detected when he got close.

And when he sat next to her, it was true. She breathed him in,
dizzy. It was almost enough to dismiss the niggling feeling in the pit
of her stomach.

The woman she'd hurt tonight . . .

But that's partly why she'd come here: to forget. So she was going to do it.

He offered her popcorn, then sat on the couch, not minding the
smell of garlic on her skin—he never did—and reached for the remote with his other hand, stealing it from her.

He caught her smiling at him, but continued to surf until he
landed on an entertainment channel.

"What?" he asked.

"You. Such a guy. You *have* to be in control of the remote, almost like it's a car or a barbecue or something. I guess I'll give it to
you, just this once."

He laughed, and the sound brought her the comfort of a childhood day when the only worry was which game you were going to
play outside or what color Popsicle you'd snack on. Or, at least,

that was her idea of a decent childhood day—one when Frank wouldn't have gone on an Eva-inspired crying jag or a whiskey bender.

"Well, thank you." He made a show of tucking the remote into the large pocket of his khaki shirt. "I appreciate your prideful sacrifice."

They both laughed this time, just plain relaxing together. This was nice.

"You into all these star-muckraking programs?" she asked, nodding at the late-night entertainment special.

From the screen, Tamsin Greene and her gorgeous Josephine Baker vibe glowed back at them. She'd been a superstar who'd committed suicide on the Internet last month, and the media hadn't let up on the coverage since.

Matt reached into his pocket and presented her with the remote, but not before faking her out by pulling it away again. She snatched it before he could reconsider.

"You pick then," he said, tossing a popcorn kernel at her. "Just don't make me watch Lifetime."

At that, both of them cracked up, knowing the Lifetime channel didn't have a chance in hell with Dawn.

She hesitated in her surfing. "Sorry I can't hang with the biography. It's too depressing to hear about that girl's suicide again."

Especially tonight. The last thing she needed was reminders of mortality.

Matt stared at the screen, head tilted as he took in an image of Tamsin singing at a concert, dressed in a flowing white dress. "All the big interest in Tamsin Greene's career, all the TV reports and big-time magazine spreads. Everything's become a shrine to her, hasn't it?"

"Purchased with her blood."

"Sometimes, people get what they ask for."

Dawn's eyes went wide at his callous remark. But why was she surprised? This wasn't Mr. Sensitive she was hanging with—not if he was the hunter she suspected him of being.

But his remark still stung. That homeless woman hadn't asked to be injured by Dawn's weapon tonight.

"You don't feel sorry for Tamsin Greene?" she asked.

"I do, but she was asking for the press to exploit her by the way she went out. I saw her suicide. You could access it just about anywhere on the 'Net."

"But wasn't she trying to make a statement about the paparazzi by throwing the ultimate story back in their faces? She wanted to make sure she scooped them by airing the suicide, at least that's what she said before she did it. Sure, it backfired, but . . ."

"She had to suspect that the press wouldn't be able to shut up about it." Matt didn't say anything for a moment, merely watched the TV. "Who knows what she was thinking."

The television played on, but Dawn wasn't paying a bit of attention.

She cleared her throat, ready to start work. "So why'd you really call me over here? Does it have anything to do with the discussion of Jessica Reese we didn't have back by the Cat's Paw?"

"Right. Jessica." He nodded to himself, staring at the table now.

"I mean, I know you don't reveal sources"—especially when it came to Frank, the man whom an anonymous client had hired Matt to find—"but I got the feeling you were kinda willing to share."

"I am. Kinda." He turned very serious. "I'm going out on a limb here, but . . . I think Jessica might not have been murdered by a vampire."

She leaned back at his honesty because she wasn't used to it. "And what does Jessica have to do with Frank? Why would you even look into her death if it didn't have anything to do with my dad's case?"

"I thought, based on the similarities to Klara Monaghan's murder, there might be a connection."

"And how do you know Jessica wasn't killed by a vamp?"

Matt drilled a gaze at her. "Take the information for what it's worth. Sometimes that's the only choice we have."

If she knew for sure whether or not he was a bad guy, the decision would be easier. Of course, she had no idea. She was just willing to take a chance that he was on their side.

"There are some details I find striking about both Klara's and Jessica's murders though," he said, "besides the whole vampire angle."

This was a start. "Shoot."

"First, it's like the murderer wants notoriety, whether it's the public kind or even a special, secret kind that gets them off in private. I was reading up on other cases, like the Black Dahlia murder. That killer dumped the body in an obvious place, like he was making an announcement. And he left it in a grotesque, sensational state, just like *our* genius."

"Our killer wants to be famous?"

"That's why everyone comes to L.A., isn't it?" He tossed another popcorn kernel, this time at the table. "Our killer isn't exactly writing taunting letters to the police, but the signature is flashy enough."

"Like they're begging to be noticed, even if it's in a demented, passive-aggressive way."

"Exactly."

"And this has nothing to do with Frank."

"I . . . Damn it, I don't know." He dumped the rest of his popcorn on a napkin that rested on the table.

Why wouldn't he tell her about the reason all this mattered in an investigation of her dad? What was *his* agenda? Was it as crazy as her own?

The remote felt alien in Dawn's hand. She tried to think up ways to get more information out of him, first of all because she'd promised Breisi. Second of all, because she knew she needed to do everything possible to make up for Kiko's psychic blindness with Milton Crockett and the Tomlinsons—

Crack.

Just like that, her vision wavered, like something had disturbed the solidity of her world. Right on its tail, her peripheral vision caught a flash of silver? . . . red? . . . outside the window—

She whipped her gaze there, catching the orange sway of a bird-of-paradise. Not silver at all. Not even red.

Had the movement come from the Friend who'd been sent to watch her?

Uneasy, Dawn put her popcorn and water down on a napkin. Her stomach felt light, queasy. Her body felt heavy and exposed—watched.

It was a Friend, she told herself. That was all.

"What's wrong?" Matt asked. "You look the way you sounded on the phone earlier."

"And how did I sound?" She tried to smile as she faced him, her back now to the window.

She knew she wasn't wearing her emotions freely. Because of training and life experience, he'd never know anything she didn't want him to.

"Scared," he said. "You're scared of something."

"Bullshit."

She started to laugh it off—a nerve-laced compulsion—but he quieted her with a touch to her cheek. Immediately, she stopped with the bravado, jolted by the caress of his fingertips.

Real, she thought, thinking how much different this was than being with The Voice. She could feel, *see* how Matt's skin was rough, tangible, how it brushed against her own to cause friction.

The need for stimulated comfort took her over, jarring her heart to an erratic pump, sharpening the air in her lungs.

She wanted him to make her forget, like all the other men had.

Forget the homeless woman, forget Frank and Eva, just for a little while. . . .

His fingers traveled her face, sweet deliberation. When he got to her right lobe, where her long blood-moon earring used to hang with ruby-and-silver negligence, he stroked, as if mimicking the phantom fall and shimmer of it.

"I wish you'd tell me everything," he said.

"Same here." Was this one of their cat-and-mouse standoffs? Is that why he'd invited her over? She couldn't exactly be angry, because she was here for ulterior purposes, too.

"I'm not just talking about our work." He slipped his hands down her jacketed arms, coming too close to her shoulder-holstered gun while taking her hands in his.

She hadn't doffed her jacket because weapons were still in her pockets, plus, she didn't want to showcase the gun, even though he already knew it was there. In back of her, the window seemed to loom with whatever was watching her—Friend or foe. A chill flew down her spine and, not for the first time, she was glad she'd kept her arsenal handy.

But the reminder didn't chase away any of the heat churning through her. Steam bathed her, prickling her skin, making it painfully aware of what might happen between her and Matt, now that he'd gotten over some of the bashfulness.

"Right now," she said, "I'm all about work. There's not much left of me."

As if to prove her wrong, he leaned forward, molding his lips to hers in lingering question. Wet, warm. She couldn't think anymore, not with the excitement of him mingling with the shivers of being watched from outside the window.

Impulsively, she parted her lips, demanding more while pressing forward. She wanted to wipe away the violence she'd faced earlier with violence of another type: something she'd dealt with so many times before, something she could control. Skin to skin, she came out the winner every time, whether it was over a partner or Eva or even herself.

As she entered his mouth with her tongue, engaging his with ravenous insistence, he fisted her hair, moaning. She levered him backward, intending to straddle him, to grind into him and make him her goddamned slave.

"Wait," he mumbled.

"No." She sucked at his lower lip, sliding a hand down his chest as she kept pushing him back.

With just as much force, he grabbed her wrist, the one that had never been injured. He grabbed it hard.

Good. Her body remembered how, one night, he'd lost a fraction of control, at the hospital, when she'd been devastated by Kiko's back injury and had been yearning for someone to take her away from it. Matt had responded to her rough kisses, her prodding seduction.

In the thrall of memory, she groaned, the sound vibrating in her chest, in a place that echoed with emptiness.

Jonah, she thought. *Be like Jonah again. Use me as much as I use you. You were almost there that one night. . . .*

"Hey," he said again, voice garbled, familiar in its lust.

So familiar . . .

The shock of longing stimulated her, and she nipped at his neck. Her heart pounded like a broken, out-of-control machine stamping steel into jagged shapes. Condensation from its urgent thudding trickled down and down, lubricating her.

He seemed to sense that she was about to attack, as she'd done that time at the hospital. Maybe that's why he slowed things down now, loosening his hold on her wrist. He slipped his hand behind her head, cradling it, deepening their kisses.

At first, Dawn didn't know exactly what to do. Usually, she'd be down a guy's pants by now, guiding him out, shucking off her clothes to get him inside of her as soon as possible. After that, she'd be cleansed of him.

But Matt wasn't letting her do that. He was slow driving, taking his time with each suck, each nip, running his other hand over her neck.

Dawn tried to calm her breathing, but it was impossible. Her heartbeat skittered, her body becoming one long throb after another, one long melt.

Making out, she thought. Is this what it was?

When she tried to take things a step further, stroking her hand up his thigh, he blocked her, weaving his fingers through hers and ending the kiss with an easy sip of her lips.

His breath bathed her ear. "I've got something for you."

Lust nudged at her. "I'll bet you do."

"Dawn." He laughed, the vibrations of it tapping over her skin. "Humor me. You like games. You like pushing things, don't you?"

She did a half wince, half purr, and he laughed again.

"Come here." He pulled her up to a stand. "I've got something that'll . . . You'll see."

God help her, but her gaze traveled right to his zipper, where she hoped to find an erection waiting. But his untucked shirt covered the details, damn it.

He held up a finger, grinning, then went to his bedroom.

Without her.

"Am I supposed to follow you?" she asked, mentally crossing her fingers while fidgeting in pained frustration.

"No, stay out there." He was clearly amused.

Great. She waited, body belting out SOS codes in the most uncomfortable places.

What was he do—?

One of those shivers attacked her again, and she reached for her revolver, spinning toward the window, hoping—and not hoping—to discover something there.

Shoot, shoot! her dark half said, loving the power.

But . . . there was nothing. Nothing but the wind and the bird-of-paradise.

"Okay," Matt said.

Adrenaline screeching to a halt, she shoved her weapon back into the holster before he could see it, then turned around to find him walking out of the bedroom.

You almost lost it again, she thought. *Get it together, Dawn.*

He was clueless to her drama. And it was pretty cute how he was just standing there with a grin, holding some folded material.

"Um," she said optimistically, "lingerie?"

"Not quite." He was blushing. *Blushing.*

Endeared by his shyness, stumped by it, she shook her head. "Come on, what is it?"

"I thought . . . It's . . ."

"Good God." Dawn strode forward, all her aggression surfacing. "It doesn't look like a French maid's outfit."

He made as if to keep the material away from her, but then he held up a hand. "Let me explain first—"

There was no stopping her. She grabbed at the material. It belled out, filmy and flowery, into a dress.

It took a moment for her mind to wrap around what she was seeing.

"I found it in the window of a vintage store," he said, blushing even more furiously now. "Can you believe it?"

She was trying not to.

Dawn reached out, fingering the sheer material, not accepting what she touched.

It was a copy of the dress Eva Claremont had worn in her most famous movie, *Daydreamer.*

She remembered how his gaze had gone all goofy that day at lunch when she'd said Eva's name. Remembered how most men got that way with just a mention.

"You're not expecting me to put this on," she said, voice quavering, in what she told herself was only anger.

"Oh." He awkwardly looked at it. "I just—"

"Tell me this isn't the only way you'll find me attractive."

"Dawn, wait, wait. I didn't mean—"

"Is this a joke?"

He just shook his head, the dress hanging from one hand like the most loaded weapon she'd ever encountered. If it wasn't for the gleam of something in his gaze—disappointment?—she would've felt sorry for him.

Would've.

Ire surged, unreasonable, all consuming. She'd fought so hard against being her mom's daughter; it was the only way she could justify never living up to Eva's beauty. But now, even if she wasn't here, Eva was winning again. She'd taken over Jac and now, more hurtfully, Matt.

"Maybe that explains everything," she said, backing away. "You're one of those guys who gets off on my relation to Eva, right? Were you closing your eyes when you were kissing me? Did it shut out my less-attractive face?"

"No, I—"

Pressure built in her temples. "Was putting me in a dress like hers going to make it easier to get it up, Matt?"

"Dawn—"

"Why did you bring this thing out just when we were getting somewhere?"

He heaved out a pent-up breath, gaze to the ground, shaking his head. He obviously had no other explanation.

Disillusionment had never hit her so hard. Not even when she'd found out that Frank was a monster hunter. Matt's betrayal was personal.

"That's your answer," she said, backing the rest of the way toward his door. "Nothing. Because I've already explained it all, haven't I? When you said you'd become interested in me before even meeting me, it was because of Eva. You, out of all people."

She wanted to throw up. This wasn't happening. Just after she'd built up some hope. . . .

"I want you for *you*, Dawn. This"—face wracked with regret, he held up the dress—"was wrong. You're so adventurous, so into games, I thought you'd laugh or . . ."

He stopped there, but it didn't matter. She was already out the door, the night surrounding her with its unknown enemies.

Yet, when the scent of jasmine floated over her, almost like a calming embrace, Dawn knew that at least one Friend was around.

TWELVE

BELOW, ACT TWO

ALMOST done," Sorin said to the Guard bound to a steel table in its cell.

They were in the bowels of the Underground, where the granite-hollowed dormitories of the Guards festered in deep, clinging cold. The lower-level vampires had already been fed with Groupie blood, which had either been voluntarily given or even left over from the meals of the Elite citizens.

In the cell opposite Sorin, a Guard pressed against the iron bars, his pale, hideous face framed. "More . . . more food, Master, more, more . . ."

The others took up this one's chanting. "Food, food, food—"

Over the patter of gnarled voices, one Guard yelled out in supplication. "Groupie blood!"

Sorin did not even deign to glance up as he continued preparing the Guard on the table for duty. A new centurion, made for defense and perhaps, these days, offense.

"Enough," he said to the other shouting creatures.

Not a one continued. It was the way of the Underground: Guards existed to obey. They were meant to be relatively weak-minded and weak-blooded, without power, save for what Sorin had bestowed upon them.

Efficiently, he kept on with the task at hand, tightening one last leather strap around the thick torso of his newest acquisition. Then, before continuing, Sorin paused to assess his creation thus far.

Bald, clawed, outfitted with iron teeth and black clothing to blend with the night. The new Guard still closed his eyes to this fresh world he would awaken to, as soon as Sorin performed one last trick of transformation.

As with all the Guards, this one had disappeared through the crevices of life Above. He had been noticed nearly a month ago during spy work and brought to Sorin's attention. This large-bodied specimen, a drunk with no family and no real friends, had been deemed strong and fit for Guard duty. Therefore, he had been quietly captured near the time of Robby Pennybaker's security breach, just before the resulting Underground seclusion. Sorin had only recently been able to turn his attention to transforming this subject, bringing it into the ranks of Underground Guard duty. A duty that might, someday, include having to obey even the most suicidal of orders if it indeed came to war.

Brushing a hand over his creation's brow, Sorin thought what a waste that would be. It took great energy to bring every Guard to life, just as much as it had all those years ago when he had been a young man, cast out of his family home because of talents no one could explain. Talents such as controlling small animals, bending them to his will, shaping them into creatures who, at some point, became what Sorin wished them to be.

But Benedikte, the Master, had appreciated his abilities. He had loved him for what others deemed wicked and unnatural. And, ultimately, Sorin had put his so-called witchery to good use. For defense of his true home.

His hearing picked up the corridor footfalls of a Groupie—always light on their toes, they were. Soon, the exquisite creature appeared, holding a silver bowl sloshing with the blood she intended to donate for a Guard's meal. A sacrifice was required of a Groupie nightly.

Sorin paid her the honor of turning away from his new Guard. "Galatea." He had given her fellow Groupies who manned the control panel instructions to allow her in without a fuss.

She saluted him, bowing until her dark, wild hair rolled over one shoulder, blocking her face. Today she wore it in tight curls, beads shimmering through strategic locks. A sheer purple robe revealed a petite figure accessorized with merely a network of fine silver chains. One of them, Sorin could not help noticing, slipped through the cleft of her sex, no doubt rubbing her with each movement.

His blood thrashed at the notion of slowly sliding it back and forth until she moaned. Her throat would hum as he bit into an engorged vein.

She stood upright again, hair falling away from high cheekbones and slanted, silver-tinged eyes. A pang of parental loss—one of the only deep emotions he had ever felt as a vampire—stole over him. Long ago, he had taken two vampire daughters. Before they had left this Underground to return to the Old World and eventually go missing without another word, they, too, had produced preternatural children. Consequently, the Groupies of today were his own daughters' progeny.

Unfortunately, generation to generation, the blood weakened through exchange, leaving each succeeding child less powerful. Their talents paled in comparison to Sorin's, leaving them exposed to elements such as religious symbols. Even their Awareness was a mere shadow—a feeling as opposed to words spoken mind to mind. It was nonexistent from a distance.

This helplessness was the reason Groupies were the pets of the Underground: lovely, useful decorations who existed on blood and pleasure alone.

"You're working too hard, Master," Galatea said with a sparkle in her eyes. "Don't you have any time for play?"

"Play." He laughed. "It has been nothing but that for your kind since the lockdown."

"Maybe we haven't done any spy work lately, but I hear that might change with the threat of that Jessica Reese murder."

"You hear too much. They say, 'loose lips sink ships,' yes?"

That would also apply to what only he and the Master had heard tonight via spy work: Limpet and Associates' recent efforts at cornering Milton Crockett, plus Lee Tomlinson's family and lover, had proved futile, thank the day. It seemed that Limpet's little psychic had not obtained valid readings from any of them. However, Sorin still knew trouble was ahead. As a realist, he fully expected it, taking the precaution of directing spies to keep watch over the growing list of Limpet interview subjects.

"I will play after I am done here," he said to Galatea while restraining a surge of ravenous need for her. Too much labor to complete. And perhaps the Master would be calling him to conference about further strategy.

"Don't worry, I'll be waiting." Galatea grinned at him, so rash and young, a product of over three decades ago, when she had chosen to be turned.

Behind her, the Guard who had started the most recent round of chanting for food began sniffing at the blood she carried. Its nostrils flared, its eyes blaring red.

"Groupie blood," it growled.

Galatea assessed the creature, unafraid. Her kind had aided in giving birth to the Guards, lending their bite to the process. Thus, the Guards had powers equal to the Groupies, though the latter had the gift of free will whereas Sorin was the keeper of the lower vampires in every way.

Sorin cocked an eyebrow. "Galatea, please, splash the creature's mouth with your blood."

Surprised, she nevertheless did so, flicking drops from her fingers onto the Guard's lips.

The low-ranked vampire feverishly licked every fleck of moisture, grunting. "More, more, more . . ."

Sorin concentrated on its eyes. They flared with flame, excitement, the pupils expanding and blocking all color, the black center consuming the red. In that fathomless space, Sorin believed he could detect a foreign blankness. . . . A hole filled with something he could almost comprehend yet . . . could not.

Something just beyond his reach. Something he might have even known in another lifetime?

Before Sorin could grasp the meaning of what he was witnessing, the Guard's eyes contracted to red again, returning to the color of eternity.

"More, more, more," the Guard said, shaking its cell bars.

They had never shown this sort of fervor for blood until fairly recently; the Guards normally ate to survive. Had they become addicted? Or what if the Guards had developed a taste for Groupie sustenance in particular? Perhaps he needed to synthesize generic blood devoid of anything Groupie. The last scenario the Underground needed to endure was one in which the Guards craved the citizens.

"More, more . . ."

The others joined in, rattling their bars until the ground trembled. "More, more, more . . ."

"Stop." Sorin's tone was harsh. A chill traced the edges of his body, and he resented the disturbance.

One of the Guards down the hall did not heed the command.

"Home," he wailed, his voice as thin as a single wolf's cry in the distance.

Sorin would have to adjust these Guards, inspect them and repair their shortcomings. It was an ongoing process. Live and learn, as the Master might say.

"Can they break out?" Galatea asked, inching away from the cell's bars, clutching the bowl of blood to her chest.

Sorin inspected her, thinking he was close to feeling the same discomfort. Close, yes, but the vampiric years had worn off most emotion like rough wind smoothing the edges off rock.

"No," he said. "They would not survive the attempt."

She sighed, knowing he was right. "Yes, Master, you'd terminate the Guards before they would even get to the main area."

True. Even though he wasn't the real Master, Sorin alone controlled the Guards—they were subject to every whim of his sorcerer's talents. Additionally, he maintained their strength at a Groupie's level to ensure their inferiority—another precaution. Their strength was sufficient to kill a human, if need be, but not enough to overcome Sorin or the Master himself.

Galatea set down the bowl of cold blood. "Master, may I . . . ?"

"Yes, you may leave."

She wasted no time in doing so, leaving a trail of slight fear behind. It wet Sorin's mouth, whet his hunger.

But then his gaze turned toward the Guard across the hall. The creature slunk back into the darkness of its home, its red eyes becoming the only pinpoints of light.

Home, the one Guard had said.

A terrible thought occurred to Sorin. The black of the Guard's eyes, the mysterious and gaping space, the dull familiarity of it . . .

Humanity? he thought.

He mused over that. Yet . . . no. It could not be.

For the Guards, humanity had died with the first bite. It was unthinkable to leave them with memories, imaginations, reasons to return Above. They were the only members of the Underground taken against their will because no one would ever know or care that these particular individuals were gone. Sorin had infused them with the same thing he had used on his cat and other small animals during human life: thoughts of what he wished them to be.

He turned back to his new Guard. Due to the restlessness of the others, there would be no free wandering time for the group tonight. Usually, they were granted movement through the Underground tunnels, beneath the city, yet away from the vampire living area.

No more, Sorin thought. Not until the Guards were retuned.

He tested the straps on his new creation, again admiring his handiwork: years of study had allowed him to dally in physical manipulation as well as mental.

"You'll be a Dr. Frankenstein," the Master had once told Sorin over fifty years ago, shortly after he had triumphed over his fears and given in to Sorin's great wish to begin a second Underground.

Sorin had smiled at that. "My powers are much stronger than they ever were in human form, so our Guards will be our saving grace, protecting our lesser vampires during the first minutes of an attack while alerting the more powerful to prepare. We will never be caught unawares again, Master."

Now, keeping his promise, he held out a hand, then flattened his palm over the new Guard's face. He closed his eyes and performed the final step in creation: a mind wipe.

It was unlike the one the Master had subjected Milton Crockett to. Where the humans generally lost all details related to personal vampiric activity, Guards traveled the opposite road: they would forfeit everything human, absorbing Sorin's commands. In essence, they were "programmed" as the new age would say. Programmed to serve and to be vampire soldiers, willing to die for the higher ranks, brainwashed never to attack unless provoked.

He traveled inward, investing the new Guard, initiating him.

His whispered demands threaded together, tangling into patterns for the creature's brain to follow.

Ultimately, Sorin removed his touch and stepped back. "Awaken."

When the Guard opened his red eyes, the older vampire saw only complete surrender, mindless obedience.

The perfect defender.

The type of warrior Sorin wished he and the Master had possessed when their original Underground had been decimated over eighty years ago.

THIRTEEN

BERKLEY SQUARE, LONDON, 1923

Gone, Benedikte thought, huddling against the wall of an up-stairs bedroom. *It is . . . gone.*

Night peered through the abandoned house's filmy window, moonless and anesthetic. A rat's footsteps scratched over the dusty wooden floor, reminding the vampire of how he had escaped, too.

Alone now. He was alone and, somewhere below the foundation of this old building, his Underground was in ruins.

Something like a scream welled up in Benedikte's chest, but it couldn't push its way out. The vampire couldn't even move, couldn't even function, because almost everything he had loved was gone now, scattered to ashes.

Images played before his burning eyes, as if his memories were being filtered from a projector onto a screen. As if he were reliving one of the grainy black-and-white silent movies he studied and adored. Scenes of exuberant decadence, revealing how Benedikte had come to enjoy the world anew with Sorin, how he had taken resurrected pleasure from sharing a vampire's wondrous abilities with another. Sequences, centuries' worth, showing the fortunes they had charmed out of unsuspecting victims, blood kisses they had enchanted out of ladies in ball gowns and peasant clothing alike, crazed orgies of feeding and satiation.

Then . . . ah. Then came London.

More flickering pictures: tunnels and spaces they had discovered belowground, shafts that had been deserted by humans during construction for the Tube. The vampires had improved this rough matter into a palatial home, intent on obeying the recent command Benedikte had received from his own maker.

Create a community, the ultimate master had beseeched from afar. *Create and breed so I might rule a future kingdom.*

Even though Benedikte had never been raised or trained to do anything but follow commands, he had taken up responsibility and leadership. He had given birth to children, sisters and brothers to Sorin, who still had not loaned his bite to any living creature himself. Unable to forget how his human family had abandoned him, the younger vampire feared being left behind by anyone but his constant companion. For him, the pain of desertion wouldn't go away.

Benedikte, or the Master as he'd been called in his Underground, trembled. At this point, his analysis of the attack had gone beyond shock and was becoming physical, taking him over. His vampire gaze rested on the opposite wall, where a crucifix loomed, as if to chase away the evil from this house, which was said to be haunted.

At least, that's what popular gossip maintained. And Benedikte had often used these sorts of rumors, newspapers, and patterns of human speech and interaction to educate himself about fashions and trends whenever he came Above. But his newly kindled interest hadn't only become a personal pleasure—it had been vital to his home's survival.

As if challenging the crucifix to punish him, Benedikte stared at it.

Nothing. Nothing at all anymore.

No guilt at what he'd become. No cries for redemption from deep within his soul. It used to be that spiritual mementos affected him profoundly, but that had been long ago, before he realized faith was only an invisible cloak that warded off the fears of reality. Or maybe he had just seen too much in his debauched life to care anymore.

But, oddly, he did care. Too much. Terribly.

Out of desperation, he folded his hands in front of his chest, raising his head to the crucifix.

Help me. Help me to get my paradise back?

But the object merely rested in silver silence, clouding in his vision.

In a fit of profane dejection, Benedikte pushed out with his mind, swiping the item from the wall. It clattered against the floor, the persecuted figure on the cross staring at the ceiling with resigned serenity.

Benedikte contained himself, holding back an unexpected yell that could have shaken the ground. Where to turn now? Where to go after losing . . . ?

Clumsily, he reached inside his coat pocket, searching for the one item he always kept near—the only vial he'd managed to save while all the rest had perished in the attack.

He grasped the slim tube, fumbling to get it open, to hold it to his lips and drink.

Immediately, the rush of Sorin's captive soul lit through Benedikte, coloring every vein, animating him. He felt the glorious wonder of appreciating a sunset on the wealthy estate where Sorin had grown up, felt the admiration from a small audience who had been wildly entertained by the talent of snatching fire from air. . . .

Benedikte crashed to the floor, rolling to his back in shuddering ecstasy. Eyes open, he witnessed the play of rainbows as joy literally emanated from his body, flashing over the walls, reflecting off the windowpanes.

Then, when the soul allowed him to feel the sublime grief of the day Sorin had been tossed out of his home, Benedikte moaned, cried, became human again for one heavenly moment—

Furiously, the soul ripped out of him, crazed and wailing, as frightened as always. It flew back into the vial, which the vampire had enchanted with a spell that told the soul this was home, this was safety.

It clamored inside and, even while racked with agony, the Master plugged the vile, knowing he would be truly empty if he lost this one last possession, as well.

Feeling as if each corner of the room was pulling and quartering him into pieces, Benedikte shivered on the floor, clinging to the aftermath, destroyed by it.

Minutes, maybe hours later, the door groaned open. Still panting, Benedikte glanced in its direction. There, even in the darkness, he discerned the beating outline of his only surviving son.

Sorin, his tattered clothing smoked with acrid memories of the battle, walked inside, closing the door behind him. "Here you are. I should have known you would be in your beloved sanctuary."

The Master rested in this place often. Normally it was after a picture show, with the grand piping of organ music still chorusing through his limbs, or after a night of visiting clubs, with their Harry Houdini imitators or flappers dancing to the jazz music.

When Benedikte didn't answer, Sorin tried again. "Your Awareness was closed off to me—"

"We had no protection." Benedikte pressed his hands against his face. "I'm not a leader—I never have been—and we were caught off guard because of it. If we'd only had some sort of defense. . . ."

Bonelessly, he allowed his hands to fall to the floor. He stared at the ceiling, much like the crucifix figure on the other side of the room, although there was an abyss of difference between them.

Sorin slumped back against a wall, coming to sit. He'd battled valiantly, utilizing the magic he'd been born with—magic that had been honed through vampire talents, magic that he'd refined from country to country, border to border.

But all the other young, jazz-baby children hadn't been able to fight, thanks to Andre, the vampire Benedikte had once believed to be a brother in blood.

Benedikte rued the moment he and Sorin had been lured outside by Andre's cryptic presence. There had been a frisson splitting the air, a faint thrum Benedikte had not felt since leaving the old country.

Unsuspectingly, they'd gone to investigate.

Andre had been waiting, arm draped over a bench he'd been sitting on in Hyde Park. The emerging moon had made him more shadow than substance but, all the same, Benedikte had noticed that his brother's beard had been shaved off, his hair clipped to accommodate today's fashions, just as he and Sorin had done, as well.

He hadn't seen Andre for centuries, not since the brothers had discovered that each of them possessed diverse talents and had gone their own ways to revel in the discovery of how far they could take them. The others could perform feats such as commanding animals to obey or even affecting weather; Benedikte could do neither, although he was coming to believe that his immunity to religious objects might be a latent strength.

The only other time Benedikte had even been close to Andre was during their father's mental gathering of the blood brothers—when the great one had commanded all of them to begin separate communities and then had gone underground himself, gathering power until it was time to rise again. At that point, communication between the brothers had somehow stopped, cut off by the pursuit of their own quests, Benedikte had thought.

But now, he knew he'd been wrong about that.

Coolly, Andre sat back on the bench while a sense of disquiet gnawed on the back of Benedikte's neck. It was sharp enough to keep him from greeting his own blood kin.

"You never heard the rumors, my friend?" Andre asked.

When Bendikte didn't respond, the other vampire was more than happy to supply his own answers. "Takeovers among the brothers. Civil warring. Greed. You should've done better at keeping your perception open, Benedikte."

Before his brother could even fully explain, Benedikte suspected what might be happening Below.

"All I want is what you already have," Andre added, direct and businesslike. "And I'm in the process of getting it right now."

With a blast of preternatural speed, Benedikte and Sorin had whisked back to their Underground, where they discovered Andre's vampires holding the children captive.

The youngsters had cocked their heads at Benedikte, their faces reflecting heartrending bewilderment: how can one of our own do this?

All they'd wanted was an oasis. And, for good money, Benedikte had provided these heiresses and playboys a hedonistic refuge where they could indulge, where they could dance until dawn and the party would never end. Up until this night, the worst threat had been a fear of humans and their destructive tendencies when it came to matters they didn't comprehend—matters such as vampires. But secrecy had kept that particular threat away.

Who would have ever predicted that a brother vampire would be far worse?

By now, Andre had solidified behind Benedikte and Sorin, blocking the Underground's veiled exit.

"Surrender," the other said.

"Are you daring to go against our father's mandate?"

Andre had laughed. "I am daring. And do you know why, Benedikte? Because I want to. It'll be close to two hundred years before Father rises again and, by that time, *I* will be the one who welcomes him. *I* will be his right hand."

The vampire had been no such thing in the past. He had been a lower-ranked soldier for their master. Ambitious? Yes. But powerful? Not in his wildest dreams.

Benedikte had refused to surrender, and that's when Andre had declared war. But even before Benedikte could free any children, or before Sorin could use an ambush of violent magic to rip the hearts out of Andre's vampires, or even before Benedikte could behead his bastard brother and his brood, a clearly immune Andre laid fire to a curtain, most likely planning to extinguish the flame once he'd driven out Benedikte from his own home.

Now, here in this abandoned house where he'd shut himself off from reality, phantom cries of his still-bound children, burning in the inferno, tortured him.

Fire. Why did it have to be one of his progeny's only true killers, fire? He hadn't even salvaged their soul vials from the flames. . . .

Coward, he thought, remembering how he and Sorin had fled before the humans could arrive to put out the flames creeping from the Underground's hidden entrance near the park.

They had separated in the gathering crowd, and Benedikte the Master—the master of nothing now—had crept back to his favorite haunt to wonder what had just happened.

Lying prone on the hard, wooden floor, the seeds of destruction still weighed heavily inside of him—an instinct for isolation, the urge to make the world a mirror of what he'd suffered tonight.

"Master?" Sorin whispered.

Benedikte realized that his body had gone vaporous, reflecting what he felt: empty. A useless nothing who had no choice but to live out endless years unless he was destroyed first.

Out of pure mortification at being so revealed, Benedikte sucked into solid form. Through the years, he'd practiced his talent for changing into other shapes, but he had lost control this time.

Not that it mattered.

"Master," Sorin repeated, his tone careful, as if he were prodding a sleeping snake. "I am just as bereft as you, but we cannot stay here, not with all the human activity the fire has conjured tonight. We must go. . . ."

He trailed off.

"Where, Sorin?" The Master's voice was flat. "Where shall we go now?"

"Another home belowground." His son slid to his feet, vampire graceful. "We can find one. We will begin anew, perhaps in Edinburgh—"

The Master stayed silent.

"Or . . ." Sorin began, logical until the end, never giving up. "Or America, Master. You adored San Diego and Los Angeles."

"Never again."

Sorin stilled himself, Awareness vibrating, soaking into Benedikte. The older vampire batted his son's optimism away, seeing no use for it.

"I'm done." The Master closed his eyes, willing darkness into every inch of him.

"Master, I know we are at a low ebb, but there is so much more to discover in this world. Night by night, there are new inventions, new *movies* for you to see. Think of more films with little Mary Pickford."

Not even the lure of his favorite, an actress who smiled as Tereza had, could interest Benedikte.

He shut down, a broken film flapping in a projector.

Too weak to speak, the Master used his Awareness. *I will never subject myself to this failure again, good soldier or not.*

Numb, he blocked out Sorin's inevitable answer.

He just wished he had enough hate to keep himself going.

With one last attempt, he tried very hard to conjure it, to summon some emotion that would spark the will to continue. And, miraculously, his form turned from this sad lump of cynicism to something he'd never experienced before: an awful monster he should be—the picture of horror. Yes, yes . . .

The materialization of the hatred he wanted to feel.

He reached his zenith, rising in the air and growing, seething, baring his fangs to the emptiness that this world had become.

The door creaked open again.

Two men in military uniform stood in the entrance, and Benedikte—the godforsaken Master—reared on them, hissing as he stretched himself wide.

With only a gasp of terror, the men's eyes bugged out, as if witnessing hell frozen over.

Benedikte laughed and laughed, finally triumphant, until he glanced in Sorin's corner, where his son was hiding his face.

Turning away from the horror his father had become.

FOURTEEN

The Others

THE next day, the horizon was just bleeding into dusk when Dawn drove Kiko back to the office after a bout of physical therapy.

She was tuckered out. Not only had she conferenced with the therapist about Kik's progress ("We'll keep an eye on that medication," was the only lame solution for now), but earlier, the whole team had brainstormed and individually trained. Dawn had made sure that her own workout had been especially grueling.

After telling the team about Matt's take on Jessica Reese and that's all (right, like Dawn was going to mention Eva's damned dress to anyone, *ever*), she'd gotten out the old whip chain. The goal had been to stay frosty with her newly acquired skills, but the exercise had gone beyond that: Dawn had worked until the sweat washed off last night's stinging disappointment.

(The cleansing hadn't lasted long.)

After getting showered, she met Kiko in the computer room,

having decided to follow up on those links about Lane Tomlinson, Lee's brother.

"Crap," she said, clicking back to the search engine's home page when she saw that there was nothing worth noting. "Sometimes I think the only thing that's going to give us the big lead is another murder."

"Don't jinx anyone." Kiko was settled at a smaller table, ramrod straight with his back brace. "But . . . okay, I've thought about that, too, especially if the copycat killer starts getting cocky and careless. *That's* when we could get a break."

"Man, I'd hate to rely on another woman getting killed."

Her cell phone rang. When she looked at the screen to find Jacqueline Ashley's name listed, Dawn's blood pressure shot up.

They're calling me a throwback, Jac had said that day in the hospital before taking off her ball cap and revealing blond hair just like Eva's, forcing Dawn to focus on a face that seemed to conjure her dead mother's.

Jac had been excited, yet wary, about Dawn's reaction to the makeover. *They say that, even though I don't look exactly like her, I remind them of your mom. . . .*

Mom. Dawn had only known her from pictures: giddy wedding photos of Eva's ill-advised marriage to everyday-average Frank. Publicity stills of a rising movie goddess. The crime-scene photo tinted with blood.

Now, as the phone rang again, Matt's betrayal from last night lent new life to the Eva bitterness, snaking into the old fear and confusion Dawn had nurtured year after year.

Hush, little baby, don't say a word. . . .

"What's wrong?" Kiko asked.

Mama's gonna buy you a mockingbird. . . .

"Jac." The name was nothing more than a painful croak.

Kiko bounded over to Dawn. "Aren't you going to answer?"

When Dawn didn't make a move to do so, he grabbed the phone.

Immediately, he began chirping away, happy as can be. Dawn recalled that Jac had sort of made her feel that way, too, once upon a time before this whole makeover thing.

She needed to stop freaking out. For the last time, Jac was Jac and nothing more. Hell, if that wasn't true, The Voice would've stepped in already, pinpointing Jacqueline Ashley as a masquerading vamp.

Feeling her sanity whirling down a black hole, Dawn fought back, holding out her hand to Kiko for the phone. When he didn't give it to her right away, she tugged it from him.

"Party," Kiko said sotto voce. "She wants you to go out tonight, you lucky dog."

"Hey," Dawn said to Jac. She kept looking at Kiko, as if he was some kind of stabilizing force that would keep her from gurgling down the drain.

"There you are." Jac's voice, bright and sunny. "I was thinking you were avoiding me."

"Been real busy, that's all."

"Tell me about it. Buccaneer boot camp just ended, but we'll be shooting at the studio now. Maybe I'll get some time to start fencing at Dipak's again. We'll have to do that soon, before I go on location, all right? Boot camp made me a lot better. And wait 'til I tell you about all the gossip. Dawn, do you know that movie people actually call each other 'darling'? I can't get over that."

"You will."

All the golly-gee-whiz talk drove home that Jac really was a small-town girl who'd come to Hollywood via some modeling contest. Or . . .

Dawn stopped. Even Breisi had said the starlet was only a Tinseltown carbon copy of Eva and no more. *Breisi*, the steadiest person Dawn knew. So why was Dawn still thinking the worst?

"What are you up to tonight?" Jac asked.

"Work."

Kiko shot Dawn a look, probably knowing she was making excuses not to see Jac again. He'd crawled back into his chair, leaning on an elbow propped on a bigger table, lovestruck and all *Bye Bye Birdie*–ish.

"You work too much." Jac laughed. "I'm going to kidnap you. There's a party Paul Aspen is throwing, and I'm not really comfortable enough with the cast yet to show up by myself."

Paul Aspen, prince of the heartland. In twenty years, he'd be remembered as an actor who built his fortune on flag-waving movies, but he had recently branched out. Hushed gossip said that his worst vice was "deflowering" young girls on the set and off, but Joe and Phyllis Matinee didn't know that.

"Be my bodyguard?" Jac added kiddingly.

"Industry parties aren't really my scene."

Kiko lightly hit her.

"Wait, Jac." She held the phone to her shoulder.

"Call back," Kiko said.

Slightly annoyed, Dawn returned, then promised the actress she'd get back to her in a few minutes. A weight dropped off Dawn as she hung up.

Wow, she could breathe again.

But Kiko robbed her of that real quick. "You should go."

"Why's that?"

"Because *I'd* kill to see her, and I'm not going to let you cut off my Jac connections just because you hate the Hollywood status quo."

At the notion of seeing the girl again, panic welled. Foolish or not, it was time for Dawn to lay it on the line.

"Remember a few days ago when the possibility of Underground vamps having plastic surgery came up?"

Kiko looked at her sidelong.

"I can't help thinking," Dawn continued, "what, with the things we found out about Robby Pennybaker's own faked 'murder' and planned 'comeback' that . . ."

Kiko finished for her. "You think she's Eva with plastic surgery, and that Jac could have been Underground, just like Robby."

Dawn had refused to talk about that day in the hospital, but she knew Breisi had filled in Kiko and The Voice. She was glad she didn't have to go through all the details again.

"Here's the thing," Kiko said. "I don't think you should worry about Jac. She's actually been under watch, just like a lot of people we've been in contact with. So far, she's clean."

"Jac was under Friend surveillance . . . ?"

"Uh-huh, and the Friends are spread thin. We don't exactly have a surplus, and they need to get back home every once in a while to sort of refuel, know what I mean?"

"Gee, Kik, thanks for telling me about this before."

He shook his head, as if she should've learned better by now. "You're never going to know everything that happens around here. Not unless you need to, Dawn. *I'm* used to it by now."

So just accept it, he didn't have to add. *Just know that you're doing your part to save the world, Prophecy Girl.*

"Obviously," Kiko continued, "Jac isn't a concern, or else the boss would've had *us* follow up on her."

Yeesh, maybe it wasn't obvious, but at the hospital, Dawn had almost broken down at the thought of a resurrected Eva.

Couldn't they see what she was seeing—?

Wait. Good God, she'd never even looked beyond her own shock.

She calmed herself, thinking rationally for once. What if Jac/Eva could lead her to the Underground? Shouldn't she be wondering about that?

"Go. To. The. Party," Kiko was saying. "There's nothing pressing happening tonight anyway. Breisi wanted to go over what we know about Jessica Reese *again*, then she'll probably hermit up in her lab."

She saw a flash of something off-kilter in his gaze, but he looked away before she could call him on it.

"Why don't you and Breez come with me?"

"Because Jacqueline Ashley isn't . . . Dawn, you can't go around thinking everything, including Jac, is going to attack you. Believe me, you gotta get out of that phase. When I saw my first monster, I went through it, too, but you need to chill before you do even more damage."

She knew he was talking about the homeless woman. How many times had she told herself the same thing?

How damned many?

He got out of his chair. "Clear it with the boss if you decide to go. And"—he turned away—"I hope you do. I hope Jac helps you get out of this funk."

He left the room in a rush, never looking back.

But Dawn barely noticed because she was already thinking of ways to get the truth out of her starlet "pal."

Even if no one else believed in her suspicions.

JAC had gotten a new Prius and, while she drove up the Pacific Coast Highway to Paul Aspen's home in Malibu, she chattered away about her new ride.

"I decided on cherry red because I'm still such a sorority girl at heart, but the flip color doesn't scream 'tree-hugger hybrid driver.' That's what my PR guy said—buying this car, no matter what color it is, shows I'm concerned about the environment, even though I'm not giving interviews about it." Jac grinned. "Isn't all of that so major? All *I* wanted to do was save some gas."

Jac's window was only slightly gaped, ensuring that her hair didn't get messy, even though faint huffs of the summer-night breeze still played with her long blond waves. Tonight, she wasn't wearing her usual sunglasses and, at first, Dawn had flinched when looking into Jac's brown irises. The last time that had happened, Dawn had seen Eva with all the clarity of a knife shearing into her stomach. This time . . . not so much.

Maybe the shock had worn off?

As Dawn tried to return Jac's grin, she noticed that the starlet really did look like she'd been in a boot camp for the last month; it wasn't that she'd lost weight—no, she looked like the usual slender Jac in her white silk tank and a pair of tight black pants. It was just that her skin was duller than the usual pearly complexion. Or maybe it was just Dawn's vampire-steeped imagination taking over.

Jac noticed the visual inventory, so Dawn casually said, "Looks like you haven't been eating well."

"I know, I know," Jac said. "Nerves—total nerves! But that's all going to change. I've been assigned a nutritionist. Can you believe that? Someone's going to tell *me* how to eat, like I don't have a clue."

"There'll be a lot of someones telling you how to do everything from now on."

Jac nodded, respecting Dawn's own moviemaking expertise. Sure, she'd "just" been a stuntwoman, but she knew the ropes.

The ride went quiet, a little tense. As they drove along the surf-lined highway, the radio DJ talked gossip: Justin Timberlake in Vegas, Paris Hilton's most recently discovered sex video, Darrin Ryder's recovery from last month's mugging and his big night back on the town—

Jac snicked off the radio, not that Dawn cared. She wasn't a big Ryder fan; his harassment on a movie set was just one of many reasons she'd found herself on the outs in her stunt career.

Minding her seat belt, Dawn pulled her jacket tighter around her. After The Voice had given her permission to "take care of some personal business" for a few hours, she'd armed up and driven to Jac's. Chances were there'd be a security check at the door—unless

Jac had enough clout as the production's ingénue to get them out of it—so Dawn had adjusted her weapons accordingly.

Item one: if Jac were Eva, she might be like Robby Pennybaker, who'd been basically unaffected by holy objects; this meant Dawn had forgone most of those items except for a few just-in-case stand-bys, like a bit of holy water and the crucifix she always wore. Item two: Dawn might never get inside the party with a gun or blades, so she'd brought less obvious weapons. Silver, which had poisoned Robby, was her greatest ally right now so, among other things, she'd worn a necklace, bracelet, and earrings that were sharp enough to pierce a vamp's skin if they got too close. Breisi had con-structed the jeweled set a while ago, so Dawn had borrowed them. She'd also grabbed a lighter and a mini aerosol hairspray—a makeshift flamethrower in case fire could stop an attacking vamp.

So here she was—a real live vamp hunter. She hadn't even rubbed down with garlic, deciding not to offend everyone at the party tonight. Instead, she'd been sneakier, bringing along a small perfume dispenser full of garlic essence that she could mist onto her skin. It would work for lower-level vamp repulsion if she needed it. Subtle yet armed.

Jac pulled onto Malibu Colony Drive, where they came to guarded gates. After Jac's ID quickly ushered them through, she continued to Paul Aspen's mansion, which also boasted security at the entrance. As they pulled into the drive, tropical vegetation loomed above them, lush and still.

While the guards checked the car ahead, red taillights glowed through the windshield. Dawn turned to Jac, and the girl smiled brightly, washed over by the sanguine shade.

A bolt of anguish at seeing her mother covered in red again ripped through Dawn. Her stomach went sour. Still, it was time to start working. Time to solve what the hell was going on.

"Know something funny?" Dawn asked.

"I can always use some comedy."

Here it goes, she thought, primed to pay careful attention to every detail of Jac's reactions.

She let out a tiny, uncomfortable laugh, *Acting!* like her comment was about to embarrass her. "Last time I saw you in person, back at the hospital . . ."

Dawn trailed off purposely.

Jac merely tilted her head in a casual listening pose.

"I . . ." Dawn laughed again. "Well, seeing you all made over . . . For a weird second, I actually thought you were my mom, like you'd come back to life. Isn't that messed up?"

Dawn waited for the clues to surface: a gleam of understanding in Jac's gaze, a flinch, a tell.

But there was nothing. Just Jac reaching out to Dawn and patting her knee.

Dawn's instincts told her to push away, but it was a nice touch, lending her some ease. Inexplicably, she put her own hand over Jac's, but as soon as she realized it, she retreated.

Jac didn't seem to mind. "I know how that made you feel, and I understand why you needed to take some time before seeing me again. I'm still so sorry about the surprise."

"I'm over it."

Jac squeezed Dawn's knee. "Now that we've gotten the awkwardness out of the way, I'm actually flattered that you'd say I'm like her. Gosh, to even be in the same realm as Eva Claremont is just . . ."

It was like stars were shining in the girl's eyes. Stars with pointed edges that jabbed and tore.

If she *were* Eva, she was a hell of an actress. Or was Jac truly just another innocent bystander, one who was in direct firing range of Dawn's agenda?

You can't go around thinking everything is going to attack you, Kiko had said.

Once again, she thought of the throwing star speeding toward the homeless woman, the snick of it hitting her arm, the blood on the stuffed animal.

"Hey," Jac said, leaning closer. "Something's wrong, isn't it? Is it still me?"

The car ahead of them drove away, and the security officer waved Jac forward. Dawn was saved from answering as the starlet pulled up.

And when Jac rolled down her window, allowing the scent of jasmine to permeate the car, Dawn relaxed. She wasn't alone.

It didn't take long for them to clear the checkpoint. Paul Aspen's people had probably prepared an extensive list of who to let through easily. Yeah, Dawn got the evil eye, but the fact that the beefcakes let her through without more of a scene spoke a lot about Jac's status on the set.

And she went right on thinking that way, too, at least until after the valet parked their car. It was only when she and Jac got to the exquisite teak doors that she started to feel like an outcast among the beautiful people again.

Bodyguards took one look at Dawn and stopped her. Oh well, that's what she got for wearing the regular I-don't-give-a-shit gear. She was Jac's entourage, but she wasn't a star herself, so that meant she couldn't get away with the grunge.

As they patted her down, she casually checked out the exotic, chicly overgrown foliage, the torches burning fake fire from wall sconces. The house was a quasi-Mayan temple. How sacrificial nouveau.

When it was over, Jac seemed to think it was a good idea to make her friend forget all about the second-class treatment. Linking her arm through Dawn's, she guided them both into the house, clearly excited at her big movie-star party. Sad. Maybe this was the first time anyone in the cast had invited her.

"I wonder how many hearts you'll break tonight," Jac said as they walked through the foyer. The blaring recorded music—something so hip the band probably didn't even have a name—was making Jac talk loudly.

Dawn stiffened as they approached the main area. "I don't break hearts, I eat them." She was kidding. Pretty much.

Her rigidity had made Jac back off. But then, pulling an impressed face, the undaunted actress reached out and gave her friend's biceps a feel.

"Look at that. I wish I had these guns! You make everyone here look lazy!"

Even though she was oddly pleased by Jac's comment, Dawn pretended she wasn't. It appealed to the part of her that believed she *wasn't* inferior to these people, and Lord help her, she liked knowing that someone else thought the same way.

They drew nearer to the action, and Dawn tried to remain placid, keeping her rebellious facade intact, presenting the girl who'd spurned all the other Hollywood kids while growing up. It'd been one of many ways to distance herself from Eva, and it'd worked.

As the main room opened up in front of them, she saw that the mansion's interior was created to seem brittle and broken, the walls fashionably crumbling, the décor utilizing everything from long-stemmed candleholders shooting up from the floor to a polar bear rug in front of an empty grand fireplace.

But the partygoers provided a modern touch. Near a flat-screen TV, a crowd of young hipsters from *Aliantrance*, a fantasy that had scooped the number one spot at the box office for the past three weeks, yelled while maiming each other by proxy with their gory PlayStation street fighting. Scattered throughout the rest of the room, less enthusiastic men and women in silks and chunky jewelry swayed to the techno-flavored music, drinks in hand, cigarettes burning from extended fingers. They were standing against walls, draped over couches, mingling with each other and probably working deals with every breath.

Well behaved, Dawn thought. The party must've just started.

As a tabloid socialite strolled by, her boutique perfume made Dawn want to choke. And it made her realize something else: the jasmine had disappeared, replaced by acrid smoke, the expensively bad perfume, and emerging perspiration.

"I can't get used to this!" Jac said, sounding half-afraid and half-fascinated by her surroundings. "You'll protect me from trouble though, won't you, Dawn? My fencing buddy? My own personal bodyguard?"

"Why not." Dawn led Jac away from an oily guido approaching due right and headed for a private corner. Even though she didn't know what to think about her friend, she felt protective. Weird but true.

On their way, they were intercepted by the man himself, Paul Aspen. Reportedly in his late thirties, he was the type who wasn't actually a "man," but more of a "guy." A perpetual Hollywood Peter Pan, he'd shaved off his sandy hair for this buccaneer role, probably hoping to age himself, and had gotten his ears pierced, too. Tall and full of that star-making "X factor," he was a producer's wet dream.

His hazel eyes seemed friendly enough as he offered Dawn and Jac two drinks. "I heard on a security scanner that my favorite costar had arrived, and I'm not talking about Will."

Dawn belatedly recalled that Jac's other costar was Mr. *Independence Day* himself.

"Who's your friend, Jacqueline?" Paul added.

Dawn wanted to be ornery and tell Paul Aspen straight out that she was about ten years too old for his tastes, but she shut up for Jac's sake.

Just about bursting with smiles, Jac made short work of the introductions, telling Paul about Dawn's stunt work and how she wanted to get Dawn on staff.

Was Jac just starstruck or was there some crushing going on here?

Dawn shifted around, refusing Paul's cocktail offer. Jac took him up on it though, inspecting the red liquid in the martini glass before testing it.

"What is it?" she asked.

Paul sipped at the one Dawn had rejected. "Death by Sangria. Damned if I know what's in it, but it's supposed to be the same old classic with a twist."

"Mmm." Jac laughed and stopped drinking. "Good. Dawn, you sure you don't want one?"

"I don't drink, really." Frank had sworn her off booze.

"Well, I'll be . . ." Ever the social sentinel, Paul was watching the foyer and raising a welcoming hand to a well-known producer who'd just sauntered in. "There's Robert, so don't mind me while I pay homage. I'll see you girls later?"

"Definitely," Jac said.

Paul leaned in close to both of them. "Here's a tip. If anyone offers you a tour of the place, say no. We've already had one incident tonight with an anonymous supporting actress, a horny director who shall go unnamed, and a secret room behind the fireplace. Beware of these old houses, ladies."

He winked and rushed off, Jac's gaze trailing him.

Dawn got her attention. "Please don't tell me you're—"

"No. Oh, heck, no. It's just . . . I'm *working* with him, Dawn. I watched him on *Co-Ed Nights* when I was a teenager." She lifted her glass, but then lowered it when she caught something from across the room. "Oops—nine o'clock. Someone's checking you out."

Okay, it was beyond Dawn's power to resist, especially when she was surrounded by all these reminders of how she'd had to compete with Eva day in and day out. Yup, the old resentment was back and flourishing, so if a man was looking at Dawn and not Jac from across a room, that was a small victory. Disgusting, but pitifully true.

She glanced over and, what do you know. A typical pretty boy was indeed giving her the once over. But when he realized he had her attention, his gaze predictably shifted to the girl next to her.

Eva was winning again, even if she wasn't actually here. . . .

"Go get him," Dawn said to Jac, fixing her attention elsewhere.

"No, that boy likes you. I can tell."

"Forget it."

Dawn saw a chest full of iced bottled water near a couch, so she went over to it. As she grabbed one, she tuned in to a conversation between two industry types sitting nearby.

The woman had a streak of white dust under her nose and was waxing on about how Hollywood would always be "in the know." They weren't irrelevant at all, she kept saying, gesturing madly. Fuck the red states. Fuck the conservative press.

Dawn unscrewed her water and took a sip, hiding a laugh.

Jac was laughing, too, casting Dawn a knowing glance as she guided her outside, where it was much quieter. Jungle plants hovered over a glowing blue pool. Two women were skinny-dipping, watched over by a group of appreciative men discretely smoking weed.

"So how's work going?" Jac said, turning her back on the scene and taking the opportunity to make a can-you-believe-these-people face.

"Work is work. PI stuff. Top secret. All that."

"It sounds exciting."

"Not so much." Dawn took another drink. "Detecting involves lots of waiting around and running into barriers. And my boss . . ." She shook her head. "He's . . ."

Whoa. Time to shut up.

"He's what?" Jac seemed ecstatic that Dawn was actually communicating.

Suddenly, Dawn wondered if she was actually a project for this girl. Some people were like that—they gravitated toward fixer-uppers. It drove them, just like fearful bitterness seemed to drive Dawn most of the time.

"My boss is uncommunicative," she settled on saying. It didn't give anything up. "He kills me."

"Aw, just let go of it. Negative feelings suck. Life is so much easier without them."

"Is it?"

"Yeah, all the bad medicine you take in?" Jac made a dismissive motion, graceful, balletic even. "Who needs it?"

I do, thought Dawn.

Jac touched her arm, spreading a ray of comfort through Dawn's skin. Still, she couldn't help shirking away.

"Sorry," Jac said.

Dawn tried to make like she didn't know what the other girl meant.

"No, I am." The starlet tucked a strand of blond hair behind her ear. "I'm sorry I look like her. I'm sorry I make you squirm."

What was there to say? Dawn took another quaff just to have something to do.

"Can I ask?" Jac said. "What was she like, your mom?"

Shit. "I don't know. She died when I was about a month old. I was raised by my dad because she wasn't around."

"You say that like she meant to abandon you."

Dawn gripped her bottle. "She didn't. Abandon me, that is. She's always managed to be with me."

Knowing she should be marking the other girl's reactions, Dawn locked eyes with her, but Jac only seemed confused.

"What do you mean?"

Dawn drank again, waiting. Baiting.

Finally, the actress's gaze broke away. "It seems like you don't like her much."

"Why's that?"

"Look at you." Jac held her hand out, chock-full of empathy. "You scream hatred, Dawn."

That was it—an invitation to say everything she'd always wanted to, whether or not Jac deserved it.

"She's dogged me my whole life, and not in the way a mom should. It was always, 'Why aren't you as pretty?' 'Why aren't you as talented?' 'Why aren't you as sweet?' And you know what? I went the other way in every category. I got tired of competing with her as soon as I was old enough to feel inferior, and that was real early, believe me."

She felt so much better now that she was directing her wrath at the proper place, not inwardly, not at every other person who happened to cross her path.

Jac's voice quavered. "She wouldn't . . . I mean, don't you think she would just want you to be happy if she were alive? Don't you think she'd do anything to make that happen? Just . . . you've got to *stop* competing with her, Dawn. I'm sure that would've made her so sad."

Throat closing with heat, Dawn held up a finger. "There's no way I can compete—do you know why?"

"Why?" Jac said, eyes getting watery.

"Because Eva Claremont is the big winner." Dawn was shaking now. "She took the top prize in the Desert Your Family Sweepstakes, and I'll be damned if I ever compete for *that* title again."

If Jac *were* the real Eva, she'd understand that. Eva hadn't ever died. She'd literally left her family to go Underground.

Jac's empty hand covered her heart for a second, her gaze exploding with such emotion that Dawn nearly went into defensive mode, ready to fight and bring it all down.

But then, just as if the girl's response had only been subliminal—a vision spliced between the frames of a filmstrip—it was gone.

Instead, she was shaking her head, holding her drink to her chest like it was a comfort object. "Dawn, poor Dawn."

Squeezing shut her eyes, Dawn fought—what? Was it disappointment that she hadn't flushed out Eva? Or was it bottom-sucking disgust at not wanting to admit that her mom really was dead?

God, dead . . .

"Why don't you sit down, Dawn."

She felt Jac guiding her to a chair, felt the give of wicker at her back and the softness of a cushion at her bottom. She buried her face in a hand. Above her, Jac hesitated, probably knowing Dawn wasn't going to talk anymore right now.

"I'll get us something else to drink, okay?" Jac said, stroking Dawn's hair from her forehead. "I'll be right back, and we can settle in for a long chat."

As she left, Dawn intuitively knew that Jac was letting her regain composure. Wasn't that the sign of a friend? And didn't that friend deserve to be treated better?

She opened her eyes, leaning her head back, taking in the stars that blurred in the sky with the heat of oncoming tears.

I don't want to be this way anymore, she thought. *I can't keep being this way.*

She evened out her breathing, focusing on the sky until it cleared.

You've got to make things right when she comes back. Apologize and move on—

A dark, blurred figure suddenly filled Dawn's sight. Before she could react, a glowing gaze locked her in place, eyes blazing and swirling into a whoosh of indescribable colors. It felt like a burning fist was breaking into her, slicing through her pliant body, drawing her up to the edge of her chair.

Mind screw? . . . just like Robby when he attacked? . . . block it, stop it. . . .

Dawn pushed out with all the inner energy she could muster. It wasn't fast enough—

But it was good enough to smack the attacking mind halfway

out of hers, good enough to keep the other out of her deepest memories and thoughts.

Still, her limbs were pinned to her sides, not because her strength was gone, but because she couldn't think of how to move.

Where was her Friend protection? Dawn realized she hadn't smelled jasmine for a while. Had her defense somehow been driven away?

"Just relax," said the unknown assailant, the hypnotic voice becoming Dawn's everything. "Allow me to come in."

No, she thought. *Never.*

The other's power seeped into her, *turning muscle and bone to stilled liquid.*

"There . . ."

The tone, so gentle and warped, dragged her down into a watery limbo where sounds became muffled and slow, where heaviness pushed at her from every side.

Falling, floating down until she didn't have the strength to even think of driving him out anymore.

Too lazy, too surreal . . .

Triumphantly, the creature stepped forward, light from the reflecting pool below casting blue wavers over his stunning face.

"*I'd like you to accept my drink invitation this time,*" Paul Aspen said, "*but now, I'll be the one who's imbibing.*"

FIFTEEN
THE BIG DRINK

I guarantee," the actor added, "that a drink will make you feel better."

Weightless, stretched from all sides, Dawn didn't answer. She only had enough energy to push away—

Stay out. Don't come in. . . .

Her strength ebbed, and she plunged back into his sway.

"I won't do anything you don't want me to." As his eyes glimmered like a hypnotic object waving back and forth, Paul Aspen flashed that eternally boyish smile. Persuasive, trustworthy. "I only want to taste you. You're notorious in the Underground and, as you might know, I've got a yen for breaking in new girls. You'll never remember a thing afterward. No pain, just peace."

Somewhere, the phrase "mind wipe" bobbed by like an irrelevant cartoon object in a fragmented river. But she was too enthralled by what he had said to pay attention.

No pain, just peace. What she would give for some of that. . . .

Right now, as he stared into her, warming her like a fire in the cold, she believed he could give it.

But . . . Old habits . . .

She tightened her mind block, straining at him. . . .

Then lost it again.

Paul Aspen, waving up and down in his own dreamboat, sighed, slid his arms under Dawn, and lifted her. The world slanted while he carried her off, through the swollen foliage to a clearing under the same stars that had been keeping her company only minutes ago.

But, this time, those stars bent and twisted, then released, softening into reflections of Paul's swirled eyes.

"When you walked into my place tonight," he said, "it was the first time I'd seen you face-to-face. The human who brought down Robby Pennybaker, who was not only the subject of your missing persons case, but my blood brother. Your power turns me on. You're a walking goddess, Dawn, and by becoming a part of me, you can be a part of everything beautiful."

She had heard men whisper seduction to her before, then take it back as quickly as a mind wipe when they were done. Back in that other world, pretty words inevitably included Dawn's relation to Eva, the sex idol.

Yet, in this pool of emptiness, Paul Aspen had not mentioned anything about her mother.

He stroked her cheek, smiling down at her like a rogue angel, and by just looking into his eyes, Dawn somehow knew he wasn't thinking about Eva at all.

The realization made her blood float with ecstasy. No pain, just peace . . . and beauty. She was his universe, the most gorgeous woman he had ever seen, just like with . . . Jonah. Yeah, with Jonah . . .

"Good." His fingers traveled from her face to her neck, where he paused at the crucifix, then laughed, using a nearby stick to flick

that and Breisi's sharp silver pendant aside. Languidly, he contin-
ued stroking. "Beautiful, so beautiful. May I . . . ?"

Her mind block slipped, but her deepest layer, her fear—
Fought
Against
It—
But at his words, she slipped again.

"I knew you wouldn't be easy," he said, smiling. "Nothing
worthwhile ever is. You need to be eased into peace, I suppose, and
that's okay, because I want a little of you so badly I'll wait. You
won't use any of this against me anyway. You won't be able to."

Mind wipe . . .

She groaned, still fighting somewhere in the far reaches of san-
ity, but his gaze was too much, too compelling.

Paul ran his fingertips over the center of her throat and, with
only a look, she knew everything about him: how he'd been an er-
rand boy on a studio lot, fetching water for the likes of Mickey
Rooney and Judy Garland. But then a producer's wife had discov-
ered him, at first making him an extra in her husband's movies,
then giving him a supporting role that turned into so much more.

He'd been a star, seeking a place in the stratosphere with names
like Rock Hudson and Frank Sinatra.

But one day the offers stopped coming, even though he still had
his looks. He was too much trouble, they said. And that was when
Paul met him, *at the beginning of his freefall. The Doctor. He had*
saved this star, resurrected him, given him new life that he would
be able to reinvent for generations to come.

He'd stayed Underground longer than most as the Doctor had
perfected his technique in creating his first vampires. And he had
been able to stay Above as "Paul Aspen" longer than any of the oth-
ers, thanks to the use of makeup that allowed him to "grow older"
bit by bit. Now, on his last legs in this incarnation, he was antici-
pating the need to go Underground again soon . . . very soon. . . .

In this silent sharing, the vampire leaned closer, smelling of something Dawn could not name, like an exotic scent that led her into a sublime sleep.

"I'm the closest you'll get to immortal. To come into me with your blood should be an honor, Dawn. I want to be the first to have you, because even though you won't remember this moment, you're going to eventually know the Underground. You'll find paradise there, too, and beauty. Always beauty. You'll never have to worry about any of your earthbound problems again."

His smiled shimmered. "You're going to fit in with us."

He trailed his fingers to her collarbone, and Dawn shifted, body so needy, so attuned to the only anesthetic she knew.

Then, like clouds in her dream/nightmare, two thoughts wisped by:

Matt.

Jonah.

She tried to bar those out, too. But it was not as easy as a regular mind block, the one that was even now dissipating again while Paul smoothed his palm up, down, up her neck. Heavy motion, sexual, faster, harder, an innuendo making her pulse sweet and thick.

"Don't look so sad," he said. "I heard your father is missing. And I know your mom has caused you so much pain. You've fought long and hard during such a short life, so why not allow me to lift your burden for a night?"

Looking into the promising dreamscape of his gaze, moving with his rough/tender caresses, she sincerely believed he could make things better, erase all her problems and shine light all over the earth. He promised, and it had to be true.

In the liquid haze of her consciousness, he stopped stroking, his eyes boring into her with genuine care, drawing her to him. Slowly, she offered her neck, her veins pounding against skin, begging to be punctured.

He could take it all away. If he did, maybe everything would be fine.

"Yes?" *he asked, eyes brightening, heating.*

Her mind block quivered with the struggle of holding. It left the rest of her unguarded, open to what he wanted.

"Yes," *she whispered.*

Without pause, his form expanded, beginning the change.

Too late, Dawn opened her mouth to yell, but couldn't.

With a shuddering rumble, the vampire whipped into himself, just as Robby had, snapping into Danger Form with the violent speed of a storm. Milliseconds later, he was hovering, luminous and piercing to the eye, a breathtaking monster that froze Dawn to the ground even as it lured her to open herself to its bite.

He reached out, the angelic, formless fog that had once been his body revealing all her fantasies. You are loved, *the creature's mist whispered,* you are free from sadness.

Yet Paul Aspen, vampire, was not tempting her with solid images as Robby Pennybaker had done: he was luring her with whispers in the dark of light.

On the edge of screaming—at her weakness and her victory— Dawn stiffened just before he laid fang to her throat. He broke her skin with a sinuous pop, sliding into her jugular vein and making her arch and grasp at the dirt.

"Oh, G—" *She grabbed at air—freezing, hot, thick, horrifying air.*

Her head was pummeled by a million fists punching to get into her brain, hands that cried to sift through every piece of information. And, as the vampire sucked the blood from her, she went dizzy, feeling a part of herself escaping.

Reaching out to grasp anything, everything, she urged her mind block to defend her.

But . . . it didn't. Mistake, she'd made the biggest mistake of . . . Oh . . .

*He was pulling at her with erotic greed. Instinctively, she
pushed at him, but connected with nothing. Her hearing filled with
the sounds of his animal frenzy while images of his seduction kept
blipping into her:*

Beautiful. Goddess. Safe. Loved.

*The sky started going black, dimming into midnight and gutter-
ing the stars. Energy, life itself, ebbed out of her, bit by bit. . . .*

Peace . . . No . . . pain . . .

The breath left her as her eyelids closed.

*She didn't know when the vampire stopped because time didn't
exist anymore. There was quiet in this hovering world, he had been
right about that. Blessed blankness.*

*She felt a touch on her neck. Fingertips, solid, warm with the
tapping pulse of her blood in his creature's body. She felt her
wound knit together, still wet and sore.*

*"Before I say good-bye, sweet Dawn," he said, voice back to
normal, "I want to thank you, even though I didn't drink enough
to leave you terribly affected. I would've liked more, but at least I
can say I was the first. Always the first." He laughed a little. "It
was worth any hell I'll catch. But you won't be turned, you won't
even remember anything about this. . . ."*

She summoned a mind block again, but it rolled into nothing.

The Voice . . . she thought over and over.

She hadn't been careful enough.

*Then the vampire laid a palm on her forehead, and the last thing
she remembered was the stars blinking into oblivion.*

In her sleep, she heard something thudding against her brain,
pounding, pounding, pounding.

Jerking awake, Dawn found herself coated with sweat, which
stuck to her with a clammy chill.

"Vamps," she said, still hearing the pounding in her mind.

But then she blinked and looked around, and the chaos slunk back into her nightmares.

She was lying on a carpet that covered the wooden floor of a strange house. Fully clothed except for her jacket, she found an Indian blanket wrapped around her legs, telling her how restlessly she'd slept.

When she spied a fireplace, she realized she was in a living room. A further glance at the furnishings—antique paintings and mini wire reconstructions of things like the Eiffel Tower—brought it all back.

Dawn was sitting smack-dab in the middle of Jacqueline Ashley's living room.

Her head started booming out information: Jac's gingerbread house on Bedford Drive. A place that'd been built for a director from the '30s. The producer from Jac's new movie, renting it out for her during the shoot. He wanted a lovely old-time starlet PR image for Jac. He was interested in her long-term career.

Dawn tried to stand, but—damn. She felt . . . weird. Weak limbed.

After a second try, she wobbled to her feet, wondering why she felt so awful. It seemed like she should be remembering something. . . . But instead, there was only a void right in the middle of her.

She hadn't sucked down any alcohol, right? Had someone slipped something into her water then? And why couldn't she remember anything past her blowup with Jac about Eva?

Looking at the mantel clock, which read 3:22, Dawn tried to piece everything together. How had she gotten back here?

She headed toward the steps leading to a second story, her body also feeling the slightly bruised ache of a morning after. But she hadn't had sex, right? Oh, shit. What'd happened?

With a perfunctory knock at every door, she checked inside, hoping to find Jac's room. On the third try she succeeded, the faint hall light spotlighting her party buddy dressed in a lace nightie and covered by the sheet on her four-poster bed. The room smelled of historically rendered must, just like Limpet's place: memories pressed into paint and rose-patterned carpet.

"Jac?" Still noodle-bodied, Dawn crept closer.

"Mmmm." Jac smiled in her sleep.

"Hey."

Dawn gingerly touched a bare shoulder. Nothing. She tried again, but harder this time.

The blonde flinched, squinted at Dawn, then glanced around. "What time is it?"

"After three. Jac, what happened at that party?"

The starlet took a moment. Then, "You drove your car and met me here, then we went to Paul's together. We got into an . . . interesting conversation and when I left for a few minutes . . . I came back to find you passed out in that chair." Jac settled an arm underneath her head, staring up at Dawn and looking innocent enough to chase away any thoughts of wrongdoing. "You've been working hard, so I let you snooze away. It was okay though. People were coming up to me and chatting, so babysitting you actually kept me out of trouble. Paul helped me drag you back to the car and you didn't even wake up." She yawned. "Couldn't carry you by myself up the stairs to a guest room here though."

Absently, Dawn touched her neck, where the skin was tender, but not broken.

"So did you at least have a little fun?" Jac mumbled hopefully.

"I'm not sure. Did you see anyone put anything into my water?"

Jac sat up, hair ruffled. "What're you talking about?"

"Party tricks." Dawn paused. "Listen, thanks for watching over me, because if some chucklehead did roofie me up, you probably kept them away."

"Roofie?"

"Rohypnol, the Forget-Me Pill, R2-Do-U. It's like a sedative with no smell, color, or taste, and dickheads crush it up and put it into their victim's drinks."

"Are you serious?"

"Wish I weren't." But a couple things didn't make sense. First, when would someone have slipped her the drug? Second, she'd probably still be under the influence and experiencing more than just a hangover. Probably.

"I'm so sorry," Jac said. "It's all my fault."

"Why? Did you drug me?"

At Jac's awful expression, Dawn waved it away, hoping not to travel the rough roads of another "discussion" right now.

"Listen . . ." She started toward the door. "I need to get back."

Really, because, passed out, God knows what could've happened. Jesus.

"Call you later?" Jac was sitting on the edge of the bed by now, long legs dangling. "Maybe on a better night, after you've gotten some sleep. Or at a place where people aren't such . . . dickheads." She cleared her throat at the uncharacteristic word, but still looked kind of proud for saying it.

"Jac, you and the word 'dickhead' don't jive. Stick to 'weenie' or 'dumb dumb' in the future, 'kay?"

She laughed. " 'Kay."

In spite of the heaviness, they both managed their own uneasy grins. Damn, life was strange. Two months ago, Dawn couldn't stand to hang with other women. Now she was grinning and fist-bumping with two of them.

Tentatively, she lifted a hand in good-bye, then left, thanking Jac for watching over her again.

As shaky as she was, Dawn wanted to run. In fact, she was in such a hurry to get out of the Bedford house that she fumbled with her jacket, which was hanging on a coat tree at the entrance. Then she tripped on the steps outside when she put her jacket on, and everything spilled out of the pockets, splaying over the rock driveway. Graceful for a freakin' stuntwoman.

Dawn mindlessly grasped at what she could and then ran-wobbled the rest of the way to her car.

Plopping into the front seat, she winced. Had she just slept wrong?

Her mind went into overdrive doubting it.

She took out her cell from a jacket pocket, knowing she had to check in with the team first thing. Theoretically she'd be safe in her hunk of precious junk; it'd been outfitted for protection by Breisi. It was even equipped with the same type of concentrated UV lights that blazed outside the Limpet house and Kiko's place, just in case.

When The Voice picked up, Dawn raised her brows; she'd expected Breisi instead. Obviously, the brain had set her phone on forward to the boss, probably because she was sleeping.

"You sound . . . Are you all right?" were the first words out of his mouth.

Buzz, hum—her body went through the regular routine at the sound of him. And the fact that he seemed so damned concerned touched her in a different place, somewhere not so easy to get to.

"I'm fine," she said, not knowing how to deal with all this tenderness he'd shown lately. "At least, I think so."

She told him all about the party, the stars, the blank spots, the carpet that she'd woken up on in Jac's living room.

"Jac thought I'd just passed out from exhaustion," Dawn added. "She acted like she didn't know if there was anything else going on."

"And you don't believe her?"

He said it with stony reserve, giving her yet another reason not to fully trust him. After all, he was the one who'd betrayed her, luring her to L.A. with Frank's disappearance because he needed her to fulfill that asinine prophecy about triumphing over vampires.

"I don't know if I believe Jac about anything," she said, rubbing the aching spot on the side of her neck, once again feeling like a chunk of her was missing.

The Voice sucked in a breath.

"What?" Dawn asked.

Pause. Long, long, long pause.

"Dawn," he said with his usual calm, although it was sharpened by something more. "I'd like you to come back to the office now."

"I really am tired. Can't I get some shut-eye and then—"

"Please."

He'd said it with such emotion that she just sat there, hand to her neck, the same desire—yet different, too—flooding her.

"Promise me," he said.

"Okay."

"I suppose an 'okay' will have to do." She could sense him getting back to business, even over the phone. "Tell me, did you note any differences in Jac tonight?"

"Same cheery girl next door. She did look a little on the pale side, but she said it was because of her *eating habits*."

"It's well-known that starlets struggle with weight and image issues."

Before he could get too rational and talk Dawn out of her healthy suspicion, she went for it. "Is she my mom?"

Silence.

"Because I can't help wondering why the hell you would allow me to see her if all the puzzle pieces are fitting together into a picture I don't like, Jonah."

More silence. When he came back on, his tone was eerily controlled. "You just answered your own question. Why would I put you in danger?"

"Let me see . . . Maybe because you did it when you brought me out here in the first place? My first night, as you recall, I found my lucky old self dodging burning vamp spit."

"As *you'll* recall, I wasn't enthused about the prospect."

"But you let me go anyway after Kiko talked you into it. It makes me wonder if you'd put me in a bad spot again, is all. Would you?"

He paused, and she knew exactly what he was going to say.

"How far are you willing to go to get him back?"

Frank. At the beginning of all this shit, she'd naïvely told The Voice she would do anything to find Frank. But back then, she hadn't known what was involved, hadn't known she'd be putting every part of herself at risk.

When she didn't answer, he pulled out the big guns.

"Dawn."

A change, a stirring of the seduction she was so used to. Dark, low, almost irresistible. Her mind misted with the desire for him that she couldn't contain.

"Don't," she said. "Just answer my question. Is she Eva?"

"Dawn . . ."

Her mind clouded with caresses, thumb tips trailing up her inner thighs, parting her legs, exposing her.

Unable to fight anymore, she weakened, slipping down in the seat at the flash of sexual heat, the bite of agony.

At her limit, she threw a mind block to stop him, to make him answer, goddamnit, to—

Rrrrrrrooooooaaaarrrr.

The air seemed to explode, shattering with the punch of glass. She looked to the right, where a side-view mirror had webbed into a thousand pieces. She knew she'd done it, just as spontaneously as she'd done with Robby when she'd hurled him across a room.

"No more!" Her words stuck in her throat.

No more filling her spiritual vacuum with sex. No more chasing away rejection and loneliness with self-destruction. She was sick of everything, sick of herself.

Trembling, she sat up, faced the phone like it was him. And it was close enough, wasn't it?

"I'm not letting you in again. *Never* again."

It seemed like years passed in the aftermath of her eruption. Then, finally, he spoke, his voice naked of hypnotic power and steeped in something that sounded like actual sorrow.

"I'm doing what I have to, Dawn."

Unwilling to subject herself to more, she hung up and shut off her phone, tossing it away. The air died in silence, as if buried by her anger.

But then something he'd said earlier spiraled across her conscience: *I need you more than anything.*

Without checking herself, she reached for the phone, sorry for what'd happened. But then she yanked her hand back.

Screwed up, she thought. She wasn't going to keep being so screwed up.

She started the car, but didn't even think of going to the office. What she needed to do was regroup and think, goddamnit. The Voice wasn't enough to stop her from searching for her dad, even if she'd end up having to do it on her own. Which looked very likely right about now.

Damn him. Damn him to hell.

When she got to Kiko's, the lights were on. She got even more pissed because he should've been resting. Couldn't he get anything through his thick head, either?

His back brace lounged topsy-turvy on the floor as the TV muttered lines from an old noir movie. In the meantime, he was pacing while dialing his phone over and over. He didn't even seem to know she was in the room.

"What's this?" She shrugged off her jacket, then went to the back brace, picking it up. "What the hell is this, Kiko?"

He shoved the phone in the air in frustration, his voice slurred. "Can' get through to *Dancin' with the Stars* . . . gotta vote for Stacy an' Tony."

"You asshole, that season ended a long time ago."

She wanted to kick him for being so obviously stoned out of his mind. It was another betrayal because he knew what he was doing to himself. He knew it was wrong and he knew it hurt Breisi and Dawn and, yes, probably even Jonah.

She slumped, tired. Too tired. "Why do you keep taking that crap when they mess you up so bad?"

Kiko lowered the phone. "I hurt tonight, Dawn. Don't yell at me for hurting."

Damn him, damn him for being so weak. She hated weakness.

She sank to the floor, unable to conjure anything, not even her own tears. She'd been crying more lately from exhaustion, stress, and emotion than at any other time in her life. Tears were beating her up because she'd come to care too much, so she wasn't going to allow them anymore.

But . . . she'd betrayed Kiko, too, hadn't she? He'd been so proud of her for supposedly containing herself with the men, and she'd failed him just as much as he'd failed her, so she had no right to be angry or sad.

"Dawn? Dawn?" Kiko scooted over to her, patting her back. "Hey. Hey, guess what?"

Jesus, he was trying to cheer her up with that idiotic game they'd fallen into way back when they'd first started out.

She stared straight ahead, wanting to look at him, but not doing it because that's when she'd start to cry.

"Guess *what*?" he repeated.

She gave in. "The apartment upstairs has been flooded by black goo and . . ."

He kept patting her back, and her throat just got more raw, overwhelming her chest with sharp, quickened pain.

"Cool," he said. "*Dark Water.*"

At his correct answer, she sobbed once, but bit back another one. Rage and sadness surged, taking her over.

And that's when Kiko gasped and drew back his hand.

For a second, Dawn didn't think anything of it. Not until she realized she was wearing Frank's T-shirt.

Sucking in a breath, she turned to her psychic friend.

His eyes were foggy and she didn't know if that was because of the drugs or a vision.

"In one of the two red fingers pointing up to the sky," he mumbled.

Dawn got to her knees, taking him by the shoulders. "What're you talking about?" High, he was just high. "Damn it, Kiko, you make me . . ."

She pushed back from him, balling into herself, chasing away the ache in her stomach, in her chest. No crying. If it was the last thing she'd do, she wouldn't cry anymore.

And, ten minutes later, when Breisi called to let them know that there'd been another murder, it was easier than ever to ice herself over.

Because that's what she needed to do. Ice every tear.

Cope until she didn't have to anymore.

SIXTEEN

BELOW, ACT THREE

Sorin was near an entrance, the night-tinged mouth of an abandoned quarry where shadows swallowed all vision. A place so harmless to the eye that no one Above ever bothered to wander near.

"You made a valiant attempt," he said into one of the encrypted cell phones all the Underground used. As a breeze carried the scent of a human summer, he took in the aroma. It was almost a gorgeous night.

On the other end of the line, Paul Aspen's voice came through as clear as curved glass. "You don't have to say the rest: you wish I'd been successful in finding out what Dawn knows. But I couldn't get deep enough. Not with her resisting like that."

"When I discovered she would be attending your party and I asked you for this favor, I knew she would be a hard mind to read. I do wonder, however, how your encore—your need to bite her—will be received by the populace." Sorin paused, emphasizing his disdain for the Elite. "Some more than others."

"You think the bite will be the big issue? Mind wiping bugged me the most, but you asked me to do it." The actor gave a dramatic pause. "Still, it's not like I erased all Dawn's vampire experiences—that would've made her pals suspicious if she'd come home wondering about things she'd already shared with them. It was just a superficial wipe to take out what *I* did, nothing else. I took the precaution with her because you thought it was best. 'She is not a normal meal,' you said, 'and the stakes are too high to depend on just her permission.'"

What he said was true. Usually, the released Elites fed for amusement upon their Servant entourages in between monthly maintenance infusions from the Master, so the concept of mind wiping for them was considered déclassé. Similarly, to every other vampire, it was a method used only in case of emergency, a tool for serious intervention only. All the same, the bite was what bothered Sorin because it was an act of greater intimacy.

Was it not just like an Elite to take what he wanted and damn the bigger picture?

Sorin shook his head. Perhaps recruiting one of their first Hollywood Underground creations for spy work had not been wise. However, Sorin had never been content with the speed of their current spy work, so he had circumvented the Master's approval this one time and seized the opportunity to improve their information. After all, spies had indicated that Dawn was away from her team and heading for the property of an Elite who had no attachments to her, and the actor had been willing enough to perform quick spy work for the sake of the Underground. Certainly, they had experienced some initial trouble when an unknown spirit had been detected but, over the phone, Sorin had instructed the Elites at the party on how to use their given talents to charm the interloper into a holding vessel.

Sorin would soon be interrogating that captured spirit himself.

He laid his head back against the rock wall. The information culled from raiding Dawn's mind would have been their greatest asset. If only they had been successful in this reconnaissance.

On the phone, Paul Aspen sighed negligently, and Sorin could imagine the superstar leaning back in a lounging chair by his pool, sipping from a blood cocktail.

"No one down there is going to know about what I did or didn't do with Dawn Madison anyway, right?" the actor said. "You told me I was doing this for you on the hush. Say, did the real Master even know? That'd be a hoot—the second in command messing around underneath the chief's nose."

Sorin bristled. Elites were the only ones who knew of the real Master's existence. They loved to remind Sorin that he was no more than a glorified bodyguard and merely their sibling.

"I made my vow to you, Edward." It was Paul's old name, the fifties matinee-idol moniker that remained in Sorin's memory. "This must remain a secret."

"Because you *didn't* tell the Master." The star laughed. "Oh, this is entertaining."

Only now did Sorin realize how rash this decision had been. "I planned to tell him, Edward, but he is involved with important matters that I dare not interrupt needlessly."

Yet why should Sorin have to explain to an Elite? Though he was appreciative of the movie star's aid tonight, the Elite's act of biting Dawn Madison would cause trouble. In fact, there were two who would be most affected by Sorin's aggressive decision to sic Paul Aspen on the human.

"I love it," the actor was saying. "Sorin the minion. You and your superiority. Hah."

Sorin held his composure, knowing this vampire was younger and, thus, less intelligent in so many ways. An Elite did not contain half as much magic as he—not of the real sort anyway.

Just as he was about to thank the actor once again for his contribution and end their tedious conversation, a bolt of Awareness crashed through his consciousness.

Success! the real Master's voice thundered.

Standing, his loose robes fluttering around him in the night wind, Sorin closed the phone without another thought.

He melded Awareness with the Master. *Success?*

Lately, they had been exercising a higher level of Awareness, a deeper connection that had grown lax during more peaceful times. Thus, Sorin could almost feel the cold of a bare room, one of the Underground holding areas where the Master was presently standing.

Jessica Reese's killer, the Master said. *Even after my most recent miscalculations, we've found our troublemaker!*

Jarred to action, Sorin headed out of the entrance tunnel, accessing a secret door, one of many leading farther underground.

Who . . . what . . . how . . . ? There were a legion of questions streaming through him at once.

One of our Servants assigned to tail the Limpet suspects hit paydirt. They caught our murderer coming out of a second victim's apartment tonight, fresh from a new kill.

Master, this is good, very good. . . .

Hold on—the new body was found by human witnesses before our Servants could get to it and destroy any evidence that might lead to more publicity.

No.

Yes, but that's beyond our control now. But we can *control what happens from here on out.*

Questions continued to baffle Sorin. Who, why, when—?

Specifics are not my concern, Sorin, not right now. Spies have our killer in custody. And I have something in mind. . . .

What?

A plan that's going to strike a blow to Limpet, and he's never going to know where it came from. It's going to keep us safely on the sidelines, but it's also going to flush our enemy out. We can disable and expose them, and the best part is—we don't have to do any of the dirty work. I've thought of every angle.

At the very idea, Sorin halted in his tracks in front of the last rock door that led to the Underground itself. Vision breaking, he was unable to take another step.

What do you have planned, Master?

He felt his father smile. *I'm going to make an offer that any true vampire would never turn down.*

Membership in the Underground.

Yes, but that membership wouldn't last for long. I won't keep a common street murderer around.

Sorin agreed with that much, yet what of the rest?

As far as I know from initial spy contact, the Master thought, *our killer has a Lee Tomlinson fetish. Our spies were able to finesse that our buddy wants to be like Lee, and Lee, of course, wanted to be one of us. With what I have in mind, we'll make sure these murders won't shed any more light on vampire activity, and we'll indirectly disable Limpet. Two birds with one stone. We'll level a preemptive strike that won't be traced back to us once the deed is done. Afterward, if Limpet really is our enemy, I guarantee he'll expose himself—*

And we'll be waiting.

With merely a touch, Sorin coolly unlocked the door in the granite wall and entered the emporium. Instead of the usual lazy activity, the place was exploding with aggression. Near the waterfall lagoon, Groupies were practicing the change, going in and out of their vampiric forms, challenging each other in hand-to-hand combat with blades. Their speed would blur the eye of a human, but to Sorin, the battles unwrapped with clarified grace. Under a screen, a close-knit band of Elites was studying a movie, *Crouching Tiger, Hidden Dragon*, imitating high-flying aerial fight moves and taking them one step further by attaching themselves to the walls, using the planes as platforms to fight. None had altered into their most dangerous forms yet, though Sorin knew that would be in the coming.

Master, Sorin asked, seeing only the gray walls where his father waited, *where are you? I can come to represent you—*

I'm going to take care of this one.

His protective instincts stirred. The Master had been shapeshifting into solid mass more and more lately, ever since the threat to the Underground had reawakened him.

Suddenly, via the Awareness, Sorin heard a door open. The Master did not look to see who had entered the room. Instead he kept staring at the gray wall. His fury had been stoked by the presence of this killer—Sorin could feel this keenly.

Shortcuts, the Master thought. *This idiot thought it'd be possible to take a shortcut to stardom, just like Lee Tomlinson ended up doing.*

Sorin said what he knew his father wanted to hear. *Stardom is earned.*

Stars are born, the Master corrected, paying homage to his darling Elites.

In the background, a Servant private investigator greeted the Master in a deep, affable tone. "Look who we have for interrogation."

The head vampire smiled again, and Sorin knew the wheels of their fate were about to be set into motion. The day help them, this was it, the beginning of the end for either Limpet or the Underground.

Nobody is going to take it away from us again, the Master assured Sorin just before turning around to greet the murderer.

The Awareness scrambled, slicing colors and angles together until Sorin could not see.

"Who are you—?" began the garbled voice of the murderer.

Then the connection exploded into nothing, leaving Sorin staring at the Elite's movie screen, two warriors rising, then flying at each other over the rooftops.

The Master's reawakening was complete.

Yet, that is what Sorin had also believed over fifty years ago, back when a second Underground had seemed to be just the thing to resurrect Benedikte from his sorrows.

SEVENTEEN

LOS ANGELES,
CALIFORNIA, 1954

Now, there is a specimen," Sorin said as he and Benedikte exited the Chadwick Arms Hotel on Wilshire Boulevard. "Who would protest *his* absence?"

Benedikte glanced at the man Sorin indicated. The tattered threads of his clothing clashed with the white tuxedo jackets and black bowties he and his son wore.

A bum, they called this type. A man whose outer dishevelment mirrored the inner Benedikte: ravaged and lifeless.

At Sorin's comment, the man lifted a dull gaze and an empty fedora hat to the vampires as they passed.

"Spare any change?"

A hotel doorman rushed over. "You leave these gentlemen alone! Out. . . ." He shooed the bum away. "Go on now."

Sorin lifted a grateful hand to the employee and turned back to Benedikte, matching his pace as they headed for the sidewalk this summer's evening. "Are you certain you would not rather hail a cab?"

Benedikte carelessly switched into Awareness mode, knowing he was taking a chance on being discovered by another blood brother, but not caring. Normally, simple shielding was all they dared do Above since it wasn't easy to detect. Yet, what did he have to lose now?

I prefer to stalk at the moment, thank you. It's the only way to play tourist.

As day bowed under the coming weight of night, he noted that so much about this walk should've been a miracle: the Technicolor glamour of a city that housed all the silver-screen stars he adored, the sight of the sun, the wonder of being a preternatural creature among men.

But even as Benedikte's blood simmered at the scent of human life, he couldn't enjoy it. Not since London, when he'd discovered that everything was meaningless. It had broken his will to realize that even brothers didn't have enough honor to stand by a code.

So why have one of his own? Why not kill and pillage at random? Why protect a brotherhood that would end up destroying itself before the true maker could awaken from his deep sleep?

Not that Sorin agreed with this. No, the younger vampire still had dreams of "making a family," fantasies of another place he could call home.

Even now his son was going on about his latest idea: Guards for a second Underground.

". . . The perfect build, Master. I could take such a man, even a transient in a fedora, and mold him into a soldier who would protect our territory. A first line of defense. Imagine if we had possessed a small army of Guards when Andre attacked."

Home.

The concept floated through Benedikte briefly, but then he rejected it. Too soon for another one, too impossible. It would only be destroyed again.

To distract himself, he took up the trail of a redhead who

walked with a bluesy sway to her hips. He imagined she was rush-ing to meet a lover at a motel. Benedikte fantasized about intercept-ing her there, erasing her wanton behavior by grabbing her hair, twisting back her neck to expose a ripe vein, drinking until she was drained. Then, he could make her over into what a woman should be—innocent, inspiring, and sedate.

That sounded just about right. During the last thirty years, he'd been lucky, never getting caught in his excesses, always fleeing from city to city before his victims could be discovered. It was an exis-tence Sorin despised because he had, of course, come up with a far more civil plan to make everything easier. A plan that would allow them to settle in a place closer to Heaven than Benedikte would ever get.

Secrecy, Sorin kept saying. *Remember how well it worked in London before we grew careless?*

At the sound of Benedikte's heedless footfalls, the woman looked over her shoulder. The vampires nodded and smiled in re-turn.

Two well-heeled men out for a summer stroll. That was all.

She picked up her pace and darted into a market. My, my. Sharp instincts.

As they continued down the sidewalk, Sorin thought, *She felt us. Do you not think a woman with such perceptiveness would make a proper vampire daughter for you? Think of how she would always hide her tracks.*

Benedikte rolled his eyes. *How many times do I need to tell you I'm not interested in more children?*

Master, I see your face before you lay yourself to rest. I hear your lonely thoughts. Stop lying to me.

Benedikte kept walking.

You are reluctant, Sorin added. *You fear a new Underground will end up like the old, but I tell you, we can anticipate your blood brothers' tricks, if any should cross us again. Do you not long for a*

*rest, Master? Have you not already fallen in love with this town
and wished to become a part of it?*

They passed an Italian restaurant, garlic wafting out from the
ivy-decorated trellises. It had no effect on Benedikte; immunity to
the herb's properties was one of his personal talents, and his blood
had passed it on to Sorin. He wished he had thought to use that sort
of one-way repulsion on Andre back when—

He didn't want to think of London. Didn't want to think of
how, since those times, he'd cultivated such a shell that nothing got
through to him anyway. Feeling cancelled, he spent much of his
time in vaporous form, though Sorin had convinced Benedikte to
shift into his old body and hit the streets tonight.

"Stop wallowing in grief," his son had said. "We have collected
a fortune throughout the years, so let us enjoy it. Let us at least pretend to have a life in this town where imagination makes the
prospect so simple."

Why not, the Master had apathetically agreed. It might break
the monotony, if nothing else.

Beyond the Italian restaurant, they passed a church, which
brought a wooden laugh from Benedikte. It wasn't until, farther
down, they came to a movie theater that the Master paused under
the shining marquee.

With a mocking smile to Sorin, he bowed to the altar of film,
then set off on his stalk again. He knew his son understood the
cruel joke, the absence of rules that allowed them both to exist.
After London, even Sorin had lost some faith, becoming numb to
spiritual meaning and, therefore, increasingly immune to it, as well.

But, again, maybe the immunity was only another talent. A des-
tiny.

Before long, they arrived at the Ambassador Hotel, where a
pocketful of cash would buy them some mindless leisure, if they
were lucky. And if they were really fortunate, maybe there'd even
be something tasty on the menu.

Smile, Master, Sorin thought as they walked beneath the awning of the Cocoanut Grove. *Out of all places, I thought this should make you the happiest.*

When they paused at the entrance, a blast of music, color, and joviality hit Benedikte's vampire senses, overwhelming him.

Sorin was right. Happiness was all *over* the menu.

A band played a Tony Bennett tune onstage, leading a floor full of perfect people to dance and laugh. Palm trees from *The Sheik*, Rudolph Valentino's biggest movie, spread their leaves over what looked to be a Moorish palace, complete with gilded pillars and tables clothed in white. Small table lamps cast golden lights on the jubilant faces of men and women wearing evening gowns, minks, and diamonds.

Consumed by the lustrous haze, the vampire took a step forward, recognizing one of his idols dining and mingling. Lana Turner, using her dimples on a willing romantic victim.

As he and Sorin flashed their money and were shown to a table, the word *home* consumed the vampire again. It was all he could do to remain in his seat, taking in everything while holding his breath.

Time moved in a breeze, heavy with an intoxicating twist that he hadn't experienced since meeting Sorin—a night that had changed the path of his wanderings. And, at some point, when his son left him alone, Benedikte barely noticed.

He was too wrapped in the perfumes, the throb of a hundred heartbeats entwining through his own veins.

Eventually, when Sorin came back, presumably from dancing, Benedikte focused on his son, vision finally locking into place.

"Care to take a turn?" the younger vampire asked, arms around the waists of two beautiful women smiling with red-lipstick confidence. Twins, with their black hair worn as short as Liz Taylor's, eyes big and blue, skin pale and tempting.

Benedikte's lust suddenly reared up, beating in time to a rumba the band was now playing.

"Hey, hey, hold on there!" A man with sparkling hazel eyes, also clad in a tuxedo, came up behind Sorin. He had a wide, youthful smile with a flop of brown hair covering most of his brow. It took Benedikte a moment to absorb that he was staring at one of Hollywood's biggest actors, Edward Waters.

The star took one of the twins by the hand. "Are you stealing my partner?"

He wasn't angry, and Benedikte knew that Sorin had already read this, too. Even so, the younger vampire inclined his head toward the actor, graciously surrendering only one twin.

"Quite the gentleman," Edward Waters said, duly impressed. He stuck out his hand to Sorin and introduced himself.

When the actor turned to Benedikte, the vampire laughed. Actually laughed. "We're acquainted by way of the screen. I'm Benny." His masquerade name.

Sorin had shaken Edward's hand without deigning to offer his own moniker. "You're familiar with Geneva and Ginny?"

The girls fawned over Edward, saying they knew him well.

The matinee idol gestured to a nearby table, where slick-haired men with cigars enjoyed their steaks. With a boyish bow of the head, he said, "I'm trying to make my way over there. Dealmakers. One of them's got a part I'd sell my soul for, if you know what I mean."

Something in the back of Benedikte's consciousness flickered.

"Anyway," Edward added, addressing Sorin, "if you don't mind, I'd like to dance *both* of these lovelies past the table, just to get the conversation started. I'll get 'em right back to you though. Any objections?"

Geneva adjusted the décolletage of her gown to make it even more appealing. "If there's a role in it for me, let's go."

Edward laughed. "All business. I should've known."

As he led the twins away on a stream of pleasant farewells, Sorin stared after the women.

Their skin, he thought to Benedikte. *Did you smell their skin?*

He had; it was a vampire's curse and blessing to be aware of appetite at all times.

Their taste, Sorin continued. *I could live forever on the taste I imagine they carry. If we only had a home, where I could keep them, I would live off their blood for years.*

Although Benedikte had never seen Sorin so taken with a victim—or two—he was much too preoccupied with Edward Waters to respond. It was as if the star had showered a little bit of his presence on the vampire.

He watched the human joking with the producers, throwing his head back after he told a good anecdote. Magic. Pure magic.

Benedikte's mouth began to water, but not with the thought of blood. The soul. He craved the soul Edward Waters said he would give up for his career.

The vampire's musings crashed together, falling to pieces that magnetically rearranged themselves into a new order.

Soul. Career. A vampire's talents.

He glanced around the room again, surreptitiously peeking into the minds of the others, retreating before they could notice he'd even been inside. Benedikte didn't even need to look into their eyes he was so powerful, and it helped him to see a new world: a dreamscape of plastic surgery, casting couches, deviant schemes. The all-consuming hunger to be loved.

The search for identity.

Closing his eyes, he accepted them all, knowing he was among his own kind.

An hour, perhaps many more, went by, and the lounge slowed to a trickle of activity. The vampires were among the last to leave, though Sorin had charmed the twins into crossing the threshold with him.

I will be in my hotel room, the younger creature thought to Benedikte as they exited.

His son caught a cab and, in a rush of giggles, the twins disappeared inside, dragging an amused Sorin with them. He would be cautious about his bite, Benedikte knew. There was no need to come with him back to the hotel just yet and spoil his anticipated adventure.

There was a lot to think about, and wandering the night streets would offer clarity, as wandering often did. At least, it had back when anything mattered. . . .

Postmidnight silence captivated the town while Benedikte folded his hands behind his back, the same thoughts running through him over and over.

"Sell my soul . . ." A long career—a very long one . . .

Struck by the power of the concept, the vampire laughed, glanced around at the empty field he was in, then laughed again. Soon, he was holding his sides, dropping to his knees, laughing to the point of crying.

He peered up, finding the Hollywood sign blazing in eternal majesty from a mountainside. Lore had it that the letters had once read "Hollywoodland" and that it had undergone a makeover to accommodate the town's changes.

A makeover. Plastic surgery. If Benedikte could find a doctor, then absorb his knowledge and refine it—

Powered by his discovery, he cried out in triumph, then stood, walking at a quickened pace to keep up with the speed of his mind. He traversed streets, walking, walking until his feet hit grass, then dirt. Rocks towered above him, blocking a moon that was arcing through a sky turning lighter and lighter.

He was so engrossed that he didn't even hear the footsteps behind him.

Crack!

Something had hit his head, catching him so unawares that he stumbled back, losing his footing on rock, tumbling, back, down, darkness—

A figure jumped into the hole after him, raising a crowbar in the moonlight.

Irritated by the interruption, the vampire snapped into pure form, swelling, roaring forward to catch the man's throat in his jaws. But as soon as his fangs sank into a vein, Benedikte knew the attacker had only wanted his wallet.

Wrong prey.

Furiously, he gnawed, whipping the man back and forth, tossing him away when he grew bored. The anonymous body rolled farther into the rocky depths, but Benedikte's sight cut through the darkness. A tunnel traveling through rock.

The vampire wavered, then placed his hand against a wall, reading the history of where he was. An abandoned quarry. Its materials had been used to build the surrounding streets. Closed in the '20s . . .

With an implosion, everything came together.

He sank against the wall, laughing again until tears poured out of his eyes.

Home, he thought, clinging to the granite. *The joke's on me, but I think I might finally be home. . . .*

EIGHTEEN

THE HOUR OF
FORGET-ness

THAT night, it was the same drill after the team got the news about the most recent Vampire Killer murder: a visit to the crime scene featuring a few ineffective object readings by Stoned Kiko, plus a team meeting that came to nothing.

The murderer hadn't made any more mistakes this time out than the last, and since Kiko had been too medicated to give them any psychic edge, the team would just have to wheedle information out of their LAPD and coroner's office sources—not that the officials had been experiencing much luck in their own investigations. Still, relying on others meant Limpet and Associates would have to wait, and Dawn was weary of it.

Sure, Breisi had arranged another clandestine appointment at the morgue during tonight's witching hour. But that seemed as far away as Christmas to a kid.

It was only nine AM, and Dawn was driving to Kiko's from the newest yellow-taped crime scene, which was near Jessica Reese's apartment. Because of Dawn's weaker-than-usual disposition—one look in a mirror had shown a slightly pale complexion that had quietly freaked her out even more—she was headed back to catch a nap and drink more orange juice. She'd been slamming it for the last few hours, and it seemed to help a little, bringing her to the point where she felt decent enough to deal with everything that was going on: a new murder, the old murder, last night's party craziness, the fight with The Voice . . .

Dawn gripped the wheel a little harder. Things were still tense between her and the boss. In fact, when Breisi had said that he wanted Dawn to report to the office right away, Dawn had flat out refused. Like she would go over there and set herself up to fall under The Voice's spell again.

No way. Even if he wanted to "check her over" because of last night's possible roofie scandal, she'd only go back with the others in a few hours since she didn't trust herself alone with him. Then they'd *all* be putting their heads together about what the police had turned up about the new victim.

Annie Foxworth was her name—a mousy teacher who'd died in the same vampire way as Jessica Reese, even though the two women didn't share any connections that would reveal something about the killer's appetite for choosing a certain kind of victim. In fact, the reportedly modest Annie and the more boisterous Jessica didn't seem to have much in common at all, so far.

So what was the link? And, most important, why hadn't a Friend been able to stop the newest murder during their assigned surveillance last night?

Maybe that issue was the scariest: the ever-increasing unreliability of the spirits. They were supposed to be keeping tabs on most of the suspects, but the Friends had already been spread so thin that a lot of the regulars had gone unwatched last night: Sasha Slutskaya, Matt Lonigan, the patrons of the Cat's Paw, and most of the Tomlinson family. Or, to be more accurate, only one Friend had been assigned to the Tomlinsons, and when Marg had left the motel to sneak out and loiter in front of the Beverly Center's Hard Rock Cafe to smoke cigarettes, that had left the rest of the brood unsupervised.

But another scenario bothered Dawn even more. What if the killer was someone they were totally unaware of, someone the Friends *couldn't* watch?

And *that* led to an ever pricklier consideration: was one protective Friend even enough to guard the team members themselves anymore? Would they all have to move into the Limpet house for security on their off hours?

Shoving aside the dire possibility, Dawn pulled into a grocery store parking lot, thinking she'd pick up more juice before she got to Kiko's.

As her engine rattled to a stop, she undid her seat belt, absently checking her deep, buttoned pockets for her ATM card. She didn't do purses, and even a wallet was a stretch.

While riffling, she found her driver's license and garlic spray, which she'd spritzed on before getting to the crime scene. Then she got to the crucifix and the holy water vial. But . . . her card?

She searched every pocket, every inch of her car before finally admitting that it must've spilled onto the driveway back at Jac's. Great, this was her reward for trying to get out of the girl's house in record time. So much for a clean getaway.

Well then. There was, like, a buck in the dashboard and she'd tossed a wad of dollar bills onto Kiko's kitchen counter before weaponing up last night and going to Annie Foxworth's place. She'd been trying to make room for her throwing stars and whip chain and had thought an ATM card—which she'd assumed was in her jacket—would be sufficient. Dumb. Dumb, dumb, dumb.

She had to go back to Jac's. No choice unless she wanted to tango with her bank, and who had time for that kind of crap?

Dawn got out her phone. A call to the actress would keep her from freaking out at the sight of Dawn scrounging around the drive-way: just a quick stop, she'd say, no need to come out and talk to her.

But Jac wasn't even home, or at least she wasn't answering her house number.

Dawn tried calling Jac's cell.

"Hi!" said the voice mail. "It's August fifteenth, bright and early, and I've shut off my phone while I *take a meeting* with my producer and director." She'd said "take a meeting" with a wink in her tone. "I'll get to your message later . . . don't want to be that rude cell-phone person who takes calls and ignores the people she's with. Thanks!"

Dawn left a brief one. She needed that damned card for more than just juice, and she'd be in and out of there anyway.

As she realized that she was stressing out over such a boring, everyday problem, Dawn chuffed. She just *wished* her life were full of missing ATM cards and that was all.

Her phone rang. She checked the screen, not really wanting to get into a conversation with Jac if she was calling back. She didn't want to deal with Matt, either; he'd left a ton of voice mails that she hadn't answered because she still wasn't in the mood for his apologies.

Luckily, it was Breisi. "Glad I caught you before you fell asleep."

Dawn didn't even have time to explain the ATM card annoyance before the woman launched into the latest. Knowing this might take a while, Dawn grabbed an earpiece from her passenger seat, put it on, and plugged it into the phone. Then she started the car and got moving to Bedford Drive.

"I just talked to Kiko's doctor," Breisi said. "Right now they're together, and Dr. Walter's seeing if there's a physical reason for all the pain. He'll also be assessing if Kiko's hydrocodone intake is a case of physical dependence or if it's psychological."

"I wish Dr. Walter could just take Kik off the things."

"The boss thinks we should be ready for an intervention if the situation doesn't improve."

At the mention of The Voice, Dawn zipped her lip.

"And then there's more." Breisi sighed. "We still haven't heard from the Friend who was protecting you last night."

In spite of all the other Friend problems, Dawn knew her defensive buddy for today was still around. She'd smelled the jasmine before getting into the car.

The team had theorized about how last night's spirit could've disappeared from the party. At their lack of answers, The Voice had told them he'd be alerting all the Friends, and then planning on how to keep this from happening again.

"I hope we find her," Dawn said, pulling up to a red light.

"Likewise." Breisi didn't even stop for a breath. "I've also got a murder update, something interesting the police have already uncovered about Jessica Reese and Annie Foxworth. This might not be much, but they both patronized the same drugstore—ValuShoppe. It could be that the killer hung around the aisles to choose their victims, then followed the women from there to ascertain their schedules."

At the green light, Dawn took off with more speed than necessary. How about that—even something as insignificant as shopping could be dangerous. "So someone's checking out the ValuShoppe employees and frequent customers, then interviewing to see if there've been any weirdos hanging around—?"

"And scanning security videos. You've got it."

Breisi sounded sort of happy that Dawn was actually detecting. Dawn smiled, fine with the approval. It could end up being the highlight of her day.

"I deserve a prize," Dawn said, unable to resist. "How about you give me your bladed crossbow?" It was the coolest Breisi weapon ever, and Dawn had admired it since night one.

"Over my dead body."

"I had to ask."

"Hold up," Breisi said. "Dr. Walter just came out."

"Grill him good."

"You know it. And, Dawn?"

"Yeah?"

"After you sleep, *please* see the boss. He's concerned about what happened last night. Very concerned."

Only to appease Breisi, Dawn gave a noncommittal grunt, then shut down the line.

Keeping the earpiece in, just in case Breisi called back, Dawn hardened herself to what The Voice wanted and drove on.

She passed a convertible with a surfboard and a voluptuous blow-up doll sticking out of the backseat and tried to find it humorous. But the only funny part was that the team's foes—whoever they may be—weren't having to do much to thwart them these days. Life was pretty much doing all the attacking.

So much for hostile red- or silver-eyed vampires.

When Dawn arrived at Jac's, she kept an eye out for roving security vehicles as she punched in the code to open the gate. She knew it from last night, but that didn't mean neighborhood watch would welcome Dawn's Soda Can Special cruising the area. She'd definitely make this quicksilvery.

She shot up the drive, then, with a spray of gravel, pulled to a stop near the door, disconnected from her phone, and cut the engine. Speedy as a streaker running across an Academy Awards stage, she darted outside and to the entrance, inspecting the area where she'd dropped everything early this morning.

It didn't take two seconds to find the ATM card wedged under some trimmed bushes.

"Idiot," Dawn said to herself as she walked back to her ride. "That was brilliant."

When a jasmine breeze floated by, she glanced up. It sounded like the Friend was trying to get her attention.

"What is it?" Dawn asked.

Heeee-eeeeere . . . The breeze whistled upward, toward one of two chimneys piping out of the gingerbread house's roof.

Chimneys. Two. Red.

Something Kiko said when he'd touched Frank's shirt poked at Dawn. *In one of the two red fingers pointing up to the sky.*

In one of them?

Nah, Dawn thought, looking at the roof, at the red brick jutting up like . . . well, like two red fingers. Dawn had told Breisi, and Breisi in turn must've passed Kiko's mumbo jumbo on to the rest of the Limpet team, but that didn't mean anything he said was valid enough for them to go on. Still . . .

With a burst of hope, she forgot any fatigue and exploded into a run, heading for a tall oak that spread its branches far and wide.

In one of the chimneys, huh?

She grasped a branch, using all her strength to lever upward, pulling until she flipped around and hovered above the branch like a gymnast on a bar. Years of competition and practice had brought her to this.

She rested, climbed higher, higher, flipping and rising. Resting. Then she got close enough to the roof to crawl over a stocky branch, to plaster her body to the shingles. There, she pushed up to a crouch, getting her balance.

A soft gust of jasmine air felt like a hand barring her progress. A warning.

"Why did you tell me if you didn't want me to investigate?" Dawn said, irritated.

She had no idea what Frank would be doing in a chimney, but she forged ahead anyway.

I'm gonna find him, she kept repeating, never looking down.

The Friend swished away, screaming toward the ground.

Dawn should've taken that as a hint.

Because the next thing she knew, something pinched into her

neck, and she only had enough time to collapse to her stomach, nails digging into the shingles as she slid downward.

Her head got cloudy, fuzzed with heat and confusion.

Down, down, the world speeding by, flip-flopping, her fingers burning . . .

Before Dawn could register any more, a bed of jasmine softness scooped her up, hefted her to the ground, then winged away in a swish of speed.

Drugged, Dawn thought, the grass against one cheek, the trees and sky and house all blending together.

She started to lose consciousness, eyelids falling. But before her lights went out, she saw a tall woman with short, curly dark hair and a pistol coming around the brick corner.

Oh, fu—

Just as the woman raised the weapon again, she got slammed to the ground by an invisible force.

By a Friend.

And that's when Dawn went dark.

D AWN?"

A female voice, flowing into Dawn's dreams like hot cocoa warming down a child's throat on a rainy day.

At first she felt achy—old injuries creaking and moaning, her body heavy and shaky. Then, pushing open her eyelids, Dawn felt a crush of velvet against her temple. This wasn't grass. And when she saw walls and pictures through her lashes, she guessed that she wasn't outside at all anymore.

Falling, grasping, nails scratching over shingles . . .

Woozy, she forced herself awake, feeling some medicinal goop on the tips of her fingers, then finding Jacqueline Ashley sitting in a chair across the living room. The painting of a jazz-age rake with his hair shined back loomed behind Jac like a . . .

Friend. What had happened to Dawn's Friend?

In spite of her protesting body, she forced herself to sit up. Then she shook her head, bristling off the dizzy weakness with pure determination.

Through the visual dust bunnies, she saw that the portrait wasn't the only thing hovering over Jac's shoulder. The tall woman, maybe a Samoan, with short, dark curls, dark eyes, and a major-league scowl, was standing guard, too. She looked a little worked over with half her brown face scrubbed raw, and Dawn hoped her Friend had gotten in a few good bruises at least.

But where was she . . . ?

"So the crack shot doesn't have a gun right now?" Dawn muttered, referring to the Amazon. She was surprised she could talk with all the cotton dryness in her mouth.

"Julia, could you please give her some water?" Jac asked, gaze still on her trespasser.

Unsteadily, Dawn moved to the edge of the settee, the movement driving home that her jacket was lighter now. Without even checking, she knew that her gun was gone, her other weapons taken, too. And her phone—not a chance. Damn it, she had to call Breisi, even The Voice. Someone.

"Julia shot me with a dart," Dawn said.

"She'll do that with any suspicious characters who creep around the property. If I'd gotten your message about stopping by beforehand, I would've told her to look out for you, probably not on the roof though."

Dawn eyed Julia as the Amazon reappeared and gave Dawn a bottle of water. "Is this your new bodyguard?"

As thirsty as sand, Dawn made sure the cap was already sealed, then undid it, taking a long swig.

"She's my servant, loyal to only me." Jac motioned Julia out of the room, but the woman lingered.

The actress coolly stared at the Amazon. "Really. Go."

Grudgingly, Julia left. Dawn took the opportunity to scan Jac, noting how pale she was, how she plucked at her fashionable summer dress.

"I didn't know you had a staff," Dawn said.

"New hire. My producer says I won't have time to—"

"Why didn't Julia want me near the chimneys?"

The starlet paused, then laughed like her guest was crazy. "I told you—she thought you were maybe a stalker."

"You have that many excitable fans right now?"

Jac stopped plucking, folding her hands together instead.

All the stress and tension piled up on Dawn, all the lies and mysteries. *Enough.* "Where's my Friend?"

"Friend? There's someone else . . . ?"

"You know exactly what I'm talking about."

If possible, Jac went even paler.

Dawn's heart began to skitter, but not because she was afraid. Okay, maybe she was. "Tell me what's going on, Eva."

At first, Jac just shook her head, acting puzzled. Something hard behind Dawn's rib cage crumbled slightly, chiseled by the thrust of so many emotions. She wanted Jac to tell her she was nuts, once and for all.

But even more than that, she really did want Eva.

Maybe Jac saw that last part more than anything else, because she lost composure. "I wish," she choked out, "you wouldn't say it like that. *Eva.*"

Something boomed behind Dawn's eyes. In her blanked vision, all she saw was a white room, then a crimson flood crashing in, painting the walls with blood and taking her under until she had to claw for breath and reality.

Da-dupp, da-dupp. Her pulse. A white-turned-red room inside her falling apart, piece by piece. It was unhinging her. It was opening her up, one wall tumbling down, then another. . . .

She grabbed at the couch, clinging to what she knew: the blood on the sheets in Eva Claremont's crime-scene photo. All the years she'd thought her mom was dead, all the grief Frank had endured. And the hate. God, the hate.

That's what calmed her down. Maybe it even iced Dawn beyond shock at this point.

Weird, she thought randomly. *My own mom looks even younger than me. Weird . . .*

Jac . . . Eva . . . whoever must've seen that. A tear slipped down her face. "I didn't want you to find out like this."

"How did you want it to be?" *Da-dupp. Da-dupp.* "You weren't expecting me to rush into your arms, were you?"

"You almost did, that day at the hospital."

"That day . . ." Dawn swallowed. "Your eyes told me it was you, but I couldn't . . ." She glared at this stranger. "I thought I was going crazy. Literally. You made me doubt my sanity."

"I realized that day, too late, that you weren't ready, Dawn. I wish you had been. I've been waiting so long for the moment you'd know who I was."

In Eva's tone, Dawn heard truth. She knew that all the woman's hidden lullabies, all the mockingbird comfort, had been real. That it'd always been there and Dawn hadn't wanted to embrace it. Couldn't handle it.

Jac . . . Eva, she tried to smile through new tears. "You needed more time to accept what was happening. No matter what all the rest of them said, I know what's best for my daughter."

Rest of them? And . . . *daughter.*

Dawn was a daughter. She had a mother.

The little girl inside wanted to run to Eva like a child welcoming a parent home from work. She wanted to bury her face against her dress and feel the give of skin under her cheek.

"No matter what all the rest of them said?" Dawn asked instead, still quivering on the edge of denial. "Who are 'the rest of them'?"

Eva blew that off. "That day at the hospital, I knew I'd revealed too much too soon, so I toned down my Allure. I was able to get into your mind, just for a moment, even though I know you can keep us out. Just that one time, when you had your defenses down and you needed a mother to hold you, you were open to believing. You were ready to hope I was alive, and you set yourself up to receive me. Just that one day . . ." Eva's voice broke to a halt. She closed her eyes, then opened them. "Everything was always planned—the moment I would finally tell you I was alive. I was *promised* I could do it when I felt it was right, but I couldn't make it happen as quickly as they wanted."

"They" again.

The defensive part of Dawn emerged to take over, sheltering her just as it had when she'd told herself over and over that vampires couldn't possibly be real. "So when Breisi walked in, you had this . . . Allure? . . . under control." *Cope, cope with this. . . .*

Eva had brightened, clearly thankful that Dawn was actually engaging in a discussion instead of flying off the handle.

So civil, this conversation. So smack in the ether of a nightmare.

Mommy, you're home . . . !

Dawn shut the little girl down.

"You're right," Eva said, "Breisi was never able to see my undiluted Allure."

"And what's 'Allure'?"

Her smile dimmed. "I was hoping we could talk technicalities later—"

Dawn burst out of her chair, but when a wave of imbalance swooped over her, she fell back down. Still, she didn't let that water down her temper. "You of all people owe me the truth!"

"I . . . I would do anything to make you see that all I did was make our lives better. You'll realize that soon. I had to go to extremes, but you're going to see how wonderful things can really be. I'll show you."

"Because the second time counts more than the first?"

"I tried to show you how much I care," Eva said, "even in little ways, just to gently bring you around. Remember on the TV news, how Darrin Ryder got attacked the same night Tamsin Greene committed suicide?"

Darrin Ryder, the actor who'd sexually harassed Dawn. "What're you talking about?"

"I heard that he'd been giving you trouble, and I . . . taught him a lesson after I was released. Just a good, fast mugging. He never even saw me." Eva tilted her head.

Something about her reminded Dawn of Robby Pennybaker, but she couldn't . . .

"I had to protect my baby girl," the actress added.

Dawn's anger resurfaced at the daughter reminder. "Wow, that clearly makes you mom of the century. You mugged an asshole in my name, kind of like buying me a bracelet with 'Dawnie' etched into it for my sweet sixteen, or being there for the prom that wasn't. That *definitely* makes up for leaving us."

"Let me—"

"Explain? You found the fountain of youth, but it's filled with blood. Is that what you want to 'explain'?"

Eva played with a seam on her dress, tears streaking down her cheeks. "I thought I had this worked out. . . ."

Dawn's rigidity brought on all the questions the team had pondered. *Concentrate on them,* she thought.

And when the little girl knocked at Dawn's breastbone to let her run to Eva, Dawn was more determined than ever to keep her shut in.

Question. Find a question. Okay. Think about, early on, when Jacqueline Ashley had started her campaign to win Dawn over. Because that's what it all was, right? A scheme, a step-by-step plan to worm into her daughter's heart by pretending to be a good-natured pal.

Dawn folded her arms over her chest, gelled fingers just now starting to throb from the pain of scraping the roof. Or maybe she was just tuning in to what pain really was.

"There was a time," she said, "in that Internet café . . . Kiko shook your hand. He should've been able to read you."

Eva seemed eager to provide this simple answer. "Controlling the Allure. Years and years, I've trained to master it. Even though Kiko couldn't come into *me*, I could draw *him* in enough to win him over. I charmed him. I charm *everyone* into believing that I have what Eva had."

"You *are* Eva, so of course you have what she did." Now her vision was beginning to seep red, the color filming down like a livid, sheer curtain. "But you still haven't told me why you did it. Why you gave up your own family to be a vampire."

She noticed Eva was trembling. She looked strung out.

Mommy, what's wrong? How can I help you . . . ?

Again, Dawn resisted her own neediness, instead focusing on how Eva got up, paced to a window, and pushed her fingers through her blond hair. A wink of something silver, something tucked in a corner, snagged Dawn's attention.

Was that her whip chain . . . her weapons? Why had they all just been thrown aside? Were Julia and Eva so arrogant that they thought Dawn couldn't do any damage?

Careless, she thought, steadily averting her gaze from the pile while still keeping an eye on it.

"I've had enough of never being answered—" Dawn grated.

Eva spun around, her eyes swirling, but Dawn threw out a mind block before the other woman could get to her. She'd been expecting this, and God knows, she wasn't open to her mother anymore. Eva sure as hell wasn't getting in this time.

Immediately, the vamp covered her face with her hands. "I'm sorry," she mumbled. "I just wanted to stop all this."

"But you can't. You said you were going to tell me everything, so start."

Eva raised her tear-ridden face, holding her palms up to Dawn in supplication. "Unlike your boss, I *want* to share everything." She tried to smile. "That's who you're also thinking about, right? The boss who doesn't communicate?"

Dawn still felt a probe at her mind, even though Eva had apologized for trying before. Bitch or not, Dawn had to respect the persistence. "I've got nothing to give you about my job, so stop trying to interrogate me. I'm just your everyday, average Josie Blow with a dysfunctional family. That's it."

"You wouldn't share, even if I could tell you what happened to your . . . Friend?"

On a bolt of rage, Dawn's energy blasted outward, shattering a vase on the table near Eva. The actress jumped back, mouth agape.

"Just think," Dawn said softly, trying to hide her own astonishment, "what I could do with a relic like *you*."

Bluffing. It was all she had.

Mommy . . .

Dawn smacked the little girl quiet.

"Your Friend isn't hurt, I swear." Eva glanced at the vase and . . . smiled? "I was already home when the spirit attacked Julia, so I . . . Let's just say I've very recently been trained to captivate. We've all been instructed in how to do it because of the party last night."

So that's what'd happened to the first disappearing Friend. At least Dawn knew now. "Since we're being honest, were you the one who put me under by the pool?"

"No." Eva looked angry, or at least she was pretending to be, because maybe that's all a vamp could do—act. "And I'm going to find out who did it. Believe me."

Dawn did, and for a forbidden second, she welcomed the

mama-bear protectiveness, grasped on to it until she was holding on so hard she had to let go.

She retaliated. "So you still haven't told me *why*."

"My handlers," the actress said, backing off of the mind screws. "They told me that, when I lost my youth someday soon, the roles would dry up. I was lucky to be in the flush of beauty now and wouldn't it be nice if that could last forever? I got scared. I panicked. Frank couldn't hold a good job and he spent money like a madman, so who was going to take care of the family if I couldn't? I didn't know it at the time, but my managers had . . . connections. They figured out a way for me to keep my career successful: my life insurance and residuals would provide for you and your dad while I waited Underground to make a comeback and earn a lot of money again. A lot more since my legend would pave the way. I wanted to always provide for you, even if I had to make a sacrifice to do it better."

"A sacrifice." Such a harmless word coming out of Eva's mouth. "You did this for your own ego. You and Robby Pennybaker and Lord knows who else."

"I always meant to come back to you." Eva inched closer, seeming so much like young, fun-loving, kindhearted Jac that Dawn almost bought it. Almost. "Please. I was just released, and it's the first thing I'm taking care of, besides getting resettled in my career."

It'd be so nice to just accept everything Eva was saying and offering. Imagine, righting all the wrongs between them, starting over again as mother and daughter. Could all the empty nights of hearing Frank play old records be erased? Could Dawn even be a better person with her mom to guide her now?

So easy to fall into this emotional seduction.

Dawn's neck throbbed, still tender from whatever had happened last night.

Something deep inside warned her not to fall. To hold on.

"We're not bad." Eva stopped, tilting her head. "All we're looking for is a good life. Every single one of us."

Dawn didn't want to start wondering if creatures like Eva considered her, Breisi, and Kiko to be the bad guys. That would muddle all the righteous anger, all the justifications for vengeance.

Instead, Dawn summoned her Eva bitterness. Easy. Adrenaline surged, canceling her exhaustion.

Pretending to break down under all her mom's tempting words, Dawn wiped the medicinal goop off her fingers as she walked toward the vampire. After the gel was gone, she opened her arms as if to suddenly embrace everything Eva had to offer.

Probably because she wanted it to happen so badly, Eva's ageless face lit up at her daughter's approach.

Abruptly, Dawn dodged around Eva, diving for the first weapon she could—the whip chain. Within a second, she had it unfurled, spinning at her side. The silver could poison Eva.

The vamp seemed to sink into herself. "Oh, Dawn."

Heart fully hardened, she struck at her enemy, the silver dart on the end of the whip slicing through the air.

With mind-bending speed, Eva avoided the attack.

Dawn jerked in surprise, the flow of her chain interrupted. Annoyed, she got back into her rhythm.

"I'm telling you to put it down before you get hurt," Eva said, sounding so much like a mother that Dawn almost did stop.

But it didn't really work with a middle-aged woman bitching at her from a young girl's body. "What's the Underground, Eva?"

The vampire looked heartbroken.

"Where's Frank? *Do you know where the hell my dad is?*"

"Please put that down. . . ."

Dawn spun the whip backward so it slowed at the apex of the spin, then allowed it to fall back into her hand. But just as Eva looked relieved, Dawn quickly stepped forward, skip-stepping into a tornado kick, releasing the whip and going into a right elbow hook spin to gain enough speed to strike.

Slowly, Eva nodded, then sighed into Danger Form.

She whirled, ghost tendrils in misty motion, then snapped into a cloud of breathtaking angel-featured splendor. Before Dawn could maneuver the chain around again, Eva had zipped under the arc of the whip's spin and flashed up to Dawn's hand, jarring the handle away.

Aghast, Dawn could only watch as the vamp masterfully manipulated the handle, circling the whip and dervishing her own way across the room. When she released the chain, it cut into a wall, spitting plaster, then died to the carpet.

As if to punctuate the finale, Eva popped back into human form, wisps of silver streaming from her body like iced smoke.

"That's so not going to work," she said, sounding like Jac— naïvely disappointed.

For the first time, Dawn felt truly beaten, having no options. Her pulse vibrated, turning her stomach.

"I guess it's time to prove," Eva said, "that my intentions aren't that bad at all."

Out of nowhere, someone gripped Dawn's arm. She glanced up to find Julia shaking her head at her. *Bad dog,* she seemed to be saying. *Bad daughter.*

A rumbling filled the air, and Dawn glanced at the fireplace, which was moving away from the wall, exposing a slat.

Before she knew what was happening, Julia and Eva had taken both her arms, forcefully ushering her through the dark space, down some stairs. . . .

Toast, Dawn thought. *I'm toast. No one will ever know what happened to me.*

But when a door opened at the end of a tunnel, she saw a light. They shoved her into it, and there, in the blinding flash, she saw a well-kempt man in a T-shirt and jeans, chained to an overstuffed couch.

Dawn fell to her knees, then sprint-crawled toward him, choking on happiness and fear.

As she jumped up and collided into his chest, his beefy arms wrapped around her, cutting off what little she had left of her breath.

Then the door behind Dawn and her father crashed shut.

NINETEEN

THE RED FINGER

DAD!" Dawn cried into Frank's brawny chest, clinging to him. His familiar scent—the musk of car grease, a hint of old beer days gone by—washed through her.

He was real. She held him tighter. He was *here*.

For his part, Frank was squeezing so hard Dawn thought she'd pop. The pressure brought on a flash of memory: *Daddy, I can't breathe,* she'd said once after coming inside the house after school. A neighbor had dropped her off from gymnastics practice because Frank had forgotten to pick her up again. *You're too strong, Dad. . . .*

Big-girl Dawn pushed away to get some oxygen, but also because she wanted to see that it was really him and not some damned vampire joke. Reaching up to hold his grizzled face in her hands, she laughed a little hysterically.

"You're okay," he said. "I knew the last thing she'd do was hurt you, but . . ."

He shook his head, out of words.

Dawn kept drinking him in. Deep lines emphasized his smile, and his green eyes were clear of their usual hangover fuzz, a sheen of what seemed like relief washing over them instead. His steady gaze was surrounded by crinkles, his skin so leathered it looked like some treasure map that might actually pay off. His dark hair resembled the usual wild-grass clearing, but it'd receded more than she remembered.

She'd missed him; she hadn't realized just how much until now.

They hugged again, and she noticed that, in spite of his brawn, his tummy was slightly rounded. Eva had kept him fed.

"You *are* okay," he mumbled against her hair, "right, Dawnie?"

"Okay" was such a relative term. "I've found you, and that makes me more than okay. Now . . ." Ignoring her aches and pains, Dawn squeezed him one more time, then quickly reached down, testing one of the long chains shackling his arms. "I've got to get you out of here."

"Whoa, whoa . . ." Frank smoothed back her hair with both hands, then kissed her forehead, pressing her to his chest until she was gasping again. "I almost want to think that this is one of Eva's mind tricks."

Like father like daughter. "We've got a lot to talk about, but . . ." She backed away, tugged at his chains anchored against the wall. They held like a mother, but Dawn wasn't exactly at her strongest right now.

"Ain't these somethin'?" Frank yanked on one, too. No give from its base. "You don't know how I've fought 'em. They're some kind of impossible silver. Only the best from Eva."

Was he actually joking around? That took her aback until she realized that Frank had found ample opportunity to get used to this captivity, that he was probably able to yuck it up all he wanted because it'd become so real to him. Yup, just a part of his everyday life, being chained to a wall by a vampire, aka his wife come back from the dead.

She glanced around the room, noticing how nice it was. A fireplace that probably hadn't seen flames for years, the type of couches and chairs you'd find in an L.L. Bean catalog, a door halfway open to expose a clean toilet and shower, a mini refrigerator, a television.

"I get to watch all the sports I want," Frank said, touching Dawn's head again, "and no one nags at me about it."

He jerked his chin up to one of two cameras perched in the corners.

"Ah," Dawn said. "That's how she keeps tabs."

"I think my audience is Julia, mostly. You get a load of her? Every once in a while when she brings a meal, she'll tell me what an honor it is to have Eva chain me up. Batshit bozo."

As Dawn's heart rate began to smooth out, she marveled at Sober Frank. She wasn't used to complete sentences or articulate thoughts from him.

She'd think about all that stuff later. Right now, she just wanted to stay glad to see him and figure out how they were going to get out of here.

He motioned to a couch. "Looks like you need to sit. It'll be a while before the welcoming committee comes through that door again."

Was he kidding? "There's got to be an exit somewhere, and I'm going to find it."

"Hell, if you wanna crawl up the fire chute, give it a go. It's blocked off except for a tiny hole in the center." Frank shot one of his patented charming/cocky glances at her. "I've tried everything else."

Well, hey, so she might as well give up then, right?

Ambling toward the fireplace, Frank demonstrated the boundaries of his chains. They were long enough to allow him freedom on this side of the room, but short enough to keep him away from the faraway door.

Smart move, Eva, Dawn thought. When she or Julia entered, Frank wouldn't be able to ambush them. But, at the same time, he had a certain amount of movement.

Dawn stuck her head into the fireplace and peered up, squinting. Indeed, there was only a tiny hole.

One of the chimneys. A red finger.

She pulled out, flabbergasted that Kiko had actually seen something. His prediction had been cryptic as hell, but he had some of his mojo back. If Dawn hadn't been stuffed into a secret room by her mother-cum-vampire and her Amazon lackey, she might even say things were looking up.

"I used my fork to make that," Frank said, plopping to the sofa. He kept looking at her and smiling as if he couldn't believe she was with him. "That hole just popped up last night, so I tried to yell in the chimney, just to see if anyone would notice my voice, like maybe a Friend on patrol. Or even you, Dawnie. I knew Eva would be bringing you home at some point, and I always imagined you coming over and hearing me before she got to you. Some warning system I am."

"I'm surprised she didn't repair the hole lickety-split. A Friend could've gotten through."

"True enough."

At the same moment, both of them seemed to realize they were talking about really messed-up things. This wasn't baseball chatter or an attempted conversation about the electricity bill. This was Friends and vampires.

Frank gave her one of his funny, screwy looks. It was the type of expression that'd make her laugh when she was younger, the type that had made her love him even when she was angry enough to spit.

"So, I kind of climbed on the roof to investigate," she said.

"You did what? Dawnie—"

"Don't lecture me on safety, Frank. I was checking out something Kiko predicted."

"Kiko? Well, I'll be—how *is* he? And . . ." Frank's throat worked and his eyes caught a glimmer. "And . . . Breisi?"

Dawn knew who he really wanted to hear about. "Breisi's fine. She talks about you all the time—misses the crap out of you—but she's worried. *Everyone's* worried."

She wouldn't go into details about the boss. Dawn felt too rushed for that now, and she wouldn't be telling Frank most of it anyway. Her dad would probably get all protective and pull out a shotgun, then order The Voice to marry Dawn and make her an honest woman or something. Frank was weird in a lot of old-fashioned ways; he didn't like "Dawn's men."

Not that he knew about a fraction of them.

He was smiling to himself, probably hearing the name "Breisi" reverberating through his head. With that one little tell, Dawn realized just how much he missed the other woman. How deeply he felt for her.

"Breisi and I have talked," Dawn said.

"Good for you two."

He lowered his gaze at her, and she understood right away.

Quiet. The cameras. No talking about Limpet and Associates allowed.

"I'm just chatting about your new girlfriend." Dawn took warped pleasure out of Eva's probable reaction to Frank moving on without her. "I don't care if the vamp gets offended."

"Dawn." He'd used the un-nickname, which meant he was pretending he could discipline her. "She's your *mom.*"

She reared back. "You're sticking up for her?"

He looked away, and the bottom fell out of her world.

"Tell me you haven't forgiven her."

"I . . ." Frank shot another glance to the camera, but Dawn could tell it was only so he wouldn't have to talk.

"Goddamnit." She laughed bitterly. "She's tooled with your mind. What do they call this . . . the Stockholm syndrome?"

"She's the woman I fell in love with."

The woman who'd driven him to drink with her death, the woman who'd haunted him with her senseless "murder."

"She must've done a number on you to even have you thinking of forgetting everything she put you through."

"Yeah, she has." Frank held up a finger and pointed to his head. "She's tried to get inside the whole time, ever since that night I thought I saw someone who looked like her and followed them into the Bava nightclub."

She remembered what The Voice had told her about Frank's last contact: *he called me from what I now think to be Bava and said that perhaps it was time for you to come out here and fulfill your place, Dawn. Yet before he could continue, the phone went dead, and I didn't hear from him again.*

"You saw Eva there." Dawn got to her knees. "She mind screwed, then captured you."

"I didn't gain consciousness for a while. I don't know where she took me—somewhere cold and dark—but then I fully woke up here, in chains."

"Getting you back was her first project. She told me she wants the family together again."

"And she's serious. Hell, is she ever serious."

They both glanced up at the cameras.

"She's a vampire." If Eva's betrayal wasn't enough to turn him against her, maybe this would be.

Her dad only nodded, face unreadable.

"Doesn't that mean anything?" There he was: simple Frank, good buddy to everyone, doofus supreme. So easy to take advantage of.

"Hey, I know what's at stake," he whispered. "Do you?"

"Obviously, I know a lot more about it than you do."

"She's going to turn both of us, that's why she's revealed herself to you, Dawnie. There's no going back now. That's why you're locked in a room with me. We belong to her."

Belong? Damned if she did. Eva had given Dawn up years ago. No late claims on these goods.

Frank continued. "I realized what was going on from the second I regained consciousness, and I was prepared to make life easier for myself. She didn't take the time to win me over the way she did with you, but—"

"That's 'cos she knew you'd fall for her again. She knew you'd still be a sucker, Frank."

"We've got history, damn it. A man and wife . . ."

Agonized, he bowed his head, turning one cheek away from her. All Dawn wanted to do was remember how badly she'd yearned to find her dad; she wished she could just go to him now and hold him like any other daughter would. But he wasn't making good choices—as usual. He'd disappointed her, especially with a woman like Breisi waiting for him.

Then Dawn noticed a faint redness on his neck.

Her own neck flashed heat, and she held a hand to it, not knowing why.

Suspicion about Frank crept in slowly. No. He couldn't have allowed Eva to . . .

"Like I was saying." His voice sounded dredged. "I didn't do too bad for myself down here. Except for keeping her out of my head, I stopped fighting her. Damn it all, back in the day she just about ruined her career to marry me, Dawnie. And the less I fought, the more chain room she'd parcel out. I even got a TV. She told me just how much she wanted a family again, how much she missed you, too."

Dawn wouldn't dwell on that last part; she was just happy Frank had been mind blocking Eva. "You didn't want to escape?"

"More than anything. To you and . . ." His gaze went soft, but when he glanced at a camera, he hardened up again. ". . . other people outside. Part of me wanted to warn you, but I couldn't."

"Does that mean the other part of you is on board with this whole wonky family-reunion idea?"

He gave her a look that said, *Aren't you? Don't you want what we never had?*

Dawn didn't react, instead forcing him to continue with her jaded silence.

"She's been having me sleep during the day while she works, then she'll wake me up when the sun goes down. Every night, I've screamed at her out of pure frustration. *Every* goddamned night."

The lightbulb went on. Kiko had always gotten the best readings from Frank's T-shirts after dusk. Was it because of this nightly upheaval?

"Don't you think I want to throttle me just as much as you do right now?" Frank asked.

"You have no idea what I want to do."

"Same here. You have no idea." He shifted, and his chains clanked. "The worst thing is, I was afraid all my . . . friends . . . would get hurt because I know Eva isn't alone in this. I have the feeling she's got something else planned, but I don't know what. I've wondered if she answers to a higher authority."

There he was: Frank the PI—the man he'd become while she was away. In spite of everything, it made her kind of proud.

"Ever hear of an Underground?" Dawn sent a nasty look at the camera again. "The old woman and I touched on the topic."

"Can she be saved from it?"

What?

"Well, can she?" he repeated.

She couldn't fathom this. He wanted to rescue the woman who'd calculated her own murder and left a heartbroken family behind. Seriously?

"Yeah," Dawn said. "I can decapitate her. That'd save her real good."

Frank went pale. In his eyes, she could see him assessing the stranger she'd become.

Saying it hadn't felt right at all; it made her guts tighten. But

Eva wasn't her mother. She wasn't sweet, nice Jac, either. She was one of them, a Robby Pennybaker, the mini motherfucker who'd violated her and tried to kill her.

"This Underground . . ." he began, face flushing slightly.

"Let your beloved wife tell you about it." Dawn hurt for Breisi, hurt for what should've been justice but wasn't. "I need answers from *you*."

"Like what?" He sounded so resigned, the loser of round one. Back to the Frank she knew, the pre-Breisi ne'er-do-well.

"For starters, how did you get involved with all this?"

As he hesitated, Dawn realized her right arm was throbbing. Great—the old injury letting her know it wasn't happy. And she was really tired. It was all crashing in on her now.

"Careful what you say—she'll hear us," Frank whispered. "Eva's hearing is that sharp."

Holy . . . Was she ever going to get answers? What kind of situation would actually allow that to happen?

"But I'll tell you what I can," Frank said, and she saw that he really wanted to help her.

"Then tell me what the boss would want me to hear."

Frank seemed to get it: they were with a PI agency that'd been hired to look into Robby Pennybaker, and that's it. They'd talk in a private code Eva wouldn't understand.

"How did I start?" Frank stared straight ahead. "I guess it was when a local magazine did one of those 'Remember when . . . ?' stories about Eva. They had pictures of the three of us, then me and you, then updates on what we both were doing."

For Frank, that would've been hanging out at the Cat's Paw and singing about glory days with the other guys. For her own part, Dawn recalled being contacted for an interview, but she never did those. Career success had always been based on her skills; she refused to use her mother's name to get ahead.

More important . . . what was Frank saying here? She recalled that The Voice had found Kiko through a newspaper article that detailed his psychic thwarting of a serial rapist. Had a magazine feature brought Frank to Limpet's attention in the same way? Why? Because he was the father of Dawn the Prophecy Girl and Jonah would do anything—including hiring Frank—to reel her in?

"I really needed a job," Frank added, "even though I wasn't . . . trained . . . for this type of work. When Jonah contacted me, I accepted, few questions asked. It was a gold mine and I didn't want to turn my back on it: a gig with great pay. It wasn't until later that I found out there were definite . . . reasons . . . Jonah hired me."

From Frank's expression, Dawn knew she'd been right about Frank being the bait for her. "So why did you stay on?"

"Because I got good at the detecting stuff, and my muscles came in handy. For the first time in my life, I wasn't being sneered at for being useless. And . . . Breisi . . ." He swallowed.

Dawn did, too, wishing Breisi would bust through that door right now. She was really the only person out there who came through every time, wasn't she?

Chest aching, Dawn said, "Jonah took advantage of your need to have a purpose."

At Frank's warning look, she realized they were approaching too-much-information ground, so she shut up.

Speaking of being careful, wasn't it odd that she hadn't felt any hint of an Eva mind screw yet? She wouldn't have put a trick like that past a vampire. Or maybe a creature of the night needed to be looking into her eyes to get any info.

Eager to get on with it, her brain paged through a thousand notes, freezing on one that was high on the bothering-Dawn list. "You kept Eva's crime-scene photo. Why?"

Frank looked ill at being called on retaining it. "All those times I locked myself away with the bottle, I was keeping myself company with that picture. Thought I should've been able to save Eva and beat myself up about why it'd happened. Now I know it was all a part of the vampire act, but back then, her murder was real to me. I felt so guilty whenever I started to throw that picture away, so I never did. It would've been like tossing her out, too, and I couldn't." He glanced up at Dawn, shame filtering his gaze. "I *can't*."

She'd spent so long clinging to Eva, too. But it wasn't right, forgiving her, allowing her back in.

"You were questioned for her murder," she said. "You're not angry about that? She could've gotten you jailed or worse."

"She told me everything was taken care of—it was guaranteed that I wouldn't get into trouble with the law. And I *was* cleared."

Underground Servants. Were there any on the police force? Had to be. "So that makes what she did all hunky-dory—"

"I'm sorry." Now he was watching her with pity. "I'm sorry for making you this way."

Struck so hard, she couldn't say anything.

"I'm sorry," he added, "for making you so hateful and self-destructive. I tried to protect you from becoming her. But I made you hate her, didn't I? I gave you . . ." He searched for a phrase.

"An inferiority complex?" Dawn bit out. "You loved the dead Eva more than you did me. That's what I thought half the time. But"—she held up a hand—"I'm over that, Frank."

Are you? his lingering gaze asked.

She glared. *Yes.*

"You grew up with a lousy drunk for a pop, at any rate."

Almost silently, the door clicked open, and Dawn went on alert. Frank remained calm and resigned.

Julia stood in the entrance, armed with the dart gun. Hopefully it was a dart gun. All the same, it kept Dawn from charging ahead.

Then Eva glided past the Servant—Dawn had no doubt about what Julia was—and into the room. Her stylish dress rustled to a standstill, so cool and chic. She had a hopeful tenseness to her posture.

Dawn just stared at her, hard as rock.

Clearing her throat, Eva made a conciliatory gesture to her daughter. "Breisi keeps calling on your phone."

Fishing for more information about what exactly Breisi was to them both, huh? Eva had been listening in.

"I want to talk to her," Dawn said. "She might have news about Kiko. I would think you might care about that but . . . oh, yeah. You're *dead*."

"Not now, Dawn." Eva sounded so damned maternal. There was even a flash of worry about Kiko somewhere in there. "You know I can't give you the phone."

"Why? Because I'm your captive?"

"I wish you wouldn't look at it that way."

Dawn laughed, sending Julia into a grimace so horrendous that she almost turned Dawn all the way to stone.

"Right." She shot Frank a glance. *Can you believe this woman?* "I'm your 'guest.' Thank you for your hospitality. It rocks."

Now it was Eva's turn to give Frank a look. It was an expression between parents who didn't know how to handle their willful child.

Then Frank met Dawn's horrified reaction. His shoulders sank.

"Don't you want me to talk to Breisi?" Dawn asked him.

"Yeah." He lowered his head. "I do."

Eva took a loaded step forward. "Frank?"

"Don't get on his case," Dawn said. "Breisi's the best thing that's ever happened to him—and that's including your heartwarming resurrection."

Julia, half of her face now a hardening field of sores from her tussle with the Friend, finally spoke up. "Eva could've been a queen Underground. But she just wants you two back."

"Imagine that." Dawn aimed her temper at Julia. "And I want to discover my very own gold mine. I want to rule Texas and make all the beauty queens run around with donkey ears. But most of all, I want to get the hell out of here with my dad. Do you think *I'll* get what *I* want?"

Julia actually raised the gun at Dawn, but Eva slapped it down.

"I'm sorry, so sorry," the Servant quickly said, bending her head.

Clearly flustered, Eva opened her arms to her daughter. "You'll see how much I love you. Maybe it'll take time, but I made the right choice for all of us."

"You want to make us all like Robby, your little pervert costar, Eva. Don't tell me that's the pinnacle of happiness."

"But—"

"*Get. Away.*"

Mouth agape, Eva hesitated, then gathered composure. "Okay. All right, then, I'll give you a rest. It's been a strange day."

And with that, she left in a flutter of flowing skirts.

Still looking down, Julia bolted the door behind her while Dawn sat on the floor near Frank.

"Delusional," Dawn muttered, hoping her dad would agree.

But he didn't say a word. Not a goddamned word.

TWENTY

THE SOUND OF LAUGHTER

By some miracle, Dawn fell asleep on a couch. She was too exhausted, and when Frank wouldn't talk to her, a retreat into herself was the only logical way to deal.

She must've slept for hours—at least her grogginess made her think so after a jarring sound woke her up.

Muffled laughter.

At first, Dawn just stared at the back of the couch since she was facing it anyway. Something was telling her not to turn over and see what was going on.

Shifting, she heard a slight clink, then felt metal bracelets on her wrists. Through the stretched void of after-sleep, she remembered how Julia had come back in to remove Dawn's leather bracelets and slap restraints on instead, then put more medicinal goop on her while she was resting. Dawn had barely even known what was happening she was so out of it.

Giggle.

There it was again—intimate and gentle. This time, she couldn't help looking.

Frank and Eva stood near the fireplace. The vampire woman was cuddled up to him, pulling dopey faces in an effort to make him laugh. It was all very Jac, and it made Dawn wonder just how much of the starlet was really a part of Eva.

For Frank's part, he had his chained arms crossed over his wide chest, immovable, jaw clenched, but Dawn could tell it was because he was playing some sort of twee game with the vamp and not because he was discouraging the interaction.

When Eva tickled his stomach, he jerked away, chains clanking as he burst into a laugh, too. He teasingly put a hand over her mouth and shushed her.

Nausea made Dawn grimace as she sat up, leaning her arms on her thighs while fixing a glare on them.

Amidst their gaiety, Frank noticed the attention, his face going serious as he saw his daughter. He must've caught on to the betrayal Dawn was exhibiting for both her *and* Breisi's sakes, because he let go of Eva, gaze crushed and disconcerted.

Dawn knew the emotions were genuine, but that didn't mean anything when he was over there canoodling with the enemy.

Still, as he backed away from Eva, something ate at the edges of Dawn. Part of her wanted them to be together, for them to be tickling each other and cracking up at inside jokes.

"Morning," Eva said. "Or evening, actually. Your dad and I were just—"

"I saw what you were doing." Dawn looked up at one of the cameras, knowing Julia was spying on them. Suck up.

No one said anything for a minute. One big happy family.

With an anxious glance at Frank, Eva took a seat near the door, hands folded in her lap. Dawn noticed she was even paler than she'd been earlier, and that she was trembling again.

"Out of pure curiosity," Dawn said, "are you seriously this great of an actress? Because I always thought vamps had little or no emotion."

Eva's mouth opened then closed at the sucker punch.

"Dawn . . ." It was a papa warning from the peanut gallery.

"It's only fair for her to ask a lot of questions, Frank." Eva's smile wobbled as she aimed it at her daughter. "Believe me when I say that I feel emotions now more than ever. That's *not* how it is with all our community though. I know one individual who's prone to depression and manic episodes, but I also know another who's levelheaded and calculating. Maybe it depends on the person you were before the change and what you bring with you into the new heightened life."

"You mean new death. Because, *again*, you're dead."

"Debatable." Now Eva's smile evened out. "I actually feel more alive than ever. Maybe it's because I'm in control now."

Dawn paused, then got up, minding her chains as she went to the mini fridge and rooted through it to find a bottled water. Taking it out, she mockingly saluted Eva. "You were expecting me."

"I told you, it's what I've always planned."

"You're going to make me one of your kind—that's your big mustache-twirling scheme."

"I . . ." Eva tilted her head. "Well, yes."

This could work to Dawn's advantage. When she escaped—and she would, especially when the team realized she was gone and they sent backup—she could use Eva's arrogance against her. The vamp was parceling out crumbs about life in the Underground, and Dawn could work with that, stringing out as much info as possible then reporting back to Jonah.

Right? Isn't that what she should do?

Her mother was giving her a weird look, one that Dawn couldn't stand for too long. It could've been affection, if a creature like Eva was capable of it.

"I'm sorry," the vamp said. "I don't mean to make you uncomfortable. It's only that . . ." Eva bit her lip, eyes going teary again. *Acting!*

Or was it?

"It's only what?" Dawn used her shirt to help undo the cap, then took a sip, casting a sidelong look at Frank, who was staring at the carpet. She tried to find the redness on his neck again, but couldn't.

Had he ever exchanged blood with Eva?

Jesus, Dawn didn't want to even consider the scenario. But she had to. What if Frank was already one of them, just as Eva had planned?

The actress sniffed, tucking a strand of blond hair behind an ear, hand quaking now. "Over the years, I saw your movies, read about you in published articles, heard about you from . . . well, connections Above. You make me so proud. You grew up to be such a beautiful, capable woman."

Dawn tried not to let on how much she'd fantasized about hearing this kind of thing from Eva; the years had been filled with a lot of imagined conversations, pep talks, mother-daughter chats about boyfriends and growing pains.

"You can stop putting on such a show," Dawn said, forcefully twisting the cap back on her water. "You don't have to compliment me."

To tell me I'm beautiful or wonderful. Because I'm not.

Frank cleared his throat, shuffled his boots. "Why don't you hear her out?"

That earned another glare. "Why don't you get your head out of the past and think of what's waiting for you in the present?"

The name "Breisi" spiked between them.

Frank shut up again, but Dawn wished he would show more fight. She wanted her dad to put his daughter in her place, to tell her he had this all under control. But he didn't.

"Tell me," she said, swiveling her gaze to Eva, "how do you stop Frank from screaming during the night? One of your attempted mind screws? Can you soothe him like that?"

The vamp seemed unfazed, even with her sickly cast. "I think of it as a sharing of sorts. An intimacy between husband and wife."

Out of the corner of her eye, Dawn caught Frank's hand going to his neck. That bitch.

She threw the water bottle to the ground, taking a step forward, but Frank stopped her by grabbing her shoulders. Their chains rattled chaotically.

"Calm down and I'll tell you as much as I can," Eva said. "That's what you want, right? I want you to be excited about your new home. You'll learn more about it eventually, but I'll answer almost anything you ask now."

"It's not like you can get me pumped up about moving to a different school district or something, Eva."

Dawn shrugged out of Frank's grip, but he hovered behind her anyway. Didn't he get that this . . . thing . . . wasn't really his wife?

"The sad truth is this." The actress's brown gaze went soft, worried. "There might be a war, and if my suspicions are right, you'll be stuck in the middle. Frank would've been, too, but I've made sure he's out of the way now. I'm going to have to answer for taking him, but it was worth it." She lifted her chin. "Now I know enough to choose family over anything else, even the Underground."

She smiled at Frank, and Dawn shrunk away, left out in the cold.

"See," Eva continued, "no one knows I have Frank, and I've had to do some tap dancing to convince them that he's really missing. I said to them, 'Maybe he's on one of his benders or on a road trip that's lasted a little too long.' They didn't want me to reclaim him yet because his disappearance might trigger this war I'm talking about. But . . ." She glowed like a bride. "After I was released from the Underground, I couldn't wait to see him. I had to break rules and then lie by telling my master I'd search for Frank later, and he believed me. I . . . he *favors* me, and he truly thinks I'd never put my family above the interests of our home. . . ."

So she'd been *Acting!* with this master. One more reason not to trust Eva, because if she could do it to him, she could do it to anyone.

"My master's always protected me from anyone who doubts my loyalty," Eva added. "But, when I left, I needed to promise him I'd contact Frank only after I had *you* in hand, Dawn, because that's all that matters to him. You."

Dawn furrowed her brow. "Why?"

"Because you work for a monster."

At first, Dawn didn't process that. But as she backed up, then hit the couch with the back of her legs and slumped onto it, the possibility slipped into her. Jonah, the question mark who never gave her any answers. Jonah, with his lies and betrayals, his baiting and secrecy.

"What do you mean?" she said.

"The Master calls him a usurper. He believes Jonah Limpet wants to take over our Underground, and he's using you to accomplish that."

In her bafflement, Dawn looked to Frank. He was watching her closely, probably already having heard this from Eva night after night. He'd lied to her about not knowing anything of substance, maybe because Eva had told him to. Maybe he thought it best that her mother be the one to explain everything.

Did he believe his vamp wife? Or was he biding his time, pulling Eva into his good graces so an escape would be that much easier? He was still on Limpet's side, right?

"Poor Dawn." Eva stood, her thin dress surrounding her like a nimbus. "I promised I'd leave the heavy explanations to the Master. He's looking forward to welcoming you."

"Hey, I think you're not getting it—I'm not going to be a vamp." The words sounded so sure, but they were only cardboard, fake background scenery misdirecting the audience.

"Yes, you will be." Eva said it matter-of-factly. "He wants you with him, just as much as I do."

Dawn's mind spun, a carnival ride that was only starting. Or maybe it'd just picked up speed, making fragments out of what used to be real and blurring it all into a mass of colored disorder.

Eva moved closer. "He loves every one of his progeny, and when we take you into our family, you're going to feel that adoration."

For an indulgent moment, Dawn amused herself by pretending she was open to these ridiculous promises. "And what kind of vamp would I be? Aren't there a few . . . subspecies?"

"Sure—we're evolved to the point where different members fulfill different niches Underground. With the Master's bite, you'd be like me, Dawn. He thinks that much of you. You'd be *just like me.*"

Dawn shivered, not in fear but in need.

Just like her mother.

Eva seemed to understand, walking even closer. "You're too good to be a Groupie, one of the lower-level vampires."

Without even realizing it, Dawn had unshuttered her mind, and Eva flowed inside, filtering into every brain cell. Within a few bent seconds, Dawn knew how the beautiful ones—the Elite—had always come to be: the arranged deaths that made a regular superstar into a legend, the transformation as performed by Dr. Eternity, the final stage of becoming an ethereal being who lingered Underground until the comeback Above.

No ugliness, Eva thought to Dawn. *Just paradise. I'm what you've always wanted to be. I'm your mother, come with me. . . .*

Absorbing more, Dawn also saw how an Elite could walk in the sun and feel it on their face as long as they didn't expose themselves too intensely. She saw many other answers, like how blessed objects were just that—objects—and that garlic was just a nuisance because the Master had been born with this immunity, too, and the Elites had inherited a good measure of what his blood carried.

She told Dawn so much . . . but not everything. It would all come, Dawn knew, if she only allowed Eva to continue.

In her dream state, Dawn felt her mother touching her hair, weeping at the privilege of finally being allowed in. A roar grew in the back of her mind, a gathering wave of something Dawn should be remembering—

The good guys, Eva interrupted, we're *the good guys. Come to our side.*

But the wave collected more liquid thought, gathering in strength. RememberJonahrememberBreisirememberKiko. . . .

When it crashed, it sopped Dawn in cold reality, pushing Eva out with a thunderous heave.

Her mother stumbled back, teary eyes wide. Frank was at her side in a heartbeat, holding her, his chains clattering.

"What're you doing?" he said.

Dawn stared back at him, asking him the same thing.

When he didn't answer, she deprived him of her attention, but that only meant she was back to square one. Just because she was having a crisis of conscience, that didn't mean she trusted The Voice now. She needed to think about everything, needed to glue it all together until it made sense.

As Frank held Eva, she touched his chest. "It's okay. This isn't an easy choice for her."

His face didn't show any emotion as he nodded, then stepped away from his captor. Damn it, why wouldn't he clue Dawn in on what he was thinking? Or didn't he want her to know because he realized she'd hate his decision?

"Anyway," Eva said, running her shaking hands down the front of her dress, "I have to go." She wet her lips with her tongue. "Julia will have a late dinner down soon."

With the way she said it, Dawn wondered if Eva was going out to feed from her master—from what Eva had shown her, Dawn knew this was how she survived.

"You realize," Dawn said, "that my absence is going to tip off my coworkers and the authorities? Don't you think they're going to come looking for me here? Kiko's smart enough to tell them that your house is a possible location for me."

"That's been taken care of." Eva smiled like Jac used to—light and pretty. She pointed to herself. "Actress?" Then pointed to the door, altering her voice. "Your phone?"

She sounded like Dawn. Holy crap. She'd pretended to be Dawn to Breisi, or Kiko, or . . . God, she hoped The Voice had answered. Maybe he'd be able to read what was going on or do whatever he did.

Looking oddly discomfited with her own sly games, Eva turned to go, hesitated, then said one last thing. "When it comes to who the good guys are, think of who just offered the information you wanted and who's been withholding from you."

The rest of it was implicit: would you trust a boss who used your dad as bait or the mom who was taking such a chance to get her family back?

"We're not the villains, Dawnie," she said.

Dawn flinched at the nickname. Then, automatically her inner smart-ass kicked in, and she held up her hands, showcasing the chains to remind Eva of who was playing jailhouse warden here.

With a touché glance, Eva nodded sadly, as if admitting that the ends justified the means. Then she turned to Frank, lavishing a look of such profound affection on him that Dawn blushed. It got even worse when he turned away, a man caught between two impossible forces.

"Breisi," Dawn whispered to him, encouraging her dad to take a side.

Abruptly, Eva flew at Dawn, catching her T-shirt in her fists. *"Don't—"*

But when she realized what she was doing, she cocked her head, gently let Dawn go, and backed away. "Don't say that name in my house again."

Then she let out a long breath, as if destroyed that Frank had found someone else. As if deflated that her daughter actually liked the woman who'd replaced her.

Then she turned around and went through the door, closing it behind her.

No doubt taking great care to slip quietly back to her real family Underground, as all Elites did.

TWENTY-ONE

SUPERSTARRING

SOMEONE had made the deal of all deals last night.

This time, while waiting in a rental car that Someone always took great care to clean, the Vampire Killer wouldn't even have to go through the trouble of choosing a victim from the ValuShoppe parking lot. No, everything would be different with this next murder because . . .

Well, last night, "Servants," as they'd called themselves once they were belowground, had caught Someone leaving Annie Foxworth's apartment. Thank heavens it'd all turned out for the best though, because after they'd brought Someone to "the Master," he'd made an astounding offer.

Someone still couldn't believe it. A vampire. A *real* vampire!

"Fame," the compelling man had said, his eyes a swirling, visual promise of that one elusive word. "We've heard about your killing talents, and we want to put them to good use. Would you believe that we have the power to make you a fixture on every TV set in

America? Yes, it's true. *Everyone* is going to forget about Lee if you pull off what we have planned." He'd smiled then—so godlike, so loving. "You'll last in everyone's minds forever. Lee was just a flash in the night, but you'll be a star."

Someone had given in to the seduction: the glory, the spotlight, the lure of being just as special as a creature like the Master. He'd offered all of it, and Someone knew it would kill *the* Lee.

The only catch was that the Master had selected tonight's quarry, calling this murder a "favor" that would benefit all of them, including Someone. Right now, the hunt wasn't as gut-level satisfying as the real thing, but after it was over, the Master would welcome Someone into the Underground, and the satisfaction would go way beyond a thrill kill.

This was the ultimate way to best *the* Lee.

While Someone watched the next victim walk out of a now-closed hardware store and to a parked vehicle, juices ran hot again. The grip of a weapon was clammy against a palm sliding with sweat. Tonight, the vampires had given Someone a Taser, because they wanted their victim alive.

At least for now.

This performance would take place in front of a crowd. A ratings monster, Someone thought. A swan song before retiring Underground to drink blood with real fangs.

Blood had started to taste so good.

Through the windshield, Someone could see that the victim already had car keys in hand, the other hand hidden.

Someone slipped in the set of fake fangs purchased from a Goth store on the Internet with a borrowed credit card, then made sure they were secured tightly.

Open the car door. Quietly, so quiet. Eyes always on the prize, wig off and head scrubbed so as not to leave fibers; clothing black and common enough to deflect any attention.

Tonight, even *the* Lee Tomlinson would be a fan because he'd never reached these heights. The Master had told Someone that *the* Lee had wanted to be a vampire so badly he'd killed for it.

Feeling superior, Someone crept toward the victim on stealthy feet, masked in the dark. Around the empty parking lot, Servants watched to make sure everything went smoothly. This kill was that important.

The Lee would never talk down to Someone again because he'd have no right to. Fuck him. Fuck him for fucking—

Brutal images slashed through Someone: Lee wrenching Someone's arm up between shoulder blades, whispering, "I'm stronger and smarter than you'll ever be. I'm *the* Lee Tomlinson, and you're nobody." Someone had bit their pillow the whole time, mouth full of linen, spit, and bleach, belly scraping the mattress during each thrust—

Someone shook their head to dislodge the flashes, then got closer to Victim Number Three.

It was only at the scent of jasmine that the killer lost step, recalling the Master's warnings about other forces at work. But the hesitation didn't last long, because an "Elite" who'd been summoned just in case of this scenario ripped the ghost away, captivating it.

Then Someone struck quickly.

But the victim whirled around first, whisking a gun out from under a jacket.

Someone was ready, ducking, firing the Taser.

As the victim flopped to the ground, convulsing, Someone stopped being a no one.

And started to feel like the true, glamorous vampire star *the* Lee Tomlinson would never be.

TWENTY-TWO

BELOW, ACT FOUR

THE seductive music video on the Master's television screen was not only bothering Sorin, it was clearly not adding to Eva Claremont's mood, as well.

"I'm going to kill Paul Aspen," she said, standing up from the divan. "Sorin—I'm going to kill *you*!"

"Eva," the Master said, wearing his inhuman form—dark, nebulous, and outlined with the energetic red neon that spoke of good cheer. "Let's hear him out."

The head vampire guided his favorite Elite back to the pillows, unable to take his gaze from her. He stroked her hair, clearly in awe of the blond waves.

Sorin stood his ground in front of them, hands folded behind his back. They were in the Master's private quarters, where he was preparing to gift the actress with her first monthly infusion since her release. Though they received only enough blood to possess a fraction of the Master's own powers, it was enough. Without it, they would become what they feared worst: ugly, old, average.

Not that Eva Claremont was entirely focused on that matter. Unlike many Elites, who priced human attachments below fame, she had family concerns. And the Master had preyed upon those fears, utilizing Underground recruiters—Servant agents and managers—to win over the mortal actress he worshipped from afar.

Sorin somewhat respected her love for family. He had always retained an inkling of memory for his own, as well.

Eva was still glaring at him, her Allure getting away from her and causing her gaze to break apart into multihued shards. "You asked Paul Aspen to wipe my daughter's memory! *And* he bit her. Bit her, Sorin! He had no right—"

"I regret that." Sorin's tone remained even. "I did not anticipate his foolishness."

She turned to the Master. "You promised I could ease her into this life, Benedikte. If I'd known what would happen when I left Dawn alone at the party, I wouldn't have brought her. I thought it was safe."

"You're upset. I understand." The Master kept smoothing back her hair. "Don't be angry."

Sorin's posture stiffened as he witnessed the Elite slowly wrapping the older vampire around her tiny finger once again. She was the Master's weakness.

Thank the day Sorin had carried his streak of human logic with him into this world. From years of observance, he believed many other vampires clung to a semblance of mortal emotion, unable to desert it. Sorin was admittedly guilty of that, but it had faded with time, embedding itself deeply, where it was not simply accessed.

Eva had not calmed down. She was kneeling next to the Master, holding one of his darkly hazy hands. "I know Paul facilitated my return to Hollywood by getting me this big new role. He's a mentor, but I didn't realize he'd take Dawn in exchange for his efforts."

"Eva, I'll handle this."

Although Sorin could not clearly see the Master's face, he knew how the old vampire would be longing for her. It was an eternal heartbreak that Sorin did not comprehend.

The Master turned to Sorin. "Didn't you think of how this would affect Eva?"

From the sharpness of tone, Sorin knew that his maker was sickened by what had happened to Dawn, as well.

Sorin anticipated this. "I gambled and failed. Yet I still believe the risk would have been worth the reward, had I succeeded. Dawn Madison is an untapped resource, and we have waited too long to fully mine her." He paused. "And it is not as if Eva would ever extract the information we need from——"

"She's my daughter!" There was fire in Eva's eyes now. "You've both gone far enough in using her as a toy of war."

"At this point, we are all toys."

"Enough." The Master's aura throbbed. "Sorin, you know extracting information from Dawn has not been Eva's job."

"Yes, Master, I am sorry." His maker was clearly upset by Sorin's analysis. Yet what choice was there but to press onward? The spirit who had accompanied Dawn to Paul's party had yielded no information under strenuous examination, and Sorin doubted that more captivity would provoke her into revealing anything about why she was with Dawn or who her boss really was. Most unfortunately, Sorin was not even so certain that this most recent plan of the Master's—the so-called Vampire Killer scheme—would produce results tonight, even if their murderer was already carrying out the plan.

The Master assuaged Eva by petting her throat, laying her back on the pillows, and beginning the infusion process. She was trembling, most likely from residual anger and the craving for blood that built up in Elites over the course of a month.

"Maybe you're not thinking straight when it comes to Dawn," the Master said softly. "Even you admit that you revealed yourself too early."

"I had to." Eva rubbed a hand over her brow.

"Taking her captive is going to set off some fireworks. If we weren't making a move to bring Limpet out of the shadows tonight, I'd be very upset with you."

"We could've fooled everyone Above for at least a few days. Dawn's identity could've been assumed by y—"

"It wasn't your choice to force any vampire's hand, Eva."

She absently ran her other hand over the divan, no doubt knowing the Master followed her every move.

Wrapping the Master around her finger, Sorin thought again.

"Dawn was much too close to the truth," she added.

Sorin raised his chin, wishing he had Awareness with his sibling, just as maker and higher children—or even the original blood brothers—did. Alas, he was not so fortunate.

He had come to suspect that perhaps Dawn had somehow stumbled upon a secret that had forced Eva's hand. Perhaps Frank, her husband? Had Eva been lying to them all along about his whereabouts? Sorin did not want to believe she would do such a dangerous, selfish thing. She had sacrificed so much to be in the Underground so . . . why?

The Master's Awareness intruded. *Stop dwelling on it. She didn't take Frank. Her mind would show it, and Julia would tell us.*

Sorin shut off his own Awareness as he thought, *If Eva allowed you fully into her mind, you might know. And perhaps Julia worships Eva more than the Underground. You would understand such a thing.*

But Sorin did not share his feelings about how his father tended to fool himself when it came to matters he did not wish to face.

Sorin turned their communication back on. *I only wish to know why she would endanger our home.*

My guess is love. The elder vampire slipped a vaporlike arm under the small of Eva's back, arching her up as he nuzzled her neck. She tightened her hand over her brow.

Love, Sorin thought to himself. *A concept, really.* He applied it to his missing vampire daughters, turned it this way and that. Then he realized that his affection for them was now more memory than feeling.

As the Master used what looked to be a nail to slice open a wound on his chest, he scooped Eva's head into a palm and tenderly led her mouth to him.

Not yet dismissed, Sorin watched, thinking how Eva sucked more than just blood out of his father.

"Everything is going to be beautiful soon," said the head vampire. "We'll be together, you, me, and Dawn."

Intent on feeding, Eva splayed her hands against the Master's chest, sucking languidly, greedily. He leaned back his head, his other hand stroking her back, urging her against him.

"After tonight," he continued, "everything will be easier."

As she drew harder from him, Sorin fisted his hands. She had drunk enough; she needed to cease.

Yet the Master did not seem to care.

"I'm going to . . . take away your troubles tonight . . . Eva—"

He convulsed, and she rose up, pressing herself to him, stronger than usual. She laved in even more blood, moaning.

Just as Sorin stepped forward to drag her away, the Master glowed anew, then forcefully pulled her off himself. He was breathing heavily, erratically, his outline beating.

For a moment, Eva and he merely stared at each other, her skin flushed. Then, gently, he reached out and wiped a streak of blood off her lips, inserting a dark thumb between them.

Clearly embarrassed at the intimacy, Eva disengaged, squirming out from under the Master.

"What do you mean, Benedikte?" She smoothed the skirt of her dress. "What's happening tonight?"

With great pride in his strategic planning, the Master told her of the Vampire Killer scheme as well as her own part in it. When he finished, Eva's hand was at her throat, as if startled.

"You want me to show Dawn this murder . . . ?" she choked.

Inferior creature, Sorin thought. Elites had never killed for their sustenance, so they were soft.

"You won't have any blood on your hands," the Master said. "The new Vampire Killer is going to do it for us because fame is the big reward. The crowds will love this kind of violent exhibition, and our murderer knows it. All *you* have to do, Eva, is show a little bit of the killer's transmission to your daughter. When she sees it, she'll turn away from the life she's currently leading and leave us with one less fighter to worry about." The Master's glow dimmed. "She really does need to change a lot of things about that life of hers."

"I don't like this," Eva said. "It's not right."

"She'll never know we're a part of what's going on. In fact, this is a perfect opportunity to win her over. I'm making it easy for you. Who will she turn to in her grief over tonight's murder? Her mother, of course."

Eva was quiet.

Sorin tensed, suspicious of her reaction. "Perhaps you can persuade us of your loyalty once again with your aid in this?"

At the challenge, Eva stiffened.

The Master held up a hand, silencing Sorin. "Eva, I thought you would be happier." He sounded stung. "Dawn's grief is going to help *you* as much as it will the Underground."

"And you would help the Underground, yes?" Sorin asked the Elite.

"Of course. I'd do about anything. But . . ."

"This is just another step in persuading Dawn to come down here with me," the Master added. "Think of it that way."

Eva seemed to draw back from him, though Sorin did not detect a change in physical distance.

"You talk like she belongs to you," she whispered.

"She will, Eva. Just like you do."

The Elite stared straight ahead. "Benedikte, sometimes I think you've transferred your affection for me to her, and it . . . concerns me."

The Master's glow ebbed again. Awareness did not reveal to Sorin whether it was because Eva had shut him out or if it was because she doubted his professed love of Dawn.

Within seconds, the old vampire began to grow agitated; sparks lined the edges of his shadowed form. "You're testing me, just like you did at the beginning, when you constantly moped around for your family. Back then, I tried to make you happier by accepting Robby's petition to come Underground—"

"You accepted his dad's petition," Eva said. "Nathan Penny-baker wanted Robby to go through the change, not the other way around."

"Nevertheless, I was willing to overlook my doubts about turning such a young boy because he was your friend. I thought he would be like a little brother for you and ease the pain of leaving your other family behind."

But there was more to the Master's story than he was telling, Sorin thought. The old vampire had lavished young Robby with attention, hoping Eva would adore him for it. Yet the Elite had not seemed to notice, instead taking the boy under her own wing and calming his terror at what had been forced upon him. Naturally, her mentorship had echoed their mortal relationship: when Robby had misbehaved with Eva, she had reportedly always adjusted his behavior.

Yet that had only produced trouble, because, when Eva was

released, Robby had lost his only stabilizing influence Underground. He had attempted escape, although he had never visited Eva because of the risk that she would turn him in.

It had always been an ugly situation, and years had passed before the Master had even performed another procedure.

"I only want to make you happy," the Master repeated.

Slowly, Eva stood, strong on her feet now that she had been reinfused with the Master's lifeblood. "If this plan backfires, I have everything to lose."

The Master reached for her hand. "You'll have Dawn."

"And Frank someday," Eva said. "Frank, too."

The Master's night-shaded form contained quick strikes of lightning, an upheaval. *"Frank?"*

A rumble shook the room, and Sorin darted forward, wanting to stop the inevitable, but powerless to do so. "Master, you must prepare for tonight's work—"

With a rock-blasting crash, the old vampire burst into his most terrible visage: a looming demon-fanged materialization of personal fear, not so much *seen* as *felt* by any individual unfortunate enough to see their own nightmares come alive.

The hate of a mother, the alienation of being stranded . . . all of it attacked Sorin with unclean fervor.

Screeching pierced the room, forcing Eva and Sorin to cover their ears and sink to the floor. Neither changed into their own angel-silvered forms—even in full greatness, they were nothing next to the Master: only a rainfall compared to a howling storm.

"You need my blood, Eva," the maker keened, his voice like the scrape of claws over the downward slope from heaven to earth. "You need *me*."

And he had always needed someone like *her*, Sorin thought, arms cradling his head. The reflection of innocence in a chain of women, the echo of a wife dead and gone. Useless love.

The Master turned on Sorin and, although he would not look, the thought of what loomed before him made him quake: a horrifying variation of Elite beauty, distorted by rage.

Can't she see I'm making things so much easier for her tonight? he asked his son. *So much easier for all of us?*

No, Master. Sorin shook his head. *She does not see.*

He bowed lower, wishing the monster away.

She will never see. . . .

TWENTY-THREE

†HE UNDERGROUND
OF HOLLYWOOD,
1984

LONG live the new Robby Pennybaker," the Elite vampires said in chorus, lifting their flutes of warm blood.

As they toasted their newest member, their robes shimmered, the colors and textures reminding Benedikte of far harbors and exotic markets. Behind the Elites, in the emporium's background, Groupies applauded, strewn around the steamy room like cats, resting on and rubbing up against each other.

These newer creatures didn't have the Elites' "class," Benedikte thought. Instead, the Groupies were trendy beings, dressed in netlike material, their hair streaked with neon colors and gelled into odd styles. They'd been created by Geneva and Ginny before the equally frivolous twin vampires had adventured to the Old World years ago.

Yes, Benedikte ruled over them all, resting on a cushioned seat on a dais. He'd wanted to be here for this celebration, so he'd shifted into Sorin's shape, as he often did anyway. His real son was hidden in the private rooms so that none of the Groupies would be aware of the body doubling. However, since "Dr. Eternity" had been the one to turn every Elite into a vampire, the stars all knew when Benedikte was with them. They'd vowed never to reveal his presence—a security precaution.

He scanned all of his dear family, keeping his eye on one in particular: Eva.

His veins sang at the sight of her. It felt like his heart was cracking open and humming at the same time.

She was amidst the toasting Elites, holding Robby as the child vampire clung to her dress. When her gaze connected with Benedikte, he motioned her to him.

While she moved through her brethren—oh, how she moved— she brought Robby with her. The twelve-year-old was shrinking away from his sibling Elites as they reached out to congratulate him. But all he wanted was Eva.

A spear of . . . jealousy? . . . dug into Benedikte at the sight of her taking care of the boy. She did it so easily. Why couldn't she show Benedikte the same kind of simple affection?

Eva and Robby climbed up the steps; she bowed and saluted. The boy would learn about Underground etiquette later.

"Master," Eva said, blond hair sliding down over her face as she held her fingers to her forehead. It hid her expression.

"Sit with me."

She stood, revealed, giving her maker a friendly smile while leading Robby to a chair next to Benedikte's.

As she started to go to her master, the boy said, "Eva?" and held out his thin arms for her to stay.

Benedikte smiled at his new son. Robby, a precocious child star who had gone through a rebellious stage just before his vampiric change. He had grown his black hair into shapeless nonconformity and pierced his nose and eyebrow, too.

A boy vampire. Unnatural.

Benedikte's smile dimmed as he shifted his gaze to Eva. He'd only done this for her.

Keeping her distance, she sat on the arm of Robby's chair, resting a hand on the boy's shoulder. She seemed as content as always; in the year she'd been Underground, that's how she always behaved, even when Benedikte caught the lonely splinters in her gaze.

Still . . . "You're not pleased?" he asked.

"Of course I am." She squeezed Robby's shoulder as he stared adoringly up at her.

Benedikte nodded at the boy. "He's calmed down now. You have a good effect on him."

She'd been in the private rooms when Robby had first been brought here. Since the boy had given them trouble during his fake murder—Robby had attacked an innocent bystander and almost exposed his vampirism to the public—Sorin had been forced to ease Robby's mind to blankness as he'd been transported Underground. It was an aberration nobody enjoyed. Then Eva had met them in the private rooms and helped to pacify Robby when the shock of change had fully hit.

That had been hours ago. It'd taken that long for their new vampire to stop screaming.

Even though Eva kept smiling at Benedikte, she used their exclusive maker/high-child Awareness to express her true feelings.

Did you think of the consequences when you turned a human child? He's going to always have this body, Benedikte.

Shot down, he didn't answer for a moment.

Her smile remained for Robby's sake. Even in Benedikte's dejection, he could still imagine she was the angel who'd gazed down on him from a movie screen, flowers in her hair, wearing her purity like an elusive fragrance. For nights afterward, Benedikte had talked himself into believing that her smile was just for him, as Tereza's never would be again.

He finally answered his favorite Elite. *Nathan Pennybaker told* me that he and his son had discussed Robby's future, and that Robby wanted a new, even more successful child-actor career. He can have that with my help, Eva. As a vampire, he can have a second life, a third one, a—

Did you ever ask Robby?

With her sharp question, Benedikte could discern her own hurt. Deep down, Eva felt that she'd made the wrong decision in being here, that she'd been talked into the Underground by silver-tongued agents and managers who'd preyed on her fear of growing older and losing a career that supported her family.

I love you, he said, and you know I'd do anything to avoid hurting you.

Love. Eva's smile slipped as she stared at him. You don't know anything about love.

I know enough to feel it.

You don't have feelings. You think you do, but they're only wishes. You want what you can't have.

The Elites finished their drinks and called to the Groupies for more. Benedikte gazed at them. His children. His dreams.

Most of the Groupies crawled over to their social betters, skin smooth underneath their netted shirts and dresses. In the meantime, one of them turned on the small televisions stacked in modern-art disarray around the emporium, bringing to light multiple images of MTV dancing in tandem.

The performer, Madonna, wiggled across the screens, and the Groupies moved their hips in imitation, rising in front of the Elites in a sinuous dance.

But when the TV revealed that Madonna was wearing a crucifix, the pets all gasped at once, averting their faces.

After a stunned pause at seeing the jewelry, the Elites laughed. They'd inherited their master's immunity but, since they weren't old enough to lose as much faith as Benedikte, the first sight of something like a crucifix still took them aback.

But within seconds, the shock was forgotten.

Hungers stoked, most of the higher-level vampires grabbed their choice of pet, running their hands below the netted clothing, exploring flesh and priming it for their playful bites.

Immortal gods, Benedikte thought. His progeny, ever-living idols in the eyes of society. And that made *him* a part of their heavenly rotation, too. They reflected what he was, just like moons sharing light from the sun.

He heard Eva's silent laugh. *Look at you. If you're so in love with all of us—with our "specialness"—why haven't you ever tried to be famous yourself?*

He blocked her out, not wanting to admit that maybe he was the moon and they were the sun. He didn't have the courage to do what they did, to find out if he would "make it" in their Above world.

You're avoiding all the hard questions again, she added.

Slowly, he turned back to Eva, wounded by her anger.

She cradled the boy's head. *Aside from everything else, you can't pretend Robby's never going to give you grief. I know him. I've worked with him. He's a troubled kid and what you've done to him is going to create a monster.*

I thought a companion—

A companion? Her eyes flared. *What're you going to do next? Try to turn my husband? Or maybe even my daughter someday?*

At the mention of Frank Madison, Benedikte steeled himself to take more punches.

Don't even think of touching anyone else I was close to, she continued. *Do you understand?*

Each word was another illusion shattered. Benedikte's vision fragmented until he felt like he was looking out of a cracked mirror.

What you saw wasn't always what you got. He'd always known that. So why was it killing him to admit it?

He reached out to her, but she moved away. The only closeness she allowed him was during her monthly infusions. That was all. He might never get anything more.

But he hoped. He couldn't stop.

Strangely, that hope heated up in the pit of his temper. It melted, twisted, shaped itself into hideous fury. He wanted to strike out in any way possible.

Maybe, he said, *down the road, your husband will find someone else, Eva. And maybe your* daughter *could love me if you can't.*

She flew up from her seat. Robby shrank into himself, his widened gaze raised to her.

"Don't ever threaten anyone I love," she said out loud, voice quivering. "I'll hurt you beyond comprehension without even a second thought."

Then, gathering Robby, she guided the boy away, never even looking back at Benedikte as she disappeared in the direction of her room.

Never even looking back.

In the chasm, the Elites and their pets enjoyed themselves, a sea of skin and blood undulating on the floor. Mouths on bellies, red and slick, fangs scraping over thighs. Legs parted, hips arched and rocking. A temple of pleasure.

Dispassionately, Benedikte watched them, Master of it all.

His body sank, even though he physically remained stiff postured in his chair. He seemed to leak out of the form that resembled Sorin, a puddle on the floor, dirtied and diseased.

For the past thirty years, he'd lived the high life with this emerging Underground, adding to the numbers of his precious Elites, watching Groupies come to exist, seeing to it that Sorin's Guard corps would be ready to defend them when and if the next blood brother attacked.

Yet it'd only taken a woman's smile to slay him.

From that point on, he died a daily death, wanting her. His hope started to wither, spiraling downward into a chasm of worthless wishes. Long nights, endless, empty . . .

Then, finally, over twenty eternal years later, everything changed.

One night, his television sparkled with a picture shown during an Eva Claremont entertainment special: Dawn Madison, all grown up.

Slowly, Benedikte sat up on his divan.

Hope stirring.

Resurrecting.

TWENTY-FOUR

The Bargain

THE oppression in the hidden room told Dawn it was late, but more rest wasn't an option. She'd already gotten enough to revitalize, even though she wouldn't say she was fully back to Xena fighting form yet.

Frank obviously didn't agree so much with getting a move on. He was leaning against the wall near the fireplace, messing around with the wire innards of an old radio that would've been right at home in the seventies. Apparently, it was one of Eva's "antiques" and he'd taken it upon himself to play Hero of Domestic Bliss by making the piece of junk work.

"Why haven't you been putting that kind of energy into devising some makeshift weapons?" Dawn was wandering around in search of anything she could use to bully Julia. "You could even be trying to yank that chain out of the wall."

"Why would I run off when you just got here?"

Hah-hah. "Because Wifey has you chained up? Some people might consider that a threat."

"It's a . . . what do you call it? Formality. It's Julia's idea more than Eva's, really. This Underground is obviously suspicious of me 'cos I worked with Limpet. Jonah ain't one of their favorite people. Eva asks me about him all the time."

Dawn remembered the mind probe Eva had put on *her* about The Voice. "She asks you about Jonah, or she mind screws you?"

Frank kept on working, never looking up, even though his rough complexion went ruddy. "She's fiddled with my head, but I can keep her out."

Training from Limpet.

It made Dawn wonder. . . . Had she inherited Frank's blocking abilities? Is that why she'd been a natural from the start?

"Anyway," she said, scanning the baseboards, "I'm glad to hear you're still on our side. I wasn't so sure."

Now her father glanced up from the radio, baffled.

She motioned to her neck, her chains chiming. Then she gestured to him. When Dawn had allowed Eva into the superficial areas of her mind, her mom had shown her that she could heal things like bites, among all her other talents, so Frank wouldn't have much of a mark right now.

Even so, exactly how powerful would Frank's kind of vamp be? Less than Eva, for sure, but more than a Groupie.

Clearly surprised, her dad put a hand over his jugular, almost like he was pressing a love letter into a secret book.

It explained a lot, even why he would betray Limpet and Associates, a group he'd supposedly been loyal to—as loyal as Kiko. And Breisi.

Dawn chuffed. "Do you think Breisi'll be just as understanding with you as you are with the wife? I mean, when she finds out you're Eva's vampire boy and all. . . ."

Dropping his hand from his neck, Frank went back to work. He had a look on his face that said he couldn't believe Dawn would think he'd ever give in so easily. That he would ever give up on Breisi.

Dawn didn't back off. "Did you exchange blood? Is Eva your poison of choice now?"

Without warning, he heaved the radio to the ground. It vomited parts, then rattled to stillness.

Father and daughter stared at each other, needing to say so much, yet . . . there was a line to be crossed here. She didn't want to know about her parents' private lives—what child did?—but it'd come to so much more than that now.

Didn't Frank know what he was doing?

Or *did* he know? Maybe Dawn had spent so much time distancing herself from him that he'd truly become the reformed, savvier man Breisi talked about.

Who the hell was he?

Who were *any* of them?

Their impasse cracked apart when the door opened. Julia entered first, holding her dart gun and aiming it at Dawn. Always the primary target.

Eva came in next, rosy-cheeked and dressed in a new flowy summer dress. The style was her signature—one that captured Frank, if his adoring gaze proved anything.

But the actress herself was anything but flowy. She actually seemed more nervous than ever. "There's something on the news. . . ." She trailed off, watching her family's faces. "Julia, I'd like to be alone with them."

The Servant left the room, but Dawn knew she'd be watching the monitors, guarding her lady.

As if to address that point, Eva said, "The cameras are off. This is family time." She jammed a lock of hair behind an ear. "I don't really want to be showing you this, but I . . . I just think I should. You're . . ." She fidgeted. "You're both involved in this situation."

She blew out a breath then picked up the remote from a slot on the side of the TV, pressing a button. It flashed on, warming up, clearing to a solid picture.

A tilted room. Someone was behind the camera, fumbling with it, trying to adjust the aim upright.

Based on the tweed upholstery and cheap wood paneling, Dawn guessed that they were seeing the inside of an old camper.

"Almost got the perfect frame," said an anonymous female's voice from the TV.

Now Eva talked as the camerawoman played with the focus some more. "It's a live feed from the new Vampire Killer. That's what the newscasters are saying."

Dawn stepped closer to the screen. "The murderer's a woman?" She turned to Eva. "Did you know we were investigating this?" Is that why she was showing it to them?

"As you're so fond of reminding me, *I'm* a vampire. I keep abreast of these things." Evasively, Eva looked at the TV again. "I don't know anything about technology, but she's managed a live broadcast. When this started, she said she's sharing her 'finale' with the world, that she's going to kill someone at the stroke of midnight—the demons' play hour."

One look at the clock on the TV—11:36—and Dawn wanted to punch something. Even if the only reason she'd been investigating this killer was because the solution might lead to Frank, she felt like she could've saved another woman's life.

Then déjà vu hit her. Wait. Tamsin Greene had broadcast her death on the Internet. Had the Vampire Killer taken inspiration from that? Death made public, a spectator sport . . .

My God. This was the killer's letter to the press, the ultimate performance to gain fame. She didn't even care if this got her caught. But punishment wouldn't exist for this person—not if she were in it just for long-lasting celebrity.

Isn't that what Matt Lonigan had hinted?

Frank's chains rattled as he moved away from the wall, closer to the TV and nearer to Dawn. "I don't wanna see this. It's like one of those terrorist beheading tapes."

The Eva-vamp put her hand over her mouth.

On the TV, the camera stabilized. "There," said the Vampire Killer. Then she turned the lens on the victim.

Even though the picture was clear, it took Dawn a few moments to comprehend it. And when she did, the floor seemed to veer. She grabbed on to Frank to stay standing.

He grabbed her, too.

There, in living color, sat a bound and duct tape–gagged Breisi, her bobbed hair splicing over one cheek like dark, open cuts. Although she was sweating, her gaze was steady.

She didn't want them to worry if they happened to be watching, Dawn thought. Nausea made her weak when she pictured the crime-scene photo that might come out of this.

Not another photo, God, no, not another one.

Dawn leaned against Frank, who held her tight.

Eva was watching them both, eyes round and fearful. She wanted to see just how much they cared, didn't she?

"I didn't know," she said pleadingly. "I didn't realize Breisi was the one—"

"Liar!" Dawn ground out. "This is probably a repeat of another broadcast that they're playing over and over, and you knew damned well it was Breisi."

Wrapping her arms over her chest, Eva stared at the floor. "I told you, this is a live feed. That wasn't a lie."

The Vampire Killer was talking again, still off camera. "Look what I caught—a genuine vampire hunter. And, wouldn't you know, I'm the Vampire Killer. But that doesn't mean I *murder* vampires. It means I'll *be* one. So . . . the more suspected hunters I can do away with now, the better life will be later. Understand?"

She took the camera and moved it up and down, making Breisi's entire bound body nod in pretend agreement.

Breisi merely flicked the killer a glance and that was it. Dawn had never been so proud of anyone: the way Breisi kept her cool, the confidence she displayed.

Hang in there, Breez, just until . . .

Hold up—was Breisi calm because she knew The Voice would finally come outside for this? He'd never let Breisi die. He and Kiko were probably already on their way to wherever she was, and thanks to Eva's faked calls from Dawn, they were no doubt wondering why their third hunter wasn't answering their summons. But they wouldn't have time to deal with that—not right now.

11:40.

Dawn began twisting her chain bracelet, like she could work her way out of it.

As the Vampire Killer started taunting her victim in earnest—prey teasing its failed hunter—Eva raised her head again, eyes on her family.

"If your friend is a slayer—if you're all slayers—this Vampire Killer might go after *you* next. This is what you would have to face if you went back out there."

"Thanks to you and your Underground," Dawn said.

"You really think I had some sort of hand in this?" It sounded like Eva was on the cusp of tears again. "You truly believe I could ever be a part of this perversity?"

A perversity? Didn't that describe *vampires* in the most basic language?

Instead of starting another useless argument, Dawn glanced up at Frank. His face was a mask of horror as he watched Breisi, but his eyes . . . His eyes were bloodshot, full of love, proving that he didn't fully belong to Eva.

"Do you see how much he loves her?" Dawn said to the vamp.

And that's when she saw a revelation on her mother's face: Eva yearned for Frank to close the book on his old life, and Breisi's death would do that, hopefully bringing him to her once and for all. *That*'s why she was showing them this broadcast, to let him know Breisi was truly out of the contest.

"You *want* her dead," Dawn said.

"No, I don't. I don't want this to happen at all." Eva stopped, shocked, as if realizing how much she did want it. But then she vehemently shook her head. "I hate what's happening!"

"Do you know that standing by and just watching—whether you want it to happen or not—makes *you* dead to me? As dead as you've been my whole life? Or . . . it's even worse, because now I know what kind of . . . person . . . you really are. You're nothing like the mom I always wanted." Dawn bent closer to Eva. "I wish I didn't have *any* part of you inside of me."

"Don't say that. . . ." Eva came forward to touch her daughter, just as she'd done when she was masquerading as Jac. Comfort from a false friend. It wasn't going to work this time.

Dawn dodged the vampire actress, near tears again.

"You and your Underground," she added. *"Dead."*

Eva raised her arms and wrapped them around her head, covering her ears. "Do you realize how much it hurts to hear you talk like that?" She was sobbing now.

Frank was still watching the TV, as if he could protect Breisi with just a look. Prayers were probably running through his head, blocking out his daughter and wife.

But as Dawn watched her mother cry, the little girl inside of her was weeping, too. *Mommy, I love you. I've idolized you so much that it hurts to know I'll never be as good as I thought you were. It hurts to know my perception of you was never real.*

Furiously, Eva sprang to the remote and pressed the TV off. The image of Breisi disappeared, retracting into the center of a blackened screen.

11:44.

Frank went stiff, sweat dampening his T-shirt against his skin. "Where is she, Eva?"

Taken aback, Dawn looked at both her parents. They were watching each other as if they were in one another's heads. It went beyond a "parent look." It was something much different. . . .

"Eva." Frank's body was visibly wobbling. "Tell me. If it's the last thing I ever ask, please tell me where Breisi is."

"You know I can't." There was a fear in her gaze. "The Master wants this. I can't risk disobeying him a—" She cut herself off.

Had she just about said "again"? What did that mean?

"And if you don't obey," Dawn said, "your punishment would be mortality—you'd get old, just like the rest of us, God forbid."

A greater level of terror filled Eva's eyes, but Dawn wasn't sure if it was because of her mom's ego or because Dawn was firing a round of hate bullets into her chest.

Frank fell to his knees in front of his wife, wrapping his arms around her legs and burying his face in her dress.

Now, Dawn felt the tears pushing at her. They weakened her more than all the physical crap she'd already suffered. "Mom . . ." She deliberately used the endearment. "If you can stop this from happening, please, tell us now. If you really, truly don't want this to happen, convince us by putting an end to it. Please."

But when Dawn reached out for her mother's hand, it was out of pure love. For Breisi.

Eva clung to the touch her daughter had finally allowed, resting a hand on Frank's head at the same time. Then she raised Dawn's fingers to her cheek, leaning against them and wetting Dawn's skin with tears.

"I know you have enough power to help," Dawn whispered.

Eva jerked, not looking at her daughter.

"And if you did it," Dawn said, encouraged, "you'd at least give us a chance to have some kind of relationship from now on."

"If I helped," Eva said, "you wouldn't fight me anymore?"

"I'd do anything." Even march into hell.

As Eva peered up, a decision balanced in her agonized gaze.

Stunned that it might possibly happen, Dawn watched her mom carefully, trying hard to summon what she had once thought was so good about Jac. She caught a flash of kindheartedness. Maybe it was just an illusion but it was something.

"I know how much you'd be risking," Dawn said, "but it'd be worth it. I'd know you were truly the mom I thought you'd be."

With a small yet air-shattering demolition, the scales of Eva's decision tipped.

Robbed of her defenses, Dawn kissed Eva's hand, holding her face there and breathing in the scent she'd always hoped a mother might have.

Eva was going to do it. Or was this just another way to draw them in and then crush them at their weakest?

11:46.

Eva clung to her, but even in their reunion, Dawn could feel a tautness, a torn guilt for betraying her vows.

"They don't know I have Frank," Eva said, referring to the Underground. "So if I told them your missing father suddenly barged in here to rescue you, it would sound real. I could say I wasn't here when it happened, and he overwhelmed Julia—"

"And he got back my weapons." Was she pushing her luck here? "Isn't that how it could've happened, Mom? Frank supposedly got back my weapons and he wheedled Breisi's location out of your Servant. But what about Julia—?"

"She's beholden to me. She's kept secrets before and she'll do it again." Eva looked like she was being dragged toward a stake to be burned. "There're ways of making her . . . forget . . . too. But remember, this doesn't mean I'm letting you go. Not you or Frank. The Master will believe anything I say, and nothing about our future has changed. In fact . . ."

As Eva's speech faded, Dawn could imagine her words.

In fact, what I'm doing for you now binds you to me.

She'd remember. "Where's Breisi?"

"An abandoned field in the woods over at—"

"You're taking us there," Frank said from his spot on the floor. "We're almost out of time."

The vampire seemed even more torn now.

"Please," Dawn said.

That was all it seemed to take. "I won't be there to help you. I could never get away with that."

11:47.

"Mom?"

Eva closed her eyes. "You have to know—the killer's broadcast to the public wasn't real. It was fed live into *my* TV, but it's also being taped so it can be sent later to Limpet, after the deed is done. Breisi's murder was never meant to be aired publicly, it was just a lure to get Jonah Limpet out of hiding."

More goddamned luring, but so what? Eva had just confirmed that Breisi was still alive.

"We need to move," Dawn said.

"Wait. You have to be prepared for Guards, even though they . . . Let's just say you're going to come out alive, okay? They're positioned around the area to make sure the killer has the opportunity to take out Breisi, and then to clean up after her before going back Underground."

"Just Guards? Why didn't you guys bring out your higher-level vamps?"

"This isn't the big stand, Dawn. Limpet isn't meant to see the broadcast until the murder's over. The Master wouldn't dare send the better vampires for this little errand, not unless he knew your protective spirits would be around. But he knows that won't happen—Breisi's Friend was already taken care of and Limpet wouldn't know where to send any others."

Dawn wished Jonah would've had the chance to save Breisi: he'd always told them that he would take over if they found a vampire lair. That made Dawn think he could deal with a bunch of pissed-off Guards in a blink.

But she knew there was no way Eva would allow Dawn to call him. She was taking enough of a risk already.

Eva continued. "This is all designed to provoke Jonah into showing himself and attacking the Underground—which he will when he finds Breisi's body."

Dawn held out her hands so Eva could take off her chains. Superhuman yanks on the steel links did the trick.

"Why was *your* broadcast live? Why not just tape Breisi's death for *us*, too?"

Eva looked at a loss, as if she realized how selfish she was going to sound. "I knew I'd have to obey the Master's whims. He wanted Dawn to see what could happen to a vampire hunter—it's part of making the Underground a more attractive option than staying with Jonah. But showing Dawn the broadcast wouldn't give away anything to Jonah, either: the Master doesn't want Limpet to know that he's the one behind Breisi's death—that's where the Vampire Killer takes the fall—but he knew Dawn wouldn't be able to tell Jonah anything because I have her. I couldn't get out of going along with this plan of his, so I ended up asking a favor from him instead. . . . I just wanted get my part over with." Eva went to Frank, deftly liberating him from his chains, too. "I couldn't sit here waiting for the murderer to finish. I wanted to move on and forget what was happening with the rest of them. And the Master liked that I want to forge ahead with life, so he agreed."

Incredible, but could Dawn blame her? All Eva wanted was to get Breisi out of the way, leaving the Madisons free to reunite. The sooner that happened for Eva, the better. Screw the big war, right?

"You're lucky you're his favorite," Dawn said, already at the door. Because if the Master found out what Eva was doing to win back her family's love, he'd probably go ballistic.

Eva undid the locks.

Frank was right behind them as they started up the stone stairs. "So why not give Jonah a live feed, too, and just get this big confrontation over with?"

"For the Underground to continue prospering in secrecy, the fight has to take place Below, where humans won't know about it. Besides, the Master's confident on his home turf. He just hasn't been sure that Jonah is a foe. All he wants is to bring him into hostile territory away from Above, where he doesn't have to worry about being caught by mortals."

As much as Dawn wanted more details . . . "Where's our stash?"

With one last indecisive look, Eva complied. The next minute was a blur as she headed for Julia while giving directions about where to find their weapons, including personal effects. They gathered them rapidly.

"Remember, I'm getting those back," Eva said before they rushed into the night.

While Dawn sprayed herself and Frank with garlic, it didn't escape her notice that he flinched, and that he seemed stronger out of his silver chains.

He'd tucked a revolver into a hip holster and slung a big leather man-purse over his burly chest. Just as Dawn was tempted to ask what was in it, she saw Eva pause, close her eyes as if in desperate prayer, then whoosh into Danger Form: heart-stoppingly celestial, a silver cloud of insidious beauty.

The vampire wrapped around her family, veiling and lifting them. It felt like a storm cloud had iced around Dawn, suspending her in numbness and differentiating what Eva was from a Friend or anything else in Dawn's studies. There was a muted humming, unsettling and primal, robbing her of most senses—touch, scent, awareness of time. And, before she could connect one thought to another, Eva had deposited them on the ground.

Her glow revealed that they were at the lip of a forest, in a deserted campsite. A burnt-out fire ring and the skeleton of a lounge chair were the only signs of life.

Eva hovered away from them, sublime and misty, her tendrils weaving in and out of her form as she gave them directions to the hidden camper.

"I'm coming back for you," she vowed, raising a tendril in the direction of the camper as if to complete one last mysterious task.

Dawn couldn't stop herself. "Or you could stay and help."

"I've done enough. The killer's transmission and recording have been interrupted. Go."

Then Eva cracked like lightning, rising, rushing off again, disappearing into the midnight sky.

Of course she wouldn't stay. She didn't want to take a risk that the Underground might hear about her participation. Hell, she'd already been foolhardy in using Danger Form here Above.

"Let's go." Frank had pulled out his revolver. It had a tiny light near the muzzle that he didn't even flick on.

Was it because his sight was already good in the dark?

Dawn took out her own nightlight, a headset that could fit into a jacket pocket. She geared up, readying her own revolver.

Then they darted into the woods, leaves crackling under their boots as her pulse thundered.

The camper was right where Eva said it'd be, its windows burning like night eyes amidst the trees.

Outside the door, Frank held up his revolver, waiting for Dawn to assume position on the other side.

The trees shook, and a *screech* rocked the air. Red-eyes.

Dawn raised her revolver.

With a heave, Frank opened the door and jumped up into the vehicle, Dawn following and aiming around for the killer.

"Breisi!" she heard him say, and she whipped around, targeting, targeting . . .

Frank had rushed toward his bound girlfriend, past the waiting camera, making a desperate dive for her.

But Dawn was far enough away to get perspective: Breisi's tied, stomping feet, her widened eyes trained on something in back of Dawn—

When she whirled around, something pierced her jacketed arm, and the world electrified, plunging her to the floor in spasms and making her drop the revolver.

Above her, she could barely make out Cassie Tomlinson, head bare, sharp fangs decorating a razored smile as she held a Taser in one hand and brandished a knife at Dawn with the other.

TWENTY-FIVE

The Last Victim

As Dawn writhed, Cassie turned off the Taser and yelled at Frank. "Drop your gun, sit down, keep your hands up!"

Dawn heaved for breath, nerve endings fried. No energy. It felt like her body had been used as a baseball bat against a metal pole, but twenty times worse. And even looking at Cassie through half-lidded eyes reminded Dawn of a film-school trick shot Hitchcock might've used—a solitary figure with the world spinning around her. Vertigo.

"If any of you move," Cassie said around her fangs, "I'll filet this girl."

She bent, positioning the knife blade near Dawn's throat.

Fighting to focus, Dawn saw enough to know that Cassie, Lee's sister and the woman they'd interviewed back at the Adventure Motel, was gone. What was left was a horror show.

No more hippie scarf or cornrowed hair. Wig, Dawn thought, seeing the camper lights gleam off the woman's bald head. Generic jumpsuit, like a maintenance worker's, covering her body. Latex gloves. Fangs.

At Dawn's perusal, Cassie's mouth stretched into a smile, fangs sparkling just like her threatening knife.

A thud on the roof shook the trailer. Then another. Another, another, another.

Guards.

From Dawn's angle, she could barely see Frank because a table blocked his upper face but, next to him, the bound and duct-taped Breisi was in full view as she stared at Cassie, eyes wider now with something like growing dread. Frank had his hands in the air, his revolver on the floor.

"There's my protection," Cassie said. "All I have to do is tell them to come into my family's RV if there's trouble. And you guys are."

"Inviting the Guards in would stop your broadcast," Frank said, making Dawn wonder if Eva had prepared him for what the hell a Guard even was.

Breisi glanced at Frank. Her heart was in her eyes.

"Don't invite them in," Frank repeated.

Dawn could tell he was leveling Cassie with a steady gaze, but, from here, she couldn't see his eyes directly.

For some reason, she had a bad feeling about this.

"You don't have to prove anything to Lee," Frank added.

At those words, Cassie startled, her knife a little less poised now. But that was nothing next to the shock Dawn felt. It was like she'd been Tasered again.

How would Frank know anything about Lee and Cassie?

Training, she thought. *Jonah gave him training for months.*

Or was he mind screwing, like a . . . ?

The notion was too terrifying, too impossible.

Cassie stared back at Frank, as if enthralled. "My brother thinks I'm a nothing. He's wrong, *the*—"

"*The* Lee is wrong," Frank finished. When he continued, he wasn't addressing Cassie; he was talking to Dawn and Breisi and, weirdly, he was using Cassie's more educated speech cadence.

"That's what all the kids called Lee. *The* Lee, because he thought he was special. And when he went off to Hollywood to prove it, Cassie was afraid he would succeed. She hated him more than ever because he would become a star and she would never have what it takes to make it."

God, Frank *was* inside of Cassie's head.

Shivers traveled under Dawn's skin, bringing her to, reminding her to detach the Taser probes from her jacket. Carefully. One false move and Cassie might come out of it.

"Almost all of the family was starstruck," Frank continued. "Cassie had dreams of acting, just like Marg and Lee. But Lane, their older brother, was too levelheaded. He took care of everything after Dad died, so he didn't have time for movies and idle goals. But if there was one thing they all knew, it was that Lee was going to be famous one day. And that meant he'd lord it over them even more than usual."

Footsteps pounded the roof. Red-eyes. Emphatic thumps made Dawn imagine their barbed tails, beating time in the night.

Screeeech!

Dawn braced herself for Cassie to snap to attention, but the Vampire Killer didn't remove her gaze from Frank's.

He paused. "I don't know why Lee killed Klara Monaghan. The Tomlinsons just knew that he was heavily involved with something secret, but he wouldn't tell them what it was. It could've been Sasha he was hiding."

Shit, another dead end. The Underground did a hell of a job covering their tracks.

Dawn saw her revolver near Cassie's feet, about a yard away. It seemed like a mile. Should she use that or a different weapon to take the killer out? Dawn had gotten her sharp silver necklace back from Eva—could she slip *that* off and plunge it into Cassie's neck before the girl had a chance to call the Guards?

Deciding that she'd rather be safe than sorry, Dawn began to inch toward the revolver, knowing this was her best chance to silence the human Vampire Killer by shooting Cassie in the throat to damage her vocal cords, then quickly in the heart.

As Dawn crept her hand over the floor, her lighted headset slipped off, already loose from her fall.

"The last straw," Frank continued, "was when Lee the murderer became more famous than any of them ever anticipated. Every time he was on TV, it was hell, it was all of his bragging coming true. Even from jail he was superior. *The* Lee. And soon after the family arrived in town, they each had a chance to talk with him alone. When it was Cassie's turn, he looked right at her and reminded her about all those nights"—Frank wrestled in a breath—"all those *nights*. He told her how he'd start them up again after he got out of jail because he was going to get away with *Klara's* crime, and that meant he'd be able to get away with doing anything—especially with a nobody.

"Cassie lost it. She was a *somebody*, and she wanted to show *the* Lee she was stronger than that, to mess him up just as much as he'd messed up her. Most of all, she wanted to prove she was a person—a special one—just like him and she was worthy of more than being his inferior.

"So, on the sly, she planned everything, watched all the TV shows about murder, read about how to get away with it on the Internet, spent hours with books like *Crime and Punishment* to see what she had to do, how to act. She knew about trace evidence and, since she was smarter than *the* Lee, her first time went off without a hitch. She shaved her head and hid the deception with a wig and a scarf—a new style for a new state, she told her family. For her victims, she picked women because, realistically, they were the only ones she could physically overcome with the help of one thing: surprise.

These were symbolic victims—at first they were just used to prove a point to Lee. But that's before she got to like the blood. . . ."

Dawn held her breath, inches away from the revolver. But when Cassie leaned slightly toward Frank, Dawn paused.

"After finding them in the ValuShoppe parking lot," Frank continued, "Cassie would follow the women around to find out their schedules. Then she'd ambush them in their homes—all she had to do was pick locks and be careful about being seen. Then she'd slit their throats before they could defend themselves."

Frank was breathing harder now. "*She* was the real Vampire Killer, not *the* Lee. She was going to take the spotlight away from him by being more successful, racking up more numbers. After Jessica's murder, it was easy to take any lingering evidence like the dresses and dry cleaning bags from the closet. She burned those things, plus her own clothing, in a homeless person's bonfire near the motel. Cassie could finally use *her* acting skills, too, by pretending she was one of them and that she just wanted a warm fire."

He hesitated, then seemed to be overtaken, words rushing out, harder, more jagged. "Cassie wanted to dominate *the* Lee like he dominated her—*thrust, thrust*—she hated him, but she loved him, and maybe by imitating his murders she could also keep him safe from conviction, mislead the jury. . . . Oh, he'll owe her big if she saves him and *then* who'll be the superior—?"

Bang, bang on the roof. *Screee-ch!*

Dawn stretched toward the revolver again. . . .

"Dear God." Frank was still enthralling Cassie, but it looked like he was trying to pull away. "What Lee did—"

Closer, closer . . .

"—to her . . . Marg would turn her back on them when *the* Lee would creep into the room at night. She knew—she had to know. He'd get into bed and tell Cassie not to make a sound. He was the superior, she was nothing."

Frank jerked back in his seat, but Dawn already had her weapon. It weighed in her hand as she aimed it.

Groaning awake, Cassie blinked, then saw Dawn. Frank's connection had been severed with his shock at what he'd seen in her mind.

With a cry, the killer raised her knife, face arranged in a fanged grimace.

"I'm Somebody!" she screamed, the blade coming down.

Dawn rolled away just in time for Cassie to stab the floor. Frank bolted up from his seat.

Shoot her before she can—

"Get in here!" Cassie screamed in invitation to the Guards as she sprang to her feet.

Bang!

Knife tumbling from her grip, the pseudo-vamp flew backward, hitting a paneled wall and slumping to the floor, her chest smoking from Frank's bullet.

Then it began.

First it was the roof, moaning as it was torn off like the lid of a can, exposing them all to the night sky.

One pair of red eyes in a pale face peeked in.

Dawn had imagined this so many times before that she should've been more afraid. But fear wasn't what was driving her now. It was so much more—something hella more dangerous.

Erecting a mind block, Dawn stared down a red-eye, adrenaline escalating her heartbeat. Lifting her revolver, she got ready to target the heart with her silver bullets, but anywhere else would at least slow these clowns down. Ready, aim—

Three walls went flying to the elements, whizzing into the night. It left just the cab, with its weak light underscoring the horror.

The Guards descended.

Five of them. Five freakin' maniacs with pale bald heads, burning eyes, iron fang teeth, and black clothing belled out like death's wings.

One zoomed toward Dawn, claws outstretched.

Calmly, she squeezed the trigger. The Guard jerked backward, abruptly vacuuming into itself, its clothing falling to the ground and puffing to a quick, disappearing burn.

Four.

Panting, Dawn crawled to a better position, limbs liquid. She noticed Breisi trying to maneuver her arms from behind her back down to her feet, where she leveraged her sneakers against the rope to get the binding off.

Dawn couldn't help her. She had just enough presence of mind to notice that Frank had taken down another Guard in midflight before the last three crashed to the trailer's floor, shaking it. They rose in their stop-motion heartbeat rhythm—*ba-ba-boomp, ba-ba-boomp*—and leveled their red eyes on the team.

We could be fucked, she thought, pushing off of the floor.

One of the vamps flashed out its long tail, accidentally catching Dawn's weapon as it went for Frank's gun. Her revolver flitted to the ground. The Guard slammed away her dad's weapon, too, spinning it over to one of its partners.

The other red-eye opened its jaws, catching the revolver between its iron teeth, then crunching the weapon to debris.

So fucked.

For some reason, the three Guards didn't flick open their machete tails, and Dawn couldn't say she missed the show of steel-edged blooms. Instead, the red-eyes merely tracked her and Frank with their gazes. The one nearest Dawn tilted its head as if it recognized her. Didn't they all by now?

Not giving up, she dove for her revolver, grasping it.

A red-eye spit at her hand, and she instinctively flinched from what she knew would burn.

On her belly, she just stared at her abandoned weapon—so close.

Wasting no time, she started to reach for a crucifix in her jacket but a second blob of flying spit changed her mind. It barely missed her, too.

"What're they doing?" she asked, hoping her dad was aware enough to answer.

While the Guards waved their tails in Frank's face and hissed, her dad stood with his hands up in surrender again.

"Maybe they're thinking of all the fun ways they could use our bodies for Play-Doh?" he muttered.

Breisi moaned against her duct tape, wiggling around as if she knew the answer. She probably did, the brain.

"Eva," Dawn said. "She wouldn't have brought us if she knew the Guards might kill us. And if we're captured? No problem. She wants us Underground anyway. Maybe these red-eyes have been instructed not to ever harm the family of Little Miss Master's Favorite."

Frank laughed harshly. "I'll be damned if we get taken."

Something awful occurred to Dawn. "If we're protected, then what about . . ."

She glanced at Breisi. At the same exact time, Frank seemed to realize the danger his girlfriend was in, too.

He reached into his man-purse and pulled out another gun, but this one was longer, the nozzle flared. What the—?

He pulled the trigger. Fire scorched out of it, consuming the Guard nearest to him in one swallow.

Dawn and Breisi both hurled themselves away, taking shelter behind seats and fallen tables as the Guard screeched and flailed, running, going nowhere but the dirt as it dove off the side of the camper.

With a sick sucking sound, it moaned into a charred memory.

As a seat caught on fire, one Guard yelped away from the flames, using its machete tail to slash the conflagration off the camper.

Meanwhile, the third one attacked Frank, and Dawn reached into her pocket, whipped the velvet cover off her throwing stars, grasped one and used the motion of her body and wrist to flick it outward. The holy-water-covered silver blade swooped through the air, embedding itself into the red-eye's neck.

At the same time, Frank aimed his weapon at the other Guard—the fire scaredy-cat. The ticked-off freak easily cuffed the gun away from her dad, then wrapped its tail around him.

Concentrating, Dawn flicked another blade at her own red-eyed attacker, grunting as it swicked into the Guard's temple.

Slowly, it reached up to the wound in its neck, then its head. It bared its iron fangs. Shook its head.

Y-ah. Dawn grasped another star.

But then the Guard went stiff, dropping to its knees and banging face-first to the floor.

Convulsing, its head smacked the ground over and over again until its forehead turned to mash.

One sucking instant later, it was air, a victim of the silver plus the holy-water poison.

That *really* pleased Frank's Guard. It got feisty, opening up its tail to full extension, the blades coming just inches from Frank's surprised face as it raised him aloft.

Whick, whick, whick.

Blade after blade, it revealed a bouquet of machetes, screeching, body flickering with its *ba-ba-bomp* movements.

As the creature fixed on Dawn, she grabbed her revolver from the floor, targeting the heart.

In defiance, it lifted up both hands—*throw down, bitch!*—and basically unwrapped, then flicked, Frank out of its tail.

Right away, her dad jumped toward Breisi, then whisked her into his arms, holding her as if she was all that existed for the quickest, longest moment he could probably manage. He put his face against her hair, and she pressed against him.

Then he prepared to jump to the ground with her.

Dawn should've known it was too easy.

A hurricane seemed to fly down from the black sky, crying bloody murder.

Eva?

The silver-misted vampire flashed wispy tentacles, a heavenly storm of violence. Without preamble, a million strands seemed to wrap around the last Guard's neck, lifting him as high as a sacrifice before he could threaten Dawn anymore.

In the face of Eva's power, the creature opened its mouth, not in fear, but in . . . loving awe.

Then, with powerful thrusts in every possible direction, Eva tore the lesser vampire apart, its body scattering, meat hitting tree trunks with vulgar splats.

"Mom?" Dawn cried. "Mom!"

She'd come back. Why? Who cared—she was *here* and she was helping them!

The little girl in her danced around, squealing.

But when Eva twirled toward Frank, pushing him from Breisi and tossing her to the dirt outside, Dawn's little girl died.

"What're you doing?" she screamed, looking to see that Breisi was okay. She was, already working frantically to unbind herself again.

Eva floated, wisps of sparkling glamour mingling in her silver death-angel form. "We're going back now," she said in a shudder-inducing tone.

Dawn opened her mouth to ask if Breisi was coming, too, but by then it was too late.

In all the excitement, nobody had seen what Cassie was up to: they hadn't noticed that she'd tumbled off the camper during the commotion, that she'd somehow salvaged the camera—which had probably flown off the trailer's platform during the fight.

Then—chest wound or not—she'd crawled from beneath the camper and over to Breisi, still intent on finishing her finale and becoming a star.

Frank was the first to see what was happening. *"Breisi!"*

Eva's light illuminated it all: the camera's passive gaze while it sat where Cassie had put it on its bent stand, the knife blade flashing as Cassie darted over to Breisi and pinned the still-bound victim to her back with one arm and a leg.

All Dawn could think to do was yell to the most powerful being in their midst—her mother, the woman who'd been perfect in Dawn's dreams.

"Mom?!" she screamed.

She was begging, and when Eva's form shifted, just like a bed of stars colliding into each other, Dawn knew her mother realized it: she knew how much Breisi meant to both Dawn and Frank, and it disturbed her.

I just want my family, the actress had told Dawn. . . .

Eva loomed, refusing to engage.

On a choke of disbelief, Dawn started to get up, to go to Breisi herself. Frank frantically dug in his satchel for a weapon. . . .

But Cassie's knife was already slicing down, aimed at Breisi's throat. The start of the Vampire Killer ritual. After that, she'd use her fake fangs to rip into Breisi's neck . . . it all had to be played out for the camera. . . .

Stop!

At Dawn's mind-blasting rage, the cab of the trailer burst apart, wires sparking and buzzing. At the same time, in a boom of heat and speed, Eva tardily zoomed forward at Cassie, as if to put on a show of caring.

But the Vampire Killer had already lifted a blood-edged blade toward the lens, her fangs shining like white sacrificial knives as she assumed a profane swan-song pose for the camera.

Viciously, Eva stabbed Cassie with her multitude of tendrils, lifting the killer high above, then smashing her to the ground, reducing her to paste.

Vision blurred, Dawn sprinted forward, slicing past her mom to where Breisi lay jerking, bathed in Eva's light.

There was . . .

Dawn couldn't believe there was a wound. Flailing, she pressed her hands to it, tears and shock making it impossible to say anything. In her friend's . . . her surrogate's . . . eyes, Dawn saw utter confusion.

Where was Jonah? Breisi seemed to be asking. *Wasn't he supposed to save me?*

Frank stumbled over, frantically trying to help Dawn staunch the bleeding.

"Oh, no . . . no . . . I couldn't get a shot off in . . ." He burst into sobs, touching his girlfriend's face. "Don't die, don't die. . . ."

Breisi's eyes got duller. *Jonah?*

Even though it wasn't right to blame him—how could he have been here in time?—Dawn did. She blamed him for this. And Eva . . . goddamn her, Eva, most of all because she hadn't stopped it.

Even worse, Dawn hadn't been able to stop any of it, either.

In the near distance, the wail of a siren pierced her hearing, but she didn't know what it meant. Didn't know what any of it meant.

The lights in Breisi's eyes dimmed as she jerked and stared at Dawn. Affection. Sisterhood. So many chances missed.

"Don't go," Frank yelled, "God, don't go! I love you, Breisi—" He turned to Eva. "Save her, Eva! You can heal her!"

The sirens got louder.

Eva's light was waning, her voice soft. "This injury would take a long time to heal—it's so deep I don't know if anyone but the Master could even help with it. . . ."

Sirens . . . closer . . .

Frank raised his face, his eyes crazed. "Try!"

On what sounded like the pulse of a sob, Eva swirled her mist around him, maybe to comfort him, maybe to take him back.

Breisi's irises had been taken over by her black pupils. She choked one more time, then stopped spasming.

Instead of a baffled tint of horror in her eyes, Dawn saw something else. An . . . answer?

Under the duct tape on her mouth, Breisi smiled, her head falling to the side.

No. Dawn shook her head, throat hot and tight. No, this wasn't happening—

Sirens . . .

Then the smell of jasmine.

A blanket of mingled screams swept down from the trees, surrounding Dawn in protection, wrapping her in a womb.

Dawn tried to tell them, *Keep the cops away so Eva can heal Breisi!* but she couldn't form words.

The sirens blasted, right outside the trees.

With a silvery blast, Eva barged up against the Friends to get to Dawn, but the vampire couldn't get past their spirit shelter.

Then, wasting no more time, Eva's form enveloped Breisi's body, sweeping it into an embrace along with Frank, who pushed at the cloudy walls like a prisoner, mouth open in what Dawn thought was her name.

They zipped away, over the trees.

"*Go, go* . . ." It was the Friends, nudging Dawn away from the blood-soaked dirt where Breisi had just lain.

Hazily, Dawn stumbled away with their help, crashing through the trees just before the sirens wailed to a stop behind them.

Why had Eva taken Breisi? She couldn't heal her. So *why?*

It was as if the Friends were holding her up, pushing her along as branches slapped her face, forcing her into seclusion and never letting her rest until she got to a main road where she found a convenience store. Before going inside, they pushed her toward a washroom where she barely remembered straightening herself up. Then, numbly, she used the ATM, then a pay phone, which allowed her to get a taxi.

All the while, something was embossing itself in Dawn's vision, hissing over Eva's old crime-scene photo.

Breisi's own death pose, eyes staring up at Dawn and asking how this could have happened.

TWENTY-SIX

THE GO-TO

Dawn couldn't do much. But vague instinct told her that she needed to do *something* before the Friends escorted her back to the Limpet house: she was pretty much a fugitive who'd flown a crime scene. She had to get as much done as possible now in case she was called in for questioning by the cops.

Maybe the Friends felt sorry for her, this deadened girl who was only just now beginning to operate normally as she shakily drove to Beachwood Drive. Or maybe Dawn had more power than she was aware of over the ghosts trailing her car and they had no choice but to follow her wishes.

After the carnage, she'd caught the taxi. Luckily, the driver had cared more about some gossip he'd picked up at the store than his passenger. Had she heard about the strange lights reported around the area by campers? Probably UFOs. There'd also been gunshots— no doubt rednecks who wanted to scare off those aliens—so the cops had gone out to the location, where they'd set up some sort of secret investigation already.

Dawn knew they'd found a real crime scene, too, filled with Cassie's oatmealed body and a camera that'd recorded everything. Would a vampire video surface somewhere soon?

Then she recalled something about an interrupted transmission by Eva. . . .

Yes, Eva, and all Dawn wanted to do was catch up with Breisi's *real* killer. Eva. And then there was this Master. . . .

Right. What was she going to do with him? Throw down with this even more powerful vampire? *How?*

That's where plan B came in. After the taxi ride to Jac . . . Eva's, where she'd picked up her car, Dawn had used another pay phone to call the man who'd suddenly moved down on her list of those to avoid.

Matt Lonigan.

Sounding very surprised and even relieved that she'd contacted him, he told her he was home if she needed him.

And she did need, but not in the usual way.

As Dawn walked up his drive, most of the Friends surrounded her. A few had already gone straight to Limpet's.

"Daaaa-aawn?" one of them asked while she knocked on the door. *"Too late . . . we were . . . too late . . . he didn't know. . . . "*

They'd been telling her that off and on, apologizing, hinting that they'd been out searching for Dawn all over the county. Due to Eva's impulsive activities, they'd been able to finally lock onto her location but hadn't arrived in time.

No explanation mattered. All Dawn could see was Breisi choking on her own blood.

Matt answered the door on the second knock. The sight of his bruised everyman looks got to her, but she shut him out. If there was one thing she'd learned, it was that emotion was useless, that sex wasn't going to solve anything.

"How much is your fee to hunt down vampires?" she asked, voice flatlined.

His forehead furrowed, but he opened the door. She stepped through, past him, back turned so she wouldn't trip over his troubled pale gaze and talk herself back into feeling again.

She came to the front window and stared out of it, her hand rubbing her aching right arm. Outside, the bird-of-paradise plants lurked in the darkness, leaves scratching the panes in small bursts of dying color.

"I thought you'd want to talk about the Vampire Killer, Dawn, but it sounds like you've got something else in mind."

She could feel Matt behind her, probably unsure of how close he should get.

"First, I'll tell you why I'm *not* here. We're not going to talk about what happened the other night with Eva Claremont's dress. We're never going to mention that again. I just need your help to hunt down some problem vamps."

She remembered how Frank had read Cassie, how he'd touched his neck. Maybe he'd end up being one of her enemies, too, but right now, Eva was the biggest one. Eva and her master.

She could hear Matt breathe out a deep huff behind her. "I thought you had all the help you needed with Limpet."

"If what Jonah Limpet offers is help, I'd hate to see the opposite." After all, he'd put Breisi in the position to die tonight by hoarding information, by even *having* this mission to find an Underground.

Dawn needed to know that she had backup if Jonah wasn't going to be there to support her own vendetta. That's where Matt was coming in.

Something flashed by the window—not quite there, but there all the same. A Friend on watch. Were they keeping tabs on how much Dawn said to Matt?

In back of her, he moved forward. "Dawn—"

She spun around, anticipating his touch on her shoulder. Left arm up, she attempted to block him, but instead accidentally caught his skin with her nails. He jerked his hand back, then wonderingly looked at the scratches she'd left.

"I'm sorry," she said, voice gritty, "but this is business. Just . . . business."

And that's all it'd ever be.

His jaw clenched as he glared at the kitchen floor and planted his hands on his hips. The scratch was nothing to him, but she'd set him off by striking.

"I want to hire you to back me up, Matt. How much do you charge?"

"Too much." He looked at her from beneath a lowered brow. "Why don't you just tell me what's going on and then we'll talk about what happened with the Vampire Killer?"

"I'm not being a drama queen, if that's what you're getting at. My friend just got her throat cut open and—"

It felt like blades were slashing into her on all sides, and Dawn raised her arms to shield her face, to hide from Matt as she sank to her knees.

Breisi.

Dawn could still feel the slickness of blood under her palm, the futile pumping in Breisi's neck as she fought to stay alive.

"She killed her," Dawn said, emerging tears warping her voice. "Breisi died, and then the Vampire Killer . . ."

She trailed off. The real killer was Eva, because she'd only made a token effort to "save" Breisi, but she hadn't wanted to—and that hesitation had made all the difference. Now, the only person Dawn could take at face value was dead.

"Who killed who . . . ?" Matt got down on his knees, too. "You found the Vampire Killer? I saw what was on TV."

Something gnawed at Dawn about what he'd just said, but it

was beyond her. Instead, she uncovered her face, airing her rage as she struggled for a breath to help her stop crying. Her face was wet, exposed.

"I'm going to cut her in two." Eva . . . she was going to kill *Eva*. "And all her vamp buddies. Then I'm going to take care of . . ."

Jonah.

Horrified, she halted before she could say his name. Why couldn't she go on? Was all her training making her refuse to tell Matt about her boss? Or was it the soreness around her heart, a deep wound caused by his failure to save Breisi?

Or was it . . . shaken affection?

The realization shook her. Affection? She was going to make him pay, too. Breisi deserved better than to die because of Jonah's damned causes.

Matt was leaning forward by now, his gaze wide, as if he was a mercenary staring at glistening gold. "You're going to do what, Dawn? *What?*"

Chest tight, she allowed herself to breathe. To hesitate and think about what she was doing for once.

She licked her dry lips. "I'm going to find out why this happened." Why Jonah had *let* it happen.

Yes. That made much more sense. Maybe she shouldn't be here at all right now.

"You're going to cut the Vampire Killer in two? Didn't you already say she's dead?" Matt was shaking his head, reaching out to her but knowing better not to touch. "I have no idea what you're talking about. Can you explain everything to me? Now, *who* died?"

"Breisi." The name was a coiled tightness in her throat.

"I'm sorry, Dawn. I'm so sorry."

He made as if to touch her again, but she jerked back. One sear of his skin against hers and it was over. She'd melt into him and dilute her hate. Dawn didn't want that because the hate felt too good, too just.

"Don't be sorry," she said, "just hunt with me."

His hands looked useless from the way he held them. "I want to help, but I'm still not sure what you're asking me to do. I need you to tell me everything. I won't go out there unarmed with a lack of information."

Her mind locked up. She wanted to argue that he should tell *her* everything, too, but it'd be fruitless. She was the one who needed his aid.

There was a gusting whoosh outside, a chop of wind. Matt fixed a glance on the window.

"The more you reveal," he said, "the better off we'll be."

A prickle of unease stole over her. He sounded too demanding.

"Dawn?" he asked.

At that moment, she knew how stupid she was being. Coming here had been a strike against Jonah, a screw-you caused by the shock of Breisi's death.

Or was she finally in the right place?

She stood, cuffing at the sticky tears, wanting to erase them. She needed to think some more, needed to get away.

"I've got to take care of something first."

"Don't go." He seemed eager, rising to stand beside her. "Just talk to me. Don't allow Limpet to control you. He's done enough damage. Trust me."

Eva's dress floated past her mind's eye, flowered poison.

She held up her hands, getting it together. "I'll come back."

And she would. God help her, being around him was sending off flares of need under her skin; she didn't know how long she could keep herself off him in this moment of desperation. She wanted to feel life because death had struck her such a blow. She wanted to know that there was still some good around.

But . . . no. Not with Matt. He was Eva's. How many times did she have to remind herself of that?

"I'll call." She rushed toward his door.

He reached out for her again, but she yanked her arm away, sending him a hurt glare.

It was enough.

He turned around, his broad back to her as she left.

Shaken, she shut the door behind her and took a deep fill of oxygen. What had she almost done?

As the Friends surrounded her on the walk back to her car, her doubts set in again.

Should she have talked to Matt? Or was Jonah really on the right side? There wasn't anyone to turn to now. . . .

Dawn got into her car, starting it. She had to ask The Voice, once and for all, what the hell was happening.

And if he wouldn't answer, that's when she'd know what to do.

İNSİDE Matt Lonigan's house, the "private investigator" turned away from the window as Dawn's taillights streamed into the distance, disappearing from view like the extinguishing of red eyes in the night.

Glancing at the back of his hand, he inspected the blood-thick scratches she'd given him during their spat, but even if she'd been angry, he knew she'd be back again. Dawn was caught between the Scylla and Charybdis, and she needed him.

He walked to the bolted door, removing the basketball backboard before unlocking it and opening the entrance. Welcome darkness. The scent of dank comfort. He stepped inside, shutting the door behind him and securing it. While climbing down the stairs, his boot steps echoed against the tunnel walls.

The walk was a long, subterranean stroll. His form tingled, reacting to the nearing proximity of his home, shifting degree by degree. The scratches Dawn had given him healed because he willed them gone. In fact, whenever he was in Matt's body Above, he could choose to delay any patch-up work, just to seem more human—prone to injury. He could also be seen on film, in mirrors. He could slow vitals on others, too.

Step by step, his shape quivered, the illusion of clothes seeping into his core, his features disappearing into the vaporous blur he preferred most times.

But when he arrived at a holding chamber, he shifted back into the body he'd been doubling Above. On second thought, he wasn't quite ready for his fun to end yet.

Scratching at the rock, Benedikte—also known as "Matt"— waited for the door to open.

Inside the holding room, the real Matt Lonigan turned away from Tamsin Greene, holding her jeweled fingers in his cupped hand. He was being entertained by the Elite while waiting to switch off with Benedikte and go back Above to do his own Servant work.

"Done already?" Tamsin asked as Matt let go of her.

The Master nodded. "Sounds like there were some snags, but the most important parts were taken care of. Breisi Montoya and the Vampire Killer have been reported dead."

He gestured for Tamsin to leave, knowing her Underground vows would keep her from spreading news about these activities to the lower vampires.

With one last saucy glance at the human Matt, she pulled her sheer, filmy white peignoir around her and exited.

The Servant saluted his master, never losing any of his affable ease. "You *were* quick this time."

"I had to get back—all this nonsense about the Guards not return-ing from their watch duty is causing concern. The Vampire Killer's camera transmission hasn't helped to clear up what's going on, either, since we couldn't see anything that happened after it cut out."

Benedikte knew why the broadcast had been sliced short. Ear-lier, after Dawn had surprised "Matt"—the Master—on the phone, he'd contacted the Underground to see why she was out of Eva's care. Interestingly enough, a breathless Eva herself had just come

Underground and revealed a wild story to Sorin: it seemed that Frank Madison had rescued Dawn, then had gotten wind of the whole plan and taken his hunter daughter with him out to the woods in order to save his coworker Breisi. The fighters had no doubt been the reason for the Vampire Killer's transmission interruption.

Luckily for the Underground, Frank and Dawn had ended up playing right into the most important parts of the plan.

Across the room, human Matt was putting on his long coat. He was a PI who'd been lured to the Underground nearly a decade ago—one of their most loyal Servants, always cooperating to the fullest. That's why it'd been so natural for the Master to double him.

"So everything's in place?" the human asked.

"Seems so. Breisi Montoya, Limpet's best fighter, is gone. Kiko Daniels, their psychic, has mental powers no decent team would depend on at this point, and he's physically unable to stand against us. Many of their spirits are neutralized, too, because now that we know how to captivate Limpet's main resource, his little army is nothing."

"So Limpet's all alone now," Matt said.

"Almost." Something inside of Benedikte throbbed—a craving, a wounding hunger. "You'd probably agree that Dawn is the wild card, but I can tell you that she's primed to come to our side."

"All ours." The PI smiled.

The Master's hackles rose. "Not quite."

The Servant obviously knew what that meant. Dawn didn't belong to human Matt at all. In fact, he'd never even come face-to-face with her. Bringing her Underground—and using her to take down Limpet—had been the plan all along, ever since they'd heard she was back in Hollywood.

"Let Limpet attack now," Benedikte added. "We'll be ready for any ineffectual attempts."

"Congratulations." Matt reached out to shake hands, but pulled back when he realized it was too familiar. "We're almost done with the enemy. Pretty soon, it'll be back to good times."

Benedikte accepted the handshake anyway. "Now, I need you to go Above and fetch Charity Flynn, otherwise known as Amanda Grace. We're gathering all Elites, and she might need an escort to tear her away from her big premiere tonight."

"Got it."

The Master went on to brief the Servant as much as he could since the PI needed to know every interaction with Dawn so the masquerade would be complete, in case he ever *did* run into Dawn himself. He even went so far as to strike the stalwart human with wounds that matched the ones Dawn had inflicted on Benedikte. Then Matt took his leave.

Like Tamsin, he cast one last look back, bemusement clearly written all over his face.

It must've been strange to see your own body doubled—a walking, talking mirror reflection in life's funhouse.

And that's what existence had indeed become since Dawn Madison had arrived—bright, intriguing, and hopeful.

Within minutes, the real Matt finally left to return to his home Above, where he'd take up where the "other Matt" had left off, discretely going about life as usual in his regular job at the private investigation firm. He'd never been hired by any "mysterious client" to find Frank Madison—that had only been the Master's ruse to get close to Dawn. A good ruse. And Matt also wasn't a vampire hunter, as she clearly suspected. But there were a couple of truths to the charade: the real Matt's parents *had* been murdered, even though Servants had gone on the Internet and planted news stories to dramatize the circumstances. Using Bruce Wayne's mythology as a backstory had been too tempting for Benedikte to resist, but everyone Above had worked with that.

Alone now, the Master took a moment to compose himself. Preparation, the actors called it. Finally, he'd become one of them, no longer a coward who didn't want to see if he had what it took to "make it." With this body he'd assumed for Dawn's sake, he was performing the most award-worthy role in existence.

Eva would be proud.

He left the room, closing it up, then continued his tunnel walk toward the Underground. All the while, he transformed back into his most comfortable form: vapor-thick darkness.

As he transitioned, he thought of Dawn again, as he did more and more every day. *His*. She wasn't terribly pure, but that could be changed. Like the movies they made Above, the right props and scripts could make her the perfect woman someday.

He'd taken so many risks to be with her, made a few miscalculations, too—especially when he'd given Eva's dress to her. *That* had been idiotic, and it still bothered him. He'd been too intent on merging mother and daughter that night. But now he'd slow down, never do anything so heedless again. With Eva's help—and with "Matt's"—Dawn would be manipulated into bringing down Limpet.

Floating the rest of the way into the Underground, Benedikte went straight to a private room.

He stopped outside a one-way window, looking in from the outside. Through the pane, he could see Sorin scowling at a tentative Eva and her new guest.

As Benedikte focused on Frank Madison, his outline crackled.

Eva's story had been too strange not to be true. She'd told them that, after seeing how Frank had beaten Breisi's location out of Julia the Servant, Eva had tracked her husband to the woods. She'd been able to bring Frank back here, but only after losing Dawn to Limpet's unexpected "Friends." Too bad the Underground hadn't anticipated them—one or two hidden Elites would've taken care of the protective ghosts and Dawn would be down here now, too.

Pressing against the window, Benedikte assessed his rival. Bedraggled, wide shoulders hunched, dark brown hair tufting up, Frank Madison's face was a study in blank expressionism. Not much competition there. He would've made a nice Guard, actually. So why did he hold Eva under such a spell?

One glance at the way she hopelessly looked at her withdrawn husband increased the mystery even more. It charred Benedikte from the inside out, making him steam.

Didn't Frank appreciate Eva?

Master? It was Sorin, glancing at Benedikte from the corner of his eyesight.

I'm here.

Benedikte hadn't updated his second in command about the meeting with Dawn yet. Using Awareness Above was foolish, since, over the years, he and Sorin had realized that it could be picked up on by blood brothers. It was only while they were buried under the earth's layers that vampires were free to use their powers without detection.

That's why the Master hadn't utilized more than one mind trick on Dawn. He'd tried to discover what she knew about Milton Crockett when she'd visited "Matt's" home that night, but she'd blocked him.

His Dawn was so good at that.

But here Below . . . Benedikte was tempted to infiltrate Eva's mind, just to see if she truly loved Frank as much as she said. Yet the Master wouldn't do it. His love was too pure for such games. Besides, Eva was skillful enough not to let him in if she chose to block her Awareness. She'd feel his efforts to invade, and he'd have to pay a big price for the attack.

As Sorin used his maker/high-child Awareness, he remained un-ruffled. *So Eva has returned with her new pet. She said Frank found her after a month of "tooling around" in Alaska. He had grown weary of the private detective life—as is his pattern with jobs—and tried to procure work in a new, adventurous location. But, she claims, when he could not find employment, he returned to Los Angeles. Here, he was struck by Jacqueline Ashley's resemblance to Eva Claremont, and he tracked her to the house on Bedford. When he found her absent, he used a Limpet brain trick on Julia to ferret out information regarding Eva. At the same time, he came across the Vampire Killer scheme. Then he rescued Dawn and went to save his fellow hunter Breisi Montoya. Eva punished him well enough, but it is all fairly . . . interesting.*

Can Julia confirm this?

Eva's Servant was mind altered by Frank . . . so it seems. Hence, there is no record of what actually happened tonight. Eva's story is the only one we have at the moment.

This was true: besides having no camera transmission save for the beginning of the Killer's performance, Sorin couldn't silently communicate with a bunch of distant Guards Above who were too weak to have word Awareness.

But . . . The Master went back to what Sorin had said about Eva. Was his son hinting that the Elite had brainwashed her Servant?

Eva would never do that. Sorin didn't know her at all—not like Benedikte did.

His son must've heard his thoughts. *The danger is: Dawn Madison knows her mother is alive. Eva revealed herself, and now Dawn is on the loose. That was not supposed to happen, Master. When Dawn found out, we were supposed to have her under our sway already.*

Sorin, Limpet is just about destroyed. Let him attack.

What if there is a different danger out there? What if Eva has revealed us to another with her carelessness?

Benedikte shook his head, on such a high with tonight's success that he couldn't be brought down. *Dawn won't be a threat. She's just as alone as Limpet is right now.*

Sorin paused. *Eva did say that Dawn is disillusioned with her boss. . . .*

And in this disillusionment, she's going to turn to family and also to the one man Above who offers her help. That's Matt Lonigan. And you know I've got that covered.

When Dawn had first gotten involved, Benedikte had been the one to come up with the masquerade. Since he could shift into diverse forms, it only made sense. "Matt" would be there to place doubt in Dawn's mind about anyone else except him, just as he'd done a month ago at Klara Monaghan's crime scene. "Matt" would win her over, would direct her suspicions about these Vampire Killer murders away from actual vampires.

"Matt" was invaluable.

Besides, Benedikte had longed to meet her, and when he realized just how much she could help the Underground, justifying his growing attachment to her had been simple. And when there'd been an entire month during the lockdown when he'd only been able to phone her, excuses about his absence had been easy, too.

It was all easy.

The Master was having the time of his life with this acting, even if Sorin hadn't liked this charade one bit. But Benedikte had been careful to shield himself 99.9 percent of the time, and his son had to admit that these trips had given his father a reason to exist again. Who could argue with that?

Sorin had grown quiet. He tilted his head as he considered Eva, reflecting in the usual inquisitive vampire pose.

You absolutely trust her, his son said.

Benedikte lavished a gaze over his angel, taking in her long blond hair, her pure beauty, and ignoring how she watched Frank with such delicate longing. In her, he saw everything that used to move him while sitting in a place of worship.

I trust her with everything, Sorin.

Yes, Master. But you know what Elites are capable of. They captivate the world with their acting. Do you not think she could do the same to you?

Benedikte could feel himself heating up to a sizzle.

You're questioning me again. His thoughts were as low as a growl. *Haven't I brought us this far?*

No answer. Benedikte took that as a yes.

The Master smiled. *Maybe you'll only be satisfied when I have Limpet's head on a stick?*

Now Sorin glanced over at the one-way mirror, his smile reflecting his maker's. *That would satisfy me a great deal.*

Then it's time to finally wipe our hands of our enemy . . . quietly, as usual.

When his son chuckled out loud, a ravaged Eva turned away from her nonresponsive husband to face Sorin, then the mirror.

As she cocked her head, the Master pressed closer against the glass, tilting his head, too, worshipping her from a dangerous distance.

TWENTY-SEVEN

The Scars

As Dawn all but stumbled up to the front door of the Limpet house, the UV lights blasted on, stinging her eyes.

She opened then slammed shut the door. "Kiko?"

She sounded like she was about to jump off a cliff, and maybe that was the truth. Nothing made sense, and it seemed like the only way to make things better was to annihilate herself then build from scratch.

But the only response she got was her own thin voice, chopping back at her from the corners of the house.

Why didn't she ever get answers?

Anger exploded, pushing Dawn into a run toward Breisi's lab door. She knew it'd be locked, but she needed to try to get in anyway. Pounding with her fists, kicking, she took perverse pleasure at the punishment the door was taking.

But soon, her minor kicks and punches turned into flails, then a fight to keep back more tears.

"Damn this." Dawn slammed her heel against the door, once, again. She leaned her head against it. "Damn . . . every . . . thing . . ."

A click caused her to stumble forward, the door giving way. Breathing heavily, she watched as it cracked open.

For a second, she could only stare. Breisi had always kept the door as secure as an armory's, and Dawn had only been able to imagine what was down there.

What kind of science experiments, fantastic inventions?

Holding back the sorrow, Dawn rubbed her hands over her face, preparing herself to find out.

A droning buzz escorted her down a stone staircase. It was illuminated by lifeless blue light, which only grew stronger as Dawn descended farther, hand against the granite wall.

Buzzzzzz . . .

The sound attacked her, but she didn't dare cover her ears. Ignoring her pained arm, she pulled out her whip chain.

But when she reached the bottom, she dropped her weapon.

The blue light was coming from the ceiling, which had been designed to look like a heaven, complete with painted clouds amidst soft azure neon fixtures. Below, an army of computers, plus the expected lab equipment, stood abandoned: steel tables holding the unfinished structures of projects Breisi would never fool around with again, space-agey machines Dawn couldn't even begin to explain. But there was also a trundle bed with white railing and fluffy linen bedclothes and pillows. Next to that stood a lace-mantilla-covered end table with a reading lamp and pictures of a very young Breisi and her grandmother hugging.

Dawn walked over to pick up one of those. It felt like her ribs had turned inward, bleeding her.

Breisi, so help me, I couldn't do anything. . . .

She held the picture to her chest, pressing so hard the metal frame cut into her.

When she heard footsteps, she didn't even glance up.

Silence. Then more steps. Then The Voice, his unamplified words making it sound as if he were in the room. But it was him. She knew it.

"I wanted to help her." His tone was like the aftermath of a decimated city: crumbled and haunted. "But we lost contact, and Hatsu, her Friend, disappeared. They're all disappearing, one by one. . . ."

Tautness strung the air together, linked only by the buzzing machine in the corner. Breisi had lived here. She'd made the Limpet house her home, made the team her family. Dawn wanted to cry even more.

"Can you tell me what happened?" The Voice asked.

Dawn tried to talk, couldn't, but then gathered herself and tried again. It was rough but audible. "You really have no idea? You never saw the—"

She almost said "video," but Eva had said the transmission hadn't gone public.

Something tapped at her brain. Video. The broadcast. But she couldn't hold on to it.

The Voice abolished the silence. "We only have her . . ." He stopped, then started again. "We found Breisi's body set out in the backyard, and she's being carefully seen to."

"Thanks to Eva." Dawn wasn't going to give that vamp credit for carrying Breisi away from the cops, for giving her back to the people who cared about her. Eva could apologize in a thousand different ways and it wouldn't make up for anything.

"The Friends have already told me many things about what happened." A footstep echoed. "Can you tell me, Dawn?"

"Do I need to repeat it? You've set us all up."

"What did you say?"

His voice blasted out with such wounded ire that Dawn dropped the picture. It shattered to the floor, jags of glass killing Breisi a second time. Dawn wouldn't take her gaze off that, somehow knowing she could've stopped this, too.

But it gave her an odd strength, and she felt herself whipping around to face his darkness. "You knew about Eva. Why didn't you warn me? She took me, Jonah. She has Frank, too. It makes me wonder if you knew something that could've saved Breisi, but maybe you weren't telling *her*, either—"

"Frank is with her?" Relief, pure and simple, weighed his voice. "And Eva took you to be with both of them?"

Now he didn't sound relieved so much as remorseful.

"Yes, I was kidnapped. Did you really think I ditched you and the team, even if Eva pretended she was me on the phone?"

The Voice didn't say anything, which meant he'd had doubts about her, too. How? What had she done to burn *him*? Just because she wasn't a natural do-gooder like Breisi or Kiko didn't mean she lacked loyalty or more noble qualities. Did he think that little of her?

His laden sigh filled the room, seeping into her. But she was already too soaked with grief, saturated enough to hit rock bottom and stay there.

She sank down to Breisi's bed.

More footsteps. But he still didn't come out of the shadows.

"Kiko's prophecy, where you're victorious over the vampires . . ." Pause. "He also predicted that you'd have to make a choice, Dawn, and you'd have to arrive at that decision yourself. Just know that I kept you uninformed because I couldn't afford to turn you against me until you were already invested in our cause. This meant you would eventually come to hate me. . . ." His voice cracked. "But I was prepared. I am *always* prepared because that's why I exist."

"To serve your crusade?" she bit out. "That's why you . . ." She primed herself to finally say it. "That's why you used me as bait again—to see if Jac was an Underground vampire?"

"I need you, Dawn."

No voice tricks, no hypnosis. He just sounded terribly human.

She stared straight ahead. "The good of the many outweighs the good of the few, right?"

"This is the most powerful vampire community I've ever met, and the best hidden. I've never needed more than my spirits and a few well-chosen humans to act as my eyes and ears outside. But we'll be the victors, somehow, even if there's always a price. I learned that early."

"How?"

"Through other facades, just like Limpet and Associates, which exists only to find this Underground."

She took that in. "So all our cases, like Robby's and the Vampire Killer's . . . We don't take them on unless they'll lead Underground. And when your team finds them, that's when you step in."

"As I always do."

"So there've been other . . . Undergrounds?"

"Many."

His voice seemed even closer and, only now, did it raise something up inside of her, something that had been slain when Breisi died. Raw feeling, even more than Matt had stirred. But his tone wasn't hitting her in a physical way; it was at the core of her, soothing what needed to be soothed.

She didn't want that. Didn't want him.

"So let me get this straight," she said, an edge to her tone. "About a year ago, you started collecting your lambs for the slaughter here in L.A. for *this* facade?"

"Every one of my fighters is precious to me." His voice had dragged itself back to a growl. "I had a hunch about all the strange movie-star murders—and I felt the presence of a master—so that's when I began recruiting."

"Why a new team? Do they all die before your next mission?"

"I ask every one of them what they are willing to do for a bigger cause, Dawn. They all have the same answer: anything. You said the same, too, when it came to helping us find Frank. I have to depend upon a literal interpretation of 'anything' or I have nothing."

It was a roundabout answer, goading her to ask, "Just how many times have you done this before?"

When he didn't answer, Dawn asked, "Am I on the right side? Why did you let this happen to Breisi, *why*?"

"The terrible part is that I did not let anything happen tonight. It was beyond my control. Far beyond my control."

If he hadn't sounded so troubled about that, Dawn would've attacked the dark. But there was something much more frightening at work here: maybe The Voice wasn't all-powerful. Maybe he was in over his head just as much as everyone else.

"Then why do you want to hunt this Underground?" she asked. "Why don't you just back off and stop?"

"Because I cannot."

She knew that was all she was going to get. But then, as if he wanted to make up for it, he offered something else.

"A while ago, I lost an entire team because one of them used knowledge they shouldn't have ever possessed. She knew *too* much. The team divided because of it, and we lost our quarry, so I learned my lesson and applied it this time to avoid a repeated disaster of that magnitude." He let out a breath. "Whether the world Above knows it or not, we are at war. And war is not merely physical combat—it's built on lying, torture, and mental games. It's the utilization of anything that works, and I *will* do whatever it takes to win. You would, too."

Maybe he thought he'd earned her trust with that nibblet. But he hadn't. It'd take a lot more.

Something on a steel table caught her eye. On weak legs, she managed to rise, to go to it.

When she touched the object, she couldn't hold back anymore.

It was a bladed crossbow, only half-formed like a creature caught in the middle of death and existence.

"She was making it for you," The Voice said. "Breisi knew how much you admired her own weapon."

On a ragged sob, Dawn hunched over the table, depending on it to keep her standing. She pushed at the crossbow but it was attached to the table, immovable. "Damn you to hell, Jonah."

"Well said," he whispered.

She darted a glare toward the location of his voice. Darkness. "Can't you just give me a sign of faith, just one? Can't you make Breisi's death meaningful in the least?"

"Nothing can do that."

Giving up, she rested her head in her arms, rubbing her tears off on her jacket. She was done. No more.

"Dawn?"

She heard a stirring behind her, then another sigh, this one a surrender of sorts.

Then she felt the shocking tingle of someone at her back.

Almost not wanting to, she raised her head, chills digging down her spine, skin more alive than ever. Slowly, she turned her head to find him right behind her.

Jonah.

Words vibrated in her throat but wouldn't come.

The details of him finally completed the blanks from the few pictures she'd unearthed. Dark hair that had grown out slightly, curling like soft down. Tall, lanky but filled out through the shoulders and chest. Dressed in an outdated silk coat over a white shirt and trousers. But his face—God, his face stunned her the most.

It wasn't his topaz eyes, almost almond-shaped, reddened from Breisi's death. It wasn't even his etched cheekbones and full lips.

It was the scars, long razored crisscrossing welts, angry and tragic.

A broken saint, was all she could think. A young man in his early thirties who'd already seen too much to endure.

He rendered her even more speechless when he held out a lone daisy, an offering of peace or . . . maybe something else she didn't have the strength to handle.

She didn't take the flower. Couldn't.

Jarred by her rejection, he withdrew it, looking around the room as if lost. He set the daisy on a table near him, his skin going red.

"Help me," he said simply, jaw clenching, as if he were barring himself from further agony. "I don't want to beg, but you're the only way we're going to beat them."

The enemy: her mom, the other vamps.

She didn't know who was what anymore.

"I never did get the chance to . . ." Jonah used his hands to help him formulate whatever it was he needed to say. "Last night, at the party . . ."

He wanted to check her over.

She didn't move as he came forward, hand outstretched as if to gentle her. It was only now that she saw beyond the scars.

His eyes burned with a compelling force she couldn't resist. It was as if this was where he lived—in his gaze—and that's where she should join him.

He looked into her, just a momentary flare. But then, whether it was required or not, he laid a palm to her forehead—a cool hand battered with rough, male skin. She allowed her eyes to close. Allowed her body to stop resisting, just this once.

His touch was voltage to her system, her belly tightening and heating. And when he pulled away, all her worst instincts wanted to haul him right back to her, not necessarily for the physical satisfaction, but because he understood the pain.

He might've been the only one who did.

Jonah looked at the ground, fisting his hands. And when he raised his scarred face again, his brutally forceful gaze, Dawn didn't like what she saw.

Shattered ire.

"You've been mind wiped," he said, voice ragged.

Dawn touched her neck.

"I'm going to gut every last one of them." His face had grown so red that his scars stood out like white blades. His neck veins mimicked the scars, pulsing as he turned around, addressing the room—or the world. "I *will* find out which one you are, you demon bastard! I'll—"

The room shook, the walls exhaling bits of dust.

"Jonah!"

He turned back around and the rumbling stopped. But his eyes still held the wrath of vengeance. "I don't think they exchanged with you. No blood exchange, no turning."

"I'm . . . not one of them." Thank God, sweet Jesus.

"They were trying to get information out of you. I imagine you mind blocked them, Dawn."

"What about Frank? I saw his neck and—"

Another voice sounded near the staircase. "He's gotta be a vamp." Kiko.

She turned around. His blond hair was wild, his eyes blurry, but he had a strange smile on his face.

Thinking he'd gone too far over the line of devastation, she held her arms out, getting to her knees as he came to her.

They held each other—what was left of the team.

"Trust him," Kiko whispered in her ear, voice thick. "Trust me. I've got it together now. No more meds—I don't care how much it hurts. We're going to get these guys. We're going to slay every last one of them."

Even above everything else, she worried about what he was saying. Did he think he could just cold turkey himself off those pills?

"You'll even go after Jac . . . Eva?" she whispered back to him.

"Especially her." Kiko hugged Dawn even tighter. "I should've known. That's how it is out here. Never trust what you see."

Laying her cheek against Kiko's head, Dawn glanced at Jonah, who was standing off to the side, arms empty, watching his team from a near distance that was a canyon all the same.

Could she trust what she was seeing? Or should she go back to her only other choice: Matt?

As Jonah looked at her, she thought she saw something deep and anguish ridden in his gaze—an emotion she didn't dare define.

Because that might be a trick of the eye, too.

Dawn framed Kiko's face with her hands, trying to show him she was strong enough to go on. But he was grinning again.

And when the room filled with jasmine, Dawn knew why.

An invisible force bumped against her fist, and she gaped. At another gentle nudge, Dawn's chest welled up with thick joy.

She should've known . . . Why hadn't she . . . ?

"You should have kept faith," the wisp of a familiar voice said from a dimension away.

"Breisi?" Dawn asked on a sharp sob that scraped her throat.

The newest Friend wrapped around her team.

Dawn laughed, cried, turned to Jonah, but he was already retreating into the darkness, the shadows dimming him until just the glow of his topaz eyes remained, then disappeared.

Swallowing away the lump in her throat, Dawn went back to her friend and her Friend, eyes wide open with burning, ecstatic tears.

And she was damn well going to keep those eyes open from now on.

Seeing everything for what it really was.

Look for

BREAK OF DAWN
VAMPIRE BABYLON, BOOK THREE

Coming September 2008 from Ace Books